Farrow's Patch

To Carl & Janet

[signature]

Farrow's Patch

Thomas P. Marquis

Writers Club Press
San Jose New York Lincoln Shanghai

Farrow's Patch

Writers Club Press
an imprint of iUniverse.com, Inc.

For information address:
iUniverse.com, Inc.
5220 S 16th, Ste. 200
Lincoln, NE 68512
www.iuniverse.com

ISBN: 0-595-12233-7

Printed in the United States of America

To Linda, Jennifer, Thomas, Stephen
And
Janet

Chapter 1

The plane droned on, just as it had for the last hour. Below was the green carpet of trees that hugged the contours of the Wrangell Mountains and above, the clear, blue Alaskan sky. The pilot, Cole Bryant, eased in a little left rudder and gently banked the aircraft to the left. Then he cut the power to just above idle and instantly the drone of the engine was replaced with the rushing sound of the wind as the plane decreased its speed ever so gently.

Off to the left, just below the horizon, a crystal clear lake came into sight. "Well, gentlemen, there's your home for the next week, off to your left, tucked into those mountains," Cole said. "It looks as though you picked a good week for fishin' and huntin'. The weather report on the weather channel predicts only a slim chance of showers this whole week. I'm gonna circle the lake to make sure everything is okay, and then I'll set "Lizzie" down at the east end of the lake."

Cole guided the plane into a gentle curve, counter clockwise around the perimeter of the lake, adding a little power every now and then to keep the slow winding descent smooth and safe. "Lizzie" responded to his slightest corrections as if she were a trained animal. The plane descended to about five hundred feet above the lake surface and hung there as if an eagle waiting for the right moment to dive for its prey. The water of the lake was so clear that every now and then the eye could catch the silver glint of the sun reflecting off of a large fish beneath the surface.

The sight was not going unnoticed from the four men behind the pilot's seat. "Ooh, man did you see that fish!" "Look, there's another one!" "Man, set this thing down, we gotta get fishin' now!"

The large round man sitting closest to the left window said, "How long before we'll be ashore, Cole?"

"Oh, it'll take about ten minutes to land and guide the plane to the dock, then another twenty minutes or so to unpack the provisions, Mr. Harmon," Cole responded. "Now make sure you have your seat belts snug and your feet flat on the cabin floor in front of you. I've checked the lake surface for any logs or debris, and we are going to land straight ahead in a minute or so," he said. "Is there any questions from anybody before I put "Lizzie" down?"

"Not from me, just let me get to them fish, Cole," said the skinny bald-headed man sitting next to the right side window.

"I can't wait! I've been looking forward to this vacation for years!" from the man in the last seat on the right side.

The youngest man of the group said, "Hey guys, I'm bettin' I catch the first bass!" And with that comment the cabin broke out with bragging and bets until just before the aircraft touched down on the surface of the lake.

There is something magical when a plane softly touches the water. Cole cut the power on the craft to idle. It slowed to a speed just fast enough to keep it from stalling, hovered momentarily, as if it wanted to change its mind, then gave in to the pilot's wishes and dipped the pontoons into the smooth lake surface. As soon as "Lizzie" touched the water, it felt as if Cole had applied the brakes. But the plane was still not slow enough to keep out of the air and, as it caught a light breeze, it lifted ever so slightly almost lifting the pontoons out of the water. Then a moment later, the pontoons settled back down into the water to act as two small boats carrying the passengers across the surface of the lake at an ever decreasing speed until the airplane was moving no faster than a small fishing boat gliding across the clear, smooth water.

Cole guided the craft using the foot pedals that control the movement of the tail rudder and, also, small rudders mounted on the rear of the pontoons. At the same time, he increased and decreased the power of the engine with the throttle controlling the speed and direction of the slow moving airplane as it glided toward the dock. Cole cut the power and quickly jumped out onto the starboard pontoon. Stay seated gentlemen until I have "Lizzie" tied up to the dock," he said. Cole grabbed the rope under the fuselage, waited until "Lizzie" floated to within two feet of the dock and jumped the short distance to the dock surface. Then he tied the plane snuggly against the pilings at the end of the dock.

"Okay guys, you can make your way out of "Lizzie" and put your feet on the dock of the place you're gonna spend the best vacation of your life," Cole said, with a gleam in his eyes. "In one week from now you're gonna beg me to let you stay for the rest of your lives! So, enjoy this time to the fullest, 'cause you're gonna miss it."

The scene was breathtaking. The magnificent trees came right down to the shoreline where large rocks and logs bridged the gap to the water's edge. Towering above the trees in the background were a ring of majestic mountains that cradled the pear-shaped lake. The western edge formed the bottom of the pear, while the eastern shoreline was the top of the pear, including a steeply inclined stream that resembled the pear's stem.

There was a long, silent pause as the four men stood on the dock trying to comprehend what they were seeing. None had ever experienced such rugged, serene beauty at any time in their lives.

Taking a deep breath of the cool, crisp, unpolluted, green smelling air, George Sleigman, the skinny bald-headed man said, "I think I've died and gone to heaven! I...I...can't...believe this place!"

"Paul, you've really outdone yourself when you arranged this trip," said Kevin Blanton, the youngest member of the foursome. "If the next week is as wonderful as this magnificent landscape, I know you're gonna have to hold a gun to my head, Cole, to get me to leave. It's just unbelievable!"

Paul turned around from the view and faced the other men, camera in hand, and said, "Come on guys let's get a group picture because nobody, I mean NOBODY is going to believe this place!" he said, with a little rasp in his voice.

At his command, the group lined up on the dock, and Cole focused, framed, and took the first picture of many more to follow for the next glorious week these buddies were going to share with each other for the rest of their lives. The fish stories would be repeated over and over and, even though the fish are the best in the world, they would get better and bigger as the years passed. It is hard to believe what a week in the middle of nowhere can do for the human spirit. At the end of this brief time together, these four men would have a bond that would last a lifetime.

"All right, gentlemen, let's get "Lizzie" unloaded and you can get on with your vacation," Cole said. "I'll hand the supplies out of the plane, and you guys carry it into the cabin."

After fifteen minutes the plane was unloaded and all the supplies had been placed in the cabin, a small twenty-foot by twenty-foot structure made of logs that came from the surrounding forest. Cole himself built it twelve years ago, shortly after he came to Alaska to stay.

The interior was dark and musty smelling, with a tongue and groove hardwood floor that he had brought up from Juneau, one planeload at a time. The walls were sealed with cement-like mud that filled the cracks between the rough-hewn logs. A small picture of some bears catching fish out of a stream hung on the front wall between the rustic door and a window, which looked out onto the covered porch that ran the length of the cabin. A large stone fireplace occupied the far corner of the same wall, with a long slate hearth extending to the edge of the left-hand wall.

Running down the length of the wall stood three bunk beds lined up military-style, linens stacked at the foot of each bed. A large detailed map of the surrounding mountains and the lake hung on the back wall. At the top of the map, printed in red capital letters, were the words "World Class Alaskan Experiences". Underneath this, the words "Rugged, Remote, Relaxing, Refreshing", were printed in smaller blue letters. A window on each side of the map produced a view of the forest behind the cabin.

The right side of the cabin had a very primitive kitchen that consisted of a short counter with two cabinets and a drawer for kitchenware underneath, a sink with an old iron hand pump to one side, and a bucket under the sink to catch the dirty water. Two shelves hung above the counter, which held heavy ceramic dinnerware and porcelain metal cups.

Toward the front of the cabin, on the same wall, was a closed in area without any doors that had a rod and hangers for clothes. A large four-legged oak table with six chairs sat in the center of the cabin on top of an oval rope rug that extended beyond the perimeter of the table. A wrought iron oil lamp with three yellow stained globes evenly spaced around a circular metal frame hung over the table.

All of the windows had heavy oil cloth shades that could be pulled down to keep the heat in the cabin on cold nights, something that was the norm in this Alaskan wilderness. In short, the cabin was cozy, clean, sparsely fixtured, and designed to keep the occupants safe and secure.

The cabin sat back in the woods about fifty yards from the rocky shoreline. The trees surrounding the cabin were at least one hundred fifty years old and towered 125 to 175 feet into the air. The air was filled with the evergreen odor emitted by the heavily forested hills that surrounded the lake and cabin. At the base of the trees, the earth gave off the deep aroma of soil, which never totally dried out from the frequent showers that passed through the area.

"Great place Cole, just like I pictured it. So far you score a twelve out of ten," Paul observed.

"This is the place for me, but where's the john?" asked Kevin.

"For Pete's sake, Kevin, that's all you can think about. Wait till you get to be my age," Pete Harmon mused as they all laughed.

Cole laughed and said, "Well gents, the head is about twenty yards behind the cabin conveniently located next to the large evergreen tree. It's complete with toilet paper and an oil lantern. You might even find some old "Sears" catalogs or "Fish and Stream" magazines inside, so enjoy, ha, ha."

Cole gave the men final instructions about the cabin and where everything was located. Then he showed them the material in the large handbook that was kept in the cabin to help the visitors get acquainted with being in such a remote area.

"Now fellas', I want to remind you that out here you have to fend for yourselves. All of the wildlife out here is just that...wild and untamed," he waved his arms about, indicating the surrounding area. "You must keep this in the back of your mind at all times. Everything is real! The bears will just as soon have you for dinner if you allow it to happen. Have fun, but take care of yourself and each other, and don't put yourself in the position of being in danger," Cole cautioned. "I suggest you plan everything you do. Make sure you leave plenty of time to get back to the cabin before dark. If you want to sit on the porch at night, have a fire going in the pit out front to ward off any unwanted visitors," he said, "and remember, help is about a half a day away."

"I have an antenna in that tree over there," he added, pointing out the window to a large sequoia that towered at least one hundred fifty feet above the ground. "The two way radio is kept on the shelf above the counter. Only use it if you have to get help. From this location, you can reach the ranger lookout station fourteen miles away. They will relay the message back to Chisano Ranger Station, and someone will be sent out. The rangers at the lookout station would have to come by land and that would take at least a full day," Cole explained. "So you see, gentlemen, you're a long way from civilization," he quipped. "Any questions before I leave you to the best time of your lives?" he asked.

The four men shook their heads and escorted Cole down the porch steps, past the fire pit to the dock, talking low amongst themselves and occasionally asking a question or two of him.

Once on the dock, Cole turned around, shook each man's hand, then stepped down the short distance onto the starboard pontoon. He opened the cabin door and eased himself into "Lizzie", sat at the controls and turned the ignition key. The engine groaned as the starter engaged, cranked, and then the engine caught and fired up. Blue exhaust came out of the pipes under the front cowling and the engine rumbled to life at a fast idle. After a minute or so, the engine smoothed out and started to purr. Cole set the engine rpm's back to a slow idle, jumped back onto the pontoon, untied the rope and pushed off from the end of the dock.

As the craft floated gently away from the dock, Cole stowed the rope in a compartment under the fuselage, jumped back in the cabin and closed the door. He waved to the four adventurers, pulled out the throttle a little to increase the power and carefully guided the airplane out to open water. Having noted the wind direction, Cole pointed "Lizzie's" nose into the wind, increased the power and guided her across the lake in a straight line. As her speed increased, she rode higher and higher in the water until the lake surface couldn't hold her down any longer. "Lizzie" broke free from the water and climbed steadily as the view from inside the cabin made the trees on the other side of the lake appear to speed toward her.

Once airborne, "Lizzie" climbed to one thousand feet and Cole eased in a little left rudder and aileron to guide her into a slow left hand turn that would bring the craft directly over the cabin. As the plane flew over the dock, Cole moved the wheel left and right several times to tilt "Lizzie" first to the left, then back to the right in a waving motion. The men on the dock waved their hands enthusiastically as the craft lumbered past them then climbed at an increasing angle to finally disappear from sight beyond the mountain range.

After the plane cleared the mountain peak, Cole set his course for due south, continuing to climb to six thousand feet, then set his speed at 105 mph. This would be the shortest route back to Farrow's Patch. Usually, Cole would have the previous group of vacationers to the cabin on board going back to Farrow's Patch, but since this was the beginning of a new season, the four men he just left were the first group he shuttled up to the cabin this year.

Cole needed to get a load of supplies for the new cabin he was building on an island northwest of here. He was planning to get a lot accomplished this week at the new cabin with the good weather forecast. The weather had been pretty miserable until a week ago and that made it hard to do much work outside. But that is "Alaska". The weather pretty much determines what a person does with their life at any particular time. In Cole's case, he was sacked in with bad weather and couldn't fly for four days. So he put off getting supplies till better weather came along. By then, it was almost time for the first group of vacationers at the cabin on Gakona Lake.

All of the rangers that could fly aircraft took turns shuttling the vacationers to the eighteen cabins the National Park Service operated in this area. Since one of Cole's duties was the maintenance and booking of the cabins, he had the honor of shuttling the first group of the season to one of the cabins.

So he flew down to Farrow's Patch two days early to get "Lizzie" serviced and go over coordinating all the arrangements for the seemingly endless number of groups of vacation visitors to the cabins. While he was there, he made sure all of his personal provisions had come in and placed more orders for the other groups of visitors that would follow as the weeks flowed through the end of summer.

Cole looked out the side window of the airplane on this beautiful country. Down in the valleys, the trees were that fresh green color when the leaves first emerge and look so young and new. Up near the top of the mountains, the leaves had not come out yet, so there was a contrast of light green to gray the further up the slopes the eye roamed, with patches of green where the evergreens stood. In another two or three weeks the scene would be entirely different as the new, young leaves would then be covering the tops of the mountains and the color would flow from dark green in the valleys to light green at the peaks of the mountains.

This time of year everything changes constantly in Alaska. The snowless seasons are short. Even now, May 17th, there was still snow on the tops of some of the mountains in this region even though they only rise to four thousand feet. By mid-September, snow would reappear on the mountains. Spring and summer are sandwiched in those four, short months. Not only do the mountains come alive in that brief period, but so do the people of Alaska. The heavy weather lifts which, also, lifts the spirits of the population.

The plane cut through the cloudless midday sky leisurely and effortlessly. The monotone growl of the engine put Cole's mind into motion reflecting on his life and how he happened to be flying "Lizzie" at this particular time in his life. He looked ahead of the airplane and as far as the eye could see was endless tree covered mountains. "Oh, what a great place to be living!" he thought. But, not too many years ago, a very similar sight would have made knots form in his stomach.

His mother and father, Tom and Linda Bryant had raised Cole in Philadelphia, Pennsylvania. He had a normal childhood, living in the same house all his life in a middle class neighborhood on the outskirts of the city. His parents were very supportive and made sure he did well in his school studies and extra-curricular activities. He enjoyed sports and played second string on his football team and, for two seasons, participated on the track team.

His father worked as a financial advisor and was hoping that Cole would follow that line of work for his own career. However, Cole wanted to be outdoors. He loved to hike, and fish, and hunt. Cole's father enjoyed the outdoors, too, but only as a weekend or vacation activity. Cole wanted to pursue a career in forestry, since this is what interested and excited him the most. This created a little disharmony in the family when it was time for Cole to go off to college and choose his career path.

Tom and Linda explained to Cole that he should base his career on something that would allow him to live in the style he wanted. Forestry, even though a stable career choice, would not provide that kind of income. After many late night conversations and confrontations, Cole decided to go along with his parents' wishes. He would pursue finance as his major. After all, his parents were good role models, and they lived very comfortably and were very happy over the long run.

So, off to Penn State he went and four years later had a Bachelor of Science degree from the College of Finance. Throughout his school years he was the typical student. He had a girlfriend in tenth grade and another halfway through eleventh grade almost to the end of twelfth grade. Then in college, he had a serious relationship in his sophomore and junior year, which ended during the summer break.

His girlfriend, at the time, was Jennifer MaCaulley. She was majoring in political science, and her political philosophies leaned heavily to the left. Cole was a middle of the road conservative but enjoyed debating

Jennifer on politics. The relationship basically was finished before it had begun, but outside of the difference in political views, Cole and Jennifer had many similar interests. They both enjoyed the outdoors, hiking in the warm months and skiing in the wintertime.

Jennifer became more vocal on political issues as the Vietnam War heated up, and more demanding that Cole needed to flee to Canada to avoid the draft. She thought Cole should protest the country's presence in Southeast Asia and was very upset that he would not participate in sit-ins and marches relating to the "immoral war" raging in Vietnam. He tried to explain to Jennifer that she was entitled to her opinions, but he was, also, entitled to his. He felt he should support his country, even if he didn't feel we should be engaged in a "civil" war in another country. He felt the United States was trying to bring peace to that region and, at the time, the country was afraid Communism was going to take over the world and the freedoms we had in America could be lost.

However, he did participate in a few anti-Vietnam rallies in 1966 and 1967, but nothing serious. He remembered those were very nervous and unsettling times. He knew that when he graduated from college he would either have to join the armed forces or be drafted to serve his country in this very unpopular war that was dividing the country morally and politically.

Cole's father had been a pilot in World War II. When the war ended and he had a little extra savings, he would take Cole and John, Cole's older brother, for airplane rides. As the boys got old enough, Tom would take the boys to the local grass airport and give them flying lessons. Both sons learned to fly and caught the flying bug. Usually it is too expensive for a young man to continue flying, but Cole was befriended by an acquaintance of Tom's and he let Cole use his plane whenever he wanted to fly. All Cole had to do was pay for the fuel. The man felt it was better if the plane was used, than to just sit around and get old.

So Cole had a lot of flight hours in a Piper J-3, a small two-seater covered in yellow canvass. It was a sturdy craft with a dependable sixty-five-horse power engine that propelled it at a leisurely sixty-five miles per hour and could take off and land on very short runways. Everytime

Cole would go home to visit from college he would try to find enough time to take the aircraft on a flight. Because of his piloting experience, the post graduation decision to go in the Air Force was a "no brainer". He either joined the Air Force or got drafted into the Army.

So he went to the local recruiter, discussed becoming an Air Force pilot and, with little fanfare, joined up for a four year tour of duty as a Forward Air Controller or FAC, as they were called in Vietnam. The FAC flew a single engine, light observation plane very similar to the piper J-3 in size and design. It was made on contract by Cessna, called the 0-1. It had high wings with struts to the fuselage, windows all around and even windows looking out the top through the wing. It was unarmed and carried small rockets on the wing that would fire smoke canisters.

A FAC was assigned to each army battalion. The FAC would land and take off from temporary dirt runways near the front lines, fly low over the jungle and identify Vietcong troop movements or buildups. Then, the FAC would call in an air strike to "take out" the enemy. When the thundering jets would arrive at the location, the FAC would fly close to the area and fire the smoke canisters to the exact location the bombers were to attack.

It was an extremely dangerous job because the airplane had to fly low and slow, so it was subject to ground fire at all times. Couple that with the fact that the airplane had no armor or weapons, and it was easy to see the pilot was a sitting duck for the enemy. When our troops were pinned down, the FAC would coordinate the air strike through his own observations and the directions given to him by the Lieutenant on the ground. Sometimes, the strafing jets were actually given a particular tree to hit, which required the FAC to get the smoke canister right on the mark.

Even though it was dangerous and demanding, Cole was good at it and many times it was as if he and his 0-1 were as one. The battalion had tremendous respect for Cole and trusted his support. But one sunny afternoon, after he had been a FAC for ten months, it was Cole that had to rely on the battalion to save his life.

He had come back from many patrols with dime and nickel sized holes in the wings of the 0-1 and even one time had a gash in one leg where a bullet brushed his calf. But they would patch the holes and send him up again the next day. It was part of the business and nobody really thought much about it.

On March 16, 1969, Cole was flying routine observation when his eye caught what appeared to be a dark, oblong object under a large tree next to a sandy path. He wanted to check this out, but part of the FAC's mode of operation was a game of cat and mouse. The FAC never let on to the enemy what he was doing because if he did let on, the enemy would fill the plane with bullets.

So Cole marked the spot mentally, using the surrounding geography as points of reference, and flew on in his normal erratic meandering flight path. Then, after a while, doubled back to take another look at the area where the unidentified object had been spotted.

As he approached from the down-wind side, he put the plane as close to the trees as he could. Increasing the power, he pointed the nose of the 0-1 in the air just ahead and above the large tree he used as his reference point, to gain altitude and provide an extra moment or two over the tree to gain a better look at the object below.

At that point, all he remembers is seeing a puff of white smoke and a loud whistle as the projectile slashed through the tiny airplane, then a tremendous burning in his right side and the sensation of falling, a huge crashing noise, tree limbs breaking, and the smell of fuel and earth. Finally, blackness and total silence engulfed him.

The Vietcong had been waiting for him all day. It was part of their plan to take out the FAC, then, without the use of the overhead observer, launch an attack on the battalion on three sides, taking them by surprise.

When the little airplane came to rest upside down, wings torn off, fuel leaking from the steaming engine, he was immediately surrounded by screaming Vietcong. If he had been conscious, they probably would have killed him then and there. But they were filled with a great sense of superiority since their plan worked, and they had downed the airplane with just one mortar round.

Curiosity of the American grabbed them and saved his life, for the time being. They dragged him out of the crumpled wreckage, put him on a cart drawn by an ox and took him to the closest village where they put him in a bamboo cage. They fed him rice and gave him water, but they did not dress the gaping wound in his side. He was their prisoner and they were going to let him die a slow, agonizing death caused by infection in the wound and a loss of blood.

Part of a FAC's assignment was to check in with the battalion every forty-five minutes using one of three frequencies AM, FM, or UHF. When this didn't happen, the report went out for another battalion to send a FAC to search the area. That search quickly discovered the location of Cole's downed aircraft due to the small wisp of smoke rising from the forest below.

Since the Vietcong had immediately commenced with the surprise attack on the battalion, it was three days before the Americans could set a plan in motion to retrieve Cole from the Vietcong-held village. On that moonless night, six infantry volunteers creeped into the village and quietly "took out" three Vietcong guards, put Cole on a stretcher and carried him three miles to a waiting jeep that transported him out to a clearing that became a makeshift landing area. A medic helicopter darted into the landing area, hovered momentarily, then touched down just long enough for the men to load the stretcher carrying Cole on the craft. Instantly, it rose vertically one hundred feet in the air. The nose of the helicopter tilted toward the ground as the pilot thrust the machine forward at full speed; the camouflaged aircraft disappearing rapidly from sight as it passed over the thick growth of the surrounding jungle.

Cole was treated and sent back to the States. His wounds were bad enough that the Air Force gave him an early discharge from the service. So, he went home to Philadelphia and recuperated at his parent's home for the next three months. After he was released from the doctor's care, he got a job at a mortgage company in Philadelphia.

Cole was in misery. He hated everything about working and living in the city. He hated the commute to and from work, the masses of people always bearing down on him in the streets, the noise, the endless, seemingly never ending rush to go nowhere. He pictured his life as the same old thing from now until death. He thought to himself, "I cannot do it! I will not do it. There has to be more to LIFE than this! STOP THE WORLD...I GOTTA GET OFF!"

So one day he left work early, went to the library in downtown Philly, and spent the afternoon browsing through travel books and materials on careers. In that afternoon outing, Cole cleared his head, organized his thoughts, and made notes on some possible careers and locations he thought he might want to consider.

The next day he called Mr. William Defreese, Park Ranger Administrator, Wrangell Reserve, Moose Cove Alaska. Cole spoke with Ranger Defreese about possible employment opportunities with the National Park Service in Alaska. He explained his desire to be a forestry major in college and his dreams of a career in the Park Service even though he chose finance as his college major. Ranger Defreese was impressed with this young man, but Cole just didn't have the qualifications at that time to be a ranger. Then, in the conversation, Cole mentioned three things that got him a chance for an interview.

The first, and least important, was the forestry courses he took in college as his electives. This showed Ranger Defreese that Cole really did have an interest in forestry. The second was that he had a finance degree and could handle the accounting and financial decisions for the division.

The third, and most important, was Cole's background in aviation. While talking about his experiences in Vietnam, Cole pointed out that he flew airplanes...in particular small, light aircraft such as the piper J-3 and the Cessna 0-1 as well as others. In Alaska, there are more airplanes than cars or trucks. To do anything in Alaska of importance, an airplane is usually essential. And if you know how to fly one, you're in demand.

So Ranger Defreese asked Cole to send him a resume and a very detailed letter explaining his experiences and in what positions Cole felt he would be interested. He told Cole not to hold his breath about getting a job, but he would look it over and, if there was anything he could do, he would let him know.

Cole waited patiently and after several months received a call from Ranger Defreese. "Cole Bryant, please," the man's voice on the other end of the telephone said.

"This is Cole, what can I do for you?" he asked inquisitively.

"Cole, this is Ranger Bill Defreese of the Wrangell National Forest in Alaska. How are you doing today?" the ranger asked.

"Sir, I'm fine and dandy. Are you calling about my application for employment?"

"Yes, I am. As I told you I would do, I looked over your resume and past experiences. Based on what I see, I think I might just have the position for you to start. It probably isn't what you had in mind, but it would get you into the Park Service," he added, "and then, if you follow the training outline I have developed for you, in a couple of years you could become a full-time ranger. What I want to do is to send you the notes I've made and see if you might be interested," he said. "Cole, I think you would be an asset to the Service and that is why I have spent so much time on this plan. But I want you to look the program over and, if there is anything you don't like about the plan, then you need to let me know," Ranger Defreese emphasized.

So ten days later, Cole received a thick package at his parents' house. The package was one of those large brown eleven by fifteen inch envelopes with a large number of cancelled stamps in the upper right-hand corner and numerous large, round-hand stamps in black ink from the various main post offices that the package had passed through on the long journey from Alaska. The upper left-hand corner contained the return address of Ranger William Defreese, Wrangell Reserve, Moose Cove, Alaska. The center area had Cole's name and address printed neatly in all capital letters. The envelope resembled one of those abused suit cases of someone that had traveled extensively throughout the world, with stick on labels from the various airports and customs stations it had gone through, showing the wear and tear of being handled by indifferent, uncaring workers along the way.

When Cole got home that evening, his mother was very interested in the contents of the mystery envelope. But Cole offered no explanations, took the package to his bedroom and studied the various papers, pamphlets, and notes that Mr. Defreese had sent him. The more he read, the more excited he got. The plan Ranger Defreese had set up would give Cole the opportunity he had dreamed about, a chance to pursue his dreams in forestry as a Park Ranger.

The real trick was to present this to his parents in such a way that they would listen to him and give him a chance to lay out the whole plan without the conversation turning into a blow out argument. So for the next two days, he agonized over his decision to join the Park Service in Alaska and how to tell his parents. But it was now or never, and he decided to tell them that evening after dinner.

Cole fidgeted through dinner, then asked his parents for their attention and understanding in what he had to discuss with them. "Mom, Dad, I want to thank you in advance for a wonderful life up to now. It is because of you, as role models, that I have done so well. I appreciate all your help in my rehabilitation from my war injuries," he said, "but I am all healed now and it is time for me to get a place of my own," he added. "I want to share with you my plans and my dreams for the future."

Cole's dad sat motionless, ready to hear what he had to say. But Linda, Cole's mom, couldn't hold her tongue. "This has something to do with that package from Alaska you received a couple of days ago, doesn't it?" she asked. "What is it, Cole? What have you done?"

"Mom, Dad, I have always tried to do what you wanted of me," Cole started, "and I am truly grateful for everything you have done for me and given me. Because you insisted I do well in school, I was able to get a college degree that will always provide me with a good job. You have always supported me in my endeavors and activities," he went on, "and because of that I am a better person."

"When I was asked to serve my country in the Vietnam War, I stepped up and joined the Air Force," he continued. "There are many things I have done to satisfy other people. Not that I didn't want to do it, but I wouldn't have done many things if I wasn't pleasing someone else," he emphasized.

"I love you very much Mom and Dad," he said in a softer, loving tone, "but it is time I make a decision that is my own and not be swayed by any outside influences," Cole stated emphatically. "First, the bombshell! Then, I will explain my reasoning, my plans to carry out my decision, and finally my dreams." He took a deep breath in an attempt to suck up his courage. "I have decided to become a Park Ranger in Alaska! And I have been hired, if I want the job!" Cole exclaimed.

At that, Linda cut him off and said, "Cole, you can't be serious! What is going through your…".

Tom stopped Linda in mid-sentence, "Wait a minute, Mother, give Cole a chance to explain his plans. He, obviously, has spent a lot of study and thought on this," he added. "Cole is not your little boy any longer. He has just come back from a very dangerous, man's job, wounded in the course of defending his country. This is not your little boy!" he scolded again. "I don't know about you dear, but I am anxious to hear what my son has to say and support him in what he wants to do with his life."

Linda agreed and apologized for "flying-off-the-handle." The confrontation was over and Cole could settle down into explaining his decision and going over his plans. Mr. Defreese's plan was to bring Cole in as the Administrative Assistant. This position would handle all of the books for the Wrangell Reserve district. It required someone that could do bush pilot type work because he would be needed at several locations.

"So you see, folks, I will still be using my finance background, my piloting skills, and Mr. Defreese has me set up on a study program that will allow me to become a Park Ranger, something I have wanted for a long time," he concluded. After answering many questions from his parents, they were comfortable with his decision and wished him well, giving Cole their blessings and support.

So, off to Alaska Cole went and, now as he was flying over this beautiful state, Cole was feeling pretty good. He had made the right decision for himself. Everything had worked out the way Ranger Defreese had said it would. Cole had been a good student and a hard worker, and Ranger Defreese guided Cole along the path to becoming a full time Ranger.

The plane hit an air pocket and jolted a little which brought Cole out of the deep thought of the past and back to the present. He was following the Lower Pegula River that flowed through the valley, guiding the airplane left and right to adjust for the meandering river. In about a quarter of an hour he would see the town of Farrow's Patch, his destination.

Cole checked everything in "Lizzie" to make sure the landing would be smooth, then pushed the control forward, ever so slightly, to start the craft on a descending path toward the far end of the valley ahead. The small river flowed through the valley floor with ever increasing speed as it snaked its way out of the valley, across the small, flat plain at Farrow's Patch, to Icelander Bay.

When the airplane broke free of the mountains to the east of Farrow's Patch, Cole cut the power back and added a little down flap to start to slow the speed of the airplane. Unlike the Piper J-3 on which he learned to fly, this plane required a longer landing area and the speed had to be decreased more, so more "down" flaps were necessary to slow the craft.

"Lizzie", as Cole affectionately called her, was a Cessna 207. This is a seven-passenger plane with an ample storage area or, if you aren't carrying seven passengers, the rear seats fold down or remove to haul even more supplies. This type airplane is one of the favorites of the bush pilots of Alaska because it is very sturdy, able to handle fairly heavy loads, very maneuverable, able to take off and land in fairly short distances, and easily adaptable to skis, pontoons and, of course, wheels. The airplane is powered by a 225 horsepower engine and cruises at about one hundred fifty miles per hour.

Cole had come by the airplane rather by accident when he had gone to Seattle, Washington to visit an old college buddy back in the spring of 1972. While he was there, he went out to the local grass airport at the edge of the city and spent some time chatting with the "locals" around the hangers. He noticed the Cessna sitting behind the hanger in an overgrown, grassy area.

"Hey Pete," directing his conversation to Pete Malloy the hanger operator and resident engine mechanic, "what's with the old Cessna in the back?".

Pete answered, "That belongs to widow Slineck over in Mason County. Old Doc Sly used to fly her on the weekends until he died three years ago. His wife, Elizabeth, just couldn't decide what to do about the airplane," he added. "She's about eighty now and pays the rent for the space every month. But she won't sell it and told me to quit asking her what she was doing with the bird," Pete said, as he wiped engine grease from his hands onto a shop towel.

"It sure is a shame she's letting it sit there and rot like that. I would love to have something like that up where I'm at now. Those type airplanes are so useful," Cole said. "Not getting nosey or anything, but do you think I could talk to her about it?" he asked. "I mean, if you don't mind or anything."

"Cole I'll be honest with you. There ain't no chance you're gonna change Mrs. Slineck's mind. It won't bother me a bit for you to talk to her," he said. "I don't think it will do any good, but it would be nice to get that plane out of here and back in use because it is close to being ruined from neglect of maintenance," Pete stated.

Pete proceeded to write down directions to Mrs. Slineck's house and told him to call on her after church on Sunday. That was usually the best time to get her to sit quietly and listen to what a person had to say.

So on Sunday afternoon, Cole found himself on the front porch of Mrs. Slineck's house. It was an old, white, two story house that was set back about a hundred yards off a paved rural road. The driveway consisted of white crushed stone that made that crunching noise as the car tires rolled across them. The house and grounds were very neat, obviously taken care of by hired help.

When he knocked on the screen door, a small yapping sound started in the back of the house and quickly made its way to the other side of the closed front door. He could hear the scratching of paws on the doorframe and footsteps on the hardwood floor approach the door at a slow pace. Then the door opened wide and before him stood a short, frail looking, white-haired lady wearing a flowered dress with pleats running down the front from the waist down to the hem, just above her ankles. She was wearing short-healed white shoes with flat toes and her apparel was topped off by a white sweater that was thrown across her shoulders. The dog was one of those longhaired, fluffy things that came up to just above the lady's ankles.

"Mrs. Slineck?" Cole asked.

"Yes," she answered, a quizzical expression on her face.

"Mrs. Slineck, my name is Cole Bryant," he started, "and by way of introduction, I am a Park Ranger in Alaska. I have come here today to talk with you about that Cessna airplane over at Brogan Field," he added. "May I come in, or can we sit out here on this beautiful porch and chat awhile?" he asked.

With that, Mrs. Slineck agreed to talk with him and, after what seemed to be an hour, she asked Cole to come in and have supper with her. Looking at his watch, he realized he had spent the entire afternoon talking with this very interesting lady.

Later that evening, Mrs. Slineck agreed to sell the Cessna to Cole. She was very impressed with this young man and she felt like her husband, Doc Sly, would want Cole to have the plane. She said that what she wanted for the plane all along was someone that would love it as much as her husband had. No one, until then, had even come close to wanting the plane as much as Cole did. If they had, she would have sold it years ago.

Mrs. Slineck agreed to let Cole fix up the plane and, then, pay her one thousand dollars a year for five years, at which time the airplane would be his. Cole couldn't believe his ears. The airplane was worth three times that amount. He showed up at the hanger on Monday morning with the good news and made arrangements for Pete to overhaul the engine and get the plane flyable.

Once Cole got the Cessna to Farrow's Patch, he completely refurbished the plane. When the plane was done, he called Mrs. Slineck and told her he named the airplane "Lizzie" in honor of her because that is what Doc Sly used to call her. He thanked her profusely telling her she was the one that made it all possible for him to have the airplane.

As he approached the coast, he observed the vivid blue waters of Icelander Bay, in the deeper water off the shore, gradually turning into blue-brown as the sea came closer to shore, churning up the sand from the sea bottom, then, finally touching the land with a boiling surf very similar to the boiling action of water in a pot on a stove as it froths over the top. There was virtually no beach along the coast, most of the shore being made of heavy rocks on which the sea crashed in an endless roar.

Farrow's Patch is flat and barren and juts out into the bay forming a small cove. There is almost always a steady wind blowing off of the bay. The land is high, being crossed in several places by small gully-like streams and creeks. The area is about three-fourths of a mile from the shoreline to the foot of the mountains to the east, and about one and half miles running the other way, north and south, along the coast.

The area was named after Col. Johansen Farrow, a Norwegian explorer that spent two years mapping the surrounding area in the early 1800's. Legend has it that this area came to be known as Farrow's Patch because the permafrost layer, the layer of earth beneath the surface that is permanently frozen, is not as prevalent here as it is in the surrounding areas. This allows a green moss-like grass to grow on the surface much later in the fall, as winter sets in. Thus, the area has a distinctive look much of the year with all the other areas white with snow and this small, flat area still green.

"Lizzie", once again, responded to Cole's every move as they approached the cove for the landing. Since the wind direction was from the open sea, Cole brought the airplane low over the southern part of the fishing village, checking to make sure he was the only plane in the area. Even though there are no runways when landing on the water, all of the airplanes landed in the same area to avoid any confusion in case someone missed spotting an approaching plane.

The landing area was protected from the open sea by a half-mile long stone jetty extending from the northern part of the cove, which sheltered the surface of the water from the wind. This made for ideal landing conditions because of the relatively smooth surface to land on and a steady head-wind blowing above the top of the jetty that kept lift under the wings till touching down on the water.

The airplane skimmed along the surface and the pontoons slowly descended into the water as "Lizzie" slowed down. Cole pushed his right foot on the rudder pedal after "Lizzie" slowed, turning the craft to the right, and taxied her into the air marina, that area of the cove reserved for the floatplanes.

From this angle, Farrow's Patch loomed overhead about thirty-five feet at the top of the rocky shoreline. The cove was attached to the village by an old wooden pier that was connected with winding steps that precariously worked their way up the side of the shoreline and emptied out onto the main street. To the south, in the deeper part of the cove, a second, longer dock used by the bigger fishing boats had a ramp that made the incline to the village less of a burden for hauling supplies and large barrels of fish up to the village.

Cole pulled "Lizzie" into a slip, secured the lines, cut off the fuel line supply valve and put a protective canvass tarp around the engine cowling and propeller. Then he jumped up on the old wooden pier, took a deep breath, gathered up his duffel bag and started for the stairs that would lead him to the main street of Farrow's Patch and an event that would change his life forever.

Chapter 2

Cole turned around to face the cove when he reached the top of the old wooden stairs that connected the pier below with the main street. Taking in the view, he observed the calm waters of the cove and the rough water beyond the jetty churned up by the constant wind that blew in from Icelander Bay. He reflected briefly on the origins of the wind. Perhaps it had come all the way across the ocean originating in Asia or Japan. But, in any event, the wind was very cool, or cold by most people's standards. Today the temperature out of the cool wind was a "warm" fifty-one degrees Fahrenheit. But standing here in the wind, on top of the shoreline, felt more like thirty-seven degrees.

Off to the left to the south, where the ramp met the pier, two fishing boats tied to the pier, that extended two hundred feet out onto the water, slowly rose and fell with the easy rolling swells in the deeper part of the cove. An overhead rope and pulley system on top of telephone-type poles connected the outer end of the pier with the fish processing plant at the top of the rocky shoreline. A large steel basket was slung beneath the cables that were stretched between the poles. The basket could be raised and lowered by workers pulling on the vertical cables that wound between several pulleys. The heavy weight of the fish laden basket was reduced by the use of a large electric motor attached to the basket and supplied with power provided by electricity from the processing plant.

A steady ant-like stream of workers was busy loading and preparing one of the boats for its next voyage out to sea. The voices of the workers would occasionally drift across the water, carried by the wind, only allowing segmented parts of sentences to be heard at this distance. The other fishing boat docked at the pier showed no form of life.

Looking to the right, up the coast to the north, Cole observed the wooden pier that hugged the rocky shoreline. Individual slips for each airplane extended from the pier, held in place by large pilings. The slips had large metal drums underneath allowing them to float on the water so that the floatplanes and the slips were always at the same relative position for easy unloading and loading.

At this time, there were just three airplanes, including "Lizzie" in the slips. At times, during the height of tourist season, there might be as many as twelve floatplanes in the cove, some anchored in the cove away from the pier and slips. There wasn't any activity on this side of the cove right now.

Further up the coastline, Cole could see the repair barn, as the locals called it, which was run by Tony Barsells. He was the local aircraft mechanic. As far as Cole knew, there wasn't an airplane around that Tony couldn't fix.

Cole loved this place and every time he came here always took a moment to stand at the top of the stairs to gather his thoughts and count his blessings to be able to call this area "his home". As he turned around and looked down the main street of town, he realized that if it was "neat" a person was looking for, this was not the place to be.

Alaska is a hard place to live. The weather is harsh and unforgiving. Most of the people are the same, harsh and unforgiving. You must be like that to survive. It is not to say the people are mean, but the way of life is for those rugged individuals that can make it on their own. One must learn to survive the winters if one is going to last in Alaska. If you are not a survivor, you either die or move out.

All of the buildings in Farrow's Patch were weather beaten and looked tired. Even the newer buildings looked old after a couple of years. The elements take their toll on everything. Repairs are done in the warmer months, and that only lasts four months, at the most. So, if it doesn't get done in those four months, it must wait until the next year.

Looking down the street from the top of the stairs, off to the right, Cole observed the largest building in town, the fish processing plant. They process all types of seafood from oysters, to King Crab, to fish. But fish, of course, is the largest part of the operation. The seafood is unloaded from the boats below and brought up the cable lift in the steel basket to the processing plant where it is prepared for flash freezing. Later it is loaded into trailers or boxcars to be shipped down the coast to the various seafood markets.

The outside of the building was old board and batten construction with the roof steeply peaked, to attempt to keep the snow from building up too high in the winter. On the gable end facing the cove, the cable system entered the building high up the side through a large square hole that was covered by large shutters when not in use. The front of the structure facing the street was windowless. Double doors in the center of that side, with one small window in each door, allowed entry into and exit from the building.

As Cole started walking down the main street, he noticed that the irregular placement of the buildings along the street looked as though a small child had lined up different sized building blocks, that probably came from different sets, in two rows parallel to one another. The only thing missing from the haphazardly placed buildings were the giant letters and numbers that would be on the sides of the building blocks.

The buildings were huddled close to one another on each side of the street as if to protect themselves from the cold winter winds, four stores on the south side and five on the north side. Between some of the storefronts, small alleyways led to the back of the buildings, or stopped abruptly at a door, but most of the buildings were attached to each other by common walls. A sidewalk made of cement in some areas, stone in others, and segmented with a wooden walkway now and then, provided access to the businesses on both sides of the street from the diagonal parking spaces running down the length of the main street.

Cole made his way across the traffic circle, at the end of the street closest to the cove, where vehicles turned around to head back toward the other end. In the center of the circle, an American flag hung from a flagpole, and below, stood a stone statue of Col. Johansen Farrow, a gift to the town from Bragan, Norway.

The street had the untidy look of most poor, small towns where the community budget was small and the staff of the local government even smaller. There were just three vehicles parked on the street, normal for this time of day in the middle of the week.

Halfway down the street, Cole veered to his left toward the Madison Rooming House, the only place in town to rent a room. It was a two-story building, with a weathered brick front, that sat in the middle of the row of businesses on the north side of the street. It sat back from the main street thirty feet, or so, with a raised porch running the width of the front of the building, a white banister defined the limits of the porch around the outside perimeter. A half dozen white, wooden rockers were lined up behind the front banister with potted evergreens at each of the four corners of the porch, adding the only accent color to an otherwise drab appearance.

Cole made the three steps up the porch, walked to the wooden framed door and opened it while peering through the glass panes to make sure someone wasn't trying to exit at the same time. Inside, a large, darkly lit lobby wreaked of smoke. To the left, a long wooden counter was embedded into the wall, behind which Mr. and Mrs. Stromyer, the owners, were standing.

The high ceiling was made up of heavy, darkly stained beams and tongue and grove planking, and the walls and floor were of the same tongue and groove construction. The floor was bare except for two large oriental rugs that divided the center of the room into two symmetrical areas. Various animals' heads adorned the walls around the perimeter of the lobby. A large, highly polished brass chandelier with twelve oil lamp-type globes hung from the center of the ceiling. A half-dozen chairs and as many small sofas were scattered around the room. Two large fireplaces stood on opposite walls, one on the street-side wall, the other on the rear wall that separated the lobby from the dining area. Other than the odor of stale smoke, this was a cozy place to spend a cold winter night.

"Hey, Mr. and Mrs. S.," Cole called out, as he entered the lobby. "Any messages? Anything going on?"

"No messages, Cole," Mrs. S. answered. "Greta wants to see ya' as soon as you can get a chance. But nothin' more'n that," she added.

"Well, I'm going to get the supply list from my room and head over to the general store right now. You know I'm headed to the island in the morning, don't you?" Cole asked.

"Yeah, I hope this good weather holds out so you can get a lot done the next couple of days," Mrs. S. stated, waving her arms about, describing the clear weather.

Mr. S. joked, "Cole you probably could use my help out there. I'll get my things and go with you."

"I believe Cole can do just fine by himself," Mrs. S. said, as she punched Mr. S. in the arm, then gave him a hug. "Besides, I really need you here, dear, to take care of me and this big old place," she said, looking at Cole and winking.

"Yeah, Mr. S., she really needs you around here. I might get too much done if you helped me. Then I wouldn't have anything to do with my free time," Cole smiled, turned on his heels, and headed up the stairs to the room that he and the other rangers used when they had to come into town.

The room was sparsely decorated, but extremely clean and neat, located on the second floor with a large window facing the main street. A small bathroom occupied the rear corner of the room opposite the street side, with a closet next to it and two twin beds lined up parallel to one another on the back wall, quilt comforters placed neatly on the foot of each bed. The wooden floors, made of dark pine, were left bare, being covered only by two small rugs placed beside the beds.

The room was permanently reserved for the National Park Service so it would be available at anytime the rangers needed it. Alaska is a huge area, a couple of the parks being larger than some states in the continental United States. So the room was used quite frequently to give the rangers a place to stop when they had to go from one area to another. Cole grabbed his list from the night table between the beds and headed over to Greta's General Store.

The general store was located on the other side of the street from the Madison at the end of the block, built diagonally to the other buildings, as it faced both the main street and the highway that ran up and down the coast. The highway was a very narrow asphalt-paved road with center striping that was heavily traveled by huge over-the-road trucks hauling frozen and fresh seafood to Canada and the west coast states, logs to the mills, and supplies up and down the coast of Alaska.

As Cole walked across the uncrowded street, he noted a Land Rover parked in front of the Yukon Saloon, the local bar where the transient fishermen spent their hard-earned money, and the community jeep parked in front of the general store. This was the vehicle that nobody in the community owned, but was maintained and used by everyone in the surrounding area that had a need for it. The honor system was used and, surprisingly, the vehicle was kept in excellent running condition.

"Hey, Joel! How's your wife feeling?" Cole shouted to the only person visible on the street.

"She's doin' much better Cole. The Doc says she can get outta bed tomorrow and start helpin' around the place in a coupla' more days," Joel answered.

"Great! Let me know if you all need anything, Okay?"

"Okay, Cole. Thanks."

When Cole cleared the concrete step in front of the general store and reached for the door knob of the double door that provided entry to the establishment, it suddenly swung wide open and spit out a four-foot tall kid scurrying at a fast pace. Cole's reaction was to quickly step back, reach out with his right hand and grab the loose fitting plaid patterned wool jacket by the collar to slow the running figure to a quick stop. The kid's boot-clad feet momentarily came off the concrete sidewalk as Cole's strong handgrip stopped the kid's momentum.

"Whoa there, fella! Where ya' goin' in such a hurry?" he blurted out. "You gotta watch where you're going or you might hurt someone!"

The short kid was wearing an olive and deep-red plaid wool cap that matched the heavy coat, with silver fur circling the lower edge and large attached fur-lined pull down earmuffs tied up across the top.

Dark-brown, unkempt shoulder-length hair poked out from under the cap. Across the forehead, short uneven bangs protruded out of the front of the short-billed hat. Large dark-brown eyes matched the brown freckles on the short nose and full cheeks, and the pastel-pink lips forming the mouth were shaped in a startled expression, as if saying "OOOH!"

"Hey mister, let me go! I mean it, let me go or I'll kick you where it hurts!" the kid yelled. "I said LET ME GO RIGHT NOW!" in an even louder voice. "My dad will put a bruisin' on you if you don't let me go!"

"Slow down little fella. Let's not go getting all steamed up. I just want you to slow down. You know, you could really hurt someone coming out that door so fast," Cole cautioned.

A stout woman of medium height came through the open door dressed in dungarees and a loose fitting flannel shirt yelling, "Don't let go Cole! That kid took some chewing tobacco without paying for it!"

Looking first to the lady and then back at the child, Cole responded, "Is that right? Did you take the tobacco, son?"

"I'm not a boy, mister. I'm a girl and I intend to pay for it. I just gotta get some money from my dad. Then, I'll be right back."

"Cole, you know she wasn't going to pay for it. She was stealing it," the lady stated.

"I wasn't stealing it lady, honest! My dad will pay for it! Just let me get the money!" she tugged at Cole's hold on her, but he wasn't letting go.

"Look little girl, it is customary to pay for the items before you leave the store. We run a very honest town here, and we don't allow people to just walk in and start taking things without first paying for them. What's your name?" Cole asked, as he crouched his six-foot two-inch frame down so that he was eye-to-eye with the frightened figure.

The little girl noticed Cole's Park Ranger uniform and was suddenly very scared. She looked directly into his deep-blue eyes, surrounded by long sandy-colored eyelashes, topped by matching eyebrows. Shallow crows-feet lines exited from each side of his eyes, accented by his deeply tanned skin created by his many years of exposure to the sun. A medium-width, straight nose and high cheeks, coupled with a strong jawbone and square chin, gave him a distinguished look. His thin, deep-red lips partially covered perfectly aligned pure white teeth. Thick, full, sandy-colored hair, cut to medium length, trimmed to just touch the top of his ears, was combed back from the forehead with a part on his left side, tapered at the back of the neck.

With a slightly shaking voice, she answered, "Jodie."

"Okay, Jodie, let's settle down a little and get to the bottom of this situation. First, what is your whole name?"

"My name is Jodie Patterson and I'm just passing through with my dad, Dawson. We came up from Portland a couple of days ago," she stated in a very soft voice.

"I see. Now, Mrs. Greta here says you took some tobacco from her store. Is that right, Jodie?"

"I didn't take it! I said I'm gonna pay for it!" she retorted. "I said I'm coming back with the money in a minute. Now, let me go!" She started to twist and turn to get loose from Cole's grasp.

"Hold on little girl! I told you we were going to settle down and get to the bottom of this. Give me the tobacco you took from the store." Cole kept his grip tight on Jodie's coat.

The little girl reached into her coat pocket and pulled out a pouch of chewing tobacco, placing it in Cole's muscular, callused hand.

"Now, it is the policy of this town that everything is paid for before you leave the store. I believe you meant to pay for it, so I am going to let you go get the money from your dad. Then you come back and pay for the tobacco. Do you think you can do that?" he instructed.

Greta blurted out before the girl could answer, "Cole, that girl was stealing the tobacco! She wasn't going to pay for it! She's been hanging around the store most of the day just waitin' for a chance to steal something!" then added, "Don't just let her go. She needs to be punished."

"Greta, I'm sure Jodie, here, had good intentions. We have the tobacco back and Jodie is going to get the money and come back to pay for it," still looking directly in the little girl's eyes he added, "Jodie, I want you to apologize to Mrs. Greta for getting her upset. Then I want you to go get the money from your dad, okay?"

"Yes, sir," she said, "I'm sorry for getting you upset ma'am," and then, when Cole released his hold on her, she turned and ran down the street to the Yukon Saloon, disappearing through the door.

"Cole you shouldn't have let her go. She was stealing that tobacco and you know it, too. She isn't coming back to pay for it," Greta said angrily.

"Well, Greta, she's just a little kid and sometimes all a kid needs is a second chance to prove they can do right. Even if she doesn't come back, you have the tobacco. So nothing is really lost, at this point," he added, winking at her.

"I'm sorry, Cole, I still don't like it," she turned opening the door, shaking her head in disapproval. Cole followed her through the door into the store.

Greta had come to Farrow's Patch in 1949, looking for solitude and a way to earn an income. She had lost her husband in World War II, at the young age of twenty-six. He was her "true love", and she just couldn't get over his death. They had met in the eighth grade and instantly fell madly in love. They got married when they graduated from high school. Then came the war and Joseph, her husband, got drafted into the Army. The rest of the story was a common scenario of war. Joseph, Greta's true love, came home in a casket.

Greta was devastated. Nobody could console her. She just wanted to be left alone and not have to explain over and over, again, why she could not move on with her life. So, in an effort to stop answering questions, she unknowingly moved on with her life by leaving her hometown, drifting aimlessly across the country seeking peace within herself, eventually ending up in Farrow's Patch.

Really, she wasn't much different from anyone else that came here, passing through Farrow's Patch on her way to Nome. She spent the cold night in the Madison, one of three businesses that were operating at the time, and while chatting with some of the other folks in the lobby, found out that the fish processing plant had just opened. She soon realized that what the area needed was a general store to supply the needs of the workers.

So, with her meager savings, she rented a small building and set up shop. She enjoyed it so much, and business was so good, that in three years she built the existing building. She never did fall in love again and she never, needless to say, got remarried.

"Greta, I know that girl was stealing. But I am sure she had a good reason," Cole closed the door behind him as he tried to reason with her. "This is a small town and, unless they are leaving right away, we will find out exactly why she tried to steal the tobacco. Let's face it, where they gonna' go?" Cole asked.

"Yeah, I guess you're right, sorry," she conceded, a note of forgiveness in her voice.

"Now how are we doing on my list of supplies for the island?"

"Pretty good. I think I have everything on your list."

Since the confrontation with the girl was out of the way, Cole and Greta put their minds and efforts into getting Cole's supplies loaded into the jeep. After three jeep-loads to the airplane, all of the supplies were safely loaded into "Lizzie" for the trip to the island.

Cole checked in with the ranger station using the two-way radio in the post office, which was also the Western Union and telegraph office. Then, as usual, he stopped by the large bulletin board set on the side of the post office that kept the community informed of various events, including the whereabouts of the many fishing boats that called Farrow's Patch home port. He had noticed that the fishing boat the men were loading earlier in the day had left the cove. It was not unusual for a boat to leave in the middle of the day, because the boats had to travel so far out to sea to get to good fishing grounds. Sometimes, it took several days or even a week to arrive at the fishing area, depending on where the schools of fish were located.

The bulletin board had various notices posted, divided in sections under different headings such as: lost and found, for sale, help wanted, wanted to buy, community calendar, which was mostly empty, and fishing boat updates.

Sure enough a fishing boat, Tiger Lilly, had been scheduled to leave that day, going to Area D-8, about 259 miles north, northwest. Expected time out to sea was stated as two to four weeks, fishing for tuna. The captain of the Tiger Lilly was listed as John Goole, ship registry, United States of America.

His work complete, Cole went back to the Madison, cleaned up, changed into civilian clothes, and drove the jeep out to Pastor Evans house, where he spent the rest of the afternoon with the pastor's family. After having a delightful home-cooked dinner, Cole headed back to Farrow's Patch.

He stopped at Greta's store, which was now closed. Greta had an apartment in the back of the store, accessed via the alleyway that led to the back of the building. Cole knocked on the door. After a brief pause, Greta opened the door. "Hey, Cole," she greeted him.

Cole entered her cozy apartment, "Good evening, Greta. Have you already had dinner?" he asked.

"Yes, I have. Have you heard about that little girl that tried to steal the tobacco?" Greta queried.

"No, I haven't. What happened? Nothing serious, I hope."

"Well, she didn't come back to the store to pay for the tobacco, so when I closed, I went to the Yukon to see if her dad was there," she said.

"I knew you wouldn't leave well enough alone, Greta," Cole scolded.

"Cole, I don't like no thieves and I wanted this guy to know what his daughter was up to, you know. Anyway, I went in and asked Johnny which guy was that girl's dad."

Johnny, was the daytime bartender and part owner of the Yukon. He and his partner, Tyrus, came to town eleven years ago. There was quite a stir when the two said they were opening a bar in Farrow's Patch. Of course, Pastor Evans was against it and the owners of the other businesses did not want the bar for fear the transient fisherman would get drunk and cause trouble and damage in the town.

But, after many heated town meetings, the partners were allowed to rent a vacant building on main street with the understanding that if they could not control the patrons, they would close up and leave town. The partners, needless to say, did manage to control the patrons and, as a matter of fact, turned out to be very good and gracious citizens.

"Johnny told me the girl's dad had been waiting on the Tiger Lilly to leave port and, as far as he knew, her dad shipped out this afternoon. I asked him where the girl was and he said he didn't know. He had not seen her since early this afternoon." With a concerned tone, she added, "Cole, I'm worried. Where would that little girl go? What's she going to do?"

"Let me get this straight. You're telling me that the little girl, Jodie, I believe, was left behind when her father got on the boat?" he asked, a puzzled sound in his voice.

"Yes."

"How do you know there wasn't someone else with them? Perhaps a mother, or brother, or sister, or maybe, even, a friend of the dad's? Someone?" Cole rambled on quizzingly.

"Well, I asked Johnny if he saw them come into town or if he saw someone else with them," Greta said. "He said no one he had talked to had seen Jodie or her dad hanging around with anyone in town. He said he had asked all the locals that came into the Yukon if they knew either one of them. He was worried, too!" Her voice approached a frantic state.

Cole responded in a soothing tone, "Okay, okay. Calm down, Greta. It's not the end of the world, you know. That little girl is not going to dissolve into thin air. We need to get a couple of people to help us look for her. She probably is hanging around one of the stores," he waved his arms around as if they were surveying Farrow's Patch. "Where were they staying or did they just arrive today?"

"Johnny says they came in his place around ten this morning. He says the guy was real mean and unfriendly, and the girl was in and out all day. He said, several times the old man would make the girl cry. Then she would leave and stay gone for an hour or so before coming back into the saloon," she explained.

"Did you go anywhere else to ask about Jodie or her dad?"

"No."

"Okay, here is the plan. I'm going over to the Madison and see if Mr. and Mrs. S. know anything," Cole said. "Why don't you see if you can round up a couple of people to help look for the little girl around town." With that, the two of them split up and started their task to find the little girl.

Cole was unsuccessful at the Madison. No one there had seen Jodie or her dad, and were unaware of the situation, but several people from the rooming house agreed to help in the search. No one had found the girl after several hours of searching, so they gave up looking after the groups had scoured the town several times and darkness had closed in.

Cole asked Greta to notify Pastor Evans, since he saw most everybody in the area all the time, and Doc Brunson, who came to town on occasion, but covered a large part of the surrounding area of Farrow's Patch. They had done all they could for now. As far as anyone knew, the little girl could have left town on one of the trucks that travel up and down the coastal highway.

The next morning, Cole got up at six a.m., packed his overnight bag, had breakfast downstairs in the dining room, and headed out into the street. He checked in with Greta to see if she had any new information on Jodie's whereabouts. She did not have any more news and said she would tell Pastor Evans and call Doc Brunson's house that day.

Cole took the descending steps, briskly, to the pier below, and spent the next quarter hour getting "Lizzie" ready for the trip to the island. He switched her on, allowed the engine to warm up, then released her from the slip and taxied over to the repair barn to fill up on gas.

After giving "Lizzie" her breakfast, as he told Tony jokingly, he headed the airplane out into the cove, faced her into the wind, and gave the floatplane full throttle to increase "Lizzie's" speed till she was skimming across the top of the water. It took a lot longer than usual to lift off because of the weight of the supplies that Cole was taking to the new cabin he was finishing on the island.

Once in the air, Cole throttled the engine down to the usual loping hum and headed the airplane slightly north of the path he flew into Farrow's Patch. Passing over the coast at the southern end of Farrow's Patch, Cole noted that the mountains to the east were lined up as if a giant hand was resting on the earth below. The tips of the fingers came towards the coastline and disappeared beneath the surface just to the east of the rocky shoreline. The fingers extended back to the palm of the hand, which formed the magnificent mountain ranges that made up the Wrangell mountain range, ultimately peaking at Mount St. Elias.

Following the valleys between the mountains he flew for an hour and a half, sometimes increasing his altitude to cross a mountain or decreasing the altitude to fly in the valley, again. Then, after all that time in the air, he crossed a mountain peak and, directly ahead, loomed a large crystal blue lake.

The beautiful lake covered about four miles, east and west, and one and a quarter miles north and south. Off to one side of the lake, about equal distance from the center of the lake and the eastern shore, an island protruded from the crystal clear water. This was where Cole's new cabin was located.

Cole cut the power and lowered the flaps a little. The plane responded by slowing down instantly. He pushed the control forward a little sending the craft into a descending flight path. Then he gave "Lizzie" a little left rudder and aileron, directing her into a slow gentle left hand turn, flying the plane around the island, slowing as he went and continuing to descend as the plane made the lazy circle around the shoreline.

The lake surrounding the five acre island had been formed by an ancient glacier, making it very deep in places. The island itself, had been created by an ancient volcano that had become inactive many years ago. The shape of the island was basically round and flat, except at the northern end, where volcanic rocks jutted upward about sixty feet to form a raised area occupying about one acre of the island. The other four acres were covered, mainly, by very large evergreens.

Cole gently set "Lizzie" down on the lake, east of the island, and slowly taxied the floatplane to the end of the dock he had built to receive it. After he had secured the aircraft to the dock, he gazed across the lake to make sure everything was okay. Then he turned and walked up the dock to the island, a distance of twenty feet. He knew the exact distance because he painstakingly placed each piling in the deep water himself.

Since the shoreline sloped so steeply into the water, the pilings farthest from the shore were in water twenty feet in depth. Cole needed the plane to be this far from shore to keep the wings from being damaged by overhanging trees and the rocky shoreline.

At that moment, Cole realized he hadn't checked in with the ranger station yet today. This was something he usually did as soon as he landed, so they would know he was all right. He abruptly turned around to head back to "Lizzie" and, as he focused on the craft, saw some movement within the cabin. He stopped short, the sight having taken him by surprise, and sucked in his breath.

What could that have been? He collected himself and cautiously walked to the airplane. Looking through the rear window on the left side of the cabin, Cole observed what appeared to be an olive and red-colored plaid piece of fabric.

"OH NO! This can't be happening to me…"

Chapter 3

"Come out of there! Come out right now!" Cole demanded. "I can't believe this! Geez, I can't believe this!"

The little girl began wiggling her way out of the airplane as Cole went on, obviously out of control and still in shock from the sight of the girl.

"What are you doing in MY airplane?" he said, emphasizing the word "my".

"Please, Mister...aah, please officer don't be mad at me! I...I had to have a place to keep out of the cold last night," Jodie pleaded, as she finally exited the cabin door.

Cole grabbed her hand and helped her over to the dock surface. "But why my airplane? Why not the rooming house or some house close to town?"

"'Cause I..."

Cole cut her off, "You cannot stay here! We're going to have to get you back to Farrow's Patch! You stupid little kid, you're going to spoil everything! I have to get you back to..." he roared.

Cole was stopped in mid-sentence as the little girl started to cry out-loud, big tears running down her freckled cheeks and dripping on the front of her flannel shirt. He realized he had been very self-centered and not very sensitive to Jodie's awful situation.

"My dad left me all alone, officer," she said, between heavy sobs. "I don't have no one to look after me. I don't know what to do," she looked up at Cole, her eyes stained red from tears. Then looking back down at the dock, tears flowing profusely, she cried out, "I'm sorry...but I don't know what to do or where to go!"

Cole crouched down to look at the tiny girl, face to face, and reached out to hold the little girl by her shoulders in an effort to calm her down. She immediately grabbed him around the neck, tucking her head under his chin and holding on very tight, all the while crying with big tears now getting Cole's ranger uniform wet across the front. Cole responded by hugging Jodie, and patting her back with his powerful hands. "Oh, Jodie, I am so sorry. How could I be so thoughtless? I'm really sorry," he said soothingly. "We will make this all right. I promise. I promise!"

Jodie, still crying hard, started that snubbing sound kids make when they cry real hard. She remained clinging to Cole, not saying a word. "Jodie, I'm really very sorry I got you so upset. It's just that it was such a shock to see you here. It really took me by surprise. Now try to settle down, and we will talk about this situation, okay?"

"Okay...Okay, officer," she said, between sobs. "Can you...hold me...just...a minute more?"

"Sure, sure I will. Take your time. It'll be all right, there, there," he continued to hug her, patting her tiny back.

After what seemed to be a long time, Jodie finally eased her hold around Cole's neck, and stepped back away from him a little way.

"There now, Jodie, let's start over, okay?" Cole said softly. "My name is Cole Bryant, and I am a park ranger. I'm not an officer. You can call me Cole," he said, by way of introduction.

"Okay, Cole," she tried the name out to see how it sounded, "I'm sorry for ruining everything for you. I really, really am sorry," snubbing, as she spoke.

Cole tried to lift her spirits by sounding upbeat. He said, "Tell you what, let's go up the dock and get a soda. I could use a soda, how about you?"

"Yeah, I'd like that," she said.

Cole stood up, placed the little girl's hand in his, and they both headed up the dock to the shoreline. Once there, Cole grabbed a rope that was attached to the lid of the large wooden box that he had sunk into the water and pulled on the rope opening the lid. Then grabbing another rope, he raised a smaller metal box, kept inside the larger wooden box, up the three feet out of the cold water to rest at his feet on the dock. Opening the metal box, he extracted two bottles of soda then lowered it back into the water.

He sat down on the dock at the edge of the shore and patted his hand on the planks, indicating for Jodie to sit beside him. With their feet dangling off the side of the dock, he slipped his combination knife from his pocket, opening the sodas. After both of them took several swallows of the ice cold sodas, neither of them saying anything, Cole calmly began to find out what had happened and why. "So, Jodie, why don't you tell me about yourself? What is your full name, again?"

"My name is Jodie Patterson," the snubbing had ceased, but her voice sounded congested from the crying.

"How old are you? Where are you from?"

"I turned ten years old in April. Me and my dad came up here from Portland. We got into Farrow's Patch yesterday morning. We've been hitch hiking for about a week to get here."

"Have you been living in Portland long?" Cole asked.

"Yeah, my whole life. My mommy died a couple of months ago, so it was just me and my dad."

"Oh my!" he was shocked, "I'm very sorry to hear that. Do you have any brothers or sisters?" he asked. He wanted to know more about Jodie's mother passing, but he felt he would first try to get the facts from her current situation settled.

Without a pause she answered, "No, sir. No one."

"No aunts or uncles? Grandparents?"

"No one, I said," she began to cry softly. "No one," she mumbled, as if it was now just starting to sink in that she was all alone.

"Why did you and your dad come to Farrow's Patch?"

"'Cause my dad said we was going to go out to sea on a big fishing boat. He was supposed to take me with…him," she said, as she started to cry again.

"Now, now, don't go and get upset again," Cole reached over to her, patting her on the shoulder. "Your dad said he was going to take you on a commercial fishing boat?"

She thought a moment, then answered, "Yes sir, he said we would make a lot of money on the fishing boat. He said we both could go on it."

"What is your dad's name, Jodie?" Cole quizzed.

"His name is Dawson Patterson."

"What is your address in Portland? I assume you mean Portland, Oregon, right?"

"Yes sir, Portland, Oregon. My address is 5544 North Calmon Street. But we don't live there anymore, 'cause we moved out to come up here," she moved her arms about to indicate the trip up the coast.

"You mean, you and your dad moved out of your house to come up here to go out on a commercial fishing boat?" Cole asked in astonishment.

"Yes sir, my dad said there was nothing for us back in Portland and this would be a way to make a lot of money."

"Didn't he tell you kids aren't allowed on commercial fishing boats?"

"No sir. My dad did not tell me that. You see, he gets real mean when he has been drinking. So, I try to stay out of his way when he gets drunk," Jodie began to explain. "That is why I got in trouble in town…'cause he told me that I couldn't go with him unless I would get him some chewing tobacco. I asked him for some money, but he said he had spent the last of the money on booze," she added. "So, if I wanted to go on the boat with him I would have to get some tobacco. That's when you caught me stealing from the store, Cole. I'm real sorry I did that," she lowered her eyes to avoid contact with Cole.

"So you tried to steal the tobacco so you could go on the fishing boat with your dad. What happened when you went back to the bar to tell your dad you got caught?" he asked.

"Well, I didn't tell him right away, because I was hoping he would forget about the tobacco. Sometimes, when he's drinking he forgets things," she said. "But pretty soon he remembered, I guess, and he called me over to the table where he was drinking. He asked me where the tobacco was and I told him I got caught taking it. He laughed and said I wasn't going with him on the boat." Her voice got louder and more intense as she continued to tell of the painful event, "He said I wasn't nothing but an anchor around his neck. He was gettin' on that boat and gettin' rid of his anchor. And then he laughed and laughed, and later, he got up and left," Jodie spoke with panic in her voice. "I begged him not to go. I asked him what was going to happen to me. I need my dad to take care of me!" she said, as she started to sob again. "He just laughed and said, 'Figure it out yourself, kid', and then...and then...he walked down the pier and got on the boat with the other guys." After a very long pause, Jodie added, "Soon after that, the boat left the cove." She put her soda down on the dock, got up, hugged Cole around the neck, and climbed into his lap with big tears rolling down her puffy, freckled cheeks.

Cole responded by putting his arms around Jodie's tiny body, saying, "Now, now," over and over.

Cole put his soda down and replaced his arms around Jodie's shoulders, gently stroking them in a soothing manner. After a minute or two, Cole asked again, "So, you don't have any relatives you can contact?"

"No sir, I don't have any relatives at all."

"How about a good friend that lived close to your house or school?"

"No sir, we didn't live in a very good neighborhood, so people always moved a lot, you know."

"So there isn't anyone you can call to help you out?"

"Except for you, my dad is the only person I know."

He thought to himself, "Geez, what a mess! What am I going to do now?" He sat motionless thinking what he could do to help this child and her terrible predicament. Could her father really have abandoned her? What was going to become of this kid? It was time to take action. He needed to get control of the situation.

"Okay Jodie, I am going to call the ranger station and let them know I have gotten here safe and sound. It is part of my job to check in occasionally. I'm, also, going to let them know that you are here with me," he added. "You know, we looked all over the place for you last night. I have to let them know you are safe and sound with me here, okay?"

"Yes, sir. I understand. But, please don't send me away!" she pleaded. "Please, please don't send me away, okay?"

"Now you know I will do what is right. But remember I am a ranger. I don't live in a city. I don't have any kids. So you probably will have to go live with someone that has a family, someone that will know how to take care of a little kid. Do you understand that, Jodie?" Cole said, in a gentle, caring voice.

"Cole, please don't send me away. Please let me stay with you. I promise I will be very good and not cause you any extra work. I promise!" Jodie begged.

"Jodie, the decision is not up to me. You see, there are laws that people have to follow. I cannot just say, 'Hey, you're my kid now. You stay with me.' There are laws that tell me what I can and cannot do," he tried to explain. "Let's not jump off the deep end, here. Let's call the ranger station and let them know what is going on and take this thing one step at a time."

Cole walked down the dock to "Lizzie", climbed in, picked up the microphone, turned on the radio and spoke calmly into the mouthpiece. After several seconds a man's voice came back over the radio, "Chisano Station, we receive you Cole."

"Hey, Bert, can you put Ranger Defreese on the radio. I have a situation, here. Repeat, I have a situation here. Nothing urgent but I need to speak with Ranger Defreese a-s-a-p," he spelled out the last word.

"That's a ten-four. Ranger Defreese is here at the station. I'll go get him. Any message at this point?"

"No message. Everything is under control here. I'll stand by for him," Cole responded.

After several minutes, Ranger Defreese was on the radio, "This is Ranger Defreese. Come in Cole."

"Yes sir, I have a situation here," Cole began, and slowly explained the order of events that had happened in the last twenty-four hours. After talking it over with Ranger Defreese, the immediate conclusion was to have the girl stay on the island until Ranger Defreese and the staff could track down Dawson Patterson on the Tiger Lilly.

"Look, Cole, I know you have a lot to do on your days off at the island but, for now, just pretend you have a guest with you, and work around her." Ranger Defreese said. "At least, this way we know where the girl is, and she cannot get lost on us. Then if we haven't come up with a solution, at that time, you can bring her here when you report back to work. Any questions?" he concluded.

"No sir, no questions," Cole answered. "Also, check with the Portland police at her old address and the local elementary school to see if anyone can verify her story...over and out." He replaced the microphone on the radio, switched it off and climbed out of the airplane.

He looked toward the end of the dock, where it connected with the shore, and observed the small figure sipping her soda as she gazed down into the clear water. "This was definitely going to be an adventure," he thought. Cole had never been married and did not have any children. Now he was going to be in charge of this kid until Ranger Defreese could figure out what to do with her.

Cole sucked in a deep breath of fresh Alaskan air, nervously pulled at his belt as if adjusting his pants, and walked to Jodie. Crouching down beside her, he said in an upbeat voice, "Well, it looks like we're going to be pals for the next couple of days, Jodie. What do you think about that?"

"Considering everything that has happened, I think that is the best news I have had in quite awhile. I promise, Cole, I won't be a bit of trouble," she continued. "You won't even know I'm around."

"Well, I have a lot of work to do, and you can help me. First let me show you around the island. Come on," he said, and held his hand down for Jodie to grab it so he could lift her up onto her feet.

The cabin was located about one hundred feet back from the shoreline and the dock. The thick trees in this area had been cut down and used to build the cabin. Near the back of the cabin the trees crowded in close to the structure. Out front was an open space about forty to fifty feet on average. A large fire pit encircled by large, round rocks, blackened from previous fires, with a metal spit suspended over its center, occupied the mid-point of the clearing.

The small log cabin, about twenty-four feet across the front and eighteen feet deep, had a porch across the entire front, two steps up from ground level, that extended six feet out from the main structure. The seams between the logs on the sides of the cabin were filled with a cement-like mud. Even though the logs came from the surrounding trees, the floor and roof had been brought to the island in "Lizzie" from Juneau and Farrow's Patch.

The long logs at the front and back of the cabin were broken by two windows and a door. The door on the front wall was placed in the dead center, but on the back wall, the door had been located behind the kitchen, off to the right side. One window was located on each side of the cabin, and all of the windows had heavy wooden shutters that swung back on each side allowing the sun to enter, filling the interior with a yellow-cast light. The roof and porch were steeply pitched, covered with metal, the joints sealed with tar.

Cole and Jodie stepped up the two steps to the porch, and Cole opened the wooden door, which was made out of a half dozen wooden planks attached together by a plank that ran diagonally across the door face. The door creaked on the metal hinges as it opened, revealing the dark, earthy smelling interior. Jodie popped right inside the cabin saying, "Wow, this is neat, Cole!" Cole remained outside opening the shutters to allow light to penetrate the darkened interior.

A dark wooden, rectangular table and four wooden chairs sat directly in front of the doorway with an oil lamp placed in the center of the table. To the right, a small bedroom with a single cot could be seen through the open doorway and, at the back of the cabin, an open kitchen occupied that area with the door in the rear wall that led outside the cabin.

To the left was the living area where a large, overstuffed chair and ottoman sat in front of a stone fireplace, which was centered on the side wall. A dark-pine rocker was placed at the rear of the living area with a small oval end table setting next to it. Three oil lanterns hung from the exposed rafters in the center of the cabin, which when lit gave off a warm yellow glow to the room.

Cole walked to the fireplace, retrieved a match from a large match-box and lit the oil lamps. Slowly a golden glow was cast over the cabin interior adding more light to the sunrays that pierced the windowpanes. Jodie had already walked over to the kitchen looked around a little and, then, joined Cole in the living area. "This is a neat place, it's nice and cozy in here," she said. "How long have you lived here?"

"I've been working on the place about two years. The first year I cut down the trees, built the walls and took out some of the tree stumps. Last year, I finished taking out the stumps and put the roof, porch and floor in the place. This year, I have been moving things into the cabin. It is livable now."

"Well, it is neat. Really neat. I mean it is really, really neat!" she giggled.

"Thanks, Jodie," Cole chuckled at the little girl's enthusiasm.

They were standing on a large, oval rope rug in the center of the living area. A gun rack with several rifles hung on the front wall and a hat and coat rack occupied the area adjacent to the door. A couple of pictures of family members had been placed on the wall next to the fireplace. Even though the cabin was very sparsely furnished, it gave off the feeling of home sweet home to Jodie.

Cole waved his arms in a big circular motion to indicate the area within the cabin. "This is going to be your home for the next couple of days, so I hope you like it really, really good," Cole said, mocking Jodie's comment. "Let's go outside and walk around the island a little to get you acquainted with the surroundings."

The cabin was located at the southern end of the small island, with about an acre of property behind the cabin. Walking in that direction, down a narrow path that meandered toward the water's edge with heavy growth on each side, Cole turned around to talk to Jodie, "Now this area is filled with berry bushes. By the end of this month the berries will start to come in and I will have lots of jellies and jams to can."

Ahead, they broke out into an open area that gave a spectacular view of the lake and, beyond, the surrounding mountains. "This area back here is where I like to come to fish, and on nice days, lay out in the sun." Here, the shore dropped off gently into the lake and even had a little sandy shoreline. It was a peaceful, pleasant smelling place with the wild flowers and the berry bushes nearby.

"Wow!" Jodie exhaled, "This is really nice. I'd like to have a picnic here."

"That's a good idea. We'll work on that," placing his hand on the little girl's shoulder, Cole guided her up the trail past the cabin.

The other four acres, or so, were north of the cabin. Here, two trails headed away from the cabin into the thick woods. Taking the narrow trail to the left, that hugged the western shore, Cole led the way, Jodie following closely, eyes wide with anticipation. The trail rose and fell, twisted and turned between the large trees and the boulders, at times the sun being completely blocked by the thick foliage. Near the end of the trail, they broke free of the heavy foliage into a rocky area occupied by large, black boulders that appeared to have been stacked on top of each other.

Jodie stopped beside Cole and looked up to the top of the pile of boulders, "This is spooky. What is it?" she whispered.

"Oh, this is part of a volcano...I mean it was part of a volcano many, many years ago. You may have studied about stuff like this in school. Do you know what a volcano is?"

"Yeah, kinda'. It blows up and hot stuff comes out, doesn't it?" She put her hands together, then moved them rapidly apart to illustrate an explosion.

"That's right, Jodie. Here, sit down and let me tell you about it." Cole sat down beside her on one of the big rocks, then began to explain in his usual park guide style, "Do you know what a glacier is?"

"That is a big piece of ice that floats in the ocean," Jodie answered.

"Well kinda'! Except it doesn't float in the ocean. That is called an iceberg. A glacier is a big chunk of ice that flows slowly down a mountain. Here in Alaska, a lot of the valleys and lakes have been carved out by those large blocks of ice called glaciers," he pointed toward the lake. "A long, long time ago this lake was formed when a glacier slowly slid down those mountains," he pointed toward the eastern range of mountains, "digging out the land as they moved. Later, a volcano over those mountains across the lake became very active," this time he pointed north, across the lake. "It would blow up and spew hot molten lava over the land, melting the ice, forming the lakes. Of course, they would cool down after awhile and freeze again," he continued. "Then, the volcano's molten lava found another way to the surface of the earth and it formed this island. At one time this island was much higher than it is now. The volcano kept pushing the earth up from below as pressure built up deep within the earth. Finally, the island erupted, blowing the top right off," he waived his hands in a violent circular motion. "But after a very long time, the volcano became dormant again, which means it quit erupting. Since volcanic soil is very rich in certain nutrients, it wasn't long before vegetation started to grow on the island. Next thing you know, it turned out to be this beautiful place.

"Are we in danger, Cole?"

"No, the volcano last erupted in 1867. It hasn't even quivered since then.

"Where is the hole the lava comes out?" she queried.

"There isn't any hole. The last time this island blew up, the entire top came off and the hole was covered up by the molten lava."

"So, just these black rocks are left?"

"That's right, just these rocks and all of this beautiful vegetation. Isn't this a beautiful place?" Cole asked.

"Yes, it's really, really neat!" they both laughed, as they headed back down the trail to the cabin area.

When they arrived at the cabin, Cole said, "Tell you what, Jodie, let's unload the supplies from the airplane and then we can get to work around the place." For the next hour or so, they took turns unloading "Lizzie" and lugging the materials and supplies up the dock to the shoreline. Some of the supplies were then placed in the cabin and the others were placed on the front porch.

"My first project is to build a covered stand for the firewood storage," Cole told Jodie. "So, let's get to it." At that, the two of them started to build a twelve-foot long covered storage area. Several hours later, they broke for lunch. After eating canned food, the two of them walked to the grassy area behind the cabin and Cole showed Jodie some of the smaller wildlife on the island.

By this time of day, the temperature had reached a very warm fifty-three degrees and so the two had shed their coats and one layer of sweaters. They looked under rocks to expose small critters and along the shoreline, where the water meets land, they observed tadpoles, minnows and, sometimes, a small bass as it approached to have lunch on one of the shiners in the shallow water. The time spent was very pleasant and relaxing and the two seemed to get along very well.

After the break, they resumed working on the storage area. Then later, they loaded the cut firewood into the newly completed firewood stand. "Whew, that was hard work," Jodie said, panting heavily.

"Yes it was. You're a good worker, Jodie. Thanks for all your help. The firewood will last much longer and be easier to use, since it will not be damp from rain anymore. Thanks! Let's go down to the refrigerator and have a soda."

The lake was Cole's refrigerator. Since the temperature of the lake stayed in the thirty to forty degree range most of the year, it kept food fresh as good as a regular refrigerator. He had constructed two waterproof boxes out of metal which were placed in a large wooden outer box with small holes drilled in it to allow the cold water to surround the metal boxes. The holes were covered with screening to keep small fish and other critters out of the box. This allowed Cole to store some meats and vegetables in one box, milk and other drinks in the other, just the same as you would in a regular refrigerator.

As they sat on the dock drinking their sodas, Jodie lay back on the dock and looked up into the sky. Across the lake the call of a hawk could be heard. Closer, the sounds of small chirping birds came from the trees and bushes on the island. Occasionally, the slapping noise of a fish jumping across the surface of the lake reached her ears.

"Cole, if you look at the clouds, sometimes they make faces and shapes. Look right over there," she said, extending her arm skyward, pointing her finger at a big white cumulus cloud. "See, it looks like a big white sheep."

"Yes, I see it. Now let me find one," he said, laying back on the dock surface. After a few moments, he raised his arm and pointed at a cloud and said, "That one over there looks like George Washington. See his white wig, and over there is his nose, and that blue patch is his eye. Can you see it?"

"Yeah, that's neat. It is changing shape now and looks like an Indian, see it?" Jodie added. This went on for quite a while as the two slowly sipped their sodas. Sometimes they would break out in laughter when they pointed out funny shapes in the slow moving clouds. Oh, it was a beautiful day in Alaska!

Later, Cole took Jodie to the grassy area behind the cabin and he set a fishing line for each of them. He said dinner was "on him" tonight, but they needed to catch it. "Out here you have to catch your own food or you starve to death, so let's catch dinner because I am starving. Do you like fish, Jodie?"

"Yes sir, and you're lucky, because I am the bestest fisherman around!"

In a short while, they had caught four bass and one bream, which they threw back, because the bass were more than enough of a meal for the two of them. The temperature had begun to drop by the time they got back to the cabin, so Cole had started the fire in the pit outside.

He gave Jodie the task of choosing and cleaning the potatoes and snapping the green beans that he had brought up from Farrow's Patch with them. The potatoes were put in one large iron pot with water and the green beans, also in water, in another and both hung over the fire pit from the large spit.

Cole cleaned the fish; placed them in an iron skillet just outside the flames' reach, seasoned them with his "secret" backwoods recipe and added a little left over fat that he kept in the cabin. In no time flat, they were eating a delicious home cooked meal.

By the time they finished dinner, it was getting quite late. The sun had finally drifted below the mountain range to the west and darkness was closing in. In Alaska the days are much longer than in the rest of the country this time of year because it is so close to the North Pole. In mid-summer, there are only four hours of darkness on the island. But today, the darkness would last a full eight hours.

Cole and Jodie cleaned up the dishes, then sat by the fire and told each other stories that they made up. Sometimes, they would laugh out loud, and other times, they would be very quiet to emphasize a point in the story.

"Well, Jodie, we need to hit the sack. You go in the cabin and I'll put out this fire."

"Okay, Cole."

Inside, Cole made up a sleeping bag for himself on the living room floor, and gave Jodie his cot in the bedroom. When Jodie had changed into her nightclothes, she asked Cole to come into the room. "Will you tuck me in, Cole?" she asked.

"Sure thing, honey."

"My mommy used to have me say a prayer. Can I do that?"

"Yes," he said, in a low voice.

"Now I lay me down to sleep. I pray the Lord my soul to keep. If I die before I wake, I pray the Lord my soul to take...God be with Mommy, in heaven, and be with Daddy, wherever he is..." she said, as her voice trailed off and she let out a little sob. She reached for Cole's neck, "I miss my mommy very, very much. I'm so lonesome," she exhaled deeply, then added, "and my daddy doesn't love me or want me...." she began to cry, big tears running down her freckled cheeks.

"Now, now Jodie...It...will be...all right," Cole whispered, as he held the little girl tight, and patted her back. "I promise we will get to the bottom of this and find out what has happened. And I promise, I won't abandon you," he added.

Cole was thinking, "Oh boy! What have I gotten myself into here? I cannot take care of this little girl. I live out in the woods by myself and my job requires I travel all over the place. How can I be responsible for a little kid? I'm a single guy, what do I know about caring for a little kid?" He began to perspire across his forehead.

But with a quiet, almost whispering, monotone voice, Cole said, "I told you we would take it one day at a time, didn't I?"

"Yes sir," she snubbed.

"Today went pretty good, didn't it?"

"Yes sir, I had lots of fun."

"Well, that was one day. Tomorrow is a new day and we have lots to do around the place. Are you going to help me?"

"Yeah, I'm the bestest helper. Right, Cole?" she sniffled, wiping her nose with a handkerchief.

"Yes you are, honey!" he emphasized, "And I have a special job for you tomorrow."

"What, what is it?" she asked.

"Well, I will tell you in the morning. But now we must get some sleep so we can get an early start on our projects tomorrow. Do you feel a little better now?" he asked, as she continued to wipe the drying tears from her cheeks.

"Yes sir. Cole can I ask you to do something?"

"You can ask me anything, Jodie. What do you want?" He was thinking maybe a glass of water or a bedtime story.

"Just tonight...will you move your sleeping bag in here with me...just tonight?" she begged.

After a moment of thinking this request through, Cole answered, "Yes, honey.... Just tonight."

Chapter 4

Cole brought his sleeping bag into the room and placed it next to the cot Jodie was using. After he settled in, Jodie said, in a very sleepy, soft voice, "You're the greatest Cole, thanks."

Cole did not say anything. He laid there thinking about the events of the day. This is one day that did not turn out the way he thought it would, but all in all it did turn out okay, though. After Jodie had settled down, she was kind of fun to be around. Normally, out here at the island, it was very quiet, but today was different. That little kid made the day go by easy and it was kind of neat to show her all about different things on the island.

Of course, Jodie would have to be turned over to foster parents. He could not possibly take care of a kid and do his job, too. That was going to be hard on her. Naturally, he would do the best he could to keep in touch with her. Right now, of course, he was the person she was attached to because he came to her rescue in Farrow's Patch. But someone else would step up and help her through this difficult period in her life.

Then his mind switched to Jodie's father. How could a dad just leave his kid? How cruel! What kind of man is this guy, Dawson Patterson? He had to have known in advance that he was going to leave this kid. Why not leave her in Portland? At least she would have been in familiar surroundings and, maybe, had someone to take care of her. Maybe Ranger Defreese found out something today. Cole would be checking in with the ranger station in the morning, as he always did every day.

Well, in three days he would be at Chisano Ranger Station and they would have a plan for the little girl's future welfare, not that she was hard to care for. He wondered what it would be like, taking care of this girl.

Just before Cole drifted off to sleep, he gazed up to look at the peaceful little girl bathed in the soft moonlight that drifted through the bedroom window. She looked so peaceful. His heart was heavy with worry about her future. He shook off the thought of becoming attached to Jodie. After all, he reminded himself, he was single, never been married, never had a child of his own, and his job would not permit him to care for a child. To himself he muttered, "Don't become attached. Don't get anymore involved," as he drifted off to sleep.

The next morning, the two were up early feeling refreshed and ready to take on another day. Cole cooked a full breakfast. They had eggs and Canadian bacon, toast, milk, and Cole, also, had coffee. After breakfast, Cole went out to "Lizzie" to call into the ranger station, and Jodie was put in charge of washing the breakfast dishes. This allowed Cole an opportunity to speak with Ranger Defreese without Jodie hearing the conversation.

Cole spoke into the microphone, "This is Cole, come in Chisano Station."

A moment or two later a man's voice came over the speaker, "Ranger Defreese is waiting for your call, Cole. Hold the line."

Soon, Ranger Defreese's voice came over the speaker, "Come in, Cole."

"Cole here, sir. I hope you were able to find something out," he said hastily.

"Well, we finally got in touch with the Tiger Lilly. She is headed out to area D-8, about two hundred-fifty to three hundred miles out to sea. I spoke with the captain, John Goole, who brought Dawson Patterson to the radio. Mr. Patterson, and I use the term "mister" very loosely, is a real piece of work. Are you wearing your headset, Cole?" Ranger Defreese asked.

"Yes, sir. Jodie is in the cabin washing the dishes, so she won't hear my conversation to you either, sir."

"Good! Well anyway, this Dawson told me he doesn't want to see the kid anymore. I asked him, why? He told me he did not love Jodie's mom, he was a real loner, and he knew he drank too much. He said he had even told Jodie's mom that if it were not for her, or the girl, he would go off on a boat by himself. When his wife died a couple of months ago, he believed this was his opportunity to cut himself free. He felt that if he had left Jodie in Portland, the authorities would have caught up with him before he could get on the boat and make him stay home with her. He said he was sorry to have caused us any trouble, but he was abandoning the girl, and he did not want to see her again."

"What did you say? What did you do?" Cole said, in astonishment.

"I spoke with the captain at length, Cole. But the situation is like this. First, they were out in the open sea outside the territorial waters. So, legally, there is not anything they can do. Secondly, the captain cannot turn the boat around because he has the whole crew to think about and they must complete their fishing trip. The captain is as appalled about this as we are, and he assures me that when they dock, Mr. Dawson Patterson will be dealt with, and we will be notified," Ranger Defreese concluded, disgust in his voice.

"I'm in shock! Patterson doesn't want to see his kid ever again?" Cole asked, in amazement. "How can anyone turn against one of their own? What kind of slime is this guy, anyway?"

"Well, I dunno. It is a bad situation at best. I called the Portland police and they ran a quick preliminary check on the family. They say the school knows the girl and mother. The girl was a well-behaved student and made above average grades. They were very poor and lived in a bad section of town. The family kept to themselves pretty much, and the father was known to be an alcoholic. The police had been called out a couple of times to settle domestic disputes. You know, the typical he hits her, she hits back kind of thing. The police never arrested Patterson," Defreese said, as he read his notes.

"What about the mother's death? How did that happen and when?" Cole quizzed.

"That's what I was coming to, Cole. The police state that the mother was a victim of a hit and run accident on the night of February 11th of this year. The accident is still under investigation. It seems there are some unanswered questions in the case."

Cole interrupted, "What? What kind of unanswered questions? What?"

"Hang on! Hang on just a minute and I will tell you!" Defreese said, raising his voice above Cole's questioning, "Some of the questions are: It was very cold that night, so why wasn't she wearing a heavy coat? What was she doing in the middle of the street? There was no alcohol in her blood, and the kid was asleep in her room when the police arrived. But, evidently, the old man had an ironclad alibi. He was in the bar down the street from the house."

"What time of night did the accident happen?"

"She died in the hospital at 3:10a.m. The accident happened around 2a.m. There were no witnesses. She was found in the street about 2:25a.m. by, get this, Dawson Patterson," he said, with a tone of disbelief in his voice.

"How convenient," Cole muttered.

"The police are going to do a more thorough investigation on the hit and run and they are, also, going to see if they can get us a distant relative or good friend that may be able to take care of the kid," he said. "I have a call into Judge Holcolmb as we speak. I need to find out what can be done with the girl, you know, what our obligations are, what needs to be done."

"Are we still keeping to the original plan? I am to keep her here till I come to the ranger station?"

"Yes, that is right. That still gives us two days to find out more about her and more about what we are going to do with her. What other questions do you have?" he asked.

"Well, none really."

"Okay, then, tell me how it went with you and the girl."

"Well, not bad. After the initial shock of having company aboard the island, I was okay with the situation. So far, Jodie is well behaved and a good companion. We, actually, had a good time together. However, last night she had several bad nightmares. I mentioned them to her this morning and she didn't remember them, which was good," Cole reported.

"I really do appreciate you going along with this plan, Cole. I hope it isn't too much of an inconvenience." Defreese probed.

"No, it isn't so bad. I have kind of enjoyed showing her the island and how to do things. So far, so good!" He paused a moment, then added in a serious tone, "Look! I want you to do something for me."

"What?"

"I noticed the kid doesn't have many clothes. So, this morning I made a list of some things I want you to get from Greta. Have her put them on my tab and have the next person going through Farrow's Patch pick them up and take them to the ranger station, okay?"

"Yes, I can have that done," Defreese answered, a bit of puzzlement in his voice. "What do you need?"

"I checked Jodie's duffel bag out this morning when she was out back of the cabin. The poor kid doesn't have anything to wear, really, so here is a list:

one pair of corduroy pants	shampoo
two pairs of dungarees	toothbrush
one belt	toothpaste
three flannel shirts	comb
five sets of underwear	hair brush
five pairs of heavy socks	pair of work boots

"Got all of that?" he asked.

"Yeah, I got it all. Cole, if I didn't know any better, I would say you are kind of enjoying looking after this kid," Ranger Defreese joked.

"Look, Bill," Cole responded, in a deep stern voice, "this little girl has lost everything in the world. She has absolutely nothing. How can I not feel something for her? How can I not help her?"

"I am really sorry, Cole. You are right. I'm sorry I sounded like I was making light of the situation. Thanks for getting me back on track," he said, in a serious tone. "I'll make sure everything gets done."

"I want three more items added to the list. In the general store I saw a stuffed Raggedy Ann Doll. It stands about a foot tall. Jodie needs something to care for, so I want that doll for her. Also, get her some candy or something, just for fun, and a box of crayons and coloring book, okay?"

"I got it down, Cole. Sounds like you're doing a bang up job. Thanks! Anything else?" He asked.

"No, that is all. I'll check in again tomorrow morning."

"Oh, one more thing, Cole," Ranger Defreese quickly interjected, "Allison is coming in from school tomorrow. She got her degree in veterinary science. She says she is going to spend the summer at the station, then decide where she will settle down. So we have one last summer to convince her to stay at the station, ha, ha."

"Great news! But isn't she going to attend her graduation?"

"Yes, we both are. It is in two weeks. She actually is getting out early because her classes did not require final tests."

"Well, I know you are very proud of A.J." Cole always called her A.J. instead of her given name.

"Yes, I am. Well, that's it from here. Maybe tomorrow I will have some encouraging news for you. Over and out."

"Over and out," Cole signed off.

By the time Cole had completed his call to Ranger Defreese, Jodie had finished the morning dishes and ran down the dock to the airplane. They greeted each other and joked a little, then got on with their day full of activities around the island.

It was a very pleasant day. The weather, once again, was a clear, cloudless fifty-five degrees and a soft breeze floated across the island from the west. Jodie proved to be a good helper, never once complaining about too much work. Cole tried to have plenty of free time between jobs to have fun. At one point, Jodie taught Cole the game of hopscotch. She scribed the outline of the hopscotch in the soil with a stick, selected two smooth, round rocks as markers and proceeded to show Cole the way to play the game. They both ended up laughing and teasing one another.

Cole spent a lot of time telling Jodie about the history of the area and showing her all kinds of fascinating plants and animals. It wasn't unusual to see them peering in a hole in a tree trunk or looking under rocks. Jodie was very interested in nature and enjoyed being shown all of these new and wonderful things.

Only once during the day did Jodie mention anything about her parents. When they were playing hopscotch, Jodie's eyes filled with tears as she remembered playing the game in the street in front of her house with her mother. But she didn't go into any detail, and Cole thought it best not to question her. Cole knew that, at some point, Jodie was going to let all of her inner feelings out. He just hoped that he would do a good job of helping her get through that part if he was the one she confided in.

Late that day, after dinner, Cole took Jodie to the area behind the cabin where they took turns casting a small screen net in the shallow water to catch shiners to use as fish bait. When their small bucket was full of shiners, Cole fixed up two fishing poles and they headed off to the highest part of the island.

The eastern trail ran through an area dense with trees and bushes and, at this time of evening just before sunset, it was rather spooky on the trail. So, Jodie hung close to Cole's heels as they traveled the narrow path to the dormant volcano.

When they reached the large boulder field making up the side of the volcano, they took turns passing the bucket and fishing poles to one another as they worked their way up the steep incline. Finally reaching the top just as the last light of day faded away, the lake view, surrounded by the majestic mountains that kept the water captured, was splended in its pristine, unpolluted, natural state.

Slightly out of breath from the hard climb, Cole asked, "How about this place? What do you think?"

"Man, oh man, this is really, really neat!" Jodie whispered, almost afraid to make any noise because it was so quiet and still.

"Tonight you are in for a treat. We are going to fish from up here. You see, tonight the moon will go behind the mountains in about an hour. This is going to allow us to do two things in one night. Do you know what they are?" he quizzed.

"No sir, I don't," she answered, with mystery in her voice.

"Well, as it gets a little darker, the light from the moon is going to shine down into the water and allow us to actually see the fish swimming beneath the surface. We should be able to see the bigger ones in about a half-hour, or so. Then, if we are lucky, later we will be able to see many, many more."

"Really? Boy, that will be neat. Then what is the second thing that will happen?" Jodie asked, excitedly.

"After the moon disappears behind those mountains," he said, pointing to the mountain range at the western end of the large lake, "it will get very dark out here. When that happens, the sky will light up with beautiful lights that look like giant curtains hanging down from heaven."

"Wow, really? Where do they come from, Cole?"

"They are caused by the magnetic fields of the earth colliding with electrons in the sky. But for now, let's just say it is one of God's many wonders. They are called the aurora borealis."

"Area Buri...what are they called?" she tried to repeat the name, then started laughing when she knew it wouldn't come out right.

"Let's just call them the Northern Lights," he added.

"Okay. I can't wait to see them," and then, at that moment, she saw her first big fish reflect the moon's light in the lake below. "Look! Look down there! A big fish just swam by!"

"Well, we can't catch anything unless we get our hooks baited and in the water, can we?" Cole exclaimed.

As the night progressed, it was just as Cole said it would be. The pair caught two large bass for dinner the next night and a bunch of smaller ones that they threw back. In any other state, the smaller ones would have been good-sized catches. Cole explained to Jodie that out here you only take what you can eat. You never waste any natural resource. That way the resource will never be depleted and the cycle of nature is never broken.

Later, the Northern Lights put on a fabulous display for the newest visitor to the island. Jodie was very impressed with the wavering lights as they changed color and switched on and off as if attached to an invisible power source.

"Ooh! Aaah!" she exclaimed, "Wow! They look like sheets that are coming out of the sky. And sometimes, it looks like they will come down and touch me on the nose." She touched her index finger to the tip of her nose to demonstrate the feeling.

"So you think you like those lights?" Cole asked.

"Yeah, they are..." and in the middle of the sentence the two said in unison "REALLY, REALLY NEAT!" and both laughed and laughed.

Very late that night the two walked back to the cabin through the dark woods. This time Jodie was not afraid. She knew the island pretty well by now and she felt comfortable....and at home. Cole had Jodie go in the cabin and get ready for bed while he cleaned the fish and put them in his lake-style refrigerator to keep fresh.

He found Jodie sound asleep on the overstuffed chair when he entered the cabin. He walked over and looked down on the peaceful face of the tiny girl that had been abandoned. He wondered, again, how any human being could desert such a sweet kid. She had been able to put on her pajamas and wash her hands and face before she collapsed in sleep in the chair.

Cole bent down and picked the girl up, cradling her in both of his arms. When he stopped beside her bed, she opened her sleepy eyes and said in a half voice, half whisper, "You are..really...really..neat," and then lifted her head to kiss him on the cheek.

Cole's heart felt like a large lump in his chest. He was becoming too attached to Jodie and it scared him. He bent down and placed the small girl in her cot, pulling the covers up to her neck, then turned and left the room. "This is going to get complicated," he thought to himself.

The next morning the two awakened later than usual because of retiring so late the night before. Jodie had two bad nightmares during the night, but once again didn't seem to remember them. Cole put Jodie in charge of cleaning the cabin while he made his morning call to the ranger station.

The news from Ranger Defreese was that he had talked to Judge Holcolmb about Jodie. The judge told Bill Defreese he would find a foster home for the girl as quickly as possible and, when Cole and Jodie got to Chisano Station, someone would take over the care of the child. They were asking the other families in the area if they could take care of the girl, either on a temporary or a permanent basis. The judge, also, told Bill he was working on a court order to keep the father from getting the girl back, if Patterson ever changed his mind.

Cole caught himself feeling a little nervous. He didn't like the idea that Jodie would be taken care of by someone else. "Wait a minute!" he thought, "This is what I wanted. I don't want to be responsible for taking care of a kid. After all, I am single and travel a lot. I can't take care of this girl."

Then his thoughts went more short term, thinking, maybe he could take care of Jodie at least through the summer. After all, there wasn't any school, and she could accompany him on his trips to the other ranger stations. Some of the other rangers took their kids along with them during the summer. It was an educational experience for the kids and gave the rangers time to "bond" with their children. It was good for the Service to pre-train future rangers and lead the youth, possibly, into a career in forestry or park management.

In that brief moment, Cole realized he was becoming hooked on the tiny girl. Oh boy! He was hooked...hook, line and sinker. This little girl had, in this brief time together, undeniably and successfully attached herself to his heart. But now, because he had not spoken up, the judge was going to honor "his wishes" and take the little girl away from him. He felt emptiness and sadness instead of gladness and relief that he wouldn't have to look after her.

In that brief moment, he thought maybe he should tell Ranger Defreese that he wanted to keep the child at least for the summertime. He could say it was for her benefit. You know, to give her a chance to acclimate herself to her new situation...to give her some semblance of a stable environment.

But Cole was still not ready to "go public" with his feelings. Jodie may not want Cole to be her guardian. "Guardian!" What was he thinking? This is going too far. No, he was not ready to discuss this yet. Besides, when he arrived at the ranger station, all of this would be taken care of anyhow. He simply was not ready to discuss any future plans of caring for this kid.

There was no new information from the Portland police. They had told Ranger Defreese it might take awhile to get the investigation up and running. But all indications were that there were no relatives or even close friends to care for Jodie. With that, the two signed off. It was agreed Cole would make his usual contact in the morning when he and Jodie were ready to leave the island.

The rest of the day was pretty much the same as the first two days. Cole continued to make improvements on the cabin and the grounds as well as allow time for fun and games. A bad thunderstorm passed across the lake and surrounding mountains late that afternoon. The pair sat on the front porch of the cabin and watched a wild display of lightning as the storm passed over the tops of the mountains to the west and proceeded eastward across the lake toward the island.

When the lightning bolts were approaching the island, Jodie quietly and quickly climbed into Cole's lap, grabbed his arms and put them around her waist. "Hey, little girl. You're not scared are you?" he said, soothingly.

"Yes...yes, sir!" she said, nervously.

"Well I won't let any of them things get you. As a matter of fact, since they scare you let's go inside and fix some hot chocolate. What do you say?"

"Sounds great!" Jodie jumped out of his lap and ran inside the cabin.

They made some hot chocolate, started a fire in the fireplace, because the storm had dropped the temperature outside into the low forties, and sipped the hot liquid. Jodie, feeling all warm inside and secure within the thick walls of the cabin, blurted out that her nightmares all seemed to be the same. Cole knew this could be the time he was worried about. The little girl may choose this moment to unleash all of the horrible memories she may have locked up inside her mind. The experiences of this girl's past few months, or even past few years, were going to have to come out for her to fully free herself from the past in order to move on to the present and future.

"What do you mean all of your dreams seem to be the same, Jodie?" Cole asked, trying not to sound too probing.

"They have the same people in them. You know, it is the same dream over and over," she said, twisting her hands together, her fingers interlocked in an awkward tangled sort of way.

"Do you want to tell me about the dreams?" he asked, his voice calm and controlled.

"No, not really. They are scary. I...I just...I just wish they would go away," she muttered.

"They will, Jodie, they will. It may take a little time but I know they will go away," he said, as he leaned toward her putting his arm around the little girl's shoulders, squeezing them gently. "When I was a little kid just about your age, I remember I would have some bad dreams. Really scary ones."

"Really? But, I bet mine are scarier than yours!"

"Maybe. Let's see. I remember one time there was this great big guy, Frankenstein, that was after me. Do you know who Frankenstein is?" he asked.

"Yeah. He is a monster that some scientist made out of old body parts," she answered, in a giggling little voice.

"That's right. Well, Frankenstein was coming to get me because he needed one more body part to make him complete. He needed a good head of hair. He felt that if he had nice hair he would be normal, and he would be able to get a date for the prom."

Jodie laughed out loud, wiggled free of Cole's arm and turned to face him, "That ain't scary! That is funny!" she exclaimed.

"To you, maybe," he chuckled, "but to me, it was very real and really, really scary!" Cole stressed. "You see, what is silly to you was very serious to me at the time. That is why, sometimes, it is good to share your feelings and fears. Another person can shed 'new light' on a subject and put it back into perspective so it isn't too scary anymore," he coached. "That is what my mom did for me. After I told her about the dream, she convinced me it was just some silly stuff I had seen at the movies and didn't mean anything. And she was right. There is no Frankenstein. It is just a 'make believe' story."

"Well mine is much, much scarier than that!" Jodie said loudly, "but I don't want to talk about it, okay?"

"Okay. Lets see, what should we talk about?" he asked.

"Well, all I can say is my dream makes yours look..," they both said in unison, "REALLY, REALLY silly!" They both laughed.

"You better quit picking on my dream young lady!" Cole joked.

Then the mystery dreams began to flow out of the little girl's mind. Slowly at first, then with increasing intensity as she got deeper and deeper into the unusual reoccurring nightmare. "The dream starts when I'm sleeping in my bed at home. It's like I'm watching a television show. It's me in bed, but I'm watching myself sleeping. Then, I hear some loud talking in the hallway by my bedroom door. I get out of bed and walk through a fog on the floor of the room to the door. It's very dark, except for a blue light coming through the window blinds."

Her eyes got round and large as she continued to describe the dream, "When I open the door, I'm standing in a dark tunnel. The tunnel is the kind you see in cowboy and Indian movies. You know, the ones where they're looking for gold. The sides and top of the tunnel are held up by big beams," she said, moving her arms above her head and then down each side to her waist.

"This is where it starts to get weird," said the little girl, standing up in a dream-like fashion turning to face Cole, who was still seated on the floor in front of the chair. "My mom is just down the tunnel a little way. She doesn't see me and when she speaks it's hard to make out her words. She's talking to somebody. I can't make out the person's face. I don't know who it is," she said, getting more and more agitated. "The person is big and dark," and then, trying to explain better, she said, "I mean, the person is wearing black...all black."

"I think it's a man because when the person talks he has a very deep voice. So he says something to my mom in that deep voice, but I can't understand. It's like my hearing has gone bad. But, in the dream, I have to hear what he said. It is like if I don't hear his words, something bad is going to happen to Mommy," Jodie said, getting very upset.

"Whoa, there little girl. Let us slow down a little. There is no need to get all upset," Cole said, soothingly. "Come here. You set yourself in my lap." He reached out, turned the child around so her back was to him and placed her on the floor in a sitting position in his lap with her back against his chest. "You know, I think you are right. That is a more interesting dream than the one I had. Let's just take a moment to settle down then you can continue when you feel like it, okay?"

After several minutes of total silence, Jodie continued her story. "My mommy, or the dark person, couldn't see me for some reason and, like I said, I could not hear what was being said. They started down the tunnel, the fog still at their feet, and I followed them a little ways back, like I was hiding or something. Every now and then, as we walked down the tunnel, a very bright light would blind my eyes so that my mommy and the dark person would sort of disappear."

"My mommy was struggling with the person. Pushing and shoving and trying to get away. All the time they were yelling at each other, but I couldn't make out most of the words. It was all I could do to keep up. I wanted to help my mommy, but I could not catch up to them" she said, breaking out in tears and sobbing heavily.

"Now, now. Take it easy Jodie. Take it easy. There is no hurry. It will be okay, I promise," Cole coached, while stroking her hair from front to back and squeezing her shoulder gently.

Another long pause, this time the silence broken by the sobbing sounds from Jodie. Finally she began again, "They stopped walking and facing each other, I heard my mom say, "Not my curls!" Then, she repeated, "Not my curls! You cannot take my curls! You don't know the first thing about caring for my curls!" And the big, black person grabbed Mommy behind the neck with one hand and took a pair of scissors with the other and cut off a big lock of hair," she said, putting her hands in her hair showing the clipping motion of the scissors.

"Then the big dark person made a quick motion. I couldn't see what he did, but when my mommy turned her face in my direction, she had black ink all over her face. After a couple more jerking motions, there was even more ink all over my mom's face. It was running down her cheeks and chin, and dripping onto her nightgown," Jodie used stroking motions down her face to illustrate the dripping fluid.

"After this, the two of them left the tunnel and walked out into a field that was covered in snow. It was nighttime and very dark. The dark person threw my mom on the ground. She just lay there. I couldn't get to my mom! Something was holding me!" Her voice raised in panic, "Something was holding me back! I could not leave the tunnel!" she shouted.

"Okay, okay. Settle down a little, Jodie, then we will start again," he said, calmly. "Just take your time. Easy now." This story was very deep rooted in the little girl's mind and Cole knew it might be his only chance to figure out why it was so vivid in her mind.

Once again, with a sigh, Jodie began, "So, I was being held by something, I dunno what, and couldn't get to my mom. The big black person quickly walked away and in the distance I could see him get on a white horse. He made the horse run very fast toward my mommy. The horse had lights where its eyes were supposed to be. The lights were very bright, making sharp pointed streaks through the darkness."

"I hid behind a bush so that the lights would not find me. I felt very scared and was afraid the lights would see me and hurt me. So I hid. Whatever was holding me let go and I could have gone to my mommy, but I didn't because I was so scared," she said, weeping quietly now, her head hung down in shame.

"Just before the white horse got to mommy, she raised up facing the running horse that was carrying the dark person. Mommy yelled, 'Nooooo...,' and the horse and rider ran over the top of her. Then, I wake up," she concluded, sobbing heavily and appearing wasted from the story telling experience.

"Boy, that is quite a dream! You say you keep having the same dream over and over?" Cole asked.

"Yes, sir. I know I told you I did not remember my nightmares, but I have," she admitted. "I just have felt so bad not helping my mom when I could have."

"You shouldn't feel bad, Jodie," Cole quickly answered, "because this is just a dream. It is not real! It is just a bunch of made up stuff that floats around in our minds at night. It doesn't mean a thing. Just a bunch of mixed up ideas that come together to make a dream, honest," he tried to reason with her.

"But Cole, my mommy is dead. And I could have helped her...I should have saved my mom from the big dark person on the horse!" she sobbed.

"Jodie! Jodie, this was a dream. Your mother did not get killed by a horse. You know that, don't you?" he asked.

"Yes, but I feel the dream is telling me something. Why do I keep having this awful nightmare?"

"I don't know why we have dreams. Maybe because it is stress or just us missing our loved ones," he said, being careful not to mention guilt as a possibility.

"Whatever it is, they scare me real bad and I am afraid to go to sleep. Can you make them go away? Please?" Jodie begged.

"Well I cannot, personally, but I wish I could. If I could make them go away you would not have another bad dream in your life," he explained, "but I will say this, you have taken the first step in getting rid of the nightmares.

"Really? How?"

"Usually, when you confide in someone else, the nightmares begin to disappear." This last point he made up to make Jodie feel better. "I do have just one question, Jodie, and if it bothers you, you do not need to answer it, okay?"

"Yes, sir."

"When was the last time you saw your mother alive?"

"The night before I started having the nightmares. That is why I feel I should have saved my mommy," she answered, in a very soft voice. "The very next night I started to have the nightmares. I feel it has something to do with my mommy dying. I wish I could go back and save my mommy, Cole!" The sobbing began again and lasted a very long time.

Cole spent a long time talking with Jodie about the nightmares and found out more about her family life. She loved her mom very much and they were very close. Cole could see that Jodie's mother meant everything to her. Nothing else in Jodie's life seemed to be very good.

The family had lived in a very bad, poor part of town. Jodie's mother, Evelyn Patterson, was very protective of her. She made sure any friends Jodie played with met her high standards. She was determined that her daughter would not get mixed up in drugs or gangs. This meant, of course, that there wasn't very many kids Jodie could play with. So, Jodie played games with her mom and her mother spent a lot of time helping Jodie with her schoolwork and inexpensive crafts.

Jodie very rarely mentioned her father, Dawson. About the only time she talked about him was in reference to something Jodie and her mother had done, and he would be briefly mentioned as having been along. Cole tried once or twice to change the subject to her father, but Jodie would answer that question and move on to another subject, or ignore the question entirely. Cole decided he would not probe anymore and hoped, eventually, Jodie would confide in him about her father.

"Wait a minute!" he thought, "Jodie was not going to stay with him anymore. "Remember? Jodie would go to a foster family because, in all his infinite, selfish wisdom, he had told Ranger Defreese he could not possibly keep the child." This was a wake up call for Cole. It was time to make a decision. He either was going to accept the decisions others, like Ranger Defreese and Judge Holcolmb, were going to make or he was going to take control of the situation and make some of his own decisions. He opted for the latter. "I cannot leave this little girl! I...I need to help her through this. Nobody will know all of the problems she has had. She would have to start all over again to explain her situation adding more insecurity and instability to her already shaky life. She may hate the family they place her with. It will be too hard for her to adjust to being passed around from place to place and family to family. I cannot let this happen. I will sacrifice and keep the girl with me," he rationalized. Oh yeah, he was hooked all right! And his heart was now controlling his mind and any rationalization he made would come out with the same conclusion: Jodie was going to stay with him.

That evening, after the storm had passed through the area, the pair decided they had enough "heavy" talk and decided to get outside in the cool fresh air. They donned their coats and Jodie put in with Cole to go exploring. She ran around the side of the cabin and headed to the grassy area beyond. Suddenly, she stopped. Something had crossed the path up ahead.

"Cole!" she whispered loudly. He walked quietly up beside her and crouched down.

"What, honey?" Cole said, very softly.

"Up ahead...I saw something big move up ahead by those two bushes. It crossed the path," Jodie whispered.

"What do you think it was?"

"I dunno. It was big and gray. Kinda' shaped like a fuzzy dog," she said excitedly, standing as close to Cole as she could get.

"You know, I have an idea. Come with me and I think I can show you what that animal is." He got up, took Jodie by the hand and headed for the cabin. He got two slices of bread from the kitchen, and both of them headed back to the grassy area.

Once there, Cole had Jodie place the slices of bread at the edge of the trail next to the berry bushes. Then the pair went to the far edge of the grassy area at the shoreline of the lake and waited patiently. In less than five minutes a shadowy figure, low to the ground, could be seen moving toward the bread from behind the bushes.

Not making a sound the raccoon made its way to the food. Taking the bread slice in its hand-like front paws, it gulped the bounty down hastily while sitting back on its hindquarters.

"Ooh!" Jodie whispered.

"What do you think that animal is?" Cole quizzed.

"I know now, Cole. I saw one of those in the nature films at school. It is a raccoon!" she answered, in a very proud manner.

"You are absolutely right!" Cole exclaimed, and patted her on the back. "Out here we don't touch the animals. You see, this is their country and we are the visitors. The animals are untamed and wild," he lectured, in his typical ranger-guide style. "If we went over to the raccoon it would probably run away. But if it felt threatened in anyway, it would take a stand and bite us. We don't want that to happen, do we?" he asked.

"No, sir!" Jodie answered, in a stern voice.

After a little while, the raccoon moved on down the trail, stopping here and there, to grub for food and finally disappeared out of sight in the thick berry bushes. From across the lake, an owl could be heard hooting. Smaller birds on the island chirped occasionally, as if glad to see that the storm had passed by and night was close at hand.

To the north, a baying sound drifted across the lake. "What was that?" Jodie asked, her eyes wide and darting.

"That is a wolf. Listen!" Cole whispered, in anticipation. Soon, the wolf howled again. It sounded sad and possibly in pain. Then it was quiet for a few moments after which the howling started again.

"That doesn't sound real good," his trained ears picked up the distress in the howl. "That is a wolf. Sometimes they howl at the moon or howl to let other animals know they are 'on duty'. But that howling gives me a feeling that there is something wrong over there," he explained.

"What do you mean, Cole?"

"Well, I don't know exactly what is wrong, of course, but that howling sounds like one of the pack might be in danger or hurt or something."

"What is a pack?" Jodie asked.

"Oh, a pack is a bunch of wolves that run together. You see, wolves are a lot like humans. They have families that stay together for life. Instead of calling them families, we call them packs. They live together, hunt together, do everything together."

"And you think one of them is hurt?" she asked, her voice quivering slightly.

"Yes. Well maybe one of them got hurt, or died, or even one of them might have gotten sick. Something like that. Wolves really care for one another, and when one of them gets hurt or dies, the others mourn for the lost one. Just like people, Jodie."

"Really? Is a wolf bigger than a dog?"

"Bigger than some dogs and smaller than others. What is your favorite dog, Jodie?

Putting her finger up to her nose the little girl thought awhile, and then said, "I think a Collie or maybe a German Shepherd. Yeah, a Collie or German Shepherd," she decided.

"A German Shepherd would be about the same size as a wolf. As a matter of fact, they look a lot alike from a distance, other than the coloring is a little different. Both types of animals are very smart and crafty, too."

By this time darkness had fallen, and it was time for Jodie and Cole to pack up their things for the flight to Chisano Station the next day. "So have you enjoyed staying on the island, Jodie?" Cole asked.

"Yes sir, I really have had a good time. I wish my mommy could have been here with us. She tried to show me all kinds of things, like you have been doing," she said.

"What about your daddy? Did he show you lots of things too?" Cole took a chance and asked the forbidden question that Jodie had successfully dodged all this time.

"My daddy...my dad...did not have anything to do with me. He didn't like kids. I was just in his way. My dad doesn't love me!" she finally said, putting the last sentence in the present tense.

"Maybe, just maybe you're wrong, Jodie. Some people show their love differently. Maybe he just did not know how to take care of a kid, or how to be with a kid. I am sure your dad loved you very much, Jodie," he said, in a consoling manner.

But Jodie cut him off, and said in a loud, harsh voice "No! No! He didn't love me! He even told me he wished I had never been born! And now, I don't want to talk about him anymore!" Then, after a very brief pause, "I mean it! I don't want to talk about him anymore!" and ran into the bedroom slamming the door behind her.

Cole could hear big sobs coming from behind the door. What had he done? This was a big mistake. He shouldn't have mentioned Jodie's father yet. What a stupid idiot he was. Jodie wasn't ready to share all of her misery yet.

He decided to let Jodie have a little space of her own for now. He had probably done enough damage for one day anyhow. He spent this quiet time cleaning up the kitchen and making sure everything was in the proper place. This way, when he returned to the cabin he would not spend all of his time looking for things.

About forty minutes later, Cole heard the bedroom door slowly open, and a puffy-eyed Jodie came out into the light of the living room. She squinted as her eyes tried to adjust to the brightness of the room. Slowly, she made her way to the big chair where Cole was sitting as he read an old "Field and Stream" magazine. Without saying a word, the tiny figure crawled up in the chair next to Cole.

She looked up into his eyes, with her big, brown, tear-filled eyes. The whites of her eyes had been stained red from the long cry and her cheeks were puffy. Jodie took the magazine from Cole's hands and let it drop on the floor in front of the chair. Then, she wiggled her tiny body into his lap and placed his strong arms around her shoulders. Facing Cole, she said in a very soft voice, "I'm sorry I got mad. I am really, really sorry." Taking a deep breath, the snubbing sounds started. "My dad hated me, Cole. I know he hated me and so did my mommy. She would try to make me feel better about it, but she knew it was true, too," she said, very softly, "But my mom protected me from him. He was a mean, mean person. My mommy was planning for us to get away from him…but she died first," she began to cry silently.

"Sometimes he would come home and hit mommy. She would grab me up, and run into the bedroom, and lock us in the room. Sometimes we would run out of the house until he would calm down. Other times, he would be okay, and talk real nice to mommy, and they seemed to get along good," she said, matter of factly.

"But my daddy never, never liked me. Usually he would act like I wasn't even there. But other times, he would yell at me, call me no-good-for-nothing. He said I was a big mistake," she paused briefly, and then continued, "He said he wished I was never born!" more tears.

Cole wiped the tears from her eyes with his shirtsleeves. Before he could say anything Jodie added, "Why was I born, Cole? I wished I had never been born. Maybe then, he would have been happy."

"Now, now Jodie, I won't have you talking like that. You're a great kid. You know that, don't you? You're smart, fun to be with and an all around good kid," he consoled her. "Every person is a little different from the next. You know your mother loved you very, very much. From what you have told me, I know you meant everything in the world to her."

"Your father is a different story. He might have had a bad childhood of his own. Maybe his parents didn't love him. Maybe he didn't even know his parents or, perhaps, he was ill and did not feel good," he said, and then added, "He could have been angry with something else and just needed someone to blame it on. For instance, he probably didn't earn much money, so he needed someone else, not himself, to blame for his lack of income. And, possibly, that was you. Yet, you know, you did not have anything to do with how much he earned," Cole paused, then concluded. "You know, Jodie, not every person in the world makes a good parent."

"You're nice, Cole. You say the nicest things." The little girl laid her head on Cole's shoulder, and he stroked the back of her head gently with his hand. And then, came the question from Jodie he did not want to hear, "What's going to happen to me?"

Cole did not answer right away. He was hoping she would forget that question and ask another, easier to answer question. Cole thought a moment before attempting to answer, then decided to ask a question of his own. "What would Jodie want? If you could start fresh right now, what would you want for yourself?"

"Well...gee, let me see. Could I bring my mommy back?"

"I wish we could, honey, but let's say everything is the same. Starting right now, what do you want to do for the rest of your life? You know, like when you are in school and they ask you what do you want to be when you grow up? Except this starts right now and goes on till you grow up."

Jodie thought about this for a long time, then put her hands to her cheeks and, with a studious look on her face, gazed into Cole's eyes and began, "When I grow up I want to take care of animals. When they get sick or get hurt I want to make them all better," she said, waving her fully extended arms in a big semi-circular motion. And then, grabbing Cole around the neck and hugging him with all her might, she said, "I want to stay with you the rest of my life!" And before Cole could say anything, she added, "Please don't say no! Please, please don't say you won't!"

Oh boy! How was he going to pull this off? He couldn't make a promise he did not have control over. And he did not have control over who would take care of this child. So, he answered in the only way he honestly could, "Honey, I am not the one that will make that decision. When we get to the ranger station we will find out what is to become of you and where you will go...."

Jodie interrupted, "No Cole...No! You don't want me either! See, it would have been better if I was never born! You act differently but you are just the same as..."

"Stop it, Jodie! Stop it right now!" he placed his hand gently over her mouth. "You listen to me! I never want to hear you say that ever again!" he said firmly, and then removing his hand from her mouth added, "You think I do not want you to stay with me? You're wrong! Dead wrong! Of course I would like to be your guardian. Maybe at first I had different ideas, but having you around these past several days has changed all of that," he confessed. "But, honey, there are legal issues that I don't have any control over. That is why I cannot say I am going to be the person to take care of you, you see?"

"No! I don't see. If I want to stay with you and you want to be my guad...garden," she tried to say the word.

"Guardian," Cole helped, "It is a person, like a parent, that is totally responsible for someone else."

"Yeah! Anyway, if we agree isn't that all that matters?"

"No, it is a lot more complicated than that. Just let me say this, for now. I will do everything that I can to make sure that your life from here on out is the best it possibly can be. If that means you stay with me, then I will fight, tooth and nail, to make it happen. But if someone can prove to me that you would be better off somewhere else, then, reluctantly, I will consider it." Then, in conclusion, he said with a frog in his throat, "You have changed my life in these few, short days. I will always take care of you...even if you have to go somewhere else!" They hugged each other.

Chapter 5

The next morning, Cole and Jodie were up early. They quickly ate breakfast, packed a lunch and some emergency provisions and, then, finished packing their duffel bags for the short trip to the ranger station. Of course, a short trip here would be a long trip in most states. But here, in Alaska, the trip by air would take about an hour, which was like taking a short drive to the market elsewhere.

At the end of the short dock, Cole began his usual check out of "Lizzie". When Jodie arrived, Cole introduced the two ladies. "Jodie, this is "Lizzie". She is my personal airplane."

"She is really neat. How long have you had her?" she asked.

"About ten years now. She was abandoned in Seattle, and I was able to buy her and fix her up. It took me a little over a year to get her finished, thanks to a lot of help from my friends," he said, his pride showing in the expression on his face and in the tone of his voice.

"When we came up here she made a lot of noise, you know, rumbled a lot," she said.

"Yeah, she is a real nice running machine. Well, now we have to get her ready for the flight," he instructed. "First thing, let's go ahead and load our things into "Lizzie", what do you say?"

With that, the two took turns loading the four bags and various other essentials into "Lizzie". After they were done, Cole checked the fluids and controls on "Lizzie", like he always did before taking off. Then he switched the power on, the starter engaged, and the big engine groaned a low raspy sound. The engine caught and fired up blowing blue smoke out of the large exhaust pipes underneath the fuselage. At first, the engine ran rough and even sounded as if it sneezed a time or two but, finally, settled down to a nice purring, rumbling sound.

Cole eased the throttle back to a fast idle, stepped out onto the port-side pontoon and looked up to Jodie standing on the dock. Above the noise of the engine, Cole shouted, "How about that? Is it scary? Kinda' noisy, isn't it?"

"Yes, sir. Really noisy," she yelled back.

"Well, come on, let's get you in "Lizzie"." He reached up, taking Jodie by the waist with both hands, and gently lowered her into the cabin. She climbed over his seat and took the right-hand, forward space. Once in, Cole showed her how to buckle up and opened the window to let in a little fresh air.

"While "Lizzie" gets up to running temperature, I am going to call into the ranger station," he informed Jodie.

A few moments after he called into the ranger station, the radio speaker crackled the answer from the station. "This is Chisano, do you want to speak to Ranger Defreese?"

"I want to inform you that Jodie is in the airplane with me at this time. Please keep that in mind," he informed the ranger on the other end of the radio.

"Roger, Cole," the voice came over the radio.

"I don't have to speak with the ranger on this end. Does he need to speak with me?" he asked, into the microphone.

"No. The message here is, Ranger Defreese will update you on yesterday's activities when you arrive. Are you headed straight here?"

"If there is nothing urgent in your area, I will meander through my section, since I have not been in the area for several days, and then head in. Do you copy?"

"That sounds good. What is your ETA?" meaning estimated time of arrival.

"My ETA should be about two to three hours. Ten-four?" he concluded.

"Ten-four, over and out," the voice on the radio signed off.

"Okay Jodie, you ready to take off?" he asked the little girl, whose eyes were all aglow with excitement.

"I've never flown in a airplane before!" she exclaimed.

Cole laughed and said, "What do you mean you have never flown in an airplane? How do you think you got here, anyhow?"

"I mean, I have never flown in an airplane and been able to look out the windows," she said, laughing.

"Ooh! Well, young lady, you are in for a real treat. Let's go!" Cole jumped onto the pontoon, unfastened the ropes from the dock, stored them in the compartment under the fuselage, and shoved "Lizzie" away from the dock.

He climbed into the cabin, secured the door, and pushed half right rudder with his foot to head "Lizzie" in a slow clockwise arc across the smooth lake surface. Easing in a little more throttle, the engine rpm's increased and the craft slipped toward the open water, as he straightened out her path using the pedals on the floor to guide her.

"What I want to look for now, Jodie, is any logs or obstructions that may be in our take-off path, and at the same time, figure out which way the wind is blowing," he instructed. "How can you tell which way the wind is blowing?" he quizzed.

"I don't know. How?"

"Well you can look at the trees, if you are close enough to shore or you can look at the ripples on the surface of the lake." Pointing out the right front window, he continued, "Where we are now, the lake is perfectly smooth, so that means no wind is stirring here. But over there, the ripples are coming from the north," and then added, with a sweep of his arm, "from those mountains on that side of the lake, see?"

"Yes, sir."

"We always try to take off into the wind or, in other words, against the wind."

"Okay, Cole," she said, with excitement in her voice.

Cole maneuvered the plane to his imaginary runway, increased the throttle to seventy-five percent power, and guided the craft across the lake surface at an ever-increasing speed. Finally, the craft had reached

the necessary velocity to go airborne, and Cole eased back on the controls to pull the craft loose from the grasp of the lake. "Lizzie" purred
like a kitten and flew smooth as silk as she gained altitude at a steady
rate. The sky was crystal-clear blue this morning, and there was virtually no wind to disturb the airplane's flight path.

"Ooh! Wow!" Jodie exclaimed, her nose pushed hard up against the
right side window, "Wow, this is beautiful!"

"You ain't seen nothing yet, young lady!" Cole chimed in. "Let me
take you for a tour of the area and a look at my home-sweet-home." He
leveled "Lizzie" off, and initiated a slow right hand turn that would
allow Jodie to see where she had spent the last couple of days.

"Down there, about one-thousand feet, is where you have been staying. See over here, closest to us is the high part of the island. Those black
rocks are where we looked at the northern lights and fished," he said,
pointing out her side window. "Notice that on this side of the island the
shore drops away fast and the lake gets very deep right away."

"Yeah. Is that why it gets deep blue real close to the rocks?" she asked.

"That's right, Jodie. When the volcano blew up it leveled the ground
back towards the other side of the island. Notice how the big rocks get
fewer and fewer as you cross the island?"

"Yes, sir, kinda'. The trees get in the way of seeing the rocks over on
that side of the island," she said, pointing south across the small chunk
of land surrounded by water.

The plane was still in a slow curving flight path around the island
and, now, was headed down the eastern shoreline. "I always say the
island is shaped like a home-made hamburger. It is basically circular
with real raggedy edges," Cole mused.

"Ha, ha, that's funny Cole. It looks like the water is not as deep starting on this side, is it?" Jodie asked.

"Good observation, honey. It isn't." Then, as the plane continued the
slow curve around the southern end of the island, he asked, "Recognize
that area?"

"Yes, sir. That is our grassy area. Boy! The land goes way out into the
lake here, doesn't it?"

"That's right. It is the only sandy area on the island. Too bad the water stays so cold. It would be a nice place to swim."

Finally, "Lizzie" completed the circle and they could see the dock area and, beneath the trees in the little cleared-out area, the cabin, fire pit, and the well beside the cabin. "What do you think?" Cole asked.

"I think you are really lucky to have such a beautiful place to live. Thank you so much for showing me all the things on the island and spending so much time with me," the little girl said, and leaned over to hug Cole's shoulder, the seat belt restraining her from a full body hug.

"You're welcome, Jodie," sensing she was pouring on the guilt should he change his mind about taking care of her. "You don't have to try to win me over, young lady!" emphasizing the last two words. She looked at him with that typical female expression that says, "Who me?"

Cole kept the plane on the same flight path around the island a second time so Jodie could take it all in, then headed northeast across the lake increasing "Lizzie's" speed and altitude until she was cruising at about one hundred-thirty miles an hour at four thousand feet.

"This whole area as far as you can see is my section of the Wrangell Reserve. I have six men that help me manage this area, which works out to about one man for every four hundred square miles. That is not very many people, but the area is very isolated and there usually are not more than two or three dozen visitors to the area at any one time, on average." Once again, Cole had fallen into his park ranger-guide mode.

Just then, something caught his eye to the port side, the left side, of the airplane about three-fourths of the way up the mountain. He gave the plane left rudder and aileron and headed in the direction of a small plume of smoke wafting up from the evergreens below.

As he approached the area, he reduced the speed of the aircraft and brought the smoke up on his side of the aircraft. He made a pass over the area and saw quite a bit of damage to the immediate area.

"What is it, Cole?" Jodie asked, in a high pitched voice.

"I am not sure yet, honey, I thought it might be a camper, but it appears there is some tree damage down there," he said, as he peered out the left window. "I'm going to take "Lizzie" down for a closer look." He guided the airplane across the peak of the mountain, turned the craft around and headed back to the area where the smoke had been spotted.

As he crossed the peak of the mountain coming back, he cut the power back to a fast idle, and forced the plane to follow the tree line down the side of the mountain, keeping the craft about seventy-five feet higher than the trees. The area in question was about fifty yards in diameter. Trees were laying on the ground in every direction. Some of them had smoke rising from underneath. Cole didn't see any fire at this time, just a lot of smoldering wood.

Then, he saw what he was looking for. Two of the trees were splintered badly and the trunks were black and smoldering. The top sections of the two trees were with the others, lying haphazardly on the ground. Cole eased in a little more power. The engine came to life pulling the aircraft out of her descent down the mountain and into a graceful gentle climb.

Okay, I know what that is, Jodie. Yesterday afternoon, when that thunderstorm came through, one of the bolts must have hit here. It caused all that damage and started a little fire, as you can see. Some of the fire is still smoldering and may start up again," he said, matter-of-factly. "I'm going to radio in to the ranger station to let them know."

Cole told the ranger station of the situation and suggested that he go up to the area and make sure it was all out. They agreed that was what needed to be done. It was determined that it would take Cole about an hour and a half to get to the area. The station would send one of the other rangers closest to the area to do a "fly over" so Cole could radio the results of his search.

"We will have Kyle fly by in about two to two and a half hours, ten-four," the voice on the radio said.

"That's a ten-four. Over and out." Cole signed off, speaking into the microphone.

Once again, Cole cut the power on the craft and gave her left rudder and aileron to bring the airplane parallel to the mountain ridge. As they passed by the damaged area, Cole told Jodie, "Okay, we are going on a little hike this morning. The first thing we need to do is determine the best way to get to that area from the lake below."

"Can't we just walk straight up?" she asked.

"I wish we could. From up here it looks easy, but once we are on the ground you'll see it will be a relatively strenuous climb. Okay, see that rock face going diagonally up the mountain, there," he said, pointing to a ragged looking scar running halfway down the slope.

"Yes, sir."

"If you look real hard, you will see a little stream that follows that down to the lake over there," his arm moved across the front of the airplane. "That is going to be our trail most of the way. Then," he rapidly moved his arm back to the top of the rock face, "we will have to find a path through that heavy growth to the lightning strike area, okay?"

"If you say so, Cole," she answered.

Cole brought the airplane close to the lake surface, inspected it for debris and checked the wind direction. He landed the floatplane and taxied it close to the rocky shore, having chosen the best location to moor the plane. After he secured the craft, the two unloaded the items they would need for the hike.

They took the lunches, machete, hunters knife, axe, shovel, emergency medical supplies, pistol and rifle, and portable two-way radio so they could communicate back to the ranger station via the over-flight by Kyle in a couple of hours. If they found a problem, such as fire out of control, they would use Kyle to call in reinforcements.

Cole carried all of the equipment, except the small backpack that contained the lunches and some of the emergency supplies, which Jodie strapped to her back. He instructed Jodie to follow him and take her time in the more difficult areas. He wanted to have them be injury free so it was important to make sure each step was a good foothold to keep from scraping themselves up or twisting an ankle.

The narrow stream they followed up the lower portion of the mountain was heavily littered with all sizes of rocks and boulders. On each side of the stream, thick bushes and huge evergreen trees crowded in close, sometimes blocking out the sun's rays. In most places, the water depth was only several inches to a foot deep, but occasionally, the stream would flatten out forming a large, slow moving section of deep water dammed up behind some large boulders, fallen logs, or in some cases, a beaver dam.

In these areas, fish could be seen swimming in the clear, cold, mountain water along with other small creatures such as, crawfish, salamanders, snails, and water-skimming insects. But the two hikers were on a mission, so not much time was spent looking at the sights around them. After the lower part of the mountain was traversed, the incline became steeper and the woods on the left, or elevated part of the mountain, began a new steeper ascent creating a larger and larger exposed rock face. The rock face was almost vertical and soon grew to be a cliff-like feature about thirty feet higher than the river bed Cole and Jodie were following. The stream became even smaller the farther they traveled up the mountain, eventually diminishing until they were walking down a narrow trail which was filled by the swift moving, shallow water of the stream.

After noisily walking and stumbling up the stream for about forty-five minutes, Cole called for a brief break to catch their wind. They sat on a large, flat boulder in the middle of the gurgling stream, drank some water and checked their equipment to see if all was well.

"You doing all right, honey?" Cole asked.

"Yes, sir. This is fun. I've never been in woods like this before."

"Really?" he asked, not expecting an answer. "How many animals have you seen this morning on our hike?"

"Well, I saw a squirrel or two and some birds, some fish and things. That is about it," she answered, her eyes darting around as she projected the images in her mind.

"Have you seen any large animals? You know, maybe a rabbit, fox, deer?"

"No, silly. They all come out at night!" she said, laughing.

"That is not necessarily true. Most of those animals come out at some time during the daylight, also. It is hard to see them because when they hear us coming, humans that is, they hide or stand real still so we won't notice them."

"You mean, we could have passed some of those animals on our way up here?" she asked, with excitement in her voice.

"Yes, I do." Then slowly raising his arm and pointing his finger toward the woods below he whispered, "Slowly turn around and look at the base of that tree right there."

Jodie turned around and to her amazement, less than twenty feet from where she sat, laid a yearling deer. It was perfectly motionless except for a slow chewing motion of its jaws. "Wow!" Jodie said, softly.

"See nature protects all of the wild animals out here by giving them a camouflaged body. We don't belong here and therefore the animals know how to hide from us. If the animals went to the big city, they would be the ones looking out of place."

Jodie laughed, and said, "Yeah! Really funny!"

The break was over and it was time for the hardest part of the hike up the mountain. The rock face on the left became the source of the small stream as more and more small water falls cascaded down its shear, cracked surface the farther up the mountain they hiked. Eventually, the rock face rejoined the general slope of the mountain and the stream gave way to a trail created by the animals of the area as they traversed to the water source.

Cole chose an area to the left to make the last push up the mountain to the burned-out section. As he headed straight up the side of the mountain, using the machete to cut away the thick brush, Jodie followed a short distance behind, occasionally losing her footing on the loose soil and rocks making up the very steep terrain. Finally, Cole emerged from the undergrowth into an open area, still filled with trees, but with much less undergrowth. Changing course again to run parallel with the mountain crest, Cole broke out into the burned-out area they had spotted from the air.

"Ah, success!" Cole exclaimed. "We have arrived at our destination, young lady. Now some rules before we proceed. First, watch out for hot spots. They could burn you and we, also, need to put them out," he instructed. "So, if you see any let me know. Second, don't wander too far away from me. I don't want you to get hurt way out here in the middle of nowhere, okay?"

"Yes sir!" Jodie responded.

"Okay, see over there?" Cole said, pointing to the far side of the burned-out section of landscape. "Over there, do you see the large tree that is badly burnt and has been splintered by the lightning? That is where the fire started. The wind probably was blowing diagonally down from the top of the mountain, which made what little fire there was come in this direction toward us. Since it was probably raining hard at the time and this area is so sparsely covered with growth, the fire burnt itself out before it could get a good start. That was really lucky for this side of the mountain."

"You mean a fire can get started that easily?" Jodie asked.

"Yes it can. You see, a lightning bolt is very, very hot. When it strikes something that can catch on fire, like a tree, not only will it sometimes bust it apart like that tree over there, but it will catch it on fire. And if there is enough foliage around the tree, it will easily spread the fire to the surrounding bushes and other trees," he explained, using his hands to describe the explosion of the tree and the flames that followed.

Jodie's eyes were wide with imagination and a little fright, too. "You mean, this whole mountain could have been burned up?"

"Yes, it could have. But, in this case, nature didn't destroy the beautiful landscape."

"Will it catch on fire again, Cole?" she asked.

"Well, that is why we are here. You and I have to make sure the fire is all out, so it won't start up again."

"Okay, then let's get to it, mister!" she exclaimed, jokingly.

Cole and Jodie removed all of the items they had backpacked into the area. Then Cole grabbed the shovel and axe and headed to the upper edge of the circularly shaped burned-out area. He made sure the soil was turned under and the brush was totally free from any hot areas, occasionally chopping a limb off of a tree to cut it away from any area that might pose a fire hazard.

It was very peaceful way up here on the mountain. The view was spectacular looking down to the big lake. Across the lake, the blue tone of the crystal, clear water gave way to the dark green of the mountain, on the far side. The clear blue sky above was swiped with occasional clouds that looked like they had been painted on a blue background with a brush that had been lightly dipped into pure white paint.

Jodie, at first, stayed in the center of the area watching Cole and tried to mimic the work he was doing. But, as all kids' attention spans are short, she slowly drifted further away from Cole as her attention was drawn from one object to another.

Cole continued to concentrate on making his way around the outer edge of the fire damage and his thoughts, too, paid less and less attention to Jodie and more and more on the work he was doing. He had found two hot spots that could have, possibly, started another fire. So it was a good decision that he decided to come look over the damage.

Jodie, meantime, had discovered a grasshopper on one of the burnt bushes. It amazed her that anything could be living in the area consumed by the fire. The grasshopper, not pleased with Jodie's presence, jumped from bush to bush to escape being caught by her. As the grasshopper made its way to a fallen tree close to the one that had been struck by lightning, Jodie reached for the grasshopper with both hands outstretched and cupped to receive the trapped bug. The most startling thing happened in that split second of total concentration.

A loud, vicious, snarling growl emanated from beneath the fallen tree just three feet from where Jodie was standing. The menacing deep guttural sound continued, interspersed with the barking sound of a dog that had the fever of rabies and had been backed into a corner of an alley with no escape in sight other than to attack and kill.

With her whole body frozen in fear, Jodie jerked her head violently to the left and gazed into the frenzied, evil-looking, brown eyes of a wolf, whose mouth snapped open and shut as the wild guttural sounds continued to emanate from deep within the wolf's throat. The hairy flesh around the mouth was pulled back to expose sharp, menacing teeth, and a foamy drool cascaded out past the gums, dripping onto the dusty dirt below. The wolf's evil looking head was low to the ground and, as it breathed between maniacal outbursts, blew bits of ash and dust into the air.

Jodie, still in shock and not comprehending anything other than the fact that she had not been bitten by the wild-eyed, crazed wolf, instantly jerked back away from the fallen log and the vicious animal. As she pulled back, she fell over a branch that caught behind her retreating feet. But she quickly rolled over onto her knees and hands and began to stumble away from the wolf on all fours, looking over her shoulder to see if the attacking wolf was getting any closer.

As soon as Cole heard the first sounds from the wolf, he dropped the shovel he was holding and, in one fluid motion, unclipped the holster attached to his belt and pulled out the Colt 38 with his right hand. Swinging around to face the vicious, growling sound, he pointed the gun directly at the wolf, squeezing the trigger. But he did not fire the pistol because, at that moment, Jodie was too close to the wolf. A slight error in his aim and he would be sure to hit the little girl. Then, as Jodie reacted to the snarling animal and backed away tripping over the branch, Cole realized the wolf was trapped beneath the fallen tree and Jodie was not in immediate danger. So he did not shoot the animal. Instead, he kept the pistol pointed at the raging wolf as he ran to Jodie and picked the little girl up from the ground as she scampered away on all fours.

As soon as she was safely in Cole's strong arms, she began to cry uncontrollably. "Now, now, it's all right! We are okay! It will be all right!" he kept saying, over and over, all the while keeping his eyes on the wolf.

After a moment or two the only sound that could be heard was Jodie's crying and snubbing. The wolf had become quiet and, from this vantagepoint, seemed to be unconscious. Every so often, a spurt of dust and ash would be blown into the air by the wolf's nostrils as it breathed heavily, its head flat on the dusty soil.

Jodie began to shake uncontrollably from fear and shouted, "I'm sorry, Cole! I didn't see that big dog lying there! "I didn't mean to wander off from you." She clung tightly to Cole's neck.

It's okay now, honey!" he said, soothingly. "I didn't know the wolf was there either! It took me by surprise, too!" He stroked the back of her head and patted her back to help comfort her.

"That's a wolf?" she said, startled, and now even more scared by the thought that a wolf almost got hold of her.

"Yes, that is a wolf. It must be caught up under that fallen tree or else you would have been wolf food!" he said, jokingly, his voice shaking a little now that the adrenaline was beginning to wear off.

"Yeah...wolf...food," Jodie repeated, a slight rasp in her voice. Her tears had subsided now and only occasionally snubbed aloud.

Cole lowered Jodie to the ground and crouched down beside her, keeping his arm around her shoulders. "I think the wolf is badly hurt. Evidently, when the lightning struck that tree over there," he said, raising his right arm and pointing with the pistol to the splintered tree, "it fell over onto this tree, knocking it to the ground. The wolf must have been running away from the lightning strike and got caught by the falling tree, trapping it beneath the trunk."

"You really think that is what happened?"

"Yes, I do. The wolf just ran in the wrong direction at the wrong time," he answered. "Jodie, the wolf is hurt really bad. See, it isn't growling anymore. It doesn't have enough strength to even raise its head," he paused. "I'm going to have to put it out of its misery."

"No!" Jodie said, adamantly.

"What?"

"No! You cannot kill the wolf. It didn't hurt us! It was just scared and hurt, Cole!" she said, forcefully.

"Jodie, honey, this animal will die in a little while anyhow. All I am going to do is put it out of its misery, so it won't suffer anymore."

"No, Cole! If we get it out from under that tree, it will be okay, don't you see?" she said, matter-of-factly.

"Honey, the wolf has been under that tree all night. It is dehydrated and probably has crushed rear legs and maybe some broken ribs. It won't make it for very long, even if we do get it out from under the tree trunk. It would be better to put it out of its suffering, honest!" he pleaded.

"No! You told me a ranger's job is to make sure we save everything for future generations, didn't you?" she asked.

"Yes, but..."

Jodie cut him off, "And didn't you say that all natural resources, including all the animals, belong to each and every person in the world?"

"Yes, but..."

She cut him off again, "Then, as the owner of this wolf, I want to save it. I want it to be able to go back to its family. I want it to roam free. Just like we do!" she summed up her argument.

"That is all true, Jodie, except not all things can be saved. If we go to all the work of removing the tree from the wolf and it has crushed rear legs, which it probably does, we WILL have to destroy the animal to keep it from suffering. So, all of that work would be wasted and prolong the wolf's misery."

"But, what IF it doesn't have crushed legs? Then you would have killed an animal that should be set free. Please give the wolf a chance to live. I'll get the wolf out from under that tree myself and then you won't have to waste any of your PRECIOUS time!" she said, obviously mad because of his last statement.

"Okay, okay!" he said, reluctantly, "I'll get the wolf out from under the tree, but we will do it my way, okay? And if the animal is too badly hurt to live on its own, then I will destroy it, and you won't say anymore about it, agreed?" he asked, obviously annoyed.

"Agreed. Thanks, Cole! You're the greatest!" she said, happily.

"Okay, I am going to give the wolf a drug that will put it to sleep so we can get close to it without being bitten." Cole opened the knap sack, and pulled out a vial and hypodermic needle. He extracted a small amount of the fluid from the vial with the hypodermic needle and handed it to Jodie to hold. Then he picked up the rope and both of them walked over to the wolf, which was still so weak it didn't seem to care the pair were coming toward it.

Cole made a small noose at the end of the rope and slipped it over the wolf's nose and mouth, sliding it tight to keep the wolf from biting them. Then taking the needle from Jodie's hand, stuck it in the animal's left front leg, just below the ankle. Slowly, he injected the fluid from hypodermic needle into the wolf.

After several minutes, the wolf was completely relaxed and safely asleep. With the danger removed from the wolf, the two inspected the animal's condition. The wolf had a large gash just in front of the left rear leg area and below the rib cage. Quite a lot of blood had been lost from the wound, but right now, the wound was kind of scabbed over and oozing just slightly.

Cole stood up and tried to lift the tree off of the wolf, but the thirty-five foot long trunk was too long and heavy. The wolf had gotten trapped beneath the fallen tree about twelve feet from the top. He got his axe and shovel, and came back to where Jodie was stroking the wolf's course fur.

"Jodie, you take the shovel and try to remove some of the dirt and rocks from underneath the wolf. Be real careful, so you won't hit the wolf with the blade of the shovel, okay?" he instructed, taking the shovel and digging a little earth out to demonstrate the method.

"Yes, sir."

Then, he went over to another fallen tree and with his axe cut off a two-foot chunk of that trunk. He wedged the cut off portion under the fallen tree, as close to the wolf as he could. Next, he chopped off the top ten feet of the fallen tree, reducing the weight of the trunk on the wolf.

By this time, Jodie had discovered that the wolf was permanently held under the trunk by a very jagged rock that had caught the animal just in front of the hipbone, at the joint, and below the rib cage. The weight of the tree was holding the rear legs pinned against the rocky surface, and the jagged rock had trapped the wolf's hips behind it, making it impossible for the wolf to wiggle forward out from under the tree.

"Hey, Cole! Look here! It looks like good news. I can see underneath the log to the other side!" she exclaimed excitedly, "I think it is just this one rock and some of the tree that is holding the wolf."

Cole came over and took a look. "Yeah, I think you are right." Then he chopped off a heavy limb, about twelve feet long, and dragged it over to the fallen trunk placing it just below where the wolf was trapped. Placing another large chunk of tree under the cut-off limb, using it as a fulcrum, Cole instructed, "Jodie, I am going to push down on this limb way out here on the end. It will raise the tree trunk ever so slightly. What I want you to do is to shove this smaller limb under the trunk as far as you can. Can you do that?" he asked.

"Yes, sir. Go ahead."

Cole grasped the long heavy limb as if he was going to jump over it using both hands. He slowly lifted himself off of the ground using all of his body weight and the leverage of the twelve-foot limb to raise the heavy fallen tree off of the wolf. The fallen trunk moved upward about three inches, and Jodie quickly shoved the small limb under the heavy trunk.

"Got it!" she shouted, as she moved back out of the way of the trunk.

"Good. Now, let's try to get the wolf out from under the tree." he bent down on his knees, and ran his hand gently under the wolf's right side. He could feel the jagged rock that Jodie had discovered in her excavation. "Jodie, put your hand under the wolf over the top of the jagged rock, and I will try to pull the animal out from under the tree."

Gently holding the sleeping wolf's head in his lap, he grasped behind the front shoulders, pulling steadily. Slowly, the animal was extricated from underneath the trunk. Cole immediately inspected the hindquarters and, miraculously, nothing was broken. The only other injury that he observed on the wolf besides the gash in the left side, was a similar gash in the wolf's right side where the jagged rock had cut through the skin as the wolf tried to free itself from the trunk.

The animal had lost a lot of blood and was dehydrated from having been trapped under the tree for such a long time. The wolf had one additional problem not related to the freak accident and Cole was going to have to break the news to Jodie.

"Well, Jodie, you were right! The wolf doesn't have any broken bones, but she has lost a lot of blood and is very dehydrated."

What does de...hy...drated mean?" she sounded out the word.

"It means her body is very thirsty. If you don't get enough liquids, it is real bad for your body, and you could even die from that."

"Did you say...'she'?" Jodie asked, a twinkle in her eye.

"Yes, I did. This wolf is a female. A girl! And, Jodie, she is pregnant."

"Pregnant? You mean she is expecting babies?" her voice raising with excitement.

"Yes, I felt her tummy and counted at least five babies."

"Can I keep them Cole? Can I? Can I, please?" she begged, jumping up and down.

"No, Jodie, this is a wild animal. The pups must be kept in the wilderness. I am sorry, but they have to stay out here. You do under-stand, that the pups will be wild, don't you?" They wouldn't want to live with us."

"Yes, sir. I understand. But it would be neat to have a dog as a pet," she said, sadly.

"Well, maybe one day you will get a dog. I am sure you will take good care of it, too," he added.

"But, this does present a problem," Cole said. "We have a seriously injured wolf, that is pregnant. If I leave her out here, even if I doctor her up, she probably will die. Or even if she lives, the pups probably will be still-born because of this shock her body has taken."

"What do you mean, still-born?"

"Still-born means the pups could be born dead...not alive."

"That is really sad," she said, leaning over to pet the unmoving wolf. "Its fur is so soft when you rub it toward the rear and really stiff when you rub it backwards toward the front," she said softly, admiring the wild animal.

"You know, Jodie, I was just thinking a little. Do you remember last night when the storm came through?"

"Yeah, that lightning scared me!" she said, holding her hands up to her ears.

"Well, I was just thinking. Just after the storm passed through the area, do you remember the wolves calling across the lake as we were walking back to the cabin?" he asked.

"Yes, I do. Do you think that was this wolf?" she asked, patting the wolf's front shoulders.

"Well, I think it was the wolf pack that this animal belongs to. Remember, one of them seemed to be in pain or something. I think that sound came from this wolf," Cole concluded.

"Wow, that is really something. And we heard her all the way across the lake," she said, her eyes frosted over as she thought back in her mind.

The two of them sat there for several minutes petting the wolf. And then, Jodie blurted out, "Let's take her back to the ranger station with us."

"I dunno' about that. I need to think through the next step in this scenario," Cole said, scratching the back of his neck in deep concentration. "While I think what to do let's clean up these wounds and get some medicine and liquids in her so she won't get any worse than she is right now. Then we can finish what we came up here to do. But this time, you stay close to me when we check for hot spots, okay?"

About three-quarters of an hour had passed when the pair heard the drone of a light airplane clear the mountaintop. Cole went to the backpack and pulled out his walkie-talkie. "This is Cole, do you read me?" he spoke into the mouthpiece.

"Yeah Cole, I read you," came back through the speaker.

"Hey Kyle, what does it look like from up there?" Cole asked.

"I've just found the area where you are. Let me take a look," Kyle responded. They heard the engine speed of the airplane reduce to a fast idle, then the whooshing sound of the air as the small craft glided down the side of the mountain about three-hundred feet above the tree tops. As the bright-yellow airplane passed overhead, Jodie read the big black letters painted on the bottom of the wings, "PARK RANGER". Then a minute later, the engine came to life and the airplane could be heard climbing out of its glide path down the side of the mountain. Kyle had the small airplane perform this maneuver two more times before his voice came back over the walkie-talkie, "It looks good from up here. Any problems?" he asked.

"No problems. I feel confident we have killed all the hot spots. Over," Cole said.

"Roger, let me report to Chisano Station."

After a minute or two, the circling plane flew directly overhead and the walkie-talkie came to life once again. "Cole, the station says to wrap things up here, and head directly to the station. Ranger Defreese has everything set up, so you should get back ASAP. He did say don't kill yourself gettin' back, just don't dawdle. He asked me to survey sector G-8 and G-9 for you. Do you copy?"

"Yes, that is a ten-four, I copy. Thanks for coming out, and have a safe day, Kyle."

"Roger, over and out." The plane picked up speed, did a hundred and eighty degree turn and pulled itself over the mountain top and out of sight and sound of Cole and Jodie.

"How come you didn't mention the wolf to Kyle?" Jodie asked.

"At this point, it really doesn't matter. Down here on the ground the wolf is our problem. Kyle would not be able to help us," he answered. "Since I think the wolf would definitely die out here by itself, and since she is carrying pups, we will try to get her back to the station and give her a fighting chance," he said, in a monotone voice.

"Oh boy! Oh boy! You're the bestest Cole!" Jodie hopped up on Cole and hugged him around the neck.

"Now, now. I am doing this for the wolf. So don't go getting all mushy on me," he chuckled, patting her on the back. "This is going to be tough to get her off of the mountain."

"Don't worry, I will help," she responded, enthusiastically.

"I'll carry the wolf over my shoulders along with the rest of the rope and one knapsack. You will have to carry the larger knapsack, shovel and axe. You think you can do that, big girl?" he chuckled.

"Yes, sir!" she quickly answered, and saluted Cole in jest.

"Okay, you follow me down the mountain, but watch your step and don't get in a hurry. The first part, going down to the stream, will be the hardest, so be real careful," he cautioned. Then, with everything in place, they headed off down the mountainside.

After a lot of stumbling, slipping and several much-needed breaks, the two emerged from the woods in front of the waiting floatplane very exhausted. They opened the portable cage in the back of "Lizzie's" cargo area, which had been folded and stored behind the fold-down seats, and placed the wolf inside. Quickly, they loaded the rest of the equipment, started the airplane and shoved off from the bank.

This time, Cole did not waste any time getting "Lizzie" in the air and once he had cleared the mountaintop, he continued to climb the airplane to twelve thousand feet altitude and set a straight course for the ranger station at 140 knots.

Jodie, of course, remained plastered to the side window viewing all of the magnificent sights below. At one point, she pointed out the window and asked, "Wow, what is that big white thing out there, Cole?"

"That is a great big mountain. It is one of the tallest mountains in the United States. It is called Mount St. Elias. Do you know how far that is away from us?" he asked.

"No, not really. Maybe five or ten miles," she answered, not having a clue even how far five or ten miles would be.

"It is a little farther than that. Would you believe one hundred miles?"

"Really? A hundred miles? That must be the hugest mountain ever! She said, spreading her arms out to describe its size.

"Not the huge-est one," Cole mimicked, "but it is a really big one. Maybe one day I will have time to fly you around it."

After and hour and a half, they approached Chisano Ranger Station. So, Cole checked in on the radio to let them know he would be landing soon and to let them prepare for the wolf's arrival.

Cole took this brief time to explain to Jodie, once again, that he was on her side and that she would have to trust him to look out for her best interest. He promised he would explain everything to her and would not let just anyone take her away. Jodie got a little teary-eyed a couple of times when Cole mentioned she may have to live with someone else, but she promised she would be good and try to accept whatever Cole felt was right for her.

Just before they flew over the ranger station, they both grew quiet. Each one was thinking of the experiences of the past couple days and what might be ahead in the immediate future. Cole's thoughts went back to just a week ago when the only person he had to worry about was himself. Now, less than one week later, he had a kid and a wolf to care for. How much more was his life going to change and how fast was it going to change?

Chapter 6

The airplane approached the range of mountains ahead at twelve thousand feet. This range of mountains was not carved out of the surrounding area by glaciers, as were the mountains around Cole's cabin. Instead, they were formed eons ago by two of the earth's plates crushing together forcing the ground upward forming the seven thousand foot high mountains. Then, many thousands of years later, the plates separated slightly causing the peaks, at this point, to collapse inward, creating a bowl-shaped valley between them.

The outside of the mountain ring sloped steeply to the outer valleys, sparsely covered with vegetation, exposing the rocky surface to the harsh Alaskan weather. This was in contrast to the inner surfaces of the mountains where the rusty-colored, exposed cliffs of the mountain peaks dropped fifty to one hundred feet vertically, in most areas, then sloped gradually toward the center of the valley, thickly covered with very tall pine and spruce trees. The valley floor was covered, in large part, by a banana-shaped crystal clear lake that was supplied with water by a stream. The stream flowed from the north, meandering its way down from the higher elevations of the mountain range, passing through the lake and out the southern end of the valley. Eventually it made its exit to the sea, 120 miles to the south.

The airplane cleared the eastern ridge of the heavily forested, blue-green mountains that form the oblong ring around Katos lake, a crystal clear mirror of the blue sky above. On the outside of the ring of mountains, the surrounding topography is one thousand feet above sea level, yet the lake surface, inside the split open mountain peaks is three thousand feet above sea level. From the air, this presents a spectacular view, and many people think the stream flowing down from the mountains has been dammed up to hold the water back. But it is the mountains that have trapped the water and formed this beautiful sight.

Unlike the areas that Cole had visited this week, Chisano station, which is the main ranger station for the Wrangell Reserve, actually has a paved road that makes its winding way up the outside of the western range of mountains, passing through the lower southern end of the ring of mountains into the splendors of Prospectors Cove, the name of this spectacular valley.

Even though the road is paved, the steep incline from the outer valley through the southern gap, Gold Diggers Notch, makes the last ten miles a hard pull for most vehicles. The large supply trucks that visit the cove occasionally crawl at a snail's pace up the winding road, finally breaking loose from the tug of gravity at Gold Diggers Notch.

Once again, Jodie was plastered up against the window trying to take in all of the magnificent sights. "Ooh! Wow! Are we going to land on that lake down there?" she asked, in a high pitched voice.

"Yes, we are. Right over there on the eastern shore. Can you see the wooden dock and two airplanes?" Cole asked, pointing out the right side window as he started the plane in its descent, tipping the right wing downward.

"Yes, sir. That is a long way down."

"That's right, Jodie. I am going to drop "Lizzie" down parallel with the side of the mountain. Then, when we reach the southern side of the valley, I will do a one eighty and bring her in on the northern half of the lake," he explained.

What is a one eighty?" she asked.

"Oh, that means 180 degrees. You probably learned in school that a circle has 360 degrees. When I say I am doing a one eighty, that is the short way of saying I will do half of a circle. Or, in other words, turn around and head back in the direction I just came from."

"I see now," she answered. "That sure is a big lake down there, Cole."

"That lake is about seven miles long and, on average, one mile wide. The mountain peaks are about six miles apart and the valley is about twelve miles long from north to south," he answered, using his hands to point out the features.

"Why are there so many trees inside the mountains and none on the outside?"

"Well, first of all the soil is very rich in nutrients inside the peaks, and since the terrain is kind of protected from the harshest weather, and there is plenty of water in the area, things like to grow here. When the pine and spruce trees drop their seeds, they are not blown away; so more trees grow in the same area. Next thing you know, you have this beautiful forest," Cole lectured, then added, "That is kind of a short version of why it is covered with trees and things. But that kind of gives you an idea of how nature works."

"Yeah, I think I have the idea. This place grows things real good."

The airplane descended smoothly, made the turn at the far end of the valley and glided down the eastern half of the long lake on its way to the landing area. Cole maneuvered the controls of the airplane and added throttle as needed to keep it about seventy five feet above the lake surface.

"Lizzie" passed over two canoes, with four waving passengers, fishing poles in hand, then Cole cut the power to idle and the floatplane gently touched down on the smooth surface of the lake, bouncing softly once and then settling down on the crystal clear, frigid water.

The noise from the rush of water under the pontoons gradually got softer as the plane slowed its pace. Cole guided "Lizzie" toward the short, wooden dock protruding into the lake from the shoreline. One lone man stood on the dock waving his arm in a gesture of greeting, as the airplane approached and Cole cut the power. He opened the cabin door, jumped onto the pontoon and opened the compartment under the fuselage to extract the coiled rope as "Lizzie" floated close to the dock. Then he threw the line to the man.

"Hey, Bert! How you been?" Cole shouted.

"Been real good, Cole. Safe trip?" Bert shouted back.

"Yes it has. I got two very important passengers with me!" Cole answered.

"Yeah, I heard. I brought the jeep. Is the wolf still asleep?" he said, as he grabbed the rope and pulled the airplane closer to the dock.

"Yes, sleeping like a baby." Cole answered, putting his foot on one of the large pilings supporting the dock and applying pressure to keep "Lizzie" from rubbing against it.

Cole and Bert secured "Lizzie" to the dock, and then Cole helped Jodie climb out of the airplane onto the dock. "Hey, little girl how are you?" Bert asked Jodie.

"I'm fine, sir."

"My name is Bert Swanson. I work around the station. What is your name?" he asked.

"My name is Jodie," she said, shyly.

"Glad to meet you. I understand we have a wolf aboard."

"Yes, sir. It is really sick, and it has babies, and Cole is going to fix her up so she won't die," she said, with excitement in her eyes.

"Well let's get the wolf out of the plane and get her all fixed up," Cole said, winking at Bert. After loading the caged wolf onto the jeep, Bert cranked up the vehicle and the three of them started up the gentle slope to the ranger station compound.

The ranger station was located in the northeast corner of Prospectors Cove. It was the largest, relatively flat area in the cove, which was one of the main reasons this location was chosen when the park service took control of the cove in 1959. The station occupied eighty-four acres, housing the main administration building, tourist center, repair and maintenance barn, storage buildings, stables, campground, and housing and dining for the staff. Separate from the main compound was a cabin for the Head Ranger, in which Ranger Defreese resided, and several small cabins used by visitors and the worker's families.

The area sloped gently upward from the lake to the main compound, then leveled off where all of the buildings stood and, finally, sloped sharply upward behind the buildings to the upper area of the mountain. The buildings appeared to be placed haphazardly on the level area, with no real plan in mind. All of the rustic styled buildings were made of materials that came from the surrounding area.

A good portion of the trees had been removed from this area, used to construct the various buildings and to allow as much sunlight as possible to get to the buildings to absorb the heat of the sun for warmth.

As the threesome motored their way toward the maintenance barn, Cole pointed out the surroundings to Jodie. "That building up there is the main administration building. That is where all of the business activities of the park take place," he explained. "You know, when I called in to the station everyday from the island? That is where they received my call. This building on the left is the tourist center. Anyone that comes up here to visit usually ends up there to get information on the area."

Bert turned the jeep onto a gravel road just wide enough for one vehicle to pass and guided it past a couple of huge spruce trees to the edge of a large one and a half story building with a metal roof and vertical wooden planks that made up the siding. There were six big windows down the length of the building and, centered in the side, a large double sliding door hung from heavy metal rails. The gravel roadway widened at the entrance to the building as it turned ninety degrees to allow easy access into the gaping hole of the big doorway, which was protected from the elements by a metal roof that extended out from the side of the building.

"This is the maintenance barn where we repair equipment and store supplies. We are bringing the wolf in here because we don't want the wolf around the livestock at the stables," Cole explained. "You see, wolves prey on other animals, and if we took the wolf over there, it would scare all of the livestock and, at the same time, might make the wolf anxious, too. So, we will keep the wolf here, away from everything, to keep all the animals calm.

"That is pretty smart. I don't think I would have thought of that," Jodie said.

Cole laughed and said, "You would think of it if it happened to you once or twice. Right, Bert?" he looked at Bert and winked.

Bert turned the jeep around in the wide area of the driveway and backed the vehicle into the open doorway of the maintenance barn. The inside was dark and smelled of diesel fuel, new rubber and oil. The floor was made of slate that was held in place with a cement-like substance and the center section, where they were now, rose unobstructed to the roof. The heavy wooden beams supported the metal roof and extended in A-frame style across the width of the building.

On either side of the center section, a second floor, about six feet high, was used for storage. Under that, on the main floor, equipment and various other projects were strewn around haphazardly. A long workbench, metal cabinets and various table saws, drills and planers were lined up along the back wall. Hanging on the walls all around the inside of the barn, were all kinds of hand and power tools.

Bert jumped out of the jeep and walked to the far end of the building, opening a wooden door that flooded the dingy interior with daylight. Then, Cole and Bert carried the cage through the door into a fenced-in area that had fresh straw laid out across the dirt floor. The fence extended over the top, but underneath a metal roof that covered the entire pen. All of the sides of the pen were securely fastened to the posts that held up the metal roof and to the outside of the maintenance barn. The fencing extended into the ground wedged between two railroad ties that had been buried into the rocky soil flush with the surrounding ground to prevent the caged animal from digging its way out of the enclosure. The twelve-foot by twelve-foot square area had a small dog-house-like structure on one side placed next to the building. A locked gate on the far side of the pen, just wide enough to allow a worker's body to pass through, was the only other opening into the pen.

Cole went back into the building, and several minutes later exited with a satchel and blanket. Laying the blanket on the ground, he said, "Okay, let's get the wolf out of the cage and onto this blanket."

Jodie held the door to the cage open as the two men gently lifted the wolf out. Once the wolf was on the blanket, Cole checked its pulse making sure the animal had come through the trip okay. "She looks no worse than when we got her out from under that tree, Jodie."

"Is she going to be all right?" Jodie asked, with a worried look on her freckled face.

"I don't know yet, honey. But, I am going to give her my best shot," he answered, not taking his eyes off of the injured wolf. "Bert, would you go ask A.J. to come over here to help me?" Cole asked.

"Right, Cole. Won't take but a minute or two." Bert quickly disappeared through the door, closing it behind him.

Cole cleaned the wound on the left side, then began to cut away the thick fur to give him room to sew up the wound and attach gauze and adhesive. Just as he finished cutting the fur and almost as if on cue, the door opened slowly and a female voice could be heard, "Is it okay to come out?"

Cole answered, "Yeah, come on out, the wolf is sleeping peacefully, A.J."

The door opened wide and A.J. stepped into the cage. A.J. was five foot four inches tall, wearing a slightly baggy ranger outfit that obviously didn't fit perfectly, work boots and an army fatigue-style billed work-cap. Her sandy-blonde hair was pulled back into a bun and tucked up under the hat. The shapeless outfit did nothing to enhance her feminine figure and the boots made her feet look large and unlady-like.

Jody looked up when A.J. entered the cage and was immediately fascinated by this young woman's facial features. A.J. had clear, fair skin, but her eyes were her most striking feature: brilliant blue that seemed to radiate their own light back to the observer. Topping off the eyes were sandy blonde eyebrows, which curved toward the center of her face and led the observer's eye to a straight, short, very feminine nose. Her lips were thin, and pale pink, curving upward in a pleasant smile, slightly parted to reveal perfectly white, straight teeth. Her cheekbones were high, with a slightly pinkish tint, and her jawbone was straight with a slight curve that accented her cheekbones and chin.

"Hey, Cole!" A.J. exclaimed, as she bent down to give him a big hug around the neck. Cole lifted one arm and returned the hug as A.J. continued, "How are we doing with our patient?"

"Hey, A.J.. So far, so good. I hope you still have your stitching skills."

"I think I do. I guess we're going to find out, right?" she answered, and then asked, "And who is your good looking assistant, Cole?"

"This, my dear lady, is Jodie. She has been my helper for several days. A good helper, at that! Jodie, this is A.J. She is Ranger Defreese's daughter and a very good nurse to sick and injured animals."

Jodie, still taking in this fascinating young woman said, "You think I'm good looking? You're beautiful, ma'am!" and held out her hand for A.J. to shake.

A.J. responded by blushing slightly, extended her hand to grasp Jodie's, and continued to hold it, as she said, "No, no, young lady. I am not a "Ma'am". My name is Allison. My friends call me Ally and Cole, here, calls me A.J. So, please call me Ally, okay?"

"Okay, Ally. It is nice meeting you. Are you Cole's girlfriend?" she asked naively, not considering the embarrassment this question might create if she were wrong in her assumption.

Ally blushed crimson, and she stammered as she answered, "No, Jodie, I am...not Cole's...girlfriend," then added, shyly, and just above a whisper, "Although that wouldn't be a bad thing to be...," and left the sentence hanging.

Cole quickly added, "I have known A.J. since she was your age, Jodie. I will explain all of that later when we have a chance. We are just good friends. Right, A.J.?"

"Right, Cole," she quickly answered, and then continued, "Looks like you have done a good job cleaning the wound. Let's have a look." She kneeled down beside Cole and the dog.

Jodie knew she had said something wrong and could sense the discomfort that her question had created in Ally. She added, "I'm sorry, Ally, I didn't mean to embarrass you."

"That's okay Jodie, you didn't know. We'll get to know all about each other in a little while. Meanwhile, I'm going to get this wolf all fixed up, okay?"

"Yes, Ma'am...I mean...yes, Ally," and they all laughed together, relieving some of the tension.

Ally opened the satchel she had brought with her extracting her medical instruments. "When I heard you were bringing the wounded wolf in, I went ahead and sterilized my instruments." She looked at Cole and asked, "Have you given the wolf any antibiotics?"

"Yes, I gave her a shot on the mountain to help stop the infection from spreading."

Ally stitched up and bandaged the gaping wound. Jodie watched the whole time, not taking her eyes off of Ally. She was mesmerized by this young, self-confident woman, wishing that one day she would be able to take care of animals that well.

After finishing the wound on the left side of the wolf, the three gently rolled the wolf onto its right side and repeated the procedure. First, cleaning the wound and cutting away the fur to get better access to the wound, then stitching up the gaping hole and, finally, covering the wound with gauze and tape.

When that was finished, Ally injected another antibiotic and a sugar solution to help the wolf restore some of its energy. Then, Cole and Ally checked the wolf for any broken bones or internal injuries including any injury that might have happened to her pups.

"If we can get her to drink some water and eat in captivity to gain her strength back, I think the pups will be okay," Ally concluded.

"I think you're right, Ally. I believe she is about three weeks pregnant, so she is far enough along that the pups should be able to withstand the trauma she has gone through. The key is to get her to regain her strength as quickly as possible."

Cole got up from the straw-covered ground, gently picked the wolf up from the blanket and had Jodie put the blanket in the covered shelter. Then, he placed the dog on the blanket. The wolf was still sound asleep.

Normally, a healthy wolf would have awakened an hour or so before this, and that is what concerned Cole a little. "I hope I didn't overdose her. She should be awake by now," he said, a worried tone in his voice.

"I don't think so, Cole. I think she will come around in a little while. Why don't you go unpack your things? Jodie and I will stay here and watch the dog. I know Daddy wants to see you as soon as you get settled in," Ally said, matter of factly.

Cole stood up, extended his arm towards A.J., grasped her hand and gently lifted her to a standing position. Then he drew her close to his body and gave her a big hug saying, "It is so good to see you back home again, A.J. It has almost been a year since I last saw my little girl," he said, affectionately. "How have you been getting along?"

"Well, I have missed you. You know, I need a big brother to watch over me," she said, cheerfully.

"Yes, yes you do," he chuckled. "I want to hear all about what you have been doing with your life, and congratulations on graduating from college."

"Thanks, Cole," she blushed, "I guess I got my training just in time to help this wolf out."

"Yeah, right! You've been doing that kind of patching up for years," he bragged on her, "But we will talk about that over dinner tonight, okay?"

"Right, over dinner," Ally repeated, and the two released their hug and stood there a moment looking in each others eyes as if looking into one another's mind and thoughts.

Then, very unexpectedly, Ally wrapped her arms around Cole to hug him a second time, saying in half-voice, half-breath, "Oh! I have missed you! It has been way too long!"

Cole, taken by surprise, reacted at first by returning the hug, then pushing A.J. away, blurting out machine-gun style, "Yeah, well we will catch up at dinner tonight!"

Cole quickly left the two girls and the wolf in the pen with these words, "Okay, Jodie, if it is okay with you I will leave you two here. I have a lot to do yet. Now listen you two, just as soon as that wolf starts to stir I want you out of the pen. Got it?"

"Yes, sir!" they said, in unison looking at each other and giggling. Ally included a salute to Cole.

The two girls talked quietly for several hours as they watched over the wolf. The whole time Jodie sat by the wolf petting its thick gray fur that had a tint of reddish-brown in places and a black streak across the forehead. Jodie never had a pet in her life. Even though Cole said this wolf would have to go back to the mountain where they found her, she couldn't help but pretend this wild animal was her pet.

Ally could sense the affection Jodie had for the wolf and, as they sat there, she reminisced about her own experiences with various animals, both wild and domesticated. In doing this Ally, also, told of her past as Jodie's interest hung on her every word.

"I was born in Alaska," Ally began. "Other than the Eskimos, not many people that live in Alaska actually were born here. Most people move here from other parts of the world to get away from the hustle and bustle, and experience adventure and live a simpler lifestyle. Little do they know, usually, that Alaska is a very hard place to live. The weather is the biggest negative factor for most people. After the first eight-month long winter, most newcomers pack up and head back home," Ally said, laughing at the last statement.

"My dad and mom moved to Alaska in 1959, the year Alaska became the forty-ninth state. Dad was sent here by the National Park Service to set up the Wrangell Reserve. They were very excited about coming to Alaska, and like most, didn't realize how hard it was to live in the harsh environment. But they managed very well and in 1960 I was born," she said, with a slight twinkle in her eyes. "Everything was fine until I was nine years old, actually almost ten. My mom was killed in a train wreck on her way back here from a trip to see her parents in Minnesota," her voice saddened by the thought as she spoke.

After a brief pause, she continued, "My daddy was devastated. He was all alone, in the wilderness, with no family around and a little nine-year-old girl to raise on his own. He told me that, at first, he thought he would ask for a transfer to a park closer to his family," Ally paused briefly to gather her thoughts, "But he loved Alaska and his work up here. He said he didn't know what to do. It seemed no one could give him the answer to his dilemma," she breathed heavily, as if the weight of the world was on her.

"I understand the staff was really great helping him out as much as they could. He missed my mom very much. I still remember seeing him cry when he thought he was alone," a tear came to her eye as she thought back to when she was nine years old. "On the outside, he remained the strong individual he always was, but on the inside, he was empty and scared. Mom was a very big part of my dad's life. With her gone, he had lost his direction in life. He later told me that the only thing that kept him going after my mom died was his desire and commitment to care for me, and to make sure that I had a good life and a secure future." She picked up a piece of straw from the pen floor and twisted it aimlessly between her thumb and forefinger.

Ally looked up at Jodie, who was watching her every move and intently listening to every word, and continued, "When he hired Cole to manage the books and oversee many of the staffing situations, it released a lot of pressure from my daddy. Cole and my dad get along very well and they both see eye-to-eye on most issues. Dad is very fond of Cole and Cole has been a blessing both to my dad and me."

"Cole has always been around to guide me and teach me," Ally's voice softened. "When Daddy had to go off on a trip, Cole was there to watch over me, kind of like a big brother. If I ever needed anything, Cole was the one I would go to for help. He is the greatest!" she concluded, and again the twinkle reappeared in her eyes.

"So you see, Jodie, when you asked me if we are boyfriend and girlfriend, the answer is no. I don't think Cole has ever considered me anything other than his little sister and probably never will." Ally looked out past the wire side of the pen to the open area behind the maintenance barn with a slight glaze to her eyes.

During the pause, as Ally reflected on her past, Jodie was very quiet and then blurted out, "My mommy died just a couple of months ago. But I don't even have a daddy to take care of me!" Her eyes began to water as she stared at the ground directly in front of her.

"I am really sorry, Jodie. Really, really sorry. I just want you to know that if I can help you in anyway please let me, okay?" Ally said, compassionately, extending her hand and placing it on Jodie's shoulder, squeezing gently. "I know how hard it is to lose one parent, but I cannot imagine not having both parents. It must be real hard."

"It is real hard at night. I miss my mommy very much. Sometimes I cry a lot before I go to sleep." She exhaled loudly. "I am so sad all of the time. But Cole has been great!" her voice perked up and she looked Ally in the eyes. "You know, come to think of it, you said Cole helped you a lot, too! You're right! He is the greatest!"

The two young ladies talked about the experiences they had without a mother around and the struggles to keep going. Another half-hour passed, and the wolf began to stir. Jodie kept petting the dog and talking in low tones to it.

The wolf would open its eyes and stare at the two girls and, sometimes, raise its head a little, then let it drop back to the blanket too weak to hold it up very long. Occasionally, the wolf would let out a soft moan. Once, it raised its paw, placed it on Jodie's hand and dragged it under its chest as if telling Jodie, "This is where I want to be petted".

"I think she likes me!" Jodie said, in a little girl's high pitched voice.

"You could be right. But remember, it is a wild animal and when she comes fully to her senses she may turn on you. So in a little while, we will have to get out of the pen. You do understand why, don't you?"

"Yes, ma'am...I mean yes, Ally." They both chuckled softly.

Soon after, the dinner bell rang and Ally told Jodie they needed to go to the dining hall. Jodie said she didn't need to go. She said she would stay with the wolf. But Ally insisted that Jodie had to go. It was tradition that everyone reported at the dining hall at dinner, no exceptions. A person could miss breakfast or lunch, but not dinner. Ally explained that her dad set that requirement in order for everyone to interact with each other. It reduced tensions and promoted the sense of family in the organization.

The two left the pen, closing and locking the door behind them, cut through the maintenance barn, down the gravel road and around the corner of the building. Ally pointed out the dining hall across the open area that was sparsely strewn with giant spruce trees that had grown to seventy-five feet tall.

"I am nervous about going in there Ally," Jodie said, as she grabbed Ally's hand and slowed down her pace.

Ally stopped, bent down to look Jodie straight in the eyes and in a calm, low voice asked, "Why are you nervous? These are just regular people. Workers here in the valley. People just like you and me."

"'Cause I don't know any of them and there will be a lot of people in there," Jodie answered, her voice shaking a little as she placed her right index finger in her down-turned mouth.

"Cole will be in the dining hall and so will I. My daddy will be there and Bert. Now, already, you have met three people and you know my daddy will be excited to meet you and the rest of the people are just like us. They are like family, honest!" she wiped the one tear off of Jodie's cheek and added, "I will stay right by your side the whole time. I promise. And I'm sure Cole will be by your side, also."

"Thanks, Ally. Will you hold my hand?"

"It will be my pleasure, young lady. Let's go eat!" The two headed straight for the dining hall where, from this distance, they could see people entering the building.

The dining hall was a long, rectangular building painted white with a high pitched, shingled roof. A wide porch ran all the way around the perimeter, one step up from ground level, made of wooden planks. A railing ran between the upright posts that supported the roof of the porch and provided a place to lean against when carrying on casual conversation after dinner, which occurred often.

The building had four windows, equally spaced, down the length of each of the two longer sides. The double doors at the end of the structure provided entry and exit to the dining hall. The doors had a pair of outer screen doors, which were rarely used, and two inner wooden doors that had nine-light upper windows and wooden plank lower panels. The kitchen occupied the rear of the building with two wooden doors leading out onto the back porch section and no windows on that side of the building.

Just outside the dining hall, the two girls met up with Cole as he approached from the other direction. "Hey, there's my two good lookin' girls," he greeted them as they approached. "I hope you two are hungry because I heard Louis is cookin' steaks tonight."

"I know I am hungry, Cole. How about you, Jodie?"

"I guess I'm hungry. It's just that I'm a little nervous right now," she said, hesitantly, still holding Ally's hand tightly.

"Yeah, Jodie is a little nervous about meeting all of these people at one time," Ally explained to Cole.

Cole kneeled down and placed his hands on Jodie's shoulders looking her square in the eyes, "I can understand that. I don't like big crowds either," and then he paused a moment to think of a solution. "I have an idea. Let's go in the back door through the kitchen. Then we will send A.J. into the dining room and pick out a table in the corner. A special table just for me and you, and A.J. and her dad. That way you will not have to walk in a room full of strangers. How's that for an idea?"

Jodie thought about this for a moment, then said, shyly, "I...guess...that would be better. Yeah, I will try that."

"Good. A.J. will you do that for us, please?" Cole stood up facing Ally and winked at her.

"I would be glad to," she answered, placing Jodie's hand in his, then patted Jodie softly on her head. She turned and walked slowly to the dining hall entering through the large front door, speaking to several people as she went.

Cole walked down the porch with Jodie to the rear of the building. He opened the first door they came to and stepped into the kitchen leading Jodie by the hand. Several workers turned to greet them as they continued through the hot kitchen area into the bright light of the dining hall.

The inside of the dining hall was the same white color as the outside of the building. It was a simple structure with exposed A-frame style trusses spanning the entire width of the dining area with no center posts for support. The dark wooden tongue and groove floor matched the tables and chairs placed around the room which were in evenly spaced rows. Other than the typical required fire extinguisher, the walls were bare, except for a large bulletin board that was placed next to the double door entrance, and the back wall, on the kitchen side of the large room was occupied by a slate covered fireplace that extended across the entire width of the building except for the areas on either side that led to the kitchen.

Ally had already arrived at the table and was waiting for Cole and Jodie when they entered the dining hall. She had spoken with the others in the dining hall as she passed through to the table so they knew the newcomer was a little shy. Cole pulled out Jodie's chair and seated her and then did the same for A.J., seating himself last. The three talked to each other about the adventure they had that day as they waited for dinner to be served.

Ranger Defreese arrived at the table several minutes later. He was a large man, about six feet tall and two hundred-twenty-five pounds. His dark brown hair was thinning on the top and cut a little thicker than military-style. His dark-brown eyes were set deep and appeared to have the ability to look right through a person, which helped him in his administrative duties. His nose was straight and of average length, and his lips were full and dark red. His most defined feature was his square jaw that ended in a powerful looking chin which contained a dimple. He had a muscular build, which was kept in shape by his long hours on the move and his constant insistence that he pull his fair share of manual labor around the park.

Cole did not see Ranger Defreese come into the dining area because his back was to the room. Ranger Defreese walked past Cole directly to Jodie, extending his hand to the little girl. Taking her hand in his he said in a deep, soft voice, "Well, well. I finally get to meet you Jodie! My name is William Defreese. Everyone calls me Ranger Defreese. Cole has told me a lot about you, and I must say, it has all been good," he smiled at her as he shook her hand.

Jodie responded in a voice just above a whisper, "It is nice to meet you sir," looking at him shyly.

Ranger Defreese released her hand and sat down across from Cole so that Ally and Jodie were on either side of him. "How do you like the ranger station, young lady?"

"It is fine. I got my wolf all fixed up by Cole and Ally and they think she is going to be okay now," still holding her head slightly down looking at her hands in her lap.

"Yes, I heard about that poor wolf. I guess she was in the wrong place at the wrong time. It was a very brave thing you did, getting her out from under that tree and saving her life. I am proud of you." Ranger Defreese patted her on the shoulder as a display of a job well done.

Jodie's confidence grew with that statement and she continued, "Cole has been showing me lots of neat things that I have never seen before. He has been really good to me, Ranger Defreese."

"I am very glad to hear that, Jodie," looking over at Cole and winking. The foursome continued talking all through dinner. After dinner, it was traditional for everyone to spend time with the other folks in the dining hall. It was at this time that everyone gradually made their way over to Jodie and welcomed her to the "family". By the end of the dinner hour, Jodie was comfortable with her new surroundings.

As soon as she could after dinner, Jodie wanted to check on the wolf. So, Cole walked with her back to the pen, this time approaching from outside the maintenance barn. The dog was still sleeping in the same position as she was when Jodie and Ally had left her. Cole unlatched the gate and the two walked into the pen, closing the gate behind them.

Jodie bent down and softly stroked the dog's head. Immediately the wolf's eyes opened and the dog moaned softly, as if she was glad to see Jodie return. The wolf lifted her head for a moment and, then, lowered it back down.

Jodie got the water bowl and brought it closer to the wolf. The wolf raised its head and took a long drink. "Look!" Jodie exclaimed.

"That is really good," Cole said. "You are a real good nurse."

"Can I stay with her?" Jodie asked.

"We can stay a little while. We still have to get you settled into your room, and I have some things I want to show you before we go to bed."

"Okay, thanks for letting me stay. I think she likes me to be with her." The wolf had stopped drinking and Jodie continued to pet the dog's head. After a while the two left the pen and headed to the bunkhouse.

Cole showed Jodie around the bunkhouse, which was located about fifty yards from the dining hall. The bunkhouse was made up of a center hallway with rooms running down the length of the building, and at each end of the building was a large bathroom that also contained showers. The layout was typical dorm-style. The small rooms contained a twin bed, desk, small bookcase, nightstand with lamp, dresser with mirror, and a closet. The floor was the same dark tongue and groove planking used in the dining hall with a small oval rug next to the bed. The room was clean and had a soft scent of pine. Heat was supplied by a gas furnace located next to the bathroom, at the far end of the building and piped to each room through ducts.

"This is your room for now, Jodie. I will be staying in the room next to this one. I bought you some things I think you may need. That is them on the bed," Cole said, pointing to the bed.

Jodie rushed to the bed and exclaimed, "What is it? What did you get me, Cole?" She quickly opened the packages one at a time to find the clothes and toiletry items Cole asked Ranger Defreese to have delivered to the station, expressing joy after opening each item. Then he opened the dresser drawer and gave her the candy, crayons and coloring book, saying, "Since you have been such a good girl, I thought you might like a little candy."

"Yes...sir!" she squealed with glee, "And a coloring book, too!"

"That's right. I won't be able to hang around with you all of the time like I was able to do on the island, so I thought you might get bored and find coloring a fun thing to do," he explained.

"Yes sir! I love to color! Thank you very much!"

In a serious tone, he said, "Jodie, when I was a little boy I had a stuffed lion that I carried with me everywhere. I loved that lion and whenever I needed a friend to comfort me, I had that lion to hold and love," he paused a moment, then pulled the Raggedy Ann doll out of the drawer, and handed it to Jodie, saying, "I want you to have this doll. I think it will help you through the tough times ahead."

Jodie jumped up on the bed, reached up and grabbed Cole around the neck, giving him a big kiss on the cheek. Hugging him tightly she whispered in his ear, "You are the greatest, Cole! I love you very much. I am glad I decided to sneak my way on to your airplane!"

Chapter 7

The next morning Cole checked on Jodie, who was still sleeping soundly, holding her Raggedy Ann doll that was peeking out from under the covers. As he looked down at her peaceful face, he reflected on his meeting with Ranger Defreese the previous afternoon. It had made for a restless night's sleep.

After tending to the wolf and unloading the rest of the items from "Lizzie", Cole had floated the airplane to the anchoring buoy and rowed the canoe, he had tied to the starboard pontoon, back to shore. He put the items from "Lizzie" into the jeep and transported them to the barracks, depositing them in his and Jodie's rooms. Then he went into the administration building where Ranger Defreese's office occupied one-half of the lake view side of the building.

The administration building was built with rough-sawn, square cut styled logs that had been coated with a dark colored pitch. A cedar shingled roof extended out to form a porch that ran the length of one of the longer sides with a waist-high railing framing the outer perimeter, only broken by two entrances at either end of the porch.

The building sat diagonal to the lakeshore, with one of the shorter sides facing the calm lake, where a row of windows provided a spectacular view of the lake from Ranger Defreese's office. Cole had found Ranger Defreese at his desk, which was on the back wall of the office facing the beautiful scenery.

The office was very neat with the décor emphasizing nature and the wilderness. Behind the desk, mounted on the knotty pine tongue and groove wall, hung eleven mounted heads of area wildlife, none of which had been killed for sport. Even though Ranger Defreese had been here for years, he never hunted for sport, only for necessity. He felt, as did most of his fellow rangers, that no wildlife should be taken unless it was necessary for survival.

Underneath the mounted animals, framed pictures of various species of animals, flora and fauna had been neatly hung. A large walnut credenza completed the area behind the desk. Two dark-brown, leather chairs sat facing the front of the desk and, off to one side next to a large, red wing-back leather chair, stood a small end table and large globe cradled by a floor stand.

A floor-to-ceiling bookcase ran the length of the left side of the room filled to the brim with books of all shapes and sizes, some of which looked like they hadn't been moved in years. Folded shutters on each side of the large windows facing the lake could be closed when the glare from the sun off of the lake surface was too great. Knotty pine paneling adorned all four walls and the floors were, also, made of highly polished pine.

"Hey, Bill! Believe it or not I have finally arrived!" Cole exclaimed. He took a deep breath, to demonstrate all he had been through, and said, "Let's see now. I have the wolf in the pen and all doctored up...Jodie and all her belongings all settled in...and "Lizzie" tied up and buttoned down," counting on his fingers as he named each accomplishment, chuckling as he spoke.

"Good! Good! Do you think you can actually do some work now!" Ranger Defreese joked.

"I'm ready, sir. I think work will be easier than what I have been doing lately."

"So, how is the girl?" Ranger Defreese asked.

"She is doing fine. Jodie has been a real pleasure to be around. And she is quite a trooper, too!"

"Really? That is good to hear!" he said, sitting back in his chair, folding his arms across his stomach. "Sit down and tell me all about it, Cole."

Cole eased into the brown leather chair facing Bill Defreese then, with a reflective look in his eyes, he related the last couple of days adventures to him. Sometimes, the tone of his voice got very mellow and Bill could sense that Cole was truly smitten with this brave young girl that had lost so much in such a short period of time.

"Cole, you do know that Judge Holcolmb is trying to locate a family for Jodie to live with, don't you?" Bill asked, leaning forward in his chair, as he put both elbows on the desk and propped his chin up with his hands.

"Well, that is what we need to talk about Bill," Cole said, a little uneasiness creeping into his voice. "I feel Jodie and I get along very well and, after having spent the last couple of days with her, I feel I would like to become her foster parent, Bill." Cole stood up and walked over to the windows, gazing out at the lake, but not really seeing anything as he reflected on the past few days. "You see, this little girl has lost every bit of security she ever had in just the past few months. She is loaded with guilt about her mother's death and about her father abandoning her. She needs something "constant" in her life," Cole paused a moment, still looking out the large window. "Someone that will spend extra time with her. Someone that will take time to listen to her and guide her." Turning around and facing Ranger Defreese he concluded, "She needs me, Bill! She doesn't need a foster family that is a temporary stop on her journey through life. She needs a permanent home. Something she can call her own. Someone she can call her own, and I think I am that person. One day, I would hope that I could adopt her and call her my daughter."

Bill sat unmoving for a moment taking in all that had just been said by Cole. Then he rubbed his hands through his thinning hair and leaned back in his large leather desk chair, exhaling deeply. "Well!...Well you have said a lot in those few sentences, Cole. But I'm not too sure you have stepped back a little and looked at the whole picture, though." Cole began to speak, but Bill raised his hand to stop him, "Just a minute, now. Let me ask you a question or two, okay?"

"Yes. Ask away."

"The first question is, I guess, you have only known this girl a couple of days, so how could you be so committed to such a long term arrangement so quickly?" Bill leaned forward in his chair again, folding both arms on the desk.

Without any hesitation, he answered, "It is kinda' hard to explain, Bill. It is as if Jodie and I have known each other a long, long time. She has begun to confide her inner most thoughts and fears to me, and she has begged me to take care of her. I have accepted the challenge to raise her."

"Does she know this?"

"The only thing I have told her is that I would do what is best for her."

"I see," Bill said. "Question two. Why do you feel placing Jodie with a foster family is such a bad idea?"

Cole moved back to the leather chair and placed both arms on the chair back, leaning down he answered, "I am not saying that placing a child with a foster family is such a bad thing, in general. I am saying that in this case, since I am willing to take on the challenge of being a permanent parent, it would be a better choice to allow Jodie to remain with me. Jodie has gone through an awful lot in the last couple of months and what she needs immediately is a secure foundation on which to start to rebuild her life. To shuffle this child off to a foster family, once again, with no sense of permanency would be the wrong thing to do. Do you see what I am trying to get at here?"

"Yes, I see what you are saying, but why you and how did you come to this conclusion so quickly?" Then standing up, Bill asked, "What I am trying to decide is are you working on emotions or do you feel you have really thought this thing out completely?"

Cole looked down at the chair seat, once again not really seeing anything. He paused, and then raised his head to look Bill straight in the eyes and said, "Bill, I have been thinking about this ever since that first night Jodie spent in my cabin. Sometimes a person must go on instinct...go on what his heart tells him is right. I am telling you, as God is my witness, this is something I must do." He stood upright and walked to the large globe and pushed it so that it rotated several revolutions, turned around and once again looked Bill in the eyes, "Jodie needs a home, a permanent home, and I feel I am the one that can give her a home and all of the security and love she needs and requires."

"But Cole, the key word here is "family". You are only one person, not a family. I think the court will want to place the child with a mother and father and preferably some other children. Why do you think the court will choose you over a traditional family?" Bill asked.

"I am hoping that Judge Holcolmb will look at all of the facts and realize I am the proper choice."

Bill walked around the desk to face Cole, took a deep breath and fired off the next salvo of questions, "Cole, you know I think the world of you. But you are an unmarried ranger. You travel a lot and you live in the middle of nowhere. What about Jodie's schooling? What about when you are traveling? She cannot stay by herself. These are all questions that must be answered. How are you going to answer all of them?"

Cole quickly answered, "I have thought through all of these things because I, too, was asking myself the same questions. I felt, if I could not answer them then I would allow Jodie to be placed in a foster home because that is what would be best for her."

"To answer your questions, let me reflect on the past for just a moment. I remember when I came to Alaska I met a brave man that had just lost his wife, and he, too, lived out in the middle of nowhere. He was in charge of setting up a ranger headquarters. He had a little ten-year-old daughter and he didn't know how he was going to raise her all by himself. But you know, he took one day at a time and he raised a very normal young lady that got a good education and a had a good family life and turned out very well adjusted." Cole put his hand on Bill's shoulder, who was emotionally moved by that statement. Cole added, "We all know that you have done a great job raising A.J."

"Thanks, Cole, but I had a lot of help," Bill answered in a soft, humble voice.

"To answer your questions, I have thought this through and have made some decisions. First, I would live here at the headquarters instead of the cabin. That way, Jodie will have some kids to play with and plenty of people around. During the summer months, Jodie can travel with me. During the other months, I will make my travel schedule day trips only, so I can be home at night with Jodie. And she can go to school with the rest of the kids here at headquarters." Then, sitting back down in the chair, he added, " I think that answers most of the questions. The only thing I need now is your blessing, Bill."

Bill came around the other chair facing the desk and sat down next to Cole. "Are you prepared to change your lifestyle that much?"

"Yes sir. I have spent a lot of time considering all of my options, and I feel these are changes that I can live with, and at the same time, be most beneficial to Jodie," he answered, enthusiastically.

Bill sat motionless thinking through what had been said then commenced, "You have a good argument, Cole. I did raise Allison out here when there wasn't much of anything around. But you were a big part of that, too, you know," Bill said, placing his hand on Cole's arm, "And I am grateful for all the help you gave me in raising that young lady. I don't think I could have done it all by myself." Then in his typical authoritative voice, continued, "I am going to support you in your decision. I can tell you have thought it through and I know you will do a good job raising Jodie. But me supporting you and Judge Holcolmb deciding in your favor are two entirely different things. I don't hold much hope out for him to give control of a ten year old girl to a single male that lives in the woods."

Cole said, "Right now, your support is the first step, Bill. Thank you. I have a plan for Judge Holcolmb. But first, I must get an appointment to see the judge. He will want to talk to Jodie before he places her won't he?"

"Yesterday, the judge told me he had a family he was checking out that might be able to take the girl. I think we should speak to him right away." Bill reached for the phone, picked up the receiver and asked the operator to put him through to Judge Holcolmb right away.

After several attempts, the operator rang Ranger Defreese back saying the judge was on the line. "Judge Holcolmb?" he asked.

"Hello, this is Judge Holcolmb," the voice came back over the receiver.

"This is Bill Defreese, are you doing all right today?"

"Yes, I am. I'm trying to get out of this office. What is it I can do for you" I hope you haven't found another stray kid," he said, jokingly.

"No, no stray kid. However, I want to speak with you regarding Jodie Patterson."

"Sure, I hope there isn't a problem," the judge said.

"No problem. Actually, a solution to your problem of placing the child. Have you placed the child yet, Judge?" Bill asked.

"No, not yet. Why?"

"Well we want the girl to stay here at Chisano Station. Cole Bryant feels the girl belongs right here with him," he said, looking over at Cole and winking.

"Say, what?" the judge's voice raised two octaves.

"Judge, it is a very long story and what I am really requesting is that you hold off on your decision to place the child until you have had a chance to talk to Jodie and Cole. Can you do that?"

There was a long pause on the phone, then the judge's voice came back on the receiver, "Look, Bill, I go through this in almost everyone of these cases. I really don't think it is a good idea for the kid to be placed with a single parent. It is, usually..."

Bill cut the judge off in mid sentence, "I'm not asking you to make a decision now. I feel it is necessary that you meet Jodie and find out about this girl. And I feel you need to speak with Cole about Jodie, too. He has gotten the girl to open up to him about her past and he feels it is imperative that she not be moved to an unfamiliar family at this time.

"Okay, okay. I will meet with Jodie and Cole. But I will not be able to see them until Monday. Be at my office in Farrow's Patch about ten or eleven. Can you do that?" he asked, in an irritated voice.

"That will be great, Judge. Thanks!" After a few more minutes of pleasantries and jokes about bothersome people, the judge hung up.

Bill looked over at Cole and, with a sigh of relief, said, "Well, at least we have an audience with the judge. But I would suggest you be prepared for the worst."

Cole knew that, somehow, he had to prepare Jodie for the worst. That was the burden he was carrying around now, as he continued to look down on the sleeping child. He hoped Jodie could handle another disappointment if the judge decided to place her with another family.

So as he looked down on her peaceful face as she slept, Cole could not help but worry that she might not be able to become his adopted daughter. He looked around the room and noticed that after he had tucked her in, she had put all of her belongings in the dresser drawers and straightened up her room. She really is a good kid, Cole reflected. He left a note on Jodie's dresser explaining where he would be, silently closed the door and headed to the dining hall for a cup of coffee.

A.J. was already seated at a table close to the large fireplace when Cole entered the dining hall. He waved his arm when he saw her, poured himself a cup of coffee and sat down across from her.

"Good morning, A.J. What's in store for you today?" he said, in an early morning, gruff sounding voice.

"Top of the morning to you, too! Daddy should be along soon and let me know if there is anything special to do. If not, I guess I will help out at the campground," she answered. "Daddy says he wants me to try to stay close to Jodie this weekend. I guess that is what you two worked out, right?" she asked.

"Yeah, since we are going to talk to Judge Holcolmb on Monday, we thought it might be a good idea to make sure it is really me that she wants to take care of her. You know, I might be the one she says she wants to take care of her, but it might be only because I have been the only one around. So we were thinking if you or someone else was close to her, she might become attached to that person because they are now the one that is closest," he explained and continued, "If I am going to become her foster parent, and hopefully one day adopt her, I want to make sure that is what she wants."

He looked A.J. squarely in the eyes and asked, "Do you think I am crazy for wanting to adopt this little girl? Please tell me honestly."

"No. No I don't," she answered quickly. "You know, you looked after me ever since I was ten and, to be quite honest, I don't think I turned out all that bad," she said, with a slight chuckle.

Cole laughed softly and said, "You're right. You have turned out pretty good. I guess your dad did a good job."

A.J. added, "And you, too! You have always been around when I needed you." She reached her hand across the table and squeezed Cole's hand, a twinkle in her eye.

Cole responded with, "Aw shucks!" returned the squeeze, then released the grasp.

A.J. looked into Cole's eyes dreamily and speaking in a low, subdued voice, "Cole, I have really missed you this whole year. For some reason when I saw you again yesterday for the first time since I have been back from school, I realized how much you mean to me. And I don't mean as just a good friend," she paused, "I mean...I don't know...it is much deeper than that. Do you feel the same way?"

"You're silly, A.J. Of course I missed you, too. You have been a big part of my life ever since I came to Alaska. I've watched you grow up. But A.J., you're sounding like some romance novel or something." Looking up he saw Ranger Defreese come into the dining hall and took the opportunity to change the subject before it went any further, "Here's your dad now."

Ranger Defreese sat down at the table greeted everyone and, after a short period of chitchat, the topics of the day were discussed. It was decided that Cole would check on the wolf with Jodie and then work in the administration building on the books. Ally would work in the campground area helping out where needed.

Soon, Jodie entered the dining hall joining the threesome at the table. "Good morning young lady. Who is that fine looking doll you have with you?" Ranger Defreese said, in a jolly, morning greeting.

"This is my new doll, Raggedy Ann. She spent the night with me," Jodie answered, holding the doll up so everyone could see it. Walking around the table she reached up and gave Cole a big hug. "Good morning, Cole."

"Good morning, Jodie. Did you sleep well?"

"Yes sir, and Raggedy Ann slept good, too!" she exclaimed, rubbing the doll on Cole's chest.

"She is a beauty. Does she behave well?" Ally asked, winking at the others.

"Yes, she does. She is a real good doll."

"Would you like some cereal or bacon and eggs for breakfast?" Cole asked.

"Cereal, please." Cole and A.J. got the food from the buffet line for all of them and the foursome ate their breakfasts as they engaged in small talk. Much of the conversation was about Jodie's most recent adventures with Cole and the rest of the conversation was on Ally's year at school: the subjects she studied, her dorm life and activities.

Cole showed a genuine interest in A.J.'s conversation, but he never let his eyes make contact with hers. He, too, had felt a different emotion toward her when they met again yesterday, and he was hoping it was because he had not seen her for almost a year. Usually A.J. would come home for Thanksgiving, Christmas, and Spring break. But this past year, she stayed at school because she had a job at the local veterinarian's office.

When she had placed her hand in his and said that he meant a lot to her, he knew the feeling was mutual. He thought to himself that if he was falling in love with her it would create a lot of problems. She was like a sister to him and, to his way of thinking, a brother doesn't fall in love with his sister. He decided he would not allow that emotion to grow any further. He was hoping that the feelings that A.J. had expressed to him were just a passing thing that would go away over the summer months and only caused by the long absence from seeing one another.

After breakfast, Jodie, Ally, and Cole walked over to the wolf's pen. Jodie had already gone to the pen before she went to the dining hall, so she knew the wolf was feeling a little better. Jodie put her hand through the wire fencing and the wolf crawled closer so she could pet the dog.

"Be careful, Jodie. Remember what I told you. This wolf is wild and may become aggressive. It may turn on you for no apparent reason,"

Cole warned her. "Make sure you don't go in the pen. If the dog acts
funny, don't put your hand through the fence."

"I will be careful, Cole, I promise. But I think she really likes me," she
answered.

"I'm sure she does. But please be careful."

Cole bent down beside Jodie and looked over the bandages he and
A.J. had put on the wolf. Then looking up at A.J., he said, "I think the
bandages are doing okay. What do you think?"

"They look good. Did Bert feed her this morning?" A.J. asked.

"I think so. I had told him to feed her at first light."

"When I came out this morning, the wolf was eating some gross looking meat," Jodie said, displaying a disgusting looking face.

"Oh that is good. Was she standing up or laying down?"

"She was standing up. When she walked, she looked real stiff, like
she was hurting a lot, and she was a little wobbly, and held her head
close to the ground," Jodie explained.

"That sounds good. That is probably why she crawled to you just
now. She is probably tired out." A.J. added.

After talking about the wolf for a while, the three split up. Ally had
asked Jodie to go with her, but Jodie said she wanted to spend time with
the wolf. Cole explained that he would be working in the office all day
and Jodie should stay close to Ally. Jodie agreed that if she left the wolf,
she would immediately go to the campground where Ally would be
working, if that would be all right. He said it would as long as she did-
n't wander around without an adult with her.

The weekend was uneventful. Cole absorbed himself in his work, and
purposefully took his time. He wanted Jodie to get used to A.J. and Bert.
So he worked as late as he could on Saturday, leaving a little time during
and after dinner for Jodie. He did not like not seeing her as much as he
had at the island, but this was a test for Jodie, as well as himself. If his
feelings didn't change and her's remained the same, he felt it would be a
sign that they would be good for each other.

Jodie spent most of her time with the wolf, spending little time with
Ally or anyone else. Four times during the weekend, Ally asked Jodie to

go somewhere with her and, all four times, she checked with Cole to see if it would be all right. The same thing happened twice with Bert. Also twice, other people asked Jodie to go with them to another part of the ranger station, and she turned them down. It was obvious to Ally that Jodie knew Cole was her guardian and respected his authority.

Sunday evening Cole had arranged for A.J., Bill, Jodie and himself to have a pow-wow concerning the meeting with Judge Holcolmb on Monday morning. They all met in Ranger Defreese's office in the administration building.

Cole started the conversation after they had seated themselves, "Well, folks, tomorrow is the big day. Jodie, I told you I would stand by you no matter what happened. As you know, it is possible that Judge Holcolmb may place you with a foster family," he looked at the little girl, still clutching Raggedy Ann close to her chest.

"I won't go!" she said, emphatically.

Cole quickly countered, "Jodie! Jodie the first thing I want you to do is to have an open mind. I know you are just a little kid, but for this meeting and the one tomorrow with Judge Holcolmb, you need to behave and not close your mind to all the possibilities. Tonight, we are going to talk about a lot of personal things, and there will be some things that each one of us may not agree with. Each one of us will be given a chance to express our view, but we must be honest about our feelings. That way, tomorrow when we speak to the judge, we will be able to speak as four people with the same united view," he paused, and looked at each of the others, then added, "I know this will be difficult for you, but you have to trust me. Will you trust me?" he asked.

"I have always trusted you, Cole. I love you and I want you to be my daddy!" she reached up to Cole with her arms extended, holding the doll in her right hand. He bent down, and she grabbed him around the neck giving him a strong hug. Then she kissed him on the cheek and whispered in his ear, "Please be my daddy!"

Cole returned the hug and kissed Jodie on the cheek, whispering, "I will. I will," then he said, out loud, "I promise I will do everything I can to be your dad!" He had a tear running down his cheek from the outer edge of his eye as he looked at Jodie. She had tears running down both freckled cheeks, dripping tears on Raggedy's red head. Then, he looked at Ranger Defreese and A.J. Both had wet eyes. Both were extremely moved by the love they saw between Jodie and Cole.

"I think we all know what we must convince Judge Holcolmb tomorrow!" Bill said. "You two belong together. I am committed to seeing that it happens. Ally was speechless. All she could do was put her arms around Jodie's tiny body as Jodie still hugged Cole.

For the next two hours the foursome talked of the pros and cons of Cole assuming the role of Jodie's father or at the very least, her guardian. They all agreed that the biggest hurdle to overcome was the one that Cole would be a single parent. But somehow, they would have to prove that Cole could raise Jodie better than the typical family.

After the informal pow-wow, Cole and Jodie went back to the bunkhouse and settled in for the evening. He told Jodie a bedtime story about when he was a kid, and Jodie told Cole a silly story about something that happened to her in school. They both chuckled and laughed a lot during the stories and, by the time they were ready to go to sleep, they were both relaxed and happy. He pulled the covers up underneath Jodie's chin, leaving Raggedy Ann peeking out the top, leaned over and kissed Jodie on the forehead, "Good night, darling," he said, softly.

Jodie said her prayer out loud and added at the end "...and please, God, make Cole my daddy! I need a good Daddy like Cole!...Amen."

Chapter 8

Monday morning started dark and dreary. The weather was overcast and, at times, a drizzle fell dampening the surrounding area. The temperature was in the low forties with a gusty breeze coming out of the east, sometimes shifting to the south-southeast.

Cole had slept fitfully and, at first light, gave up his search for the ever elusive restful sleep in exchange for a hot cup of java in the dining hall. He was the second person to enter the hall just losing first place to Rodrico, the breakfast cook.

As Rodrico prepared the first urn of coffee, Cole stacked firewood in the large fireplace and started a roaring fire, the warmth from the flames filling the empty dining hall in minutes. By the time Cole was finished starting the fire, Rodrico had two mugs of coffee sitting on the table directly in front of the crackling source of heat.

The two men spent the next twenty minutes talking of Alaska and various adventures they had experienced. Soon Ranger Defreese entered the dining hall. He, too, looked as though sleep had been hard to find last night.

Pouring a mug of hot coffee, he joined the two men at the warm table. "Well, I can't say that was the most restful night's sleep I have ever had!" Bill blurted out, as he sat down at the table exhaling a lung-full of air on the way down to the chair.

Cole chuckled saying, "Join the club. I feel like I've slept fifteen minutes, at most."

Rodrico got up from the table, leaned on the chair back and said, "Well, guys, allow me to fix you an extra special breakfast this morning. I can't do anything about last night, but I sure can get you started back on the right track this morning. Be back in a jiffy!"

About that time, Jodie and some other workers came through the doors. Soon after, Ally joined the threesome at the table. It was apparent none of the four had slept well and it was, also, apparent they were all nervous. After a hearty breakfast, they gathered their things together and met at the dock where they loaded the airplanes and prepared for the hour and a half flight to Farrow's Patch.

Cole and Jodie climbed in "Lizzie", which was resting peacefully against the dock pilings. He pushed the ignition switch and the starter engaged the engine, which groaned as it slowly cranked. The engine caught, after a moment. Blue smoke belched out from under the belly of the craft. The engine came to life at fast idle sounding rough, but strong. Soon "Lizzie" was purring and the blue smoke had drifted across the dock toward the Ranger Station.

Cole reduced the throttle to an idle and climbed out on the port pontoon into the rush of air being forced backward from the slow moving propeller. He looked over to Ranger Defreese and A.J. as they prepared to start the engine on A.J.'s Cessna 150.

Ranger Defreese had taught Ally how to fly when she was fourteen. In Alaska, one of the most useful things anyone can be is a pilot. Alaska has more pilots and airplanes than any other state in the United States. The terrain is so tough and the distances from one place of civilization to another are so far apart an airplane is the best way and the least expensive mode of transportation. Couple that with the lack of good roads and it is easy to see why the small, versatile airplane equipped right is so popular.

Ally had been a quick student. She had watched her dad and Cole fly for many years and had shown great interest in it, asking questions and observing how the plane reacted in various situations. When it was her turn to take the controls, it was as if she was born to fly. Allison was certified at the young age of sixteen, the youngest a pilot could be certified in Alaska.

When Allison started college, Ranger Defreese bought her the Cessna 150. It was a relatively new aircraft on the market but promised to be inexpensive to maintain, easy to handle, versatile, and fairly rugged. Both Ranger Defreese and Cole liked the airplane because it was faster than the Piper J-3 and the skin is covered with metal instead of fabric like the J-3, adding to its ruggedness.

Ally and Ranger Defreese had already settled themselves into the airplane and prepared it for flight when she fired up the Cessna. Allowing time for the airplane to warm up, she looked over at Cole and gave him a thumbs up. Cole untied the airplane from the small dock, stored the rope in the side compartment and knocked twice on the side door indicating everything was okay as he shoved the plane away from the dock. Ally increased the throttle a little and the small craft eased its way out into the windswept, choppy water at the center of the lake.

Cole untied "Lizzie", stored the rope in the compartment under the craft, pushed the craft away from the dock and stepped up into the cabin. Closing the door, he eased in a small amount of throttle and headed "Lizzie" out into the lake trailing A.J., who by this time had given her Cessna full throttle and was increasing the plane's speed for take-off.

"How are you holding up, Jodie?" Cole asked.

"I guess okay. I am very nervous about everything...and scared," she said hesitantly, a quiver in her voice.

Cole reached over to Jodie squeezing her left knee with his big hand in a comforting gesture. "I know how you are feeling. I'm nervous, also. But everything will be all right. I am sure of it. So don't you worry one little bit about it, okay?"

"I will try. But I think it will keep coming back to me. I promise I will try."

By this time A.J.'s Cessna had lifted off of the lake and was headed toward Gold Diggers Notch. Cole eased in seventy five percent throttle, "Lizzie" responded by increasing her speed down the center of the lake, soon escaping the lake's grasp and climbing steadily as she followed the Cessna into the sky, which was now a mile ahead and one thousand feet higher.

The two planes and their occupants winged their way through the notch, passing over the road that wound its way up the outer slope of the mountain, through the notch into Prospectors Cove, to the ranger headquarters. The airplanes leveled off at eight thousand feet, flying at a leisurely pace of 115 knots.

"Lizzie's" radio came to life as they passed over the mountain range, "November-five-niner to November-two-seven." Cole removed the microphone from the cradle, depressing the talk button with his thumb and responded with, "This is November-two-seven." The call letters on A.J.'s Cessna started with a "N" followed by 23359. She shortened the signature to N-5-9. Cole, of course, shortened his call letters from N931127 to N-2-7.

The radio crackled again, "Just checking in to see if everything is okay. Looks like we will be fighting a steady headwind all the way to Farrow's Patch," Ally said.

Cole handed the microphone to Jodie and asked her to answer A.J., "Everything is okay back here," Jodie spoke into the microphone, as she depressed the talk button.

"You make sure you keep Cole awake," Ally said.

"I will try," Jodie chuckled.

"Over and out for now."

Cole looked over at Jodie and told her to say, "Over and out," and she did.

After a little over one and a quarter hours, the planes broke free of the mountain range they had been following into the openness of Farrow's Patch. The waters of Icelander Bay lay directly ahead and three thousand feet below as they slowly descended downward across the flat plain. The head wind had now increased to thirty knots, and the little Cessna Ally was flying was being buffeted around a lot.

"This is November-five-niner to November-two-seven. Come in," Ally spoke into the radio microphone.

"Roger. This November-two seven, Over," Ally's radio cracked.

"Why don't you go ahead and land, since "Lizzie" can handle the gusty conditions better. I am going to circle the cove and descend slower. Over."

Cole responded "That is a ten-four. Good plan. See ya' downstairs. Over and out."

"Lizzie" responded to Cole's experienced hand, landing gracefully, touching the pontoons briefly on the small white capped waves blown by the gusty wind, lifting once, touching and lifting momentarily then settling down. Crashing through the foaming swells, her speed decreased and the pontoons became two boats plying the waters toward the waiting slips at the edge of the rocky coast.

Since the wind was now from the rear of the plane as they headed into the slip area, Cole had cut the power to slow idle. When the airplane got close to the slip, Cole applied power and full left rudder to swing the plane 180 degrees back into the wind. This stopped the plane from heading into the slip uncontrolled, being pushed by the wind. The plane stopped its forward motion and Cole eased off the power, allowing the wind to overcome the thrust from the propeller pushing the airplane backward into the slip. When it entered the slip, he jumped onto the pontoon, removed the tethering rope and secured the plane to the slip. Then he turned the engine off and helped Jodie out of the cabin onto the wooden surface.

By this time, Ally had just touched down on the rough surface and the Cessna was making its way toward the slips.

Cole helped with Ally's airplane, then went back to "Lizzie" and put the engine cover over the front cowling to keep the salt mist out of the engine.

They all made their way up the stairs to the main street after unloading the things they had brought with them. Ranger Defreese and Allison headed over to the post office and Cole and Jodie went down the street, hand in hand, to the general store to see Greta and tell of their adventures. They all agreed to meet at Judge Holcolmb's office at ten o'clock.

Greta had heard bits and pieces about how Cole and Jodie were getting along and was not very surprised that Cole had decided to become

Jodie's guardian. She knew Cole had a big heart and it seemed he was always looking after someone or some stray animal. She knew he would not be able to resist this little freckled-faced kid.

At ten o'clock, the foursome found themselves standing uncomfortably out front of the judge's office. The wind was blowing even harder now, driving the temperature down into the high thirties. However, their discomfort was not caused by the wind or the dropping temperature, but from a bad case of "nerves", and all of them were showing it.

"Well, guys, this is it. Let's suck it in and go inside and win this thing!" Ranger Defreese expounded.

They all took a deep breath and, one by one, went through the door. Just before Jodie entered the office, she grabbed Cole's hand stopping his forward motion through the door. She motioned for him to kneel down and he did. "No matter what happens,...I just want you to know...I love you!" her voice cracking a little.

"I love you too, honey!" he responded.

She leaned over and gave him a kiss on the cheek. He returned the gesture, kissing her on the forehead. He removed her hat and brushed her hair back with his hand, "We are going to win this thing, Jodie! You must believe it! We are going to win!" he said, soothingly, just above a whisper. They hugged and headed through the door.

As they entered the small reception area of the office they were surprised to see the judge already present. He quickly moved from the window area toward the receptionist's desk. The office area was small with a half dozen vinyl office chairs lining the left wall. The large receptionist desk occupied the area to the right with the desk chair between the desk and the front window. The office was sparsely decorated and worn looking. The rear wall of the office had a large bulletin board across the width with all kinds of official looking notices attached in a haphazard manner. To the right of the receptionist desk, stood a wall-to-ceiling bookcase about four feet wide. Beside that sat another vinyl covered office chair that matched the others on the left wall.

A hallway ran down the left wall where a door exited into the alleyway behind the building. Two doorways opened off to the right of the hallway. The closest door opened into the conference room, where the judge would hold court sessions or consultations with the various parties involved in a dispute. The second door, toward the rear of the hallway, led into the judge's chambers.

The judge spoke first, saying, "Good morning, folks! Right on time. I trust this windy weather didn't cause you too much trouble?"

Cole responded, "No, no it did not!" and then added, in a quizzical tone, "I am surprised to see you here. I didn't see your Rover out front and thought we might have beaten you here."

"Oh…yeah…well I parked the car around back. The buildings block the wind, you know, when it is blowing out of the east. So I usually park back there," the judge said, clearing his voice every couple of words. "Good morning Bill and how are you Allison? It has been so long since I have seen you. I hardly recognize you," he said, extending his hand, shaking Bill's hand first, then Allison's.

"Hey judge." Bill returned the handshake.

"It is so nice to see you judge. You are looking in very good health again. You remember the last time I saw you the flu bug had you down and under," Allison said.

"Yes, yes. I do remember that. I hate the flu! And this must be Jodie Patterson! How are you? I've heard a lot about this young, good-looking lady," he said, bending down, shaking her hand gently.

Jodie looked up into the judge's eyes. They were gray and old looking. The skin of his face was as if it were made of a wrinkled leather material, tinted tan. He had thick, silver-gray eyebrows and a thick, silver-gray head of hair that covered his ears, parted high on the left, with thick full sideburns that connected with a full beard exposing deep red full lips. His nose was bulbous with red veins running criss-cross along the surface.

Jodie responded politely in a soft, nervous voice, "It is nice to meet you, sir." Then she grabbed Cole's hand, moving slightly behind him in an act of shyness.

"Well, let's go into the conference room," said the judge, extending his arm in the direction of the first doorway. They all took their places around the large conference table centered in the room surrounded by eight low-backed, leather chairs. The only other piece of furniture in the room was a large credenza along the far wall. Once again, various notices were tacked up on the off-white walls. A large black shaded lamp hung from the center of the room directly over the table.

The judge sat down in the chair at the end of the table away from the door, cleared his throat and said, "Let me take a moment to explain the purpose of this meeting and the rules we will follow. The main purpose is to establish the welfare of this minor child, Jodie Paterson, and to give the court a little better insight into the proper placement of said child in the care of a foster family." He looked around the room at each one of them, then continued, "It has come to the attention of the court that certain individuals want to provide additional information that may allow the court to come to a more fitting decision." Once again, he looked around the room, this time with a look of boredom on his face. "The court will hear this additional testimony in the following manner. First, I will speak with Cole Bryant and Jodie Patterson. Second, I will speak with Jodie by herself. Third, I will speak with Cole by himself. And lastly, I will speak with each witness briefly, on an individual basis. Is there any questions to the order of business?" he looked slowly around the room waiting for a response from any one of the foursome. There was none, so he continued, "Good, in that case I would like for Allison and Bill to wait out in the receptionist area. Please close the door on the way out, Bill."

After the two had left and the door closed, Judge Holcolmb began the meeting between himself, Cole and Jodie. "Cole, I want to thank you for rescuing Jodie and taking such good care of her this past week. I can tell you have done a good job."

Then looking over at Jodie, the judge said, "Jodie from all of the things I have heard about you, you are a mighty brave young lady." He paused a moment, then in his deep mellow-tone voice said, "I am very sorry to hear of your mother's sudden death. I really want to express my deepest sympathy."

Jodie looked down, wringing her hands, which were resting on the table, then said in a shy, low voice that was almost inaudible, "Thank you sir. I really miss my mommy. I wish, somehow, she would come back to me." Tears welled up in her eyes. Cole grabbed a tissue from his shirt pocket and handed it across the table to Jodie.

The judge paused briefly, then continued, "Jodie we will be discussing some things in this room that may be a little uncomfortable for you. If, at anytime, you feel you cannot talk about something or need a break, just let me know. This meeting is about you and for your best interest. I want you to know that I will listen to everything each of you has to say and everything either of you tell me will remain in this room, so you can speak frankly. However, I want you to know that when all is said and done it will be my responsibility to reach a reasonable decision based on the order and charge given to me by the State of Alaska. I know that is probably a lot for a kid your age to understand, but I want you to know that I will work for your best interest, nobody else's, but your best interest," he said, emphasizing the "your" in the sentence.

Jodie had composed herself by the time the judge stopped talking and in a normal voice answered, "Yes, sir. I think I understand."

"Good, then. Jodie, in your own words, I would like you to tell me how you got to Alaska and how you came to end up with this fine gentleman here," he said, moving his closed right-hand, palm facing upward, toward Cole pointing with his thumb.

Jodie started slowly, at first, telling of her mother's death, leaving out the dream part she had told Cole. Then of her mean father's desire to go out on a fishing boat, and of the way he tricked her into thinking she was going with him on the boat. Finally, she told of the total emptiness she felt when that boat left the cove for the open sea. After several minutes of crying, she continued telling of the idea she had to stowaway on Cole's plane hoping that he would take care of her until she could find her way back home or figure out what to do. And, finally, of feeling so relieved when he told her he would take care of her. She told of the fun she had and hard work she did on the island and, of course, ended with discovering the wolf on the mountain and being able, for the first time in her life, to help save the wolf's life.

"How come you came to choose Cole as the one you wanted to take care of you?" the judge asked.

Jodie thought for a moment, then answered, "Well at first it was more out of need," she said. "Then later, it was because I knew he was a good person and would raise me right." She looked over to Cole with a bashful, yet proud look on her face.

"Could you explain that with a little more detail?" he asked.

"Well...when my daddy left me stranded I didn't know what to do. Cole had given me a chance to do right when I was caught trying to steal the tobacco. He could have arrested me or something. But he didn't. So I knew he must be an okay guy. I had seen him land the airplane in the cove. So I thought to myself that I didn't have anywhere else to go, so I would try to see what would happen with Cole. I knew he was like a policeman, and we were taught in school that policemen are good. So the way I saw it, I couldn't go too far wrong with Cole. The worst he would do is get me to someone that could help me," Jodie said, confidently.

Then, after we got to know each other on the island, I realized this guy was a hundred times better than my real dad. He takes time to show me how to do things, and he has taught me how to do new things. He cares about me, and he even bought me a doll so I would have a friend of my own," she said, holding up Raggedy Ann. "My real dad never bought me anything. He didn't care about me....He hated me!" she began to cry again.

After a brief pause to allow Jodie to compose herself, Judge Holcolmb asked, "When exactly do you feel you knew it was Cole that you wanted to take care of you?"

"Oh, I dunno. It was kinda' a slow thing, you know. The first day I was pretty much scared about what Cole was going to do with me. When he told me we were on an island and he was going to spend the next couple of days there, I was a little worried that he might be mean, like my daddy. But after the first day, I realized Cole was a nice person.

I was hoping he would feel the same about me." Once again, she looked at Cole across the table. Her eyes were wide and sparkled as she reflected on those three days at the island.

The judge leaned back in his chair and asked Jodie if she would mind if Cole left the room for a little while. She looked at the two men and said it would be okay. Cole left the room, joining the other two in the reception area.

Still leaning back in his chair, and speaking very calmly, he decided to see if the little girl had motives, other than the ones she had just expressed, for staying with Cole.

"I imagine Cole has been real nice to you this past week, right Jodie?"

"Yes sir. Real nice," she responded.

"Has Cole had to discipline you. Oh, let me put it another way. Have you done something that is not quite right and Cole had to fuss at you?" he quizzed.

She giggled a little and said, "Yes, sir."

"It must not have been too serious if you giggled about it."

"Oh, I was doing wrong. It is just embarrassing to tell about things you do wrong," she said.

"Have you been doing lots of wrong things?"

"No, sir. Not too many."

Then the judge focused in with the question, "Tell you what, why don't you tell me about the worst time you got fussed at by Cole?"

Jodie thought quite a while, then she related the story about how she wandered away from Cole in the lightning strike area and stumbled on the wounded wolf. She really felt badly that she had not obeyed Cole. But even though she had done wrong, Cole had taken the time to first make sure she was all right, then instructed her on what she had done wrong so that in the future she would not make the same mistake.

Good example, the judge was thinking. Now to see if the little girl was happy because of the things Cole had bought for her. "Jodie, I am sure Cole has probably bought you a lot of pretty things. Do you like the things he has gotten for you?"

"Cole lives out in the woods so he really hasn't bought me much. So far, he has gotten me the Raggedy Ann to care for...some candy...and a coloring book, which I colored in this weekend while I was staying with the wolf. He got me some new jeans and things 'cause mine were pretty worn out."

"I would imagine that would be a good enough reason to want to stay with someone like Cole, right?" the judge said, in a joking manner.

"It might for some people," Jodie said, "But not for me. I remember this drunk guy used to live next to us for awhile back home. He would give me all kinds of things. Sometimes money, like fifty bucks. Sometimes real neat toys, but I wouldn't want to hang around that guy no matter what he was giving away."

The judge leaned forward in his chair placing both arms on the big table intertwining his fingers together. After a moment of silence where he and Jodie looked at one another, he asked, "Jodie it is my duty not to tell any other person what you say to me. Do you understand that?"

Jodie nodded her head in agreement.

"Are you absolutely sure you want a single man, like Cole, to care for you? Wouldn't you really rather have a mom and a dad and maybe some brothers and sisters?"

Jodie looked Judge Holcolmb directly in the eyes, her big dark-brown eyes appearing to drill holes in his head. She responded with, "Sir, I have had a Mommy and a Daddy. I loved my mommy so much, and I hated my daddy an awful lot. My mommy is dead and my daddy has deserted me. I would rather have Cole than anyone else in the whole world to care for me." She thought a moment, then added, "I cannot have my mommy anymore. Cole has been able to love me as much this week as my real mommy did. I don't need brothers and sisters to keep me happy. All I need is a great person like Cole." then she added, "Please let me stay with Cole!"

Judge Holcolmb could see this was a special girl. She had gone through a lot. It had matured her beyond her years. He still felt he had to place the child with a family, but she did have a good case against it.

"Very good, Jodie, I think I have asked all the questions I need for now. Do you have any questions for me?"

Jodie thought a moment and then asked, "Do you believe that some people are just meant for each other?"

Mature past her years, the judge thought to himself. Then he answered, "Yes, I do!"

Jodie got up from the table and headed toward the door. Looking back over her shoulder, as she opened the door, she said, "So do I!"

Cole entered the conference room a minute later, closed the door and took his seat at the table. The judge was still sitting there in deep thought. After several minutes, he said, "That is some kid there!"

Cole answered, "Yes, she is. I am glad you recognize that. How could anyone not love that child?"

"Cole, you are a ranger. You live out in the woods...er, on an island. You are single and travel a lot. How on earth do you think you can care for this kid?" Holding up his hand to stop Cole from answering the question, he continued, "What about her education? What about the nights you will be away from home? What about contact with other people for the girl? Have you even considered these things?"

Cole stood up and began to pace the room as he answered all of these questions. He told Judge Holcolmb he had made arrangements to live at the headquarters, and that the girl would go to school with several other children in the area. He told him how he and Bill had worked out a schedule where the travel time would be less during the school months and Jodie would travel with him during the non-school months, which would give her vast personal experiences.

In conclusion, he said, "I just do not see a down side to this."

"Well there are quite a few as I see it Cole," the judge retorted. "A child should grow up in as normal a home environment as can be had. You know, the mother and father and another kid or two. You're not even close." Once again, the judge held up his hand to keep Cole from answering right away. "What if you decide to get married? The kid will be a problem or she may have a problem with you getting married. Have you considered that?" He leaned back in his chair folding his arms.

"Well, Judge Holcolmb, a natural family environment is always a safe bet for raising a child. But "normal" would mean a natural father and mother and a home with a lot of love in it. That situation, for Jodie, has been lost forever. The only love in that natural family environment came from the mother. The best you can provide is a foster family, which in ninety-nine percent of the cases is just a temporary stopping place on the way to another foster home, and so on. I am not just proposing to be her foster parent, but her adopted father." Holding up his hand in the same manner the judge did to keep the judge from interrupting, he paused a moment, then continued, "I feel the love of one parent can outweigh a mediocre two parent household. Life throws us all kinds of curves. A perfectly happy couple this year might be divorced next year. What kind of stress does that put on their child? Then to carry that a little further, not only does the child have to choose which parent to live with, but the child may be faced with a new parent through a second marriage. All I can tell you right now, because I am not a mind reader, is that Jodie and I have connected in a very special way. I know it has only been a week, but it seems as though I have known this little girl her whole life. You are ready to give this child to a family that doesn't even know her. Yet you question my ability to raise a child, and I am the only one in Alaska that has spent any quality time with her."

The judge sat motionless for a very long time obviously moved by Cole's argument and emotion, then said, "Cole...it is not a matter of your...ability to be a good parent. It is very unusual for a single male to become a foster parent, let alone an adopted parent. I have heard of a couple cases in the lower forty-eight where that has occurred, but this is Alaska..., a frontier. I just don't know."

The two men talked and argued for forty minutes. Finally, the judge concluded the conference and dismissed Cole. Cole exited the room with not much hope of winning the case to keep Jodie. Looking into the receptionist area he saw at least fifteen people waiting on him. It was the most amazing thing he had seen in years. They were all there to speak with Judge Holcolmb about Cole's character and why they wanted the judge to grant Cole custody of Jodie.

Cole was very moved by the outpouring of confidence all of these people expressed to him. He had always tried to do the best he could at whatever he was working on. He never did anything just to impress someone. This demonstration of approval by people from all segments of the population really made him feel like he was on the right track.

Cole talked quietly with all of them. He thanked them for their support. He was uncomfortable with all of the show of affection, but he knew that this would have to weigh heavily in his and Jodie's favor when the judge finally made his decision.

The judge listened to each and every one of them. He, also, knew of Cole's reputation as a fine upstanding citizen so the character references were not really needed. But the judge was a crafty old man, and he knew that this outpouring of concern by this many citizens could be used in a constructive way. And he intended to us it.

Out of all the people that Judge Holcolmb heard that day, Ranger Defreese and Allison had the best argument in Cole's defense, because Ranger Defreese had raised Allison by himself and she had, admittedly, turned out all right even though she had been raised in an untypical family setting.

Judge Holcolmb came out of the conference room into the receptionist area. He politely thanked everyone for coming to speak for Cole. He asked everyone, except Cole, Jodie, Allison, and Ranger Defreese, to wait outside the building while he had a quiet moment with the foursome before making his final decision.

After the crowd made their way out into the main street, Judge Holcolmb and the other four met back in the conference room for his final decision. You could cut the tension in the air with a knife as the judge began to speak, "Folks, I have listened to all of your statements and I have probed you all to get to the root feelings in this case. Now, it is up to me to apply the laws of the State of Alaska, what is right for Jodie, and what I feel will be best for all concerned."

Chapter 9

The wind blew cold and steady out of the east down the main street, swirling the dust and an occasional piece of litter as it rushed between the parallel rows of buildings lining the worn, cracked street on its way to the foothills beyond Farrow's Patch. The small crowd of people stood close together their backs hunched to the wind, some smoking cigarettes, others chewing gum or tobacco, and some just waiting patiently for the judge's decision.

Looking down the street, a stranger to the town would think that business was booming. At least one third of the diagonal parking spaces were occupied by vehicles. Most of them were old. Most were damaged from the rocks that are kicked up as they are driven down the rough, unpaved Alaskan roads, or the frequent accident when a moose stepped out into the path of the oncoming vehicle. Some vehicles were damaged when they hit a patch of ice on the roadway that was produced by the freezing temperatures, flinging the car off of the road into a ditch, or worse, into a stand of trees. At least half of the vehicles were trucks, the rest old cars.

Alaska may be beautiful, but generally, it is not a place where one makes a lot of money. Oh sure, most come to seek their riches mining gold, copper, silver or some other precious natural resource, such as, harvesting fish from the sea. But most end up barely eking out a living. Of the many that come, for whatever reason, the few that stay are rugged, generally free thinking people, that enjoy not only the beauty of

Alaska, but the solitude, the bountiful natural resources and the freedom to live life as a modern pioneer.

The gloom of the weather added to the tension the crowd was feeling. The talk among them was tense and shallow. They each had their own reasons for making the effort to travel the long distance to speak on Cole's behalf. Occasionally, several of them would wander into one of the stores lining the street, returning to the informal gathering on the sidewalk in front of the small courtroom.

Inside the warmth of the small rented space used as the local courtroom, the foursome had nervously eased themselves into the leather chairs at the large conference table and awaited Judge Holcolmb's decision. He exhaled a small breath of air as his weight was transferred from his arms and legs to the seat of the chair.

The silence in the room seemed to go on forever to everyone in the room. Jodie's palms were wet with perspiration as she wringed them in her lap waiting in anticipation of Judge Holcolmb's decision. Cole sat next to Jodie between her and the judge. He looked down at the little girl's freckled face, into her dark brown, wide-open eyes, and winked at her, nodding his head ever so slightly, indicating everything would be okay.

Across the table Allison sat between the judge and her father. Bill Defreese and Allison were holding hands, their nervousness only showing up because their grasp on one another was making their knuckles turn white. Jodie looked at Ally, who in turn was staring at Cole. It appeared to Jodie that Ally was almost reading Cole's mind. His concern was being transferred, she felt, to Ally.

Judge Holcolmb cleared his throat, leaned forward in his chair folding both forearms on the table, supporting the weight of his upper body with his elbows. He looked around the table at the unblinking eyes of the unmoving, tense audience. Calmly he said, "I am not going to hold you in suspense any longer. So I'm going to give you my decision first, then explain the reasons later." He paused, then said, "By the power vested in me by the State of Alaska, in the United States of America, my decision is to award foster parent status to Cole Bryant to care for the minor child Jodie Patterson until such time the State of Alaska deems differently.

A great roar of excitement came from the foursome. Jodie and Cole hugged one another bouncing up and down in their chairs with glee. Bill Defreese and Allison hugged each other, and then reached across the table grabbing for Cole and Jodie's arms, squeezing them in a demonstration of approval. After several minutes of exhilaration, the judge asked them to come to order.

"It is very unusual for a single man to be a foster parent...it is quite out of the norm. However, I have seen here, today, an unusual bond between Jodie and Cole. There are several areas that have tipped the balance in favor of this decision," the judge stated.

"First, there is all of the statements from the local citizens in your favor, Cole. Second, I feel you have already been a partner in raising Allison Defreese. You were much younger then, but you did have an instrumental role in the upbringing of her. You are even more mature now, and I believe that if your feelings are this strong in wanting to raise Jodie, then you already know all of the responsibilities that go with that decision. Third, Jodie seems to be on the same wavelength as you, Cole. This part I cannot explain. All of you are right, there is a special bond between Jodie and Cole."

Judge Holcolmb paused, looking around the room. He cleared his throat again, adding, "But the fourth reason is the most overwhelming. I purposely came here early this morning so that I could observe you arrive. You could say that I wanted to spy on you," he chuckled, softly. "So, I stood behind the blinds in the receptionist office and watched you all." He cleared his throat again, as if excusing his actions, then continued, "But seriously, I wanted to see how Jodie and Cole reacted to each other. I wanted to see if there was any strain between you two," he said, looking toward Jodie and Cole. "Here is what I observed. You two, Cole and Jodie, walked casually down main street talking with Bill and Allison. At the post office you all stopped and discussed something briefly and Bill and Allison went into the post office."

"Cole and Jodie continued walking down the street, chatting with each other. Jodie walked closer to Cole and reached over, taking Cole's hand." The judge looked at the foursome, "This is an important place to review. First, all of you conversed freely as you walked down the street. This means Jodie did not feel she was being dominated. When Jodie reached over to hold Cole's hand, it indicated she really does have feelings for Cole. Now to continue, after Cole and Jodie left the general store and met you all out front of the office, I observed it was Jodie that stopped Cole. She said something to him and gave him a sincere kiss on the cheek. Cole responded by speaking to her and straightening her hat and hair."

Pausing again, the judge leaned back in his chair. He cleared his throat one more time because he, too, was becoming choked up. "It is as if this is a very natural bond. I am not going to threaten that, at least for now. I am allowing you to be Jodie's foster parent...for now. As you know, Cole, foster parent is a temporary situation. I will be checking in with you two as time goes on. I will say, however, that I do not plan to move Jodie to another family." Then looking at Cole, he said, "I know you want to adopt Jodie. I will help you do that. But it will take time. We, first, must secure all of the documents from the State of Oregon, then proceed through the courts and the legal system for that."

Standing up, Judge Holcolmb concluded, "That is all I have to say. I do want to call in all of those people outside and thank them for coming here and speaking up for you Cole, even though I could have reached the same decision without them." He laughed.

"Thank you Judge Holcolmb. I take this responsibility very seriously and I will not let you, or anyone else, down. I promise to take care of Jodie," Cole said enthusiastically, as he shook the judge's hand.

Jodie walked around the chairs to where Judge Holcolmb was standing. She reached up to shake the judge's hand, saying, "Thank you, sir. I am glad you let me stay with Cole."

The judge responded by bending down to get closer to Jodie's face, "You are a very special young lady. You deserve the best."

The next half-hour was filled with the gathering of all of the people that had come to Farrow's Patch. Judge Holcolmb charged everyone in the gathering to contribute to Jodie's welfare by helping her feel at home and making sure she was considered one of their family, also. They congratulated and thanked one another and, one by one, went on their way back to their homes or work. The foursome eventually got their aircraft underway and headed back to the ranger headquarters. There was a lot of laughing and giggling on the way home. They had won their case. Cole and Jodie could, finally, get their life together started.

Once back at the headquarters, Ranger Defreese told Cole to take the next couple of days off to get the vacant cabin fixed up that they would be living in. He told Cole, jokingly, he probably wouldn't be much good to him for awhile anyhow with his mind on Jodie. So he should go ahead and get their living quarters set up.

The cabin, located on the relatively flat land at the backside of the headquarters area, abutted up to the side of the mountain. At a distance, the cabin appeared to be built right into the side of the steeply sloping mountainside. A tin-roofed porch ran down the length of the front of the small, square structure, two steps up from the ground with a waist-high railing running around the perimeter.

The walls were made of board and batten construction, painted dark green with a door occupying the center of the front side and two small windows on either side of the door. Spider webs and various insect cocoons covered the front area, as well as the eves and window openings around the entire structure. Jodie stopped dead in her tracks upon seeing the cabin. Even though there was plenty of sunlight that reached the cabin, it did have an eerie appearance.

"Gee! This place is spooky!" she exclaimed.

"Yeah, right now it does look spooky, but in a day or two it will look like home sweet home!" Cole said, reassuringly. "Believe it or not the place is in good shape. It just needs to be cleaned up a lot."

"Okay, if you say so," Jodie said, jokingly.

The interior of the cabin was very similar to the other cabins in the area. It had a large living area with a large fireplace on the left side wall.

An open ceiling across the entire width of the cabin and, on the right, a small bedroom at the front of the cabin. A kitchen area occupied the rear and across the top of the bedroom and kitchen, ran a loft.

Cole told Jodie the loft would be her bedroom, since she was young and could go up and down the ladder to the loft area easier than he could. They would put up thick drapes so she could have privacy in the loft, yet be able to leave them open when she wanted to get heat from the fireplace into the loft. The cabin was very dusty from non-use, but it would be in good shape with a good old-fashioned cleaning.

"I like it Cole!" Jodie exclaimed, as she climbed the ladder to her loft, checking out her own special area. "This is really, really neat!"

"I'm glad you like it young lady. You think you will be able to call it home one day?"

"Yes sir! When do we get started?"

"Right away. I'll go down to the maintenance barn and get some cleaning supplies and tools. Then bring them back here to get started," Cole answered.

"Can I go too? I want to see how the wolf is doing."

"Sure thing. It will probably take awhile to get all of the stuff loaded up anyhow."

The next four days were spent working hard on the cabin cleaning, repairing, and painting. During those four days, Jodie spent half of her time helping fix up the cabin and the rest of the time with the wolf. By this time, Jodie had taken over the total care of the wolf making sure it was fed the proper amount and at the right time. Cole had given her instructions on what to do, and he felt this would be educational for her at the same time.

During one quiet moment at the pen with Cole, Jodie petted the wolf softly, looked over at Cole and said, "You know, I think I am going to call her Strike.

Cole replied, "Strike? Why?"

"'Cause she has that mark on her forehead, and it is because of the lightning strike we found her."

"Well that is a real good reason." He softly clapped his hands in approval. "Strike it is, then."

Every morning Strike was glad to see Jodie, wagging her tail and coming to the hole in the fence for her morning "hello". Everyday the wolf moved with greater ease, the soreness lessening and more strength returning slowly to her body. Jodie discovered Strike would chase a thrown ball and return it to her, just like a pet dog. So many hours of playing fetch was actually helping the wolf get stronger.

Jodie found out that she could communicate with the wolf by howling the way the wolf did. Every morning when she would awaken, Jodie would dress and go outside the barracks and howl in a special "code", so to speak. The wolf would respond by howling back. This would go on for several minutes back and forth.

She found out just exactly how good a wolf's hearing really was when, one morning after she awakened, she sat up in bed and humorously howled, quietly, almost as if yawning. The wolf responded by howling in "code" to Jodie.

Thinking this might have been a coincidence, Jodie put her head under the covers and repeated the howl. To her unbelieving ears, she heard the dog respond again. She quickly dressed, racing to the dining hall where Cole, Ranger Defreese and Ally were just finishing up breakfast. Scurrying up to the table she exclaimed, "Strike just heard me call for her! She heard me from my room!"

"Really? I told you they could hear real good!" Cole said.

"Yeah, but more'n that. She heard me when I howled from under my covers! Can you believe that?"

"Wow! That is something!" Cole exclaimed, winking at the others at the table. "I bet you are really proud of her, aren't you?"

"Yes sir! I bet she's got the bestest ears of any ol' wolf!" the excitement showing in the glow in her eyes. "I'm gonna go see her now. Okay?"

"Yes ma'am. Be careful! And don't forget to come to breakfast real soon," Cole said, patting her on the back as she left.

The four days passed quickly. Friday evening, at dinner, the two announced that Saturday morning they would be moving into the cabin.

Also, at dinner, Cole told Jodie and the others it was time to take the wolf back to the wilderness. She was healing nicely, the bandages had been removed, the stitches were starting to dissolve, and the wounds had not reopened. He thought the wolf had improved to the point that she would be able to protect herself in the wild, if she had to.

Jodie really loved the wolf. Cole thought he might have trouble with her when it was time to take Strike back into the wilderness. Jodie's response was with mixed emotions. Cole felt she handled it a lot better than he had expected she would. Most little kids don't understand that some animals need to be in the wild. They feel they are cuddly and cute, and they should be able to stay with them. But Jodie was very good, realizing that Strike was not really hers to keep.

"I'm glad she is doing that well, Cole. I am really going to miss her. I wish I could see her babies when they are born," she said, looking down into her lap, twisting her fingers as she spoke.

"Jodie I am very, very proud of you. You have taken excellent care of the wolf. It is because of you that she got well so quickly," Cole said, patting Jodie on the shoulder, then giving her a squeeze across her shoulders with his arm. "I am, also, proud of you because you did exactly what I told you. You have stayed out of the cage and let the wolf come to you instead of you going to the wolf. I knew that wolf would not bite you if you let it have its own space." Looking around the table, he said, "She is really a good kid! Isn't she?"

"Cole's right, Jodie. You did a great job with the wolf. I think you might have a good career with animals ahead of you!" Ally encouraged her.

"You probably don't know it, but I was keeping an eye on that wolf and you, too." Ranger Defreese added, "And, I must say, you have done an excellent job! Congratulations!" He held out his hand for Jodie to shake.

By this time Jodie had a finger stuck in her mouth, looking shyly down at her lap in embarrassment from all of this gushing attention on her. She held her hand out shaking Ranger Defreese's hand, saying, "Thank you, sir. Thank you, Ally."

Saturday morning, the two gathered up their personal belongings from the barracks and moved them to their new home. Cole had widened the path to the cabin so it would accommodate the jeep. That way, it would be easier for a tractor to clear a path in the winter snow. The cabin was the furthest from the main headquarters, so it was important to make the distance as easily traveled as possible. At one time, this cabin was rented out to vacationers that came to the park. Several years ago the Park Service constructed new, slightly more modern cabins, along the edge of the lake. Rather than fixing up these older cabins, they only rented them out as overflow cabins. Since the last two years they were not needed, they had fallen into disrepair. That worked out nicely for Cole and Jodie, creating the opportunity to move into a place located close to Cole's main work place.

That afternoon some of the other workers, along with Ally and Bill, came to the cabin to have a little house warming. They put up extra tables out front of the cabin. Everyone brought a covered dish to share. It turned out to be a fun time for all. That evening the sun was still high in the sky as the last of the guests left. Cole and Jodie went inside the cabin to settle down for the evening. Cole started a small fire in the fireplace, and the two sat down on the rug in front of the hearth. Jodie had put on her pajamas bringing a book with her.

"Mrs. Kiawah gave this to me today, see?" she said, holding it up to Cole.

"Oh that was nice. Want to read it?"

"Yes I would. Let's take turns reading it, okay?"

"That sounds like fun." They took turns reading a page at a time from the book.

After awhile, they came to a stopping place in the book. They chatted about all sorts of things from what had happened this past week to what was planned for next week, how they thought Strike would like going back to her "home".

Cole walked Jodie to the outhouse off to one side of the cabin and, later, climbed the ladder to Jodie's loft. The bed was, of course, along the back wall. A short railing ran the length of the loft to securely keep its occupants from falling. A small rug was centered on the wood floor. A rectangular mirror hung on one wall, and a large storage closet was on the other wall. The sloping roof created a cozy atmosphere. Jodie had hung an assortment of pictures around the room, which classified it as a kid's room.

The bed, covered deep with comforters, was occupied by Raggedy Ann at the moment. "Welcome to my loft sir!" Jodie said, jokingly.

"Well, thank you ma'am! And a nice loft it is, too!" Cole played along with her. "Now hop into bed and say your prayers. It is way past your bed time."

The next morning, after breakfast, Cole had Bert drive the jeep around to the maintenance barn. Jodie had already arrived at the pen. She had been petting Strike for quite sometime. Earlier that morning, she had fed the wolf a smaller than usual portion of rabbit that Bert had killed.

Cole came around the side of the maintenance barn and approached the pen. The dog raised its head and sniffed the air to make sure this man was someone she liked. With her senses satisfied it was, she lowered her head and continued to accept the petting from Jodie.

Quietly, Cole said, "Okay girls are you ready for a little trip back home?"

"I know she will want to get back to her family, but I am going to miss this wolf," Jodie said, sadly.

"Well, I will try to make this as comfortable as possible for her. The first thing I want to do is make sure she is ready to go back. So let me have a look at her wounds," he said, as he bent down to get closer to the wolf. He stroked her side observing the long gash, then stood up holding a piece of raw meat with his fingertips. He held this above the wolf's head to make her stand up. When she did, he moved the meat down the fence and she followed the meat turning around as she did.

Cole looked at the wound that came into his view on Strike's other side. Both sides looked exceptionally well healed. The wolf could go back to the wild.

"She is doing real good, Jodie. It is time for her to go back to her pack." He looked at the little girl who was staring at the wolf. She had a sad expression on her face, but she was not crying. "Are you okay with this, Jodie?" he asked.

"Yes, sir. She needs to be with her family. I don't want to see her go, but I must. It wouldn't be fair to her to keep her in this cage."

"Right. It really wouldn't be fair to keep her in captivity any longer. We have saved her life and the lives of her pups, so we must let her go free." Cole prepared a mild sedative to put the wolf asleep for about an hour. This would not be enough to hurt the pups, but would give them enough time to put the wolf in a cage and load her into "Lizzie" for the trip back to the wilderness.

Cole had made arrangements for Ranger Defreese and Allison to make the trip with him and Jodie to the island. Ranger Defreese was using this trip as a Sunday ride and a day to spend with his daughter. After the wolf was loaded into "Lizzie", Ranger Defreese and Allison met them at the dock, boarded the plane, and they all headed for a fun day in the sun in Alaska.

The wolf had slept peacefully through the take off and was groggy for the first hour of the trip. Jodie spent the entire time in the rear of the cabin talking to the dog and petting it affectionately. The three adults entertained themselves with small talk, telling stories, interspersed with a little shoptalk.

"Lizzie" made her way through the crystal clear sky, obeying Cole's every command. The powerful engine ran smooth and effortlessly. Off in the distance many, many miles away, Mount St. Elias loomed into the sky dwarfing the huge mountains at her base. Off to the right Volcano Lake came into view, trapped between the encircling mountains. In the eastern half of the lake, was the dot formed by the ancient volcano that was Cole's island.

Cole banked "Lizzie" into a very shallow right hand turn that would bring the airplane just to the west of the island. Once the aircraft passed the peaks of the surrounding mountains, Cole cut the power on the powerful engine. The noise from the engine decreased, and at the same time, the noise from the wind that whirled past the sides and wings of "Lizzie" steadily increased.

The plane smoothly descended as Cole moved the controls slightly forward continuing to make the slow right hand turn to circle the island. As the airplane swung around the southern shore of the island, the altitude had been decreased to just six hundred feet. The trees appeared to thrust themselves skyward to meet the oncoming aircraft.

"You guys sure are silent, what's up?" Cole asked.

Ranger Defreese spoke first, "I always forget how unique this place is. It really is beautiful."

"You have that right, Daddy," A.J. chimed in.

"By the way, Cole, how did you talk me into letting you put a cabin here?" Ranger Defreese said, jokingly.

"I think it was the same idea as when we talked the Indians out of their lands," Cole chuckled, "and you cannot have it back!"

Jodie looked out the window at the island "Hey you guys. This is my island, too. Remember?" they all laughed.

Cole steered "Lizzie" around the island keeping her in the same shallow right hand turn until they were flying parallel to the outer shoreline of the lake. Slowly he decreased the altitude of the plane until they were skimming just fifty feet above the surface of the water. "Lizzie's" engine speed was just a notch or two above fast idle propelling the plane at about sixty knots. The water appeared to disappear beneath her fuselage in long streaks as the bright sunlight reflected off of the lake surface.

When the airplane approached the area where Cole and Jodie had rescued the wolf, he cut the engine speed to a slow idle and allowed "Lizzie" to set gently down on the smooth, crystal clear water. The craft touched the surface of the lake so smoothly the only way to know she was on the water was by the increased noise from the rushing water as the pontoons knifed their way through it. The craft slowed, gently gliding toward the nearby shore.

Cole switched the engine off as "Lizzie" approached the northern shore of the lake. "Okay, Bill, I'll go out and drop the anchor. I want to get "Lizzie" in as close to shore as I can."

"Right! I'll watch for rocks and overhanging limbs," Bill answered.

Cole stepped down onto the right pontoon and removed a long rope that was attached to a silver colored anchor. He swung the anchor back and forth several times, then released it, allowing it to plunge into the water just ahead of the craft as it drifted closer to shore. The airplane ran past the descending anchor as Cole took up the slack of the rope, then started to feed it out again as the craft drew away from the anchor's resting place.

When the airplane was as close to shore as it could get without hitting the rocks or becoming entangled in the low overhang of the tree limbs, Ranger Defreese shouted, "Set the line, Cole!"

Cole held the line tight stopping the forward momentum of the airplane. He tied the rope off at a cleat on the rear of the pontoon. Then, quickly grabbing a second rope and anchor, threw it toward shore anchoring the craft in that direction after he tied it off on the front cleat of the pontoon.

Cole spoke in an even, soft voice to Jodie, "Now we want to do everything calmly so as not to alarm the wolf."

Jodie answered, "Okay, Cole."

"Bill let's get on our waders, then we can get the cage out of the airplane," Cole said, then looked at Jodie and A.J. "You two girls stay in the airplane until Bill and I get the cage clear of "Lizzie". After we start carrying the wolf to the shore, you can get out of the plane, Jodie, and come to shore, also. I want A.J. to stay in "Lizzie". As soon as we get the wolf safely on shore, I want Bill to get back in the airplane. Any questions?" They all shook their heads, "Good! Then let's do it. Make sure you remain calm and quiet!"

The two men, garbed in waders, and waist deep in water, lowered the cage down from the airplane and carried the cage, above their heads, toward the shore. Occasionally, they would stumble over a rock or fallen limb, but they got the wolf safely to shore, and surprisingly, the dog did not look bothered by the whole ordeal.

Once the wolf was on shore, Ranger Defreese made his way back to the pontoon that Jodie was standing on. He carried the little girl to dry land and set her down. Then he waded back to the airplane, climbed up onto the pontoon and entered the back seat of the airplane.

Jodie bent down next to the cage. Strike rubbed her side along the wire cage next to Jodie. She reached her little hand through the large mesh of the cage and stroked the wolf's fur. The dog uttered a low sigh as it slowly paced the cramped cage, all the time rubbing Jodie's hand.

"Well, Jodie, this is it. You have accomplished what you wanted to do when Strike was trapped beneath that tree. She is healthy and it is because of you."

Jodie kept her eyes on the wolf saying in a soft, trembling voice, "Yes, sir."

"I am very proud of you. The whole time the wolf was at headquarters you made sure she was taken good care of."

As if she didn't hear what Cole said, she spoke to the wolf in a low voice, "I love you. I will miss you. But I want you to go back to your family, and I want you to love your puppies." A tear ran down her cheek.

The wolf stopped pacing and faced Jodie. She held Strike's head between her hands. The wolf looked Jodie in the eyes and let out a soft, low moan. Then, the dog let out a soft howl. The howl had several distinct inflections and ended with the low moan.

Jodie responded with the same howl, using the same inflections. Then, the wolf would howl again, and Jodie would respond. Finally, the two fell silent. Jodie looked over at Cole and said, "Would you mind going back to the airplane with the others? I want to let Strike out of the cage myself."

Cole looked a little apprehensive, then nodded his head in agreement. When Cole was in the plane, Jodie slowly opened the door of the cage. The wolf emerged cautiously, sniffed the air, looked all around the area, then moved away from the cage six or seven feet.

Jodie remained motionless. The wolf looked back at the tiny girl, turned around and cautiously made her way to Jodie's side, rubbing up against the girl's outstretched hand. The wolf sat down allowing Jodie to stroke her fur, then howled softly in the same manner as before.

Jodie returned the howl. The wolf sniffed the air several times, then sniffed the ground.

Standing again, Strike circled Jodie rubbing her fur against Jodie's body and arms and slowly walked off into the woods. Two minutes passed without a sound. Then, from a short distance away, an unseen wolf howled. Jodie, choking back her tears, returned the howl. The little girl had to let Strike go, not just physically, but emotionally, and that was the toughest part.

Jodie, head hanging down, feet softly kicking loose rocks and small twigs, walked slowly to the shoreline. Cole made his way down the pontoon, eased himself into the waist deep water and made his way to the shore where the little girl awaited him. Bending down, giving the child a big hug, he asked, "You gonna be all right?"

"Yes sir. You know it just came to me that she is going to miss me too!" she said.

"Yep. You're right about that! Come on, honey, let's get in "Lizzie" and go to our island."

Looking back over her shoulder, the little girl hoped to have one last glimpse of Strike. But that was not to be. The wolf had returned to the mountain, and was on her way to meet up with the other wolves in her pack.

Once on the island, the group had a picnic in the grassy area behind the cabin. They had laid out blankets to sit on and had brought cold drinks from Cole's lake refrigerator. It was a great time, fathers getting to bond with their daughters. They talked, and joked, and played some games.

Late that afternoon, Ranger Defreese told the others that he had decided to take the next day off. It had been a long time since he had been able to spend time with his "favorite" daughter, he joked. "Of course, this means that the rest of you will have to take the day off, too!" he exclaimed. "Now I have been hearing all of these fish tales told by you all, so I am challenging you two to a fishing contest with me and Allison," he said. "I'll make a bet with you that Allison and I can catch the biggest fish. The bet is that the losers clean up after dinner. What do you say?"

Cole took up the challenge responding, "I think you and Allison will be cleaning up after dinner because you are looking at the two best fishermen in Alaska!"

"We'll see about that, mister." A.J. countered.

"Well, Cole and I have proven we can catch fish. You and your dad are only talking," Jodie chimed in.

"Let's quit talking and get going, what do you say?" Bill asked.

The afternoon was wonderful; very pleasant weather, lots of giggling, lots of bonding. At dinnertime, the four found themselves in front of the cabin with their four largest fish they had caught. All the others had been returned to the lake, not to be wasted.

Cole and Jodie were the winners by just one half inch in overall length. After grilling the fish over the pit out in front of the cabin, the foursome enjoyed the home cooked meal. Cole had enough potatoes to go around and, of course, he had some canned beans to add to the dinner menu.

After dinner, Cole and Jodie walked out onto the dock to cover up "Lizzie" for the night. They, sat on the dock talking about all kinds of things; some funny, some sad, some new subjects, some old, just getting to know each other a little better.

Inside the cabin, Bill and Allison were carrying on their own conversation as they washed the dishes. The topics ranged from work around the national park to Allison's year at school. It was a time to catch up on all the subjects that got left untouched because of the distance created by Allison being at school and the hustle of running a national park headquarters.

"Daddy, how did you know it was Mom you wanted to marry?" Allison asked.

Bill stopped drying the dish he was holding, tilted his head slightly, puckering his lips in thought for a moment. Then he answered, "Well...well let me tell you...I knew the moment I laid eyes on your mother she would be special to me." He paused, set the dish down on the counter, turned to face Allison, continuing, "Honestly, there was something that clicked in my head. There she was holding her books to her chest walking down the main concourse sidewalk at college. I knew I had to say something to her...I just couldn't let her go by without getting her attention." Pausing again, he chuckled, then looked down at the floor as if embarrassed.

"As she approached I did the only thing I could. I blocked her path and said, "Pardon me, but your shoe is untied!" She stopped and I immediately dropped to my knee." He laughed out loud, "Since she was carrying her books at her chest, she couldn't get a clear view of her shoes. I quickly unfastened one of them and then proceeded to retie the shoe."

"You mean you untied her shoe? It wasn't untied at all?" Allison asked, chuckling.

"That's right! But it gave me an opportunity to buy some time so I could get to introduce myself." He paused again looking off into the distance, as if being transported back in time.

"We got along great from the beginning. We found a park bench nearby, and ended up talking with one another for several hours. I think she was smitten with me the same way I was for her. Oh yeah, I knew she was the one for me from the very start," he concluded.

"But I have met quite a few people at school and I have never felt like that, why?" she asked.

"Because none of them has been "the one"! I don't think it is the same for everyone....I mean the feeling I had for your mother. And I am sure not everyone actually finds "the one" in his or her life. I feel some people end up settling for someone. But, I do believe that when the right person does come along, you will know it in your own special way."

Allison stopped washing the dishes, appearing deep in thought. Bill watched her a moment or two, then asked, "Allison...tell me...what is on your mind? Is something bothering you?" He placed his right hand on her left shoulder, slightly applying pressure in a comforting manner.

She didn't answer for a long time, still deep in thought. She was asking herself if she wanted to continue this conversation. "Daddy, can we

talk freely? I mean, if I bring up a subject will you listen as my friend?
Give me your truthful answer? Not judge my motives? Just be truly honest?" she asked.

"Wow! Hold on little daughter! You must really be loaded down with
some deep feelings here!" he exclaimed. "I will answer all of your questions, honey. I have always answered your questions. The part that may
be hard for me is that I will always be your father, also. So I may have to
beg off on some subjects, if you know what I mean," he chuckled.
"Now what is on your mind?"

Allison started slowly, apprehensively at first, "I don't know if I am
way off base here, or not. And I really don't know how to get started…it
is kind of embarrassing…kind of stupid, I guess." She walked over to
the dining table, sat down rubbing her hands back and forth on the table
top, staring blankly at its surface deep in thought. Bill joined her at the
table, reached over, and grasped her hand. He didn't say anything. His
mind was racing thinking of all of the subjects he would really rather
not discuss with his daughter, even though he knew he should.

"I find myself very attracted to someone…a man, I mean." She
looked at her father to see his reaction. He sat there trying to withhold
any signs of emotion. "The problem I have is I don't know if I am
allowed to be attracted to him."

"Who is he? Why all the mystery? Why haven't you mentioned this
before? More importantly, what do you mean, be allowed to be
attracted to him?" he asked, the questions tumbling out of his mouth
machine-gun style.

"You know how you had that special feeling for Mom? Well, I have
had that special feeling for someone for over two years. At first, I thought
it would go away, but the feeling just grows stronger everyday." She
squeezed her father's hand keeping her vivid blue eyes glued to his. She
took a deep gulp of air and blurted out, "The mystery man is Cole!" She
quickly looked down at the table, too afraid to see her father's reaction.

"Cole! Cole? You're afraid to talk to me about Cole?" He placed his
forefinger under Allison's chin, raising her face upward until she was
looking directly at him.

She looked at him shyly, then said, softly, "Yes, kinda'." An embarrassed look came over her face. Suddenly she felt like a little kid.

"Geesh! I thought something terrible had happened!" he exclaimed.

"You mean you're not mad at me?" she quizzed.

"No, I'm not mad at you. But I do want to know more about this thing with Cole."

She swallowed hard, brushing her tongue across her dry, nervous lips, then pressed her lips together to remove the extra moisture. "Well, Daddy, I am very attracted to Cole. I have been for over two years," she added quickly, exhaling heavily, glad to have finally told her dad how she felt. "Not that he knows it, I mean."

"Wait a minute. Cole doesn't know you like him? So, this feeling is strictly yours. I mean as boyfriend and girlfriend?" Bill asked, a puzzled look on his face.

"That's right," she paused to catch her breath, then began again, "Let me start from the beginning. Cole has always been like a big brother to me, as you know. Actually, he is really more than a big brother to me because when I was just a little girl he was more like a second father to me. You two guys took care of me", Allison took both of her father's hands in hers, "and you both did a wonderful job. I can really say I had a happy childhood, even though I missed Mom a whole bunch, because of you and Cole."

"Thank you Allison." Bill looked a little misty.

"Well, everything was okay for a while. I went off to school and I dated some guys there. Not too many, because I was not used to having all of those people around all of the time. It isn't like living out here in the middle of nowhere, you know," she chuckled, squeezing her dad's hands gently.

"I can truthfully say I didn't meet anyone that I wanted to spend the rest of my life with. Oh sure, there were some nice guys, you know, polite and everything. But, none of them became special to me. They all lacked one thing or another. After dating them awhile, I would lose interest in them."

"When I came home after my sophomore year, something began to change for me." She gazed off in the direction of the fireplace, her mind stepping back in time, her eyes unfocused. Her voice softened and her father could feel the perspiration from her palms as her hands still held his. "At first, I didn't recognize the attraction I had toward Cole. It was just an uneasy feeling deep within my body. But, by the end of the summer, I knew I had a problem."

Allison turned her big blue eyes back to her father's face, took a deep breath releasing it slowly, as if to regain her composure. "You see, by then I realized I was in love with a man I shouldn't be in love with. At least in that way, I mean." She studied her dad's face for a reaction. There was none. Bill was doing a great acting job restraining his personal emotions.

"So, I went off to school for my junior year. I dated more that year because I wanted to release myself from the guilt of being in love with someone I shouldn't love. Plus, I wanted to see if it was just a crush that I had on Cole, or maybe puppy love, you know. Also, I wanted to see if anyone else would be right for me. Someone that had that special 'something'," she said, holding her hands above her shoulders making invisible quotation marks with the first two fingers of each hand. She stood up, paced around the room, neither of them saying anything for several minutes.

"Last summer was even harder, because I knew I loved Cole...and, to be truthful, I think he felt something towards me. But I couldn't express my feelings to him, and I knew he would never admit those kinds of feelings he may have had, to me. So, once again, I went off to school leaving my heart here, trying to rid myself of the guilt I had been feeling now for over two years, searching for someone that I might fall in love with."

"Well, guess what? I didn't find anyone that captured my heart, let alone my interest. And the "real pits" is my love for Cole remained as strong as ever. It was all I could do to stay at school, but I knew I had to in order to release my feelings for him and the guilt I felt." She came back to the table sitting down in the chair. Looking her father in his dark-brown, unflinching eyes, she asked, "Am I being silly, Daddy?"

Bill Defreese sat motionless for a moment, thinking what he was going to say to his little girl. Finally, he began, "Allison, you have really been carrying an emotional load around with you, haven't you?" he took a deep breath exhaling slowly, "You're not being silly, honey! It is natural for a young lady to be attracted to a handsome, young man. Listen, Cole is not related to you in anyway. So, biologically and legally, no, it is not wrong to be attracted to him." He looked down at his clasped hands as they rested on the table, and twiddled his thumbs thinking what he was going to say. "You know, Allison, I have always worried about you being raised out here with very few kids around to play with, but I feel you have done very well, and are basically a well-balanced country girl."

"My main fear as you became a teenager was that you would settle for someone just because they were from around these parts. So when you went away to college and hadn't found anyone by then, I figured this was good because you would have more young fella's to choose from," he chuckled.

"I never figured you would find someone so close to home that would steal your heart. That is a surprise to me!" He shifted his weight in the chair, tapped his fingers briefly on the table as he thought a moment, then continued, "Cole is a great guy. I am sure you find him attractive, but why do you feel he is the "one"?"

"Oh, Daddy, I cannot really explain it." Her eyes brightened as she looked blankly in the distance, "It is a feeling that is deep within my body...a feeling that makes my heart skip a beat...my pulse quicken...all my nerve endings tingle...a good feeling all over, and a miserable, sick feeling if I feel I must live without him.

"I know what puppy-love and infatuation are, because when I was a little girl, I was infatuated with Cole. But, this is entirely different." She paused, then concluded, "I love Cole and I cannot live without him!"

"Well, Allison, you have to talk these feelings over with Cole. You have to find out how he feels about you."

"That is the problem, Daddy. Cole will not discuss the subject with me. The only thing he has said is I am like a little sister to him," her voice cracked a little, as she looked down into her lap, a sad expression on her face.

"Maybe Cole doesn't feel the same way about you, honey. Have you thought about that?"

"Yes, sir, I have. But you know what? I think he has the same feelings about me, as I do about him. The only difference is he is not going to talk about it because he feels it wouldn't be right to fall in love with someone he helped raise." She looked at her father with a bewildered look on her face.

"Why do you think he feels the same way?"

"Several reasons. Every time our eyes meet, he looks away. So far this summer, he hasn't spent anytime alone with me. It is like he is avoiding me, except for when someone else is around. Daddy, I know he is uncomfortable when he is around me and I know he is trying to deny his true feelings."

"You know, it could be something else, too."

"Like what"?

"He has taken on a new obligation, you know. He has Jodie to think about now. I know this has to weigh heavily on his mind. He has to think about raising her, making sure she is happy and all of her needs taken care of, trying to give her a normal upbringing."

"I know that, but this has been going on for two years now. Every summer the feeling grows deeper and deeper. Cole must feel the same way about me! I just know he does!"

"I see, and what are you going to do about it?" Bill asked.

Allison shifted in her chair, ran her hand through her blonde hair, paused a moment, then looked at her dad, "Daddy, that is where you come in. Cole won't talk to me about this subject, will you..."

"Hold on there little girl of mine", Bill interrupted, "I am not going to go talk to Cole about this!"

"Please Daddy! Why not?"

"Because this is between you and Cole. I am not going to get put in the position of setting you two up."

"Couldn't you just mention that I talked briefly with you?" she begged.

"No! But if Cole ever comes to me to discuss the matter, I will listen to him. Just as I have listened to you."

"Daddy, I am so miserable! I don't know what to do." A look of despair came over her face as she pleaded to her father.

"Allison, the only advice I am going to give you is this. First, if it is meant to be, I believe things will work out for you. You need to continue concentrating on your summer job and try to have fun. Second, I wouldn't push Cole right now. He has his plate full of his own emotions right now taking care of Jodie. Third, you need to make sure if the relationship moves forward you will be willing to accept Jodie as part of the package because, one day, Cole may be allowed to adopt her. He got up from the chair reached his hands down to grasp Allison's, then gently lifted her out of the chair. They hugged each other for a long time, rocking soothingly from side to side.

Allison had that sick feeling a person in love gets when they know they are in love, but cannot carry through with that love because of some obstacle that is in the way. She felt safe and secure in her father's arms, just as she did as a little girl. She thought back to those times he had comforted her and, in a way, wished she could go back to those days when she could count on her daddy to solve all of her problems. Then, her mind raced forward to the present. She wished that Cole would put his arms around her and comfort her the way her father was doing now.

Chapter 10

A month passed and things were getting into a normal routine for Jodie and Cole. Since school was out for the summer, Jodie was able to travel to the other locations with Cole. It was a great learning experience for the little girl, and as she put it, "Really, really neat". She met new people and learned all kinds of interesting things about Alaska, the wilderness, and its people.

Jodie had shown signs of becoming closer to Allison, also. Allison brought the feminine side out in Jodie. The two would spend a lot of time talking about girl things when Jodie would hang around with Ally while she was working in the campground.

One day, while the two girls were chatting, the topic turned to clothes and fashion. Not that fashion was a big topic way out in the middle of nowhere. "You know what, Jodie? Let's ask Cole if we can go into Juneau and spend a day shopping. What do you say?" Ally asked excitedly.

"Yeah! Oh boy, that would be fun! Do you think he would let me go?" Jodie's eyes lit up with excitement.

"I think so! Well, I don't know. But we won't know until we ask, will we?" she replied. "Let's ask him tonight after dinner. That is when he is at his weakest time for saying 'no'." They giggled in unison, kind of an evil little laugh.

That evening, after dinner, Ally brought up the subject of the lack of clothes. Instantly, her dad knew what was coming. Cole listened to her talk, agreeing that Jodie would need some new clothes shortly. Then

Ally asked the big question, "I would like to take Jodie to get some clothes. Do you think it is in your budget, Cole?"

"Well now, let's see...hmmm, I think so, why?" Cole dragged out the sentence to add more suspense to the answer and follow-up question.

"Jodie and I were thinking of going into Juneau to shop for some very much needed clothes."

"Juneau? Why so far?" Cole asked. Bill cracked a smile, trying to hold it back. He knew where this was going and he knew Cole could not say "no".

"Well, there isn't any place closer with a good selection. I want to take Jodie to Juneau so she can really shop. You know, like a girl should." Ally's blue eyes gazed at Jodie, then returned to Cole. His eyes met hers and his heart did a little flutter. He hated this feeling because he loved A.J. very much as a member of his extended family. This new emotion was changing the relationship he once had with her. He wanted to be as close as they had been in the past, but he couldn't allow himself to have this new and different kind of feeling for her.

"I guess I don't have a problem with that. Just remember we need practical clothes. Not clothes you would wear in a fashion setting. When would you be going?"

"How about tomorrow? I have a relief helper tomorrow in the campground. That would work good for me. How about you Jodie? Cole?" she asked.

Jodie said that would be good and Cole agreed. Bill dabbed his mouth with his napkin, hiding his smile. He knew these two ladies had worked him to a tee.

The next morning the two perky girls headed to Juneau in Ally's Cessna. They had a great time shopping and shopping, and shopping. They laughed, giggled, tried on awful looking things and some dresses made for proms, jeans, overalls, shoes, boots, and anything else they could find. By the end of the shopping experience, Jodie had selected a very good, practical group of clothes. Of course, Cole had given the two a list of things Jodie could buy and instructions were given to Ally to follow the suggestions on the list.

Before they left the Juneau airport, Ally filed a flight plan and got a weather report. The latest weather report showed a powerful storm coming in off the Pacific Ocean, to the west. At the rate of speed it was approaching, she figured she would take a more easterly course for home. This was a common practice for light planes to fly around storms. Everyone at the airport agreed that the course she had chosen would give her plenty of time to reach her destination before the inclement weather would hit.

The trip back home was going smoothly. The airplane purred along propelling the craft and its occupants at a leisurely eighty-five knots. Ally had the plane trimmed out at an altitude of 6500 feet. Because of the more easterly course the plane had taken, the mountain ranges they crossed were higher than those closer to the coast to the west.

As they approached Copper Mountain, it was obvious this was one of the taller mountains they would pass. It thrust 6430 feet into the sky. The rocky southern exposure they were approaching was virtually treeless. The rusted copper-colored, craggy rocks that littered this side of the mountain were exposed to the harsh elements of Alaskan weather. The torrential rains that passed through the area two hundred days a year eroded deep trenches down the side of the mountain pushing smaller rocks into deep piles in areas, held back by rugged ledges or huge boulders. Today this side of the mountain was only occupied by mountain goats that fed on the sparse weeds and vines that insisted on growing here.

Most mountaintops are rather rounded, kind of flat, caused by erosion of the original looser material. Thus, it is like most mountains have been chopped off across the top. The top of this mountain, in contrast, thrust into the air forming an inverted "V" shaped peak, sharp, jagged, foreboding. Some boulders, at the top, formed both the south side and the north side of the inhospitable mountain.

The other side of Copper Mountain was in contrast to the southern side. Trees grew in abundance at the lower levels up to about four thousand feet. From the top, a sheer cliff dropped almost one thousand feet. The vertical face was heavily grooved and cracked from eons of extremely harsh weather. In the spring and summer, heavy rains eroded the surface. In the winter the moisture would freeze, expand and crack more of the surface causing more creases and deeper cracks.

The vertical surface sloped outward at a very steep angle for another 1225 feet, then went back to vertical for an additional 417 feet, where a ledge protruded out about twenty-five feet, almost horizontally, from the mountain. An additional seven to eight feet had been carved out of the vertical rock face above by nature forming a wedge-like area.

Below this area, the mountainside sloped steeply downward for another two thousand feet, or so, gradually lessening toward the base where it trapped a lake within the lower surrounding mountains. The area below the ledge was heavily forested, the ground made up of a very loose, rocky soil created over the years by the roots of the trees and other foliage crushing the large boulders into a rocky-type soil, and by rocks that had been broken loose from above, plunging down the steep incline toward the mountain base.

It has been said that a person's life can be changed in the blink of an eye. Generally, we perceive change as happening over an extended period of time. Such is the case as one's appearance changing over many years from a young child, to an adult, to an older octogenarian. But most changes in our lives happen in a split second. It is the result of the split second change that may linger for days, months, years or decades.

Allison and Jodie were about to experience change; a split-second change. At this particular moment the two girls were chatting casually as their airplane approached the mountain at just over 6500 feet. Normally, Allison would not leave just seventy feet clearance between a mountaintop and the airplane. But, even though the clearance was just seventy feet, it would occur for just a split second as the plane passed over the sharp peak, and seventy feet is quite a bit of distance from the top. A four-story office building is about seventy feet tall. So Allison was passing over this 6430 foot high mountain allowing for a four story office building on top of that, not really all that unsafe when put in perspective.

On the northern side of the mountain, at the same moment, an American Bald Eagle was in the heat of stalking a rabbit at the five thousand-foot level. The rabbit had been grazing on grass that poked out from the earth between the rocky surface. The eagle swooped close overhead and, as it did so, it made one small mistake. The eagle allowed its shadow to pass across the rabbit's back.

The rabbit, sensing this, froze until the eagle passed by. Then it moved closer to a large boulder, still close to the food source, but out of harms way. The eagle pumped its wings, climbing off into the distance, made a slow 180-degree turn, heading back toward the unsuspecting rabbit. The large bird drew in its wings, dived quietly toward the prey, increasing its speed as it approached from the opposite direction.

As the beautiful, powerful bird got within striking distance of the rabbit, it lowered its clawed feet in preparation for snagging the defenseless rodent. But at the last second, the rabbit, once again, sensed the bird. It made one hop to the left as the big bird whooshed past, missing the small animal in a rare moment of miscalculation.

Determined to bag the prey the eagle powered itself with its huge wings almost vertically using the strong wind from the east, blowing diagonally up the side of the mountain, to help it quickly gain altitude. All the time, the big bird kept its eyes and concentration on the extremely lucky rabbit. This time the eagle would not come up empty clawed. It would dive at an even faster, steeper angle and, this time, the rabbit would be the victim of the superior eagle.

At the moment the eagle crested the mountain peak, pumping its wings to gain additional altitude in preparation for the 180 degree turn and the spectacular dive to the decisive victory of bagging the unsuspecting rabbit, the eagle, ironically, became the defenseless prey as the small airplane crossed the peak at same spot.

Allison was saying to Jodie, "So, then, I put on all the makeup I could...."

Jodie screamed, "Look out!" Allison turned her head toward the front windshield. The eagle came up from below the front cowling, missing the spinning propeller, it grazed the engine cowling, smashing full force into the windshield, breaking it into thousands of small knife-like pieces, which shot throughout the cabin interior.

The huge bird passed between the girls in the front seat, part of the bird hitting Allison in the face. The bird struck the rear seat with such impact, it sounded as if a bomb had gone off in the cabin, exploding into a thousand pieces covering the interior with blood, feathers, and body pieces. Allison was covered with blood all over her face and chest caused from the bird's blood and her own blood from the shrapnel-like broken glass. Jodie had a large quantity of the eagle's blood on her face and left arm and several lacerations from the broken windshield.

The impact knocked Allison unconscious immediately, the force throwing her body backward causing her to pull back on the controls of the airplane, her hands still tightly clutching the wheel. The airplane climbed vertically upward about 150 feet, the engine still running, forcing the small craft into a "power-on" stall. Allison's hands dropped away from the controls as gravity tugged on the unconscious girl.

The Cessna rolled slowly to the right as the torque from the engine overcame the uncontrolled craft. The airplane began to shutter when the vertical motion of the airplane halted. The only thing suspending the craft in the air, for the moment, was the spinning propeller.

Jodie was confused, shocked beyond belief, and frozen in fear. She had quit screaming and, at this moment, was looking out the broken front window straight up into the sky. The plane finally stopped climbing, still slowly rotating around the vertical axis, then began to fall out of the sky tail first, as the tug of gravity on the airplane was too much for the spinning propeller to overcome. Jodie's eyes, opened wide in fear, darted about trying to figure out what was happening. Seeing the plane begin its backward fall toward the craggy, inhospitable mountain, she let out a terrifying scream.

The Cessna's momentum began to build as the plane continued to fall faster and faster, tail first, toward earth. Fifty...one hundred...two hundred...and then, as it dropped three hundred feet, Jodie, either through reaction or quick thinking, forced herself to grab the controls pulling them backward which moved the stabilizer flaps in an "up position" forcing the tail to fall upward, in relation to the airplane.

As the airplane came back to horizontal, she cut the power of the engine, her chest pushing on the controls which moved the stabilizer to the slightly down position, causing the plane to descent toward the cliffs of the mountain. Jodie, once again, tried to save the plane from crashing by pulling back on the controls, as if to make it go over the mountain, which now loomed almost 2700 feet above the heavily damaged, gliding craft.

Jodie, omitting a blood curdling scream the whole time, could not believe her eyes as the craft rushed toward the cliff. She worked the controls to no avail and, at the last moment before impact, covered her face in a panic.

The plane impacted the cliff just above the ledge that protruded out from the mountainside crushing the front of the plane back into the passenger compartment. The propeller, still spinning at idle when it struck, was bent backwards wrapping it around the crushed and crumpled engine cowling. The wings, which ran across the top of the cabin, were split apart above the cabin and forced forward, striking the cliff, still attached to the craft by the struts and the cabin sides.

After coming to a sudden stop when it struck the cliff, the plane fell another twenty-two feet to the overhanging ledge below, coming to rest with the back third of the airplane hanging in open space beyond the ledge. Jodie, slumped in her seat, was knocked unconscious by the impact with the mountain.

Allison had never regained consciousness from her impact with the eagle. She was held in place by her seat belt, her bloody face pointing upward, her head forced backward by the violent fall from the mountainside.

The Cessna remained intact. Fortunately, the airplane's forward motion at the time of impact was relatively slow, since most of the speed had been scrubbed off when Jodie had pulled back on the controls just before the plane crashed into the mountainside.

Fuel leaked out of the crumpled engine compartment, forming a pool of fluid beneath the aircraft that spread out and ran to the lower side of the ledge next to the wedge-area under the cliff. The broken wings ran from the cabin roof, forward to the cliff where the tips lay unsupported on the ledge. The fuselage was heavily crumpled in front of the cabin and twisted and bent behind the cabin area.

There was total silence for several minutes after the crash. Then as the storm the girls were avoiding approached, there were numerous lightning strikes nearby and, finally, the rains came. The downpour beat against the fragile crumpled airplane and the runoff from the rain, at first, trickled down the side of the mountain and the cliff above the airplane. Then small rivers of water cascaded off of the cliff above onto the small lifeless aircraft.

Even though the rain brought cooler temperatures with it, it also began to wash the pools of volatile fuel away from the hot engine area, preventing a fire that would have engulfed, and eventually, consumed the airplane and its occupants.

There wasn't any movement from the airplane for a long time. Its occupants were unconscious. The temperature continued to fall rapidly. The rain came down in sheets and the wind created by the onrushing storm whistled past the cliff above. Waterfalls created by the massive downpour of rain cascaded down the steep walls of the mountain, some of which pounded on the tail of the crumpled Cessna, rocking the craft precariously on the ledge, creating a loud, hollow metallic noise.

Jodie slowly regained consciousness, moving slightly at first, then jerking to alertness. She was very disoriented and tried to remember where she was. The noise created by the heavy rain and the waterfalls pounding on the fuselage echoed in her head. In her panic to orient herself, she immediately tried to stand up, but the seat belt restrained her, which created more panic. She felt terror and tried that much harder to escape. Everything was out of focus....the noise was deafening....she had to get out!

She struggled some more with the seat restraint to no avail. With unfocused eyes, she looked toward Ally, but she still could not remember how she got here. As a matter of fact, she could not remember who Ally was, at first. Her eyes continued to dart around the strange surroundings as she tried to figure out what was going on, where she was. This had to be a horrible dream, she thought. Who is this person with all that blood all over her?

Jodie lowered her head and ran her hands across her face and through her hair. Still trying to figure out what had happened, she began to cry, "Cole....Cole....come here! I am having a bad dream. Cole, come here!"

But Cole did not come. Slowly it all started to come back to her. She remembered the collision with the eagle and the long fall out of the sky. She jolted to reality, looking over to Ally, "Ally! Ally!....Ally, please don't be dead!" she cried, big tears running down her cheeks. Once again, she struggled with the seat belt. This time, more focused, she was able to release the belt.

She quickly reached over to Ally, shaking her. "Ally! Ally! Ally wake up! Wake up!" Ally was totally limp. As Jodie shook her arm, Ally's whole upper body shook like Jell-O, totally lifeless. "Ally, please wake up! I need you Ally!" Jodie called out between heavy sobs.

Then a pain jabbed at her ankle and lower leg. Looking down at her foot, Jodie saw the problem. The force of the impact with the cliff pushed the dash board and foot controls backward into the cabin space trapping her lower leg and foot under the dashboard. She tried to wiggle her foot loose, but the pain was too great, and the foot remained trapped for now.

The heavy rain and wind continued, dipping the temperature another ten degrees into the lower forties. The noise was deafening, but fortunately very little of the moisture from the rain and the water cascading from the cliff above made it to the inside of the airplane fuselage. The water continued to cool off the hot parts of the engine, and at the same time, wash the spilled fuel over the side of the ledge lessening the chance of an onboard fire.

Once again, panic came over Jodie, and she began to cry and scream, "Ally! Ally, please wake up! Please, please, wake up! I need you Ally!"

But there was no movement from Ally. Jodie quit screaming and took in the sight of Ally. Blood continued to drip from the facial lacerations on her once pretty face. Her jaw hung open at an awkward angle. The front of Ally's blue blouse was covered in half dried blood, resembling the result of someone smashing an over-ripe tomato on a blue wall. Her arms rested limp in the seat on each side of her body.

Jodie's eyes scanned lower. Horror filled her when she looked at Ally's legs. The left leg was trapped, similar to her own under the pedals and the dashboard. The other leg was, also, trapped. But the engine compartment had been pushed further back in the center of the cabin and Ally's right leg was pushed all the way backward to the seat. The sickening feeling Jodie was feeling was due to the sight of the right leg pointing in the opposite direction as it should. Jodie immediately lost her stomach, throwing up all over herself. She cried and cried, and begged Ally to wake up and be all right.

But Ally wasn't all right. She never moved. Jodie slowly cried herself out regaining restraint, once again. She thought to herself, "What would Cole do? What would Cole want me to do?" She could hear him talk to her in her mind, "This is Alaska! One must be tough!" Cole would have told her. "Jodie! Jodie! This is Cole. Can you hear me?" she imagined him say.

"Yes! Yes, sir! I can hear you," she said, out loud. Then in her mind, again Cole spoke, "You must gain control, Jodie! See if Ally is breathing, see if she is still warm."

Jodie leaned over as far as she could, her leg and foot still restrained. She reached her hand out and felt Ally's blood-covered neck. At first, all she could feel was the warmth of Ally's blood. Then, pressing a little harder on the side of her neck, she could feel Ally's pulse. It seemed to be weak, but it was steady. "Oh Ally! You are alive! Oh, thank you God! Ally is alive!" she said, joyfully. Then, she stroked Ally's matted hair, crying softly, wishing things were all better.

Again, Jodie imagined hearing Cole's voice, "Jodie, can you reach the blanket in the back seat? Try to get the blanket and cover A.J. up. The temperature is dropping and we must keep her warm." Jodie struggled to gain access between the front seats. Slowly, she maneuvered her body so she could reach between the seats and snatch the cover from the back seat. Then she covered Ally's upper body from her shoulders to her waist with the cover.

"Now what, Cole? What should I do now?" she said, out loud.

"Jodie is the radio working? Look at the dashboard. Is the radio still working? Can you see the green "power-on" light? Is it on?"

"Yes, sir. It is on." still speaking out loud.

"Call for help, Jodie. Remember your call letters? Call for help!" she heard Cole say.

Jodie looked around for the microphone. Following the wire from the radio, she pulled on it to retrieve the microphone. Once in her hand, she remembered the call letters that Ally had used many times before, "This is November-two-three-three-five-nine, come in anyone. Our airplane has gone down. Can anyone hear me? Plane down. This is Jodie will someone please get a message to Cole Bryant, Chisano Ranger Station." Then, over and over again, she would repeat the message, waiting between transmissions, hoping someone would respond.

Back at ranger headquarters, things were pretty much normal. The rainstorm that had passed through earlier was the typical summer storm. A little lightning followed by a hard rain for an hour, gradually decreasing in intensity to a soft drizzle. Bill Defresse was working in his office, and Cole had just touched down on the lake bringing his papers into the administrative building to finish up his day's work before the girls got back from the "big city" shopping spree.

In the background he could hear the two-way radio, as he always could, as various park employees reported in to headquarters. Mrs. Pitts, head clerk, usually handled the communications during the day. Cole overheard her say, "Hold on a minute. Could you repeat that last message?

The radio came to life, again, as it squawked, "This is Barrow Station reporting a possible airplane down. We are trying to find out if anyone has an overdue aircraft or has heard a distress transmission.

The message we have received is believed to have come from a pilot in the Mount Fairweather area. The message they received was very weak and only part of the transmission was understandable. The message is very broken, but we are hoping someone will be able to decipher it so we can locate the aircraft. The best we can make out the message is '...ber...3...9...plane down...Joey...Cole...park...quarters'." The voice over the two-way radio continued, "Someone has said you have a Cole that works at the park headquarters. Is that right?'

Cole dropped his papers on his desk and hurried to the radio snatching the microphone from Mrs. Pitts' hand. His heart in his throat, he spoke quickly into the microphone, "This is Cole Bryant. I think this message might be for me. Could you repeat that one more time?"

"Yes, sir. This is Fred Moses at Barrow Station. The message we have received goes something like this. Keep in mind all of the words may not be exactly right because the transmission was very weak and broken up." Fred repeated the message word-for-word ending with, "Do you think this message might be for you?"

Cole didn't answer immediately. He eased himself slowly into the nearest office chair. Looking over at Mrs. Pitts, he said softly, "Mrs. Pitts, I think you better get Ranger Defreese." Cole's insides felt like a volcano had erupted deep within his body. Holding the microphone close to his mouth, he spoke in a calm, controlled voice, "We have a Cessna 150 that is possibly overdue. On board are two females, one of which is named Jody. My name is Cole Bryant and the tail number of the airplane in question is November-two-three-three-five-nine." He exhaled deeply, ran his right hand through his hair and continued to speak into the microphone, "We are not positive this is our aircraft, yet, but enough of your message has the key words to indicate this could be a message from one of the females. Give me a couple minutes to make some calls. Do you know where this airplane went down?"

The voice on the radio answered, "Not exactly. Like I said earlier, the transmission seemed to come from the Mount Fairweather area. There are very heavy rains in that area right now, so no airplanes are flying at this time."

"Okay, that is a Roger. Give me a couple minutes and I will call you back," Cole said. Putting the microphone on top of the radio, he stood up and briskly walked over to the nearest desk. Picking up the phone he dialed the operator, asking her to put him through to the control tower at the Juneau airport.

By this time, Bill Defreese had been told of the situation by Mrs. Pitts. He stood at another desk close to Cole speaking into the walkie-talkie to Bert, "Bert, we have a possible search and rescue mission. I want you to get "Lizzie" gassed up. Then have some of the other guys load the emergency medical supplies and rescue equipment on board. After "Lizzie" is ready, have the other guys do the same thing on the Piper, and I want you to get yourself ready to fly. Any questions?"

Bert quickly responded, "Consider it done, give me twenty minutes. One question, do you want someone to be ready to go as backup in the Piper?" he asked.

"That is an affirmative," Bill clicked off.

Cole, finally, had received an answer from the Juneau airport. The man on the other end of the line confirmed that Allison Defreese, flying a Cessna 150, with tail number N23359 had filed a flight plan for her trip back to ranger headquarters. She left at four-fifteen Pacific Time. He added that she had changed the plan at the last minute to avoid a large, heavy storm coming in off of the Pacific Ocean. Bill pulled out a large relief map and they traced the route the plane had intended to fly.

Now that they knew what time the two girls left Juneau airport, they estimated the airplane's speed and the distance to Chisano Station. They soon realized the small Cessna and its two precious occupants were overdue by at least an hour. The two men looked at each other, the emotions building up inside each.

Cole spoke first, "Bill, the man on the radio said he thought the transmission came from the Mount Fairweather area." Pointing at the map, he added, "The flight plan has Allison going right through that area."

"Right, I see that. Let's get on the radio and see when the transmissions started coming in," he paused a moment, then added, "I hate to admit it, but I believe this might be our girls." He hung his head low to the map so that Cole could not see his deep concern.

Cole called Fred Moses at Barrow Station on the radio. "Fred, this is Cole Bryant. It looks like the transmission might be from our overdue airplane. We have studied the flight plan and it appears the craft should have arrived over an hour ago."

"Oh....sorry to hear that. We are unable to fly right now. I called 'weather' and they say at least two more hours till the extreme conditions leave the area," Fred responded.

"Right, what we want to know at this time is when was the first transmission received?" Cole asked.

A pause on the radio followed by Fred's voice on the radio speaker, "The first transmission was received at 6:07 PM and continued for roughly 28 minutes on and off. No new transmission has been received since 6:35 PM."

"We are going to put two aircraft in the air in about fifteen minutes. Our ETA in the Mount Fairweather area would be about one and a half-hours. Hopefully the storm will be out of the area at that time so we can start search and rescue." Cole said.

"Okay. Repeat...you are putting two aircraft in the air," the speaker rattled. "We will use band 20.25 for the rescue. Make sure you check in when you are in the air and use only that channel while on this mission. Do you copy?"

"Yes, I copy. Over and out," Cole signed off.

Looking at Bill Defreese, Cole said, "I cannot believe this is happening. Allison is a fantastic pilot. How can this be happening?"

"You know as well as I do that there are a million things that can happen. We have to be tough, buddy. We have to think of this as any other search and rescue. I'm counting on you to get our girls back." he reached his hand out, patted Cole on the shoulder and shook his hand.

The two men hurried back to the desk where the map was laid out. Bill said, looking at the route the airplane was to follow, tracing the path with his pencil, "They say the transmission was coming from the Mount Fairweather area." Using the pencil he drew a large oval representing the outer boundaries of the area. "Their flight path passes through that section here," Another smaller oval was drawn along the flight path, "They say the first transmission was at 6:07. Also, the message was "plane down", so I'm going to assume that the plane had already landed or crashed. Allowing a half hour on either side of that transmission, we are looking at this much ground to cover." Once again, Bill marked an even smaller oval on the map along the intended flight path.

"I agree," Cole said, nodding his head. "It looks like we have narrowed it down to an eighty mile stretch along the flight path. The trick now is to get that search area down to a much smaller area," he said, tapping the map with his finger.

Bill stood up straight, looking Cole straight in the eyes, "I want you to coordinate this search. You have all of the experience in finding things from the air. I want you to get it done! Any questions?"

"No, sir! Let's get the planes in the air. It is about an hour and a half to that area and the day is getting late. We may need all of the daylight we can get."

They gathered up their belongings and headed to the aircraft where Bert and Shilo were waiting. After running a quick check to make sure everything was on board, the men taxied the airplanes out into the lake for take off.

Chapter 11

The two airplanes took off, climbing to six thousand feet, leveled off and headed due south through the light drizzle. Cole radioed to Bill, "This is November-two-seven to November-six-five." Bill's Piper J-3 had call letters of N-1-0-3-6-5.

"Roger, this is November-six-five," Bill answered.

"Bill, since "Lizzie" is faster than your Piper, we are going on ahead. I will follow the path on the flight plan that Allison filed and do a quick over-flight up to the area we think they went down. I want you to fly the path up to about Rattlesnake Mountain. Then I would like you to zigzag across the flight path as slow and as low as you can still keeping a southerly course. Do you understand?"

"Yes, I understand," Bill responded.

Cole trimmed out the sturdy craft increasing the speed on "Lizzie" to ninety percent power. At this altitude, "Lizzie" would cruise at 150 knots, or so. Looking over at Bert, Cole said, "Bert, grab the relief map. I want you to study the map and get familiar with the landscape we will be flying over. Try to get the altitude of the mountains and surrounding area in perspective so we will kind of know what to expect."

"Right. Consider it done," Bert answered.

Then, Cole checked in with Barrow Station. "Barrow Station this is November-nine-three-one-one-two-seven. Come in Barrow Station."

The speaker on the radio in the airplane cabin crackled to life when the answer came back, "This is Barrow Station, Fred Moses speaking."

"Yes, Fred, this is Cole Bryant. We have two aircraft in the air heading due south toward the suspected crash area. Have you heard any new information?"

"Negative. The weather is clearing slightly in the area we feel is ground zero. The main problem is the cloud ceiling is at about five thousand feet at the clearest areas. Some of the mountains in that area get above six thousand feet. Also, no more transmissions have been received. Since there are no aircraft in the ground zero area because of the poor weather conditions, it is possible the signal is too weak to be picked up very far away. Over."

Cole thought a moment, then spoke into the microphone, "Our plan is this. I am taking my airplane straight to the area around the Mount Fairweather mountain range. It is the faster of our two aircraft. Hopefully, the weather will clear some by then. My ETA is about one hour-fifteen minutes. Bill Defreese will follow the flight plan path and start serious search activities around Rattlesnake Mountain."

"I am requesting for you to allow our two aircraft to switch over to the frequency the mayday was transmitted on. As I search the area, I will listen for any transmissions that may be sent by the girls. Also, I will transmit at intervals to see if I can get a response." He took a breath, then added, "When you add other aircraft to the search and rescue leave them on 20.25 so they will not interfere with us. You can contact us on the mayday channel and we will switch over to 20.25. That way the mayday channel will be free of unwanted chatter, okay?"

"Okay, that sounds like a good plan. The mayday came in on 26.15. That is two-six-point-one-five," Fred said.

"Roger, two-six-point-one-five," Cole repeated. "Did you copy that Bill?"

The radio cracked back, "Roger, we copy."

The two aircraft went their separate ways toward the search and rescue areas. In the cabin of both planes the pilot did his best to keep on the assigned flight path and still fly around the more severe weather areas while the copilots studied the maps giving instructions about the terrain below as they passed over the few visible points of reference.

"Lizzie" arrived at the Mount Fairweather mountain range in one hour-twenty-two minutes. However, Cole had to keep the craft at eleven thousand feet to stay out of the poor weather conditions closer to earth. He had not heard any transmissions during his trip, so he began his own transmissions to see if he could raise a response. "This is search and rescue do you copy? This is search and rescue do you copy?" Then, he would pause for one minute and rebroadcast hoping to get a response.

Twenty minutes passed as he flew "Lizzie" around the suspected area with no response to his calls on the radio.

Slowly, he decreased his altitude flying as close to the dense clouds as he could. It was still impossible to see any terrain below, and it was too dangerous to fly closer to the ground with the thick black clouds swirling below them.

Cole looked out toward the west, where the sun was shining brightly and the sky was, once again, crystal clear with small white puffy clouds floating lazily toward the east. He thought to himself, "Why can't this storm get out of our way. We have to find the girls. "He caught himself silently saying a prayer, "Please, God, please give me the necessary power to find A.J. and Jodie?'

Almost like magic, a large oval hole began to develop in the dark swirling mass of clouds. Cole could see the rugged terrain below. He looked over at Bert, saying, "You better tighten your seat belt 'cause I'm going in." He pointed just ahead and to the left of the aircraft.

Cole drove "Lizzie" almost straight down, the plane picking up speed rapidly, making Bert's stomach feel like it was going to come out of his mouth. He let out an "ooooooh", as the earth appeared to rush toward the diving aircraft.

The airplane dropped down below four thousand feet. Cole dropped the flaps to slow "Lizzie's" airspeed, guiding her just above the treetops. He grabbed the microphone broadcasting the search transmission. The rain had stopped completely in this area and it appeared the hole in the clouds was spreading rapidly in all directions.

As Cole's eyes searched the area for anything unusual, his thoughts went back to Vietnam and the similar experiences he had there. His instincts immediately sharpened and his eyes followed the terrain below looking for that broken limb on a tree or the scorched area a burning plane would create when it crashed. Anything that would give away the location of the missing aircraft.

Another forty-five minutes passed with still no sign of the girls and still no response to his transmissions. Ahead he could see Copper Mountain looming into the sky. The clouds hung low above its apex. He increased "Lizzie's" airspeed pulling back on the controls to put the aircraft into a climb that would allow them to pass over the sharp mountain ridge. Once over the peak, Cole lowered the flaps, decreased the power and put the plane into a steep dive, following the terrain as closely as possible down the steep side of the mountain.

Once again, like many times before, he transmitted the search message, "This is search and rescue, do you copy?"

Jodie had fallen into a deep sleep after transmitting the mayday signal for just a half an hour. The ordeal of the crash had taken its toll on the young girl. The adrenaline had stopped flowing and sleep had overcome her.

As she slept, she dreamed about Cole, and Ally, and herself living on the island. Everything was wonderful. The sun was shining, a soft, crisp breeze blew across the lake as the three of them spent the day fishing and playing.

In the distance, she could hear "Lizzie's" powerful engine. At first, it was idling. Then she could hear it rev up as if taking off.

She heard Cole say, "This is search and rescue, do you copy?" a pause, then, "This is search and rescue, do you copy?" This time it was much louder. In her dream, she wondered why Cole would keep saying this over and over.

Jodie suddenly snapped out of her dream and into reality. She heard Cole's voice on the radio. In the background, she could hear "Lizzie's" engine as it crested the mountain behind her. She grabbed the microphone, shouting, "Cole! Cole! I can hear you! Please come back! Cole, come get me!"

When Jodie's voice came over the radio speaker, Cole jerked back on the controls in a reaction of shock, sending "Lizzie's" nose temporarily into a climb. He answered in an excited voice, "This is Cole! I can read you. Are you okay? Repeat, are you okay?"

Jodie began to cry, answering, "No, Cole. I am hurt...and Ally is hurt real bad. We crashed the airplane...please get us out!" She sounded pitiful.

Cole answered, this time in his professional, controlled voice. "Okay, Jodie, we are coming to get you. I want you to calm down and answer my questions, okay?"

"Yes, sir. I will do what you tell me. But please get us out of here. I'm scared," her voice quivered as she spoke.

"First, I want you to describe the condition you and Ally are in," he said.

After a short pause, Jodie began, "We crashed into the side of a steep mountain. Both of us are trapped inside the plane. My foot is stuck and I cannot get out. Ally is in bad shape. She is still knocked out. Her face is swollen and her leg must be broken 'cause her foot is pointing backward, and she won't talk to me 'cause she is knocked out, or something."

Bert made notes on a pad as Cole talked on the radio. "Jodie, can you describe where you are? Do you know where you are?"

"No, sir. I don't know where I'm at. I can only see in front of me. The mountain goes straight up in front of me. I can't see below me and I cannot see behind the airplane 'cause the wing is in the way."

"Do you remember when you went down?" he asked.

"Yes, sir, I remember," she answered.

"Tell me about it. How did it happen?"

"Well we were flying along and this big bird,...an eagle, I think, hit the front of the airplane. It crashed through the windshield and knocked Ally out. Then the plane crashed into the side of the mountain," she recalled.

"Okay, do you know which mountain?"

"No sir, I wasn't paying much attention. We were just talking to each other...then, BOOM!"

Cole thought a moment, then said, "Do you think you can describe the mountain?"

Jodie thought a while and said, "Yeah, maybe. I remember two things about the mountain. It was a very tall mountain...I think it was probably the tallest one we had come across on our way home....and the side of the mountain looked all rusty. You know, all dirty. There wasn't any trees on it, like the other mountains." She thought a moment more, saying, "Oh yeah, one more thing. It was real pointy on the top."

Cole looked over at Bert who was studying the map as Jodie described the mountain. Bert said, "Cole I believe that is Copper Mountain. The one we just passed over."

"Right, I was thinking the same thing. Let's turn around, and fly back there to check it out," Cole said.

"Okay, Jodie, hang on a minute. I am coming to get you." Then, speaking into the microphone again, said, "Bill, Fred, did you copy that last series of transmissions?"

First, Bill Defreese responded, "Roger, Cole, we received it. I'm heading toward your area now."

Then Fred answered, "Good work gentlemen, I have two more search aircraft leaving in several minutes. I'll continue to monitor this channel. The other aircraft will switch over to your frequency now, if that is okay?"

"Yes, good Fred. I think the downed plane might be close to Copper Mountain. I am within five minutes of being there. Please continue to monitor," Cole instructed.

Cole slowed "Lizzie's" airspeed as much as possible as the huge mountain loomed high in the sky ahead of the airplane. "Lizzie" crested the smaller, northern mountain range. Cole initiated a gentle climb toward Copper Mountain on the other side of the valley when the radio crackled, "I can her "Lizzie", Cole! I can hear "Lizzie"!" Jodie's voice was very excited.

"Great!" Cole exclaimed.

"It sounds like "Lizzie" is coming straight at me....no wait! She is off to my left."

"Okay, hang in there! I will bring her down the side of the mountain. You tell me when I pass overhead, okay?"

"Yes, sir!"

Cole banked "Lizzie" hard to the right and began to follow the mountain parallel to its side. He kept the flaps down increasing the engine speed to drag the airplane slowly on its course, making the airplane as noisy and slow as he could.

Soon Jodie's voice came over the radio, "You're gettin' very close." Then, "You've passed me now. It sounds like you were lower down the mountain from where I'm at."

"Roger. I'll circle higher this time." Cole raised the flaps, put in full power circling the airplane hard right bringing "Lizzie" around 180 degrees. He pointed her nose skyward, following parallel to the steep side of the immense mountain.

His sharp eyes scanned the rugged surface out front and to the left of the airplane, and Bert looked out the right side as they ascended almost vertically. Soon the trees at the lower levels gave way to the vertical stone cliffs. Cole shouted, "Bingo! Bingo! I see the airplane!"

He pointed out the left window. Bert followed the path Cole's finger was pointing and exclaimed, "Yes, sir. That's the one! Yes, sir! We found it! Yeah!"

Jodie came over the radio, "Yikes! It sounds like you're going to hit me!"

Cole spoke into the microphone, "We see you, Jodie. We see you! Hang in there a little while longer. We're coming to get you, okay?'

"Yes, sir. I'm hanging!" she joked, relieved that Cole was coming to get her.

Cole, once again, put "Lizzie" into a hard U-turn, dropping her back down into the valley. He made four more passes across the crash site trying to figure the best way to rescue the two girls. Since the airplane was perched so high on the mountain it would make for a long hard climb from the valley below. But, a rescue from the top of the mountain was ruled out because of the steep, cliff-like sides and the lack of a landing area at the mountain's apex, even for a helicopter.

"November-six-five to November-two-seven," Bill's voice came over the radio.

"Roger, come in Bill," Cole responded.

"We are approaching Copper Mountain. I have you spotted. What is the plan?" Bill asked.

"The plane is about half way up the mountain. You will be able to spot it if you head toward that big crack that runs vertically off of the saddle-like boulder at the peak, about eleven o'clock from your position. The crack stops about 150 feet above a small ledge. That ledge is where A.J.'s plane is sitting. So far, we have determined we will have to rescue from the valley below. There is a very small lake that we can use for a landing area. I'm going in now. You circle and scout out the area. After I land, we will be in touch. Over."

Cole looked over at Bert, "Bert, buddy, you might want to close your eyes. This is a very small lake, so I'm going to drop this bird like a stone," he chuckled, as he spoke. Bert's eyes got large with fear as Cole first applied full down flaps, cut the power, then pulled back on the controls to raise "Lizzie's" nose skyward.

To Bert, it felt as if the plane was falling straight out of the sky. The huge evergreen trees appeared to shoot vertically toward the craft as it descended swiftly. Then it felt as if the tail of the airplane was going to hit the lake surface first as the nose of the plane pointed skyward.

At the last moment, Cole pushed the controls forward forcing the nose of "Lizzie" back to horizontal and the pontoons immediately struck the smooth lake surface with a loud slapping noise diving into the water, then popping back out to skim along the surface, as the plane slowed rapidly.

Even though Bert could feel the airplane slowing rapidly, the trees on the other side of the lake loomed ever larger, and larger, as the speeding airplane approached. Cole applied full right rudder at the last moment to turn the airplane in a sharp right-hand curve to avoid hitting the onrushing shoreline.

"Weeh! That was close!" Bert said, his voice shaking and his fingers buried in the leather armrests on his seat. "That was like landing down in a bowl of soup! Not much extra room to move around in." He wiped small beads of sweat from his forehead.

"Aw Bert, that was nothing! Wait till you see how we get this bird out of this little ol' lake!" Cole chuckled, patting Bert on the shoulder.

"November-two-seven to November-six-five. Come in," Cole spoke into the microphone.

The radio came to life, "Yes, Cole."

"Have you spotted the downed airplane?"

"Yes, we have."

"As you fly over, you should notice several rock slide areas that I feel would be a good path to reach the plane."

"Right, I agree. It looks like you can leave from the southeast corner of the lake, follow that small stream up the more gentler grade, then possibly climb the small cliff-like area or..," Bill paused, "..or better yet, follow the base of the small cliff-like area to the left. Yes, that would be better. Follow that to the left until you reach some very large evergreens. It appears the evergreens can be used like ladders to get you above the cliff area."

Cole interjected, "Great minds think alike. I had picked that route, also."

"The next part of the rescue will be tough, no matter what we do. After getting on top of the first cliff, it looks as though you will have to go straight up the next cliff to get to the ledge," Bill concluded.

"Yeah. But I don't know any other way," Cole added, "Whenever you are ready, I have cleared "Lizzie" from the lake so you can land."

"Okay, I'm coming in." Bill responded.

The Piper landed very easily on the small lake since it requires very little speed to keep in the air and a very short landing area. Once the two floatplanes were tied off at the edge of the lake, the four men prepared to ascend the mountain to rescue the girls.

Cole and Bill had several conversations with Fred Moses, at Barrow Station, coordinating the rescue part of the mission. Fred told them that two more small airplanes would remain in the area to help in anyway they could. Also, at nightfall, a helicopter would be dispatched with a searchlight to help the men if they needed it. As soon as the men felt they would be getting the girls out of the wreckage, a Red Cross helicopter would be dispatched.

The plan was set. The men had all of the necessary equipment and supplies loaded on their backs. Climbing tools hung from thick, heavy, military-style belts tightened around their waists. The only thing left was to execute the plan with as much haste as possible without jeopardizing their own safety.

Bill came over to Cole, held Cole's shoulder with his hand, saying, "Thanks for finding them, Cole, we gotta save them...we gotta!"

Cole didn't say anything, he just gripped Bill's arm nodding his head. Turning to the other two men, he said, "Okay, guys, let's make it happen."

Bert led the way for the first part of the climb. Even though this was the easiest segment of the mountain to traverse, it was slow going because of the small, loose rocks that were piled deep from years and years of rockslides. As erosion took its toll at the top of the mountain, it loosened large boulders, sending them down the steep sides crashing into other boulders on their way down breaking them into ever smaller and smaller chunks, eventually grinding them down into ragged-edged rocks ranging in size from bowling balls to as small as Ping-Pong balls.

They followed Bert single file, feet crunching and slipping on the rocks, using the plentiful large trees in this area to keep their balance and, sometimes, to wedge their bodies against to make forward progress up the steep slope. The climb up the mountain was slow, but steady, and after an hour or so they had completed the first leg of the journey.

Standing at the foot of the first cliff, the men took a much needed breather. They had climbed about three hundred feet vertically on the quarter-mile stretch. Sweat had appeared on each of their foreheads, and wet circles had formed under their arms on their ranger uniforms. They rested ten minutes, drank some water and each ate a candy bar for energy.

Bill led the group on the next segment of the journey up the steep mountain. They followed the base of the lower cliff diagonally up the mountain traversing several small streams, detouring occasionally around a fallen tree or a large boulder. Finally, they reached the large trees that would take them to the top of the cliff. Cutting some limbs from nearby fallen trees, the men attached makeshift ladder rungs to one of the large trees. Then, one by one and backpack by backpack, the foursome climbed the temporary tree ladder to the top of the cliff.

Another hour and fifteen minutes had passed. Darkness had overcome the rugged mountain. The men, once again, took a much needed break. Bill had checked in with Jodie from time-to-time on his walkie-talkie. He was becoming very concerned about Allison.

According to Jodie, Allison had not awakened since the crash. She appeared to be breathing okay and she was warm. Jodie had kept her covered up since the temperature had dropped into the high thirties. However, Jodie reported this time that Ally had aroused a little and was moaning a lot. She said, "One time Ally opened her eyes and tried to shout something. But I think her mouth is broken 'cause the one side hangs down funny. She just kind of yelled something I couldn't understand."

Bill had signed off the radio and told the men they needed to push on. "Time is of the essence!" he looked at Cole. With much concern in his voice he said, "Cole you're the one with the paramedic license, do you think the jaw is broken or could it have been a stroke or something?"

"Well, Bill, I can't be for sure without seeing her. I feel it is a broken jaw," then added, "Remember, Jodie originally said A.J.'s face was swollen. That sounds like a broken jaw."

Sounding a little relieved, Bill said, "Oh yeah, I forgot," letting out a little breath of air, as if relaxing a little.

Cole noticed a small red object lying between some small rocks. Bending down, he pushed the rocks aside and picked up the soft piece of cloth. It was then he recognized that the object was the red shoe from Raggedy Ann. Trying to keep focused, he stuffed the red shoe in his pocket, took a deep breath turning his attention to the mountain climb.

The two circling airplanes had left the area because it was determined they would not be needed anymore. The helicopter, with the searchlight, never showed up because of some mechanical failure. So, the men used the miner-style hats they wore to light their way up the third and final segment of the mountain climb.

Bert had found a crevasse down the face of the foreboding vertical surface. He had started driving large spikes in the hard rock surface at arm-length intervals. Hooking a climbing rope on the farthest spike, he pulled himself up a foot at a time. Then he would drive another spike in the rock wall, attach the climbing rope, pull himself up, and repeat the process.

This was very strenuous work. After a brief time, he handed the lead off to one of the other men. Each took their turn leading the way up the vertical face of the mountain.

Several times during the climb, one of the men would slip off of the spike holding his foot, drop several feet and dangle from the climbing rope that was attached to a spike above his head. After catching their breath, the men would catch hold of the dangling man and rescue him by drawing him closer to the vertical surface where he could again grasp the closest spike and continue the slow, exhausting climb up the mountain.

Jodie could hear the men now. They were close enough to the crash site that she could hear them talking to one another and hear them driving the spikes into the cliff wall below her. This raised her spirits, but at the same time, Ally became increasingly more restless, sometimes thrashing her body about making it hard for Jodie to hold her composure.

Every now and then Ally would emit a scream or a low deep moan. It was apparent she was in great pain. Jodie had communicated this down to Cole and Bill. They had instructed her to speak in soothing tones to Ally and to make sure she didn't try to remove her seat belt or get out of the airplane.

Another hour passed by slowly. Finally Bert, who was the lead man at the time, crested the cliff onto the ledge area. The last spike was the hardest to drive into the mountain since it had to be put on the flat surface of the ledge. This required bending the body over the overhanging ledge, holding the spike in one hand and driving the spike using the mallet with the other hand. All the time Bert's arms supported his entire body weight as his feet dangled precariously out in space.

With his whole body trembling from exhaustion, Bert attached the climbing rope to the last spike. Then he pulled himself onto the ledge using Cole's shoulders as a step to give him extra leverage to make the last push around the sharp, overhanging edge of the ledge. After a brief moment to recover from the exhausting ordeal, Bert helped Cole onto the ledge, then Cole helped Shilo up, and Shilo helped Bill onto the ledge.

Jodie was beside herself with excitement. The closer the men got to the top of the cliff and the louder the sound of their voices as they climbed ever closer, made Jodie's wait even harder in anticipation of finally seeing Cole.

One by one, as the men crested the ledge, they witnessed the mangled plane's remains. The scene was very eerie and surrealistic. The area was extremely dark. The only light came from the miners' hats the four men wore. The lights dodged about as the men twisted and turned their heads, maneuvering about on the ledge area.

The broken wings hung from the airplane fuselage drooping downward, slanting forward to the ledge surface. The front of the craft was pushed rearward crumpled in a mass to within inches of the cabin firewall. All of the windows in the airplane were broken out. The pontoons had been torn off of the airplane when it fell to the ledge surface from the cliff above. The outer skin of the airplane had been torn away halfway down the length of the side of the craft but, surprisingly, the doors had remained closed, now wedged tightly shut.

After Cole helped Shilo up onto the ledge he focused his attention on the crashed airplane. The smell of spilled fuel permeated the air. The surface of the ledge was still very wet from the torrential rains that had passed through hours earlier. Small puddles of fuel-laced water occupied the small gouged out uneven areas of the basically flat surface of the ledge.

The sight of the airplane and its condition made Cole draw in a deep gasp of air. He rushed over to the right side of the crumpled craft bending his head down to clear the broken wing. He stepped over the remains of the wing strut, which was no longer supporting the wing, turned his head to shine the hat mounted light into the cabin interior, gasping out loud at the horrible scene within the airplane.

"Oh, my God!" he muttered in a low voice. "Jodie! Jodie, are you all right?" he said, trying to control his voice.

"Daddy!" she said, "I mean, Cole!" she corrected herself. She tried to turn and grab Cole by the neck to give him a hug. When she turned her head in Cole's direction, he was shocked to see Jodie's face covered in dried blood.

"Oh, Jodie! Oh, Jodie!" is all he could say. He took a deep breath to gain his composure, then started giving instructions, "Okay guys, as soon as you can, let's figure out how we are going to get the girls out of here!"

Jodie began to cry out loud, her pent-up emotions being released in a flood of tears created first, from the horrifying crash, and then, from the long, cold wait.

"It's okay now, Jodie. We will have you out of here in a jiffy!" Cole said, giving Jodie a big hug and patting her on her shoulder.

As Cole called out the directions to the other men, his hat mounted light flashed across Allison's face and upper body. Since he was busy trying to get the men started on the task of extricating the two young ladies from the crumpled airplane he, at first, did not take note of Allison's condition. Then his vision followed the light beam to the other side of the cabin and focused his attention on Allison. He sucked in a deep breath in shock at the sight of the once beautiful face. In that first split-second impression, it was as if, in his mind, he had just seen the grim reaper clothed in black with deep sunken death-filled eyes.

Allison's face was swollen beyond recognition with dark blue-black circles under her closed eyes. Dried blood caked to her skin. Her hair was matted with blood, covered with broken glass, feathers, and other small particles of crash debris. Her jaw drooped uncontrollably from the right side of her face, blood and drool stringing down her chin, forming a pool of blood that soaked into the front of her once pretty blue blouse.

When the light from Cole's hat beamed into Allison's face, it shocked her out of her comatose state, jerking her into consciousness. "Yeeeooowh!" she screamed. Then, trying to speak, "Hellnee! Heeeee! Hellne!" she screamed, over and over, trying to say, "help me". Then she let out a horrifying scream, obviously in immense pain.

"Holy cow!" Cole exclaimed in a loud voice. "We gotta get these girls out of here A.S.A.P.! A.J. is hurt real bad!"

Bill rushed to Cole's side, peering through the broken window across the cabin at his daughter. The horror of seeing his most prized possession in that state of pain and injury was more than he could take. Cole felt Bill slump down as if he was totally exhausted, his weight bearing down on Cole's back.

"Oh my God! Oh my God!" he said, in a low voice as he exhaled in shock. "Allison can you hear me? Allison, honey, can you hear me?"

Allison kept screaming and writhing in pain. Her eyes, now open, rolled back, as sweat appeared on her forehead. Every time she tried to say something her jaw remained drooped and unmoving, and her screams got louder.

Cole jumped into action. He was a professional and his instincts kicked in. "Okay, listen to me everyone. We have to get these girls out NOW!" he said, in a commanding voice. Looking back to Jodie he asked, "Jodie where do you hurt?"

She answered matter-of-factly, "My foot is caught under the pedals down there," pointing to her feet. Cole shined his light into the crumpled foot compartment. As his light passed over Jodie to the foot compartment, Cole notice Jodie was clutching Raggedy Ann to her chest. The blood stained doll had, also, been the victim of the plane crash. It was missing one red shoe and stared aimlessly out into space as if in shock from the ordeal.

"Aw, yes, I see it." Turning to Bill, he said, "Bill get the crow bar. You and Shilo bend the pedals back. Get Jodie out." Then looking at Bert, he instructed, "Bert go around the other side, pull out the battery powered lantern and hang it where we can get some light on A.J."

Cole moved to the other side of the airplane, unloaded his backpack, and pulled out a syringe and a vial of painkiller. By that time, Bert had found a good location for the lantern. It was bathing the area around Allison in light. Cole quickly checked A.J.'s pulse and blood pressure. Surprisingly, he found her vital signs were strong, so he injected the moaning and screaming woman with the painkiller.

Bert, who had been on many search and rescue missions with Cole, dampened a cloth with water and gently swabbed Allison's face being sure not to touch the dangling jaw area. "Cole, good news! Most of this blood wipes off of her face. She really isn't cut up as bad as it looked!" Bert said, encouragingly.

"Good. While we wait for the pain killer to kick in we need to figure a way to get her out of here."

The two men noted the obviously broken leg. It was wedged under the pedals, and had been broken when the dashboard and floorboard moved rearward, squeezing the leg from the knee down toward the foot.

"I am afraid to allow the leg to twist back to the front because the bone might dig into the muscle or artery doing irreparable damage. So when we figure a way to get the leg out, I want it to be secured so we don't twist it back," Cole observed.

"Right," Bert agreed.

"Okay, first-things-first. Hand me my medical kit and I'll get her jaw fixed up. As I do that, you work on figuring out how we can pry the dashboard and cowling away."

"Right," Bert agreed again.

Bill and Shilo let out a sigh of relief as they had just gotten Jodie out of the airplane. They moved her away from the airplane and set her down next to the wall formed by the cliff above. They gave her something to eat and drink, got her covered up in a warm blanket and cleaned up her face and arms a little. Shilo stayed with her as Bill came over to help in the extrication of Allison.

The men worked feverishly trying to release the pressure on the trapped leg. Allison occasionally let out a low moan and, sometimes, screamed if they touched the leg. Cole tore some thin metal from the airplane skin, forming a makeshift cast. He padded this with a small towel, wrapping gauze and tape around the leg from just above the foot to above the knee. He did this while the leg was still in the original position so it would not allow the bone to do any additional muscle damage.

Then he helped Bill and Bert leverage the cowling and dashboard away from the leg. Next the men forced the left door open, cautiously easing her out of the twisted cabin. They gently placed Allison on one of the portable stretchers the men had backpacked up the mountain. Making sure she was firmly secured to the stretcher, they slipped a canvass sleeve up the length of the stretcher encompassing the stretcher and Allison, except for a small circular hole where only her face was exposed.

The trip down the mountain was going to be tough. After a brief break to take in some fluids and rest, the men began the task of lowering the stretcher down the side of the cliff below. Bert went down the cliff to the first landing then, as the stretcher was lowered by rope by the other three men, he guided the leading edge with another rope attached to the lower end of the stretcher. Every so often, when the stretcher would get hung up on an outcropping or boulder, it would shake or jerk, causing Allison, whom was still sleeping, to let out a moan or scream.

After the struggle to get Allison to the first landing was complete, they turned their attention to Jodie. By this time, Cole had determined Jodie's ankle was only sprained, so he had bound it with an ace bandage, then secured her in a similar fashion in the second portable stretcher, and lowered her down the cliff.

They repeated this slow, agonizing descent, carefully lowering the two precious victims down the mountain. Eventually, they met other rescuers coming up the mountain to help them. The weary foursome were relieved of the burden to move the girls further down the mountain to the lakeshore. At least another hour was spent struggling over the large rocks and boulders, and lowering the stretchers down steep inclines to finally break out into the open area at the lakeshore.

The scene at the bottom of the mountain was now much different. The sun had risen several hours before, so it was easy to take in the surroundings. The Red Cross helicopter was waiting near the shore, and there were two more airplanes on the lake. A total of six more rescuers had arrived, and had gone up the makeshift mountain trail to meet the exhausted foursome to help bring the girls down to safety.

Allison, still in a lot of pain, and Jodie, who cried uncontrollably every now and then from exhaustion, were quickly loaded onto the helicopter. Bill and Cole took seats next to the girls in the rear of the helicopter along with two medical attendants. The helicopter was pushed out into open water as the pilot cranked up the engine. After a minute or two of warming the engine and getting the rotors up to speed, the helicopter lifted off from the lake surface, climbed vertically above the surrounding trees, then headed directly for Juneau.

Jodie was in good shape, considering her long ordeal, and actually sat up leaning next to Cole, who had his arm around her tiny body. Allison, on the other hand, was not doing well. The swelling at her jaw and her right leg was worse, and her breathing had become erratic. The attendants were now spending a considerable amount of time with her. They had attached an oxygen mask to her face, and kept monitoring her blood pressure and pulse.

Bill had bent down on his knees beside her, and was talking in a low voice to Allison, "Allison. Allison this is Daddy. You gotta hang in there! You gotta hang in...just a little while longe...I love you, Allison. This is Daddy, please hang on....please......

Chapter 12

The hospital in Juneau was the typical cream-colored, one story, concrete block structure that had been built by the military during World War II. It was laid out in neat rows of rectangular-shaped buildings connected by enclosed walkways. Small windows lined the sides of the buildings with doorways at each end leading into the enclosed walkways. The roofs were sharply peaked to help keep the winter snows from collecting on them.

Inside, the once upon-a-time military presence lingered on with "cool green" paint on all of the walls and beige-colored tile in the hallways and rooms, edged with green tile where it met the walls. Fire extinguishers and fire axes adorned the walls along with a plethora of paint-stenciled notices and warnings to the occupants and visitors of the hospital.

Even though the structures were showing their age, they were maintained well. The floors in the hallways and the multitude of rooms were spotless, shining brilliantly as they reflected the yellow cast of the overhead incandescent lights that were evenly spaced down the long hallways that ran the length of each building and occupied the center of the ceiling in each patient's room.

The center area of building "D", where the girls had been taken, contained a nurses' desk and a waiting room for the visitors and relatives that spent endless hours waiting impatiently on news about their loved ones. Vinyl-covered padded chairs lined the walls around the u-shaped waiting area. A large, square coffee table with numerous dogged-eared magazines on top, occupied the center of the room. Several posters describing various ailments adorned the walls on two sides and two equally spaced windows gave a view of the grassy space to the next identically shaped building in the complex.

The nurses' desk was a beehive of activity. The phone rang constantly, being answered by the closest nurse at the time. There was a constant flow of nurses back and forth from the long row of patient rooms and the nurses' desk. A multitude of clipboards hung from racks behind the desk, each clipboard stuffed with sheets of paper that contained reports and test results on each patient.

Jodie and Allison had been brought to this building as soon as the helicopter touched down, where they worked on Allison first. The doctors got Allison stabilized, then cleaned her up and worked on her leg first. They later told Cole he had done the right thing by not trying to turn the foot around into the correct position.

The bone had been cleanly broken just above the knee. The break was kind of diagonal across the bone forming a knife-like point. This point had been pushed right next to the main artery that ran down the leg. It would have been highly possible that the broken bone would have punctured this main artery if he had twisted the leg back to the normal position. The punctured artery would have filled the leg with blood and, possibly, caused Allison to have her leg amputated, or more likely, she would probably have bled to death.

After the doctors tended to the leg and got it set in a cast, they worked on her broken jaw. Luckily the jaw, which was broken in two places, was easily set and Allison only lost one molar tooth due to the accident. The other cuts on her face and hands were very small and would not leave any scars.

Four hours after she entered the hospital, Allison was pushed down the long hallway to her room, which she was to share with Jodie. Her leg was elevated slightly above her body, hung by a chain that was connected to a chrome steel frame that was fastened to her bed. She slept soundly for the next ten hours having been heavily sedated while the doctors worked on her.

Jodie had been cleaned up and checked out by the staff. Her only injuries, surprisingly, were a badly sprained right foot and a lot of small cuts on her face and hands caused from the crash debris. She had been wheeled into the room just one hour after the girls entered the hospital where the doctors had given her a mild sedative to help her sleep through the night.

After two days, Jodie was released from the hospital. Allison's face was still badly swollen. Dark, black and blue circles remained under her eyes and over her jaw on the right side of her face. Her face was dotted with small scabs from the small cuts caused by the fragments of glass from the windshield. The doctors said they would keep her leg elevated ten days, then she could go home.

Since Allison's jaw was wired shut, the conversations with her were one-sided. Bill and Cole would merely talk to Allison, then she would nod her head in agreement or shake it in disagreement. Whenever the subject of the airplane crash would come up, Allison would become very agitated and nervous. So they decided not to push the subject for right now.

Bert was waiting at the hospital exit when Cole pushed the wheel-chair-bound Jodie through the double doors that were being held open by an attendant. They piled into an old four-door sedan that was driven by one of Bert's old school buddies, and rode the two and a half miles to the airplane basin where Bert had left one of the park service Pipers.

Having left the wheelchair at the hospital, Cole made fun of Jodie struggling with the crutches as she attempted to make the distance from the car to the plane. Because of the awkward walking surface to the airplane moored at the dock, Cole eventually ended up carrying Jodie to the airplane, lifting her into the cabin.

Bert flew the small Piper back to Chisano Ranger Station. Cole and Jodie sat in the back. Cole could tell that Jodie was apprehensive about flying again. She didn't look out of the windows during the whole flight back, and she clutched Cole's arm tightly during takeoff and landing.

"Jodie, it is important to remember that accidents happen. No matter what you are doing an accident can occur. It could be in a car, a boat, walking, or in an airplane. Accidents may happen. They are not planned, they just happen. That is why a person must take caution, and always be alert to whatever they are doing," Cole instructed in a quiet, monotone voice. "What happened to you and A.J. was an accident. There was no way for you two to avoid it. It wasn't anybody's fault, it just happened. You cannot go through life putting up barriers because something bad happened to you. It is important for you to move on and to put this experience behind you." He thought a moment, then continued, "Remember when you learned to ride a bicycle?"

"Uh huh." Jodie answered, her finger in her down-turned mouth.

"Well, you probably fell off of the bicycle several times before you mastered balancing the bike, right?"

"Uh huh."

"If you would have given up the first time you fell, you would never have known the joy of riding a bicycle! That is what a person has to do when an accident happens. You must get back up, dust yourself off, and get back to whatever it was that you were doing. Sure, you must take every step to make sure the accident doesn't happen again. Learn from your mistakes, if you made any, and continue on.

"But Cole, I didn't make a mistake!" Jodie said, in a trembly voice.

"Well that is true. Sometimes we are the victims of accidents, but the same rule applies. We cannot let our fears overcome our actions. We must continue to do the best we can, or else one day, we would be afraid to leave our houses. We all have had accidents, some big and a lot of small ones, but we keep on going. That is what you must do now. Keep on going!"

"But I am really afraid it is going to happen again!" she said, looking into Cole's eyes.

"I know you are honey, but you cannot dwell on the accident. Every time your mind thinks about the accident, try to push it out of your head, and think about something that was fun or exciting. After a while, you won't think about the crash," he said. "I know, because that is what I had to do when I had my crash in Vietnam."

"Yeah, that is right, you had a plane crash, too!" she exclaimed. "I am sorry I forgot. I was just thinking about myself." She hugged his arm, still looking into his eyes.

"Right now, that is the first priority for your inner being. You need to give yourself a little time to get over the trauma of this accident. Pretty soon, you will start to think of others, and your surroundings, more and more. All I am saying, right now, is don't allow this accident to keep you from doing the things that must be done."

"Yes, sir," she said, still clasping his arm tightly.

The following two weeks were pretty routine. However, Jodie followed Cole wherever he went. She would take her coloring book and Raggedy Ann, which now had her shoe sewn back on, and wait for Cole to finish his work. Since Cole had a lot of work to catch up on, he spent a little extra time each day at work, but the rest of his time was dedicated exclusively to Jodie.

Daylight was at the peak this time of the year, so the pair spent a lot of time taking hikes in the surrounding mountains and around the beautiful lake. Cole was always showing Jodie interesting things about nature and she was absorbing it like a sponge. It was a good, relaxing way for Jodie to release her tensions about the airplane crash. Sometimes, they would sit real still in the woods waiting for the animals to stir. This was a good time to break down any mental barriers, whispering to each other what was on their mind.

One evening, as they sat beside the lakeshore counting the number of fish that jumped out of the water, Jodie blurted out, "I'm afraid that you'll leave me!"

Cole looked at Jodie in astonishment. "Why would you say something like that, honey?"

"I'm sorry Cole. I am afraid that something will happen to you and you won't be around for me," she said, sheepishly.

"Jodie....I will always be here for you!" he answered, putting his arm around her tiny body.

"No, what I mean is, what if you have an airplane crash or something and you die? I don't want to live without you! I don't want you to die!" she exclaimed.

"Oh, boy! Is that what is bothering you?"

"Uh huh!"

"Well, Jodie, it is something you cannot let get to you. I don't want to live without you either! But, you see, I don't have any control over that sort of thing. All I can do is make sure you have a good life right now. I cannot control the future. No matter how much we care for each other, we must accept what comes our way. We must accept the good things, as well as the bad ones."

He took a deep breath, looked down at the tiny girl he loved so much and said, "I will promise you this. I will always be extra, special careful so I will be here for you and, as long as I am on this earth, I will take care of you," he said. "But I want you to promise me that you will not keep worrying about the things you cannot control. I want you to understand that even if you follow me everywhere I go, you will not be able to protect me from all of the bad things that can happen."

"What if something happens to you? I will be all alone again," she said, quietly, her eyes looking at the ground.

Cole took his hand, placed it under her chin raising her face towards his. Her big, brown, tear-filled eyes looked into his. He said, softly, "Jodie, you cannot enjoy the present if you are worried about the future. We can do something about the present...we can enjoy each other's company, the outdoors, the birds, trees, the wonderful weather, the love for each other. You and I have no control over the future. We just don't know what is really going to happen next. We can make plans, but they are subject to change. Like that time we had planned to go to the island for a picnic and that terrible storm came through, ruining our plans. We cannot control any of that. Do you understand that?"

"Uh, huh."

"Then, you tell me, are we going to enjoy the present or are we going to ruin the wonderful times of the present because we are worried about something that might happen in the future?"

"I guess I'm pretty stupid, huh?" she asked.

"No, no honey. Everyone now and then gets these thoughts. We must not let it consume us with fear. Fear is a bad thing. It limits our ability to succeed. It limits our ability to live life to the fullest. Once again, I promise to be here for you."

"I love you Cole!" she gave him a big hug around the neck.

"I love you too!" he said, softly returning the hug.

After two weeks in the hospital, Allison returned to Chisano Ranger Station. Bill had spent every other day at the hospital flying down when the weather would permit. It had given him a chance to talk at length with Allison about his work, her studies at school and both of their various adventures.

Bill had sensed that this accident had affected Allison's mental outlook on life, as well could be expected by anyone that had come that close to losing his or her life. But the mood swings that she had troubled him. Sometimes, she would go into a deep depression that would last for a day or more. Never did she have that bubbly zest for life she used to have.

He had talked several times with the doctors about this. They assured him all of Allison's vital signs were good and the depression would lift as she began to feel better and become more mobile. They said that since she had been under such duress for so long at the crash site, her mood swings would take a little longer than usual to work themselves out. They did caution him, though, that it was important to keep her occupied and around other people as much as possible.

So after much discussion about not wanting to fly back to Chisano Ranger Station, Bill won out and Allison agreed to try to let him fly her home. He had convinced her that the trip by car would take much longer, be much more uncomfortable over the bumpy roads, and not as safe since they would have to traverse several mountain ranges with very narrow winding unpaved roads. However, he did have to agree that if she became frightened he would immediately land the airplane.

Jodie met Bill and Ally at the short dock when the airplane pulled up. One of the workers secured the craft to the pilings, opened the door, and

let Jodie jump up into the cabin to greet Ally. Allison was very happy to
see her little friend again.

"Welcome home Ally!" she put her arms around Ally's neck giving
her a big hug.

"Oh boy, am I glad to see you, Jodie!" Ally said happily, putting her
arms around the little girl's shoulders squeezing tightly.

Allison's face was still a little swollen and badly bruised, only now the
dark blue bruises had changed to a kind of sick-looking, pale green. Her
jaw was still wired shut. It was evident that Ally had learned to talk better because Jodie had understood what she said.

No other injuries could be seen except for the huge cast that protruded out of the right pant leg of Allison's loose-fitting Army type
fatigues. A large white sock covered her right foot and a familiar hiking
boot was on her left foot.

After briefly taking in Ally, Jodie continued, "Boy you look a whole
lot better!"

"You think so?"

"Yeah, I do! You didn't look none too good in the helicopter on the
way to the hospital."

"You know, I don't even remember the helicopter ride," Ally chuckled, "Was it fun?"

"There wasn't anything fun about that whole deal!" they both
laughed, and hugged each other again.

"Hey, you two! Are you going to let us get Allison out of the plane
or are you gals going to talk all day?" Bill yelled into the airplane, jokingly. He was glad to see the two girls' spirits lifted, and hoped it
would continue.

"Well I don't know, maybe we will talk all day!" Allison retorted in a
wicked voice with a big grin on her face.

"Yeah, maybe we will!" Jodie chimed in mocking Allison.

"I'll make a deal with you two females," Bill added, "Let me get
Allison out of here and into the house and I will fix you the best vegetable soup dinners in Alaska with all the trimmin's." Since Allison's jaw

was wired he knew this was one of the few things she could eat. Besides, his vegetable soup was well known to all of his friends.

"Sounds great!" Jodie piped up.

"Wait a minute, Jodie! Not so fast! I think we might be in a position to deal here!" Allison said, winking at Jodie. "I think we could be convinced to accept that offer if you threw in some home-made ice cream. What do you say?"

"It's a deal! Now let's get you out of this cramped airplane," he said, shaking Allison's and Jodie's hand in a gesture of a sealed deal.

The next couple of weeks went fairly smooth. Jodie and Allison spent most of their days together. On occasion, Allison would slip back into a depression. No matter what anyone would do, including Jodie, she would not respond. Eventually the dark mood would lift and she would be back to her normal self.

Allison's badly bruised face cleared up and the swelling went down. Bill had flown Allison back to the hospital in Juneau and had the wires removed from her jaw, which made it a lot easier for Allison to talk and eat.

Cole had, finally, caught his work back up. He decided he and Jodie would go to the island for a weekend getaway while the days were still warm. So the two packed up "Lizzie" and headed off Friday evening for a little relaxation.

On the flight there, the rugged Alaskan terrain below exhibited nature in its untouched state, the wind swept hills and mountain sides giving way to huge areas of virgin forests in the valleys that were cut by rolling streams that bubbled and swirled around and over rocks as the fresh, clean water cascaded down the slopes to the larger rivers, eventually making their way out to the sea.

Cole circled "Lizzie" low around the entire shoreline of the large lake, then passed over his island paradise. Everything was just as he had left it. Everytime he looked down on this magnificent natural landscape, its beauty gave him goose bumps.

"Look! Some of the trees up there are turning colors already Cole!" Jodie exclaimed, pointing out the side window toward the upper edges of the surrounding mountains.

"That's right. Up here, winter comes very early. We could have our first snow in late September," Cole answered. "Are you all buckled in? I am going to land now."

"Yes, sir. I'm ready to land."

Cole guided "Lizzie" around the island decreasing her altitude slowly, finally touching down softly on the smooth lake surface, gliding gently across the water to the small dock. Cole jumped out, tethering the floatplane to the pilings.

The pair quickly unloaded "Lizzie", putting all of the supplies in their proper places. Next, Cole checked in with the ranger station, as he always did. After that, the two went through the woods behind the cabin to the grassy area next to the lake.

By this time, the sun had passed behind the mountains. Darkness was approaching fast. Having finished the picnic dinner they had brought, Cole and Jodie spent this time with small talk as they gazed up into the sky at the stars. Soon after sundown, Jodie heard a distant call by a wolf. That long, eerie, howling sound.

"Did you hear that, Cole?" she asked.

"You mean that owl calling to the east?"

"I hear that, too. What I mean is did you hear the wolf howling?"

"Now that you mention it, I did. There are lots of noises out here at night, aren't there?" he asked.

"Yeah, right. But what I heard I think was Strike!" she said, almost in a whisper. "I think the howling was Strike."

"You think so? Let's listen," he said, cocking his head to hear better.

Cole knew Jodie had become very attached to Strike when they had her at the ranger station, but to actually be able to say that was her howling would be stretching the truth, he felt. They waited a long time. No more howling was heard. Then Jodie said, "I am going to howl and see if she calls back."

"Okay, let's see what happens," Cole mused.

Jodie cupped her hands to her mouth, cleared her throat and howled the way she had in the barracks when Strike was still at the ranger station. "Ooowh, oooawah, ooowh." letting her voice crack in certain places just like she had done before.

Almost immediately, the howl was returned across the lake from the distant shore. Cole's eyes got big as saucers as he looked at the joyful face of Jodie. "See! I told you it was Strike!" Jodie said, excitedly.

"I cannot believe my ears! I think you are right. Can you say something else to her?" he said.

"Gosh, I dunno!" she said, flustered. "All I know is I noticed Strike has a very distinct howl. When I called her with that particular sound, she would return my call."

"Do it again. Only this time make it much softer. Let's see if she can hear you."

Again, Jodie cupped her hands to her mouth and called out in a much softer voice. Again, the howl returned from the distant shore. Over and over, the wolf and child would call across the lake. Sometimes other wolves could be heard howling. Cole notice that Strike's call was very distinct, just like Jodie had said.

The next morning, soon after Cole and Jodie had cleaned up the breakfast dishes, a howl came across the lake. This time it sounded as if the sound had come from the shore closest to the island. Jodie ran down the path to the rocks that formed the ancient volcano. She quickly climbed to the top. Slightly out of breath, she howled to the wolf.

The howl returned. She called again. The howl returned, again. By this time, Cole had made his way to the top of the rocks carrying his binoculars. He peered through them scanning the shoreline, but he couldn't see the wolf.

Jodie took the binoculars and peered through them. Nothing but trees and rocks could be seen. The howling continued even though Jodie did not answer them. The howling was definitely Strike, as far as Jodie was concerned.

"Cole, can we go over there? I am sure she is calling for me to go over there."

Cole stood there a long time not answering Jodie. He looked through the binoculars trying to see the wolf. What did the wolf want? Why would she call out so insistently? Was it a trap? He just didn't know. Finally, he answered Jodie, "This is really strange. You feel sure this is Strike?"

"Yes, sir!" she quickly answered.

Pausing a minute longer, he said reluctantly, "Okay, I tell you what. We can row the canoe over there and check it out."

"Oh boy! Thanks Cole!" she quickly jumped down the rocks, heading to the dock.

Cole followed, at a much slower pace, trying to figure out why the wolf would be so intent on calling them over to the shore. He stopped at the cabin, got his backpack, rifle, and hunting knife. Then the two pushed the canoe into the lake, boarded it and paddled off to the other side of the lake.

The howling continued off and on during the half-hour paddle across the lake. One thing that struck Cole was that no other wolves could be heard returning the call. Only Jodie, occasionally, would return the howl.

As they drew closer to the shoreline, Cole instructed Jodie, who was seated in the front of the canoe, to quit paddling. "We'll let the canoe drift in a little to try to spot the wolf. I want to see what she is up to," he said, softly.

As the canoe drifted slowly toward the shoreline, Cole noticed the absence of noise. There was absolutely no sound. No birds chirping or calling. No waves lapping at the shoreline. No animal sounds at all. No wind blowing through the trees or bushes. This was an eerie situation.

Cole, once again, put the binoculars to his eyes. Scanning the shoreline as far into the forest as he could, he searched for the wolf, or for that matter, anything that was moving. Nothing.

Jodie had remained silent the whole time. Finally, she whispered to Cole, "This is kind of spooky, isn't it?" turning around to face Cole.

"Yes, it is. I have never heard so much silence in all my time in Alaska." he paused a moment, grabbing up the oar, he began to paddle slowly toward the shore. The canoe glided effortlessly across the still lake waters, finally sliding slowly up the gravelly shoreline.

"Stay seated, Jodie," he instructed. "I'll pull the canoe up on land a little before you get out." He slid his legs over the side of the canoe stepping down into the shallow water. He waded to the front of the canoe, grasped the tether rope and pulled the canoe two thirds of its length onto shore.

"Hand me the rifle. Then you can get out of the canoe," he said, softly.

Jodie followed the instructions, handing him his rifle. Balancing herself in the canoe with each hand on the side rails, she quietly made her way to the front of the canoe, stepping out onto the dry part of the shoreline. Once onshore, she surveyed the surrounding area looking for signs of Strike.

The area they had landed at was a grassy area strewn with large boulders. The trees surrounded this area in a horseshoe-shaped fashion with the open end of the horseshoe at the shoreline.

Cole had moved into the center of the open area, holding the rifle by the stock, horizontal to the ground. He slowly turned as he looked into the wooded area, searching for the wolf. The dense Alaskan pines that rimmed the area had big thick trunks, some measuring two to three feet in diameter. It was a perfect place to hide. Some of the large boulders in the grassy area also gave good cover to hide behind. He didn't know if the wolf had planned for this, but it certainly was a good place to remain hidden until it was the right time to expose one's self.

Jodie quietly made her way to Cole's side. After standing there a moment she asked, "Would it be okay to call Strike?" her voice was soft with a little quiver.

"Yeah, try that."

Jodie cupped her hands to her mouth letting out one of the distinct howls Strike had taught her. The sound echoed back from the distant mountain. There wasn't a return howl.

The two continued to stand in the center of the grassy area peering into the surrounding woods. Jodie reached up to Cole with her left hand placing it in Cole's big callused right hand. Cole surveyed the surrounding area with his eyes, slowly passing his gaze between the large trees and big boulders.

Then with a jerk, he startled himself when he spotted the wolf standing perfectly still facing him, head low, as if ready to pounce. The wolf remained motionless, its piercing brown eyes and menacing expression striking instant fear within Cole. The beautiful coat camouflaged the animal making it difficult to get a good look at it. He could feel the power this animal had.

Jodie felt Cole flinch, and immediately turned to face in the direction he was looking. There, she saw the wolf. It definitely was Strike. She knew it was Strike by the jagged marking on her forehead. She wanted to go to the dog, but her instincts told her to freeze where she was. The evil look on the dog's face momentarily scared Jodie, too. She had forgotten how wolves have an evil expression that looks mean and menacing.

The extreme silence continued. Cole quickly scanned the perimeter of the open area. He became increasingly alarmed that this could be some kind of an ambush by the wolves. For the more he looked around, the more wolves he saw standing perfectly still facing him and Jodie. "Jodie," he whispered, "this doesn't look good. I count seven wolves surrounding us!"

Jodie had noticed all of the wolves, also. "I..know! I'm..scared!' she said, softly, her voice cracking as she spoke.

"Do you see Strike?"

"Yes, sir. She is the one over to your left. The first one we saw." She didn't raise her hand, afraid it might startle the wolves. Then, instinctively, she slowly drew her hands to her mouth, cupped them and softly howled one of the calls she used to do when Strike was staying in the pen at the ranger station, "Ooohaw...ooohow...ooooheh...ooohaw."

Immediately, Strike raised her head returning the howl as the other wolves remained frozen in their stances. Strike slowly made her way toward Cole and Jodie. Her ears stood straight up, her tail was kept high in the air. Without a sound, the wolf, with that menacing look and those evil looking brown eyes, slowly circled the pair at a distance as if making sure this was not a trap.

The second trip the wolf made around the pair was much closer. The two remained motionless, so as not to startle the wolf. After the second trip around, the wolf slowly approached Jodie briefly stopping directly in front of her. She lowered her head slightly as if bowing to Jodie, then walked beside the girl rubbing her head on Jodie's hand that was at her side, continuing on past the girl rubbing the length of her body against the small girl's hand.

Jodie immediately turned around facing the big wolf. She held out her hands in a gesture to tell the dog to come here. Strike, turning around, came to Jodie, sitting in front of the girl. Jodie petted the wolf on the head and shoulders, as Strike let out a soft moan that emanated from deep in her throat. Without any notice, the dog licked Jodie's face quickly from the bottom of her chin to the top of her forehead, two or three full-face licks.

Jodie let out a child's squeal of delight as the hot, wet, tongue left cold dog slobber on her cute, freckled face. The wolf pressed her tongue so hard on Jodie's face, it caused the tiny girl to fall over backward giggling profusely. Even Cole joined in on the laughter as he began to relax now that he knew the intentions of the wolf. He crouched down beside Jodie, as she continued to pet the big wolf.

Every now and then he would look off to the edges of the clearing to see what the other wolves were doing. Just as suddenly as they had appeared, all of the other wolves, but one, disappeared back into the heavily wooded hillsides.

The one remaining wolf appeared to be a very large male, dark in color, almost black. It stood perfectly still gazing down on Jodie, Cole and Strike from one of the more distant boulders, ears and tail erect. This, obviously, was the leader of the pack. Cole figured the wolf weighed in at a little over 120 pounds. He, also, figured if the big wolf took a mind to do them harm, they would not last four minutes. The only thing that gave him consolation was the fact that wolves don't generally attack humans unless they are cornered or threatened.

Looking back to Jodie and Strike, he observed an emotional reunion for the two. He knew Jodie had become attached to the wolf, but it was obvious that this wolf really cared for Jodie, too.

Cole spoke softly to Jodie, "She really looks healthy now." Jodie looked up at him, still giggling as she petted and played with the wolf. "Look at her coat. It really looks healthy and full."

"Yep!" she said, holding the dog on each side of the head just below the ears. "She is much bigger now, too!"

"She sure is!" he slowly leaned over extending his hand to touch the wolf on her side. "I would estimate she weighs in at about eighty to eighty-five pounds."

"Wow! That's more than I weigh," she gasped, as her eyes passed over the large animal.

The wolf rolled over when he touched her, lying on her right side. "I think she wants you to pet her too!" Jodie exclaimed.

Cole leaned over a little further and rubbed his hand down the length of the course, thick fur of her left side. She let out another low, throaty moan. "I think she really is enjoying this!" he said.

"Yeah. Look at her beautiful brown eyes!"

Continuing to stroke her fur, Cole inspected the wound they had sewn up not so long ago. "You know, Jodie, you can't even see her wound anymore." He pulled the fur apart where the wound had been. "Here, here is the scar," he said, holding the fur parted so Jodie could lean over and take a look. "She healed up nicely, didn't she?"

"Yes, sir. That looks real good."

As they sat there petting the wolf, Jodie and Cole reminisced about how they had found her and brought her back to the ranger station. A full hour quickly passed. During this time, Cole told Jodie that Strike was probably the big male wolf's mate. He told her how the dominant male wolf picks a female mate and how they stay together for life, just like humans.

"I hope Strike has picked a better mate to spend her life with than my mommy did!" she blurted out. "My daddy was a mean, ugly man!"

"Well, maybe so. But he had a beautiful little girl." He reached over and patted her on the back. "You must remember that sometimes things change in a person's life. When that happens, sometimes it can make a person mean and ugly." He looked Jodie in the eyes continuing, "I'm sure your mommy wouldn't have married your daddy if he was mean. I think he probably had something bad happen to him that made him mean."

Jodie looked back at the big male wolf still standing on the large boulder. "He looks like a good mate, doesn't he?" she asked.

"Yes, he does! The way he has been keeping watch on us proves to me that he really cares about Strike."

"Good. I want her to be happy."

Strike eased herself back onto her feet, stretched, then slowly circled them. She let out a low, kind of twirling howl. The big male wolf jumped down from the boulder, disappearing behind it. Strike wagged her tail, approached Jodie and, once again, licked her face.

The dog became increasingly nervous as the minutes passed. She made a deep, throaty sound as she looked toward the boulder. A moment later, a small white on gray wolf pup appeared beside the large boulder.

"Look! Look!" Jodie gasped, pointing her hand toward the boulder. "It's one of Strike's puppies. I can't believe it! Look at that cute puppy!" she continued.

"I see it, Jodie!" Cole answered, in a high pitched voice, "I have never, in my life, had a wolf do this!" he exclaimed in disbelief.

One by one, the puppies emerged from behind the boulder, loping and bouncing toward Strike. First, the white on gray male, then a silver on black male, an all black female, a silver on tan female, and finally a smoke-colored on black male. After the five puppies joined their mother, she walked toward Cole and Jodie with the puppies running and jumping around and between her legs. Their tails wagged rapidly and their big pink tongues hung out.

Jodie immediately got down on her knees to pet the puppies as they approached her. All five came bounding up encircling the tiny girl, licking her as they bumped into one another. She lost her balance from the force of the puppies leaping up to greet her causing her to fall over backward.

The puppies took this opportunity to playfully pounce on the little girl. They continued to lick her and tug at her clothes as she attempted to pet each one. Strike sat down watching at a distance allowing the puppies and Jodie to play with each other. Occasionally, one or two of the puppies would run back to Strike, nuzzle her, then return to the free-for-all with Jodie.

Cole, occasionally, would pick up one of the pups trying to get it to slow down long enough to get to know it a little. But the pups wanted to play, so they would wiggle away from him joining the others around Jodie.

"Yeeee! Whooa! Help!" Jodie giggled, "These little ruffians are licking me to death!" she exclaimed with joy. When she would stand up, the pups would chase her around the open area.

"I still can't believe this!" Cole said, in wonderment. "I have never heard of a wolf going to so much trouble to show off her young offspring to a human." After thinking a moment he continued, "You know, when we found this dog, she was almost dead. She realizes that you saved her life and the lives of these puppies. The puppies are the most important things in the wolf pack. If the wolf pack doesn't have offspring every year, it becomes weak. And weakness is what, ultimately, would bring down the pack."

Jodie was now sitting on the ground, legs crossed Indian-style and the puppies, somewhat tired from all of the jumping around, were now gathered quietly around her. "I don't know about all of that, but I do know that I am glad I got to see Strike again. And I'm glad that she is healthy again," she took a deep breath, "And I am very glad that she let me see her babies...eer, I mean puppies."

Soon after that, the big male on the boulder barked a command. One by one, the puppies wandered out of sight behind the boulder. Finally, the only puppy left was the smoke-colored on black male.

This puppy climbed into Jodie's lap, curling up in a circle, resting its tiny head on her left leg. Jodie took the opportunity to run her fingers through the soft, thick fur. The puppy made a low moan, enjoying the newly found attention of the little girl.

Strike stood up, slowly approaching the puppy, her head hung low, ears and tail erect. She bent down giving the puppy several licks here and there as if cleaning him up. Then Strike lifted her head, emitting a low, gurgling sound from deep within her throat. She pushed her head against the side of Jodie's face, licking her gently twice.

Jodie reached up putting both hands on either side of the wolf's neck, petting her thick fur gently. Strike, turned around and slowly walked to the side of the big boulder. Turning back to face Jodie and Cole, she let out a howl....the howl that was so distinctly her own. Then, just as quietly and quickly as they had appeared at the edge of the woods, the big male and Strike disappeared behind the boulder.

Jodie jumped up, grabbed the puppy and started to run toward the boulder, "Wait....Wait! You forgot your puppy!" she shouted.

Cole, at first, was speechless at what he had just witnessed. But when Jodie started chasing after the wolves he yelled, "Jodie! Jodie stay here, honey!" he quickly caught up with her, saying, "Strike hasn't forgotten her puppy! She has given you that puppy, don't you see?" He grabbed her by the arm, slowing her down as he spoke, "Strike has, actually, given you one of her most precious possessions! I cannot believe what she has just done!"

Jodie stopped running, the big puppy nuzzling the little girl under her chin. She looked up at Cole, who was still holding her left arm, and said, "Are you sure? You're positive she didn't forget the puppy?" she asked, almost dumbfounded by what she had heard.

Cole lowered his voice, speaking softly now, "Yes!..Yes! I am sure." He looked the tiny girl in her brown eyes that were now as big as saucers.

"Woooow!" she whispered. She looked back at the boulder, then canvassed the woods all around the edge of the clearing with her eyes looking for wolves. None could be seen. "It is sooo...quiet....again," she whispered again.

Jodie, looked down at the soft, sleepy puppy she was holding. Her mind raced with all kinds of thoughts. She simply didn't know what to make of this gift she was given.

Then she blurted out, "Can I keep him, Cole?"

Cole let out a big belly laugh, "Of course you can! As a matter of fact, I would be afraid NOT to let you keep the puppy! Strike and the rest of the pack might come and get me if I didn't let you keep him!" he said, as he continued to laugh.

The two spent the next hour, or so, getting to know Jodie's new dog. It behaved very well and seemed to be right at home with them. It was then Jodie decided she would call the new pet "Smoke" for two reasons.

The first was because of the color of the dog, the smoke-colored fur. The second, because they had rescued Strike from the lightning strike area where the patch of forest was burned away.

"You know, Cole, if those trees hadn't caught on fire we would not have been able to save Strike. That would have meant all five of those puppies would have died too!" she concluded. "And that would have been really sad. So, I am calling this puppy Smoke!"

"That is a real good name, Jodie." he patted her on the head.

After a little while longer, they boarded the canoe, paddling slowly back to the island. Every now and then, Jodie would turn around, looking back at the distant shoreline as it slowly regressed, emitting a distinctive howl, but there was never a return call from the woods. She knew that Strike had given her the most wonderful gift a wild animal could give a human.

Looking down at the big, furry puppy she said, "The bestest thing that ever happened to me since my mommy died was when my dad abandoned me in Farrow's Patch. That was the day I met you!" She slowly looked up at Cole, "And now, Strike has given me part of her life to love, too!"

Chapter 13

The rest of the weekend on the island centered on the newest member of the informal "family". The puppy was very well behaved, following Jodie everywhere she went. Even at night, the puppy curled up in bed beside the small girl.

It was like a magical weekend, as far as Cole could see. The weather was perfect, Jodie had a great time with the puppy, and there was plenty of time for fishing, exploring and just goofing off. He had a wonderful weekend and he knew Jodie had, also.

Soon after, as the days began to grow shorter, the average temperature dropped steadily. Cold, winter weather was not too far off. It, also, signaled that it was time for school to start. Judge Holcolmb had arranged for Jodie to enter school at the local school house as Cole had requested, which was a "close" twenty-two miles from the station on the other side of Gold Diggers Notch.

A total of seven kids rode the little yellow school bus to the one-roomed schoolhouse. Four kids from the station and three more outside Prospectors Cove.

So, on a crisp Monday morning, Jodie and Smoke, climbed aboard the little yellow bus at 7 a.m. along with the other three sleepy kids. She had gotten really excited about going back to school. Not only to meet some other kids and start new friendships, but, also, because she did good in school and enjoyed learning about new things. The bus, not unexpectedly, was very quiet that morning because the kids, ranging in age from seven to fourteen, had not yet fully awakened.

After motoring up the gentle slope out of the valley, across Gold Diggers Notch, and down the outer side of the surrounding mountains, the bus picked up the last three children, then headed for Pickle Hill Schoolhouse.

The name was derived from the small raised bluff area that the school building was built atop, being surrounded by a large, flat plain. From a distance the rocky covered surface, which grew a thin looking rye grass, resembled a large pickle that had been put there by an imaginary giant. Surprisingly, the rye grass only grew on the hill. The surrounding plain was barren, rust-colored rock and tan, dusty dirt that was sometimes picked up by the wind and whisped across the plain to the distant mountains.

This year the total enrollment at the school was twenty-three children. The middle-aged, gray-haired teacher, Mrs. Patty Millan, taught all of the grades, one through ten. She had two children in first grade, five in third, four in fourth, four in Jodie's fifth grade, three in seventh, three in ninth, and two in tenth.

The building was an old-fashioned, one-room school, complete with a well and an outhouse. The rectangular-shaped building had vertically planked sides that had been whitewashed many years before, showing the signs of wear and tear from the harsh weather as well as many years of under-funded maintenance from the local school district.

At one end of the building, a large wooden door permitted passage into the educational system of Picasawny County. For two decades, this small structure educated the future leaders of Alaska and places beyond. This year it would be Jodie's turn to learn. And this little, unattractive building would be a big part in developing Jodie into a fine, well-educated young lady.

Inside, the large main room contained twenty-seven very worn wooden desks that had been stained in a dark oak finish. The desks were arranged in four groups, each representing a cluster according to the grade level the children were in. Grades one through three were in one cluster, then grades four through six in another, and seventh through tenth in still another. The last cluster was filled with the four extra chairs. In this area the children did special projects that might involve more than one cluster.

A large, black, cast iron coal burning heater stood directly in the center of the classroom, which kept the whole room toasty warm, even on the coldest days of winter. Toward the back of the room, two doors, one at each corner, opened into two smaller rooms. The room on the right contained the storage area and the makeshift office for the teacher. The other door, on the left, opened into the library, Jodie's favorite part of the schoolhouse.

The library was crammed with books placed on shelves that ran from floor to ceiling. Mrs. Millan had spent years conning other schools and the superintendent of the school district out of books for her classes. She had the best resource material of any of the smaller schools in the district. As a matter of fact, some of the larger schools would sometimes borrow reference material from Mrs. Millan.

Jodie fit in well with the other kids. At first, Smoke was the topic of conversation for no one at school had a wolf as a pet. After the fear of being around a wolf wore off, the other kids really liked the well-mannered, easygoing animal.

Jodie's activities revolved mainly around school as winter moved into the area. As soon as she got home from school she would change into work clothes, have a snack, check in with Cole, who was usually at the administration building, then join Ally at the campground. After that, she would go with Ally to the barn and help feed the horses and other farm animals. By that time, it would be dark outside and the two would wash up and head to the dining hall, where they would join Cole and Bill for a family meal.

After dinner, Cole, Jodie and Smoke would head back to the cabin where Jodie would complete her school assignments. Cole was very good about supervising Jodie in her studies, giving help where needed. But, basically, Jodie proved to be a good student and needed little help. She really liked Mrs. Millan and always wanted to do her best at her studies.

As time passed, Allison's leg healed and the therapy had helped the leg come back to full potential. The limp she had, at first, disappeared and her spirits had improved over time. Only rarely did her dark moods occur and when she did have one, it only lasted for a day or less.

Allison's Cessna 150 airplane was fully insured. The insurance company had sent her a settlement check to cover the replacement of the craft. However, she gave the check to her dad saying she didn't think she wanted to pilot an aircraft again. Bill was very upset about this decision and frequently would argue with Allison to try to get her to listen to reason.

One evening Bill brought up the subject of flying again. "Allison, honey, you know that in Alaska it is very important to be able to fly an airplane. There is always a great demand for good pilots and, not only that, it will save you hours of travel time. In some cases, if you don't fly you will not be able to go to the places you need to be able to go," he explained. "You're an excellent pilot! You know you are! You took to flying like a duck takes to water."

"Daddy, I know all of that. But I don't think I should fly again," she countered, her voice trailing off. "Daddy...I...can't help think...that I used bad judgement," she paused to gather her thoughts, and to get up enough nerve to tell her dad what was truly on her mind. "I mean...I mean, I shouldn't have been flying so low across Copper Mountain!" she blurted out. She began to cry, big tears running down her cheeks, dripping onto the floor.

Bill drew Allison close to him, placing his strong arms around her, holding her tight to his chest. Several minutes passed before he spoke. Allison's tears dampened the front of his ranger uniform. "Allison, Allison, is that what has been bothering you all of this time?" He placed his right hand under her chin, gently raising her head to look in her eyes. She opened her tear-filled, brilliant-blue eyes to look into his quiet, dark-brown masculine eyes. He smiled down at her, admiring her beauty. She looked so much like her mother, he thought.

"Allison, I love you!" he said, softly. "You are so wrong. You are wrong about your judgement."

"Ooh, Daddy!" she pleaded.

Bill interrupted, "Listen! Listen to me first!" he spoke softly. He continued to look into Allison's eyes, using his index finger to gently wipe her tears from her cheeks. Still holding her to his chest with his left arm the two rocked from side to side slowly, gently, almost as if participating in a slow dance.

"Daddy...," Allison began.

Once again, Bill interrupted, "No! Let me talk!" holding his index finger over her lips to keep her from saying anything. Once again, no words were spoken. The two continued to look into one another's eyes. After several minutes, Bill began in a low, calm voice, "Allison, you have always been a responsible pilot. You have never taken any unnecessary chances! I have never seen you fly in bad weather. You have always told someone where you were flying, and what time you would leave or return," he paused, still keeping his index finger pressed to her pale pink lips. "I remember when you first started flying." He grinned, thinking back to when she was twelve. "You would take the controls so deliberately, concentrating on making the airplane do exactly what it was supposed to do." They both chuckled, she snubbed a little.

"I remember Cole showing you the finer things of flying. You know, he taught you things I would never have been able to teach you. You two guys can make those planes act like they are part of you!" he paused, looking deep within her eyes. "You two really have a gift, you know?"

"But, as for your judgement! NO! No, I will not accept the statement that you used poor judgement! And I can prove it!" he stated, emphatically.

"I don't think so, Daddy! How?" she asked, still snubbing.

"Why were you flying at that altitude?"

"Well, let's see," she thought back to that fateful day. "The weather was moving in fast from the west, so I changed my flight plan at Juneau to fly a more easterly route to miss the oncoming storm. I knew the mountains peaked higher to the east and I knew Copper Mountain was the tallest one we would fly over."

"Okay, so Copper Mountain determined your altitude?"

"Not entirely. I didn't want to waste a lot of time climbing to a higher altitude because the storm was moving in fast, so I wanted to make sure I had time to get around the storm." She thought a moment, then continued, "Also, Juneau told me the winds above seven-thousand feet were very strong out of the east. I was afraid if I went too high the winds would push me back toward the storm to the west."

Bill nodded his head, indicating he understood what she was saying. "So the height of Copper Mountain, coupled with the seven thousand foot ceiling determined your altitude, correct?"

"Yes, sir."

"How much distance did you allow to cross Copper Mountain?

"About sixty-five feet, or so."

"Why only sixty-five feet?"

"Because the mountain comes to a sharp, pointed peak, then drops away very quickly on both sides." She touched her fingers together forming an inverted "v", illustrating the mountain peak. "I would cross the peak in a split second."

Holding both of Allison's hands in his, he said, softly, "I rest my case!"

"What do you mean you rest your case? What case? All I did was tell you why I flew the airplane the way I did," she quizzed, still not listening to what she had just told her father.

"I said, I rest my case, and I do! You told me why you chose that altitude, and I agree. I would have done the exact same thing! Don't you see? You did everything properly. The only thing that happened was a freak accident," he paused a moment to gain his thoughts. "If anything happened that was wrong, it was the eagle that made the mistake, " he said, firmly. "You see, honey, you did everything right. Sometimes we do everything right and bad things still happen. This accident was not your fault!"

"But Daddy, I am the one that hit that bird!"

"No! No you are not the one that hit that bird!" he raised his voice in aggravation. "You are the one that happened to be at the wrong place at the wrong time when the bird hit your airplane! Don't you see? I would have chosen the same flight path and the same altitude. And I would have been the one to have the eagle hit me. It wasn't you, it was the circumstance. Don't you understand that?" he asked, his voice booming across the room.

Allison turned away from her father, walking slowly away, her head lowered, her mind racing. Could he be right? Was there a chance she could have missed the eagle? Her mind reflected back to the events leading up to the collision with the big eagle. Yes, yes her dad was right about her decision on the flight plan and the altitude. But could she have missed the eagle?

"Let's say you are right about all of that. I am wondering if I could have missed the eagle," she turned around facing her dad as she spoke.

Bill answered with a question, "How much time do you think you had to make a correction on your flight path?"

"To be honest, I don't remember hitting the bird. All I remember is the flight up from Juneau and us approaching the mountain peak. Then, I have no memory of anything that happened until I awoke in the hospital."

"Well, Jodie remembers the whole thing. She told us that the bird shot up from below the aircraft on her side of the airplane," he said, using his hands to demonstrate the relative position of the plane and the flight path of the eagle. "You couldn't have seen it coming!"

Allison remained silent for several minutes still slowly pacing around the room, her face pointed downward, eyes looking blankly at the floor as she remained in deep concentration still trying to remember the collision. "Daddy, do you really believe I used good judgement?"

"Yes, I do!" he said, firmly.

"Do you promise that you would tell me the truth, not just try to make me feel good about this?" her voice quivered slightly.

"Allison Defreese, this is too important to shade the truth. If I thought you had made an error, I promise I would tell you." He walked slowly to her once again wrapping his arms around her waist, kissing her gently on the forehead.

She wept and, at that moment, she cleansed her sole of all the guilt she had been carrying around these past couple of months.

In late October, Allison and Bill flew down to Juneau to pick up Allison's new Cessna 150. Allison was the pilot this time. After Bill had convinced her she was not at fault in the airplane crash, Allison had begun to fly around the area, rebuilding her piloting confidence. This, however, was the first time she had taken a passenger with her. So this trip was a milestone flight.

Allison had decided to stay with the same type of aircraft she had before because she really liked the little Cessna 150. Bill had a new Cessna ordered and, just three weeks later, Alaskan Outback Flight Center called to say they had received two Cessna's in stock as part of their regular inventory.

The day had started out cold and dreary with a light snow falling. Bill's Piper was now outfitted with skis, as were all of the others that used pontoons in the warmer months. The tiny yellow airplane cranked up hard, but as soon as the engine warmed a little, purred like a kitten.

Arriving at Alaskan Outback Flight Center, Allison and Bill were introduced to her brand new airplane already rigged with skis. Allison was very excited and couldn't wait to get her in the air. After several hours of signing papers and checkout flights around Juneau, the plane was officially turned over to Allison.

To celebrate, Bill took his daughter to lunch at the well known Aleut Restaurant, a very unattractive building that had been haphazardly added on to over the years, located just off the main street close to the fishing docks. The outer looks of the establishment did not relate to the fine cooking and the well decorated interior of the building.

Upon entering the low-ceilinged structure, the observer knew they were in a seafood restaurant. The main room had giant fishing nets strung across the black painted ceiling. Numerous booths occupied the floor area, each decorated with various deep-sea equipment, such as: large glass globes that were used to float the large nets in the water, gigs and knives used on the sea-going boats, coral from deep in the sea, diving equipment.

Bill and Allison had a wonderful lunch together. He chose big Alaskan red crab and Allison had deep-sea salmon, baked to a flaky texture with butter and the chef's secret spices. Bill joked that the secret spices were probably the cook's cigar ashes. The food was excellent, as always.

Just as they were getting ready to leave, an old friend stopped by the booth to see how they were doing. Dr. Marvin Lerner owned the All Animal Veterinary Clinic in Juneau. He was a short, slightly stooped, bald-headed man of about sixty-five. His short-cropped gray hair around the side of his head looked as if there was a line drawn horizontally around his head, above which no hair could grow.

Bill and Marv were old friends from way back. Marv used to come by the newly established park in the sixties to instruct the rangers on various new animal control procedures, medicines, and any new outbreaks of disease that may have come up. He always worked in extra time so the two could go fishing or hiking on his visits to the park.

"Hey, Bill!' he said, holding his hand out to shake Bill's. "How are you, Allison?" he asked, leaning over to give her a polite hug."

"What a pleasant surprise." Bill responded, returning Marv's handshake.

"Wow!" Marv exclaimed, looking at Allison, "What a beautiful girl you have turned out to be!"

Allison blushed beat red, "Oh stop it!" she said, waving her arm and hand forward limply in a bashful manner.

"Okay, I'll stop it, but slide over I want to sit next to you." She happily slid to the inside of the booth, still blushing. "How are you two getting along?" he asked.

"We're doing fine Marv. How about you?" Bill returned the question.

"Well, pretty much the same as always, other than I am getting too old, you know?"

"Yeah, I know what you mean!" Bill chuckled, winking at Allison. "How are things at the vet center? You know, I haven't seen you for four months, or so."

"Everything is going good," he paused a moment to gather his thoughts, "but, I guess, that is part of the problem. Everything is going too good." He looked at both of them, shaking his head.

"What, do you mean, too good?" Allison quizzed, a puzzled look on her face.

"Well Juneau is experiencing some kind of population explosion right now. People are coming in by the hundreds to take advantage of the high paying oil jobs in Alaska." He waved his arms to illustrate the influx of people to the area. "When all of these people get here, they have more pets, and more pets mean more business for me. More business for me means I need more good veterinarians," he sighed a little, then added, "and that is the rub. I need more help at the clinic." He held his hands up as if to say, "What can I do?"

"Wait a minute, Marv," Bill said. "The oil jobs are mainly on the North Slope. Why are people coming here for oil jobs?"

"That was my question, too, when this all started to happen. It seems that the additional oil workers put a strain on the supplies needed to keep them going. You know, food and clothing, and infrastructure items, like: better roads, more housing, additional demands for electricity, water, sewerage, and on and on. Not only that, but they want to spend some of those high wages on luxury items. So the chain continues to draw more and more people to supply all of those needs. And those people's needs require additional people, and so on," he said, waving his arms about excitedly. "It's great! And since Juneau is the first major city you go through from the States, we get a good portion of the new growth as a supply center."

"So all of this growth has made Marv a rich man," Bill joked.

Marv laughed, saying, "Not quite. But I am enjoying a little prosperity right now." He looked over to Allison "How about you? You ought to be out of school by now. Are you?"

"Yes sir, I graduated this year."

"What was you major?"

"Veterinary Science," she responded.

He looked over at Bill, "Bingo!" he said, holding up his hand, forming the okay sign, and pointing it at Bill.

"Now, Marv," he said, in a deep voice, "Allison is working at the station with me." He held up his hand forming a stop signal.

"I know that, Bill. And I wouldn't want to interfere with her working there." Turning to Allison he said, "I just want you to know, if things ever change for you, come see me down here in Juneau, okay?"

"You bet, Dr. Lerner. Thanks for the offer," she answered. "I am very happy being close to home."

"That is good to hear," looking from one to the other, "My son came home to work with me at the clinic, and I have enjoyed it a lot." He slowly stood up from the table, once again shaking Bill and Allison's hand, "Well, I gotta go. Some of the others at the clinic want to eat their lunch, too, so I need to relieve them. It has been nice seeing you two again. Come by the clinic anytime." With that, all three said their good-byes and Dr. Lerner left.

After lunch, Bill and Allison walked back to the flight center, and flew their airplanes back to the ranger station. The weather had cleared up for the flight back. The sky was deep blue with thin Cirrus clouds very high in the sky.

During the past several months, Cole's extra time had been spent, almost entirely, with Jodie either doing homework or participating in other activities such as playing ball, skating on the frozen lake, fishing, or tracking animals to help her learn more about nature.

Every now and then, Judge Holcolmb would contact Cole to keep him up to date on the investigation in Portland, and to make sure everything was working out between him and Jodie. The investigation in Portland was what Judge Holcolmb called a "back-burner investigation". It was not one of the top priority items on the police dockets.

Over the past few months, they knew a lot more about Dawson Patterson. They had found out that when he was a young man he was in trouble a lot for smaller petit crimes like painting graffiti on the side of buildings, shop-lifting, and fighting with others. Later, in his mid-twenties he was arrested and questioned, but not convicted, on several burglaries. Evidently this was when he met Jodie's mom, Evelyn Varsario. It was still not known why the two became interested in each other. But they did.

Dawson, evidently, had a very bad temper, which led to him being fired from many jobs. With such a bad employment history, it became harder and harder for him to find steady work. This behavior circle put additional stress on him, and led to him being arrested for public intoxication frequently.

The police had not been able to find the driver of the car that had run over Evelyn yet and, for that matter, never found the car either, or any witnesses to the crime. The most interesting thing that had been reported to the judge was that Jodie's birth certificate was a forgery. It was a very good forgery. This led to many questions like: what is Jodie's real name? What is her actual birth date? Where was she born? Why was a forgery necessary to enroll her in school? And many more.

Judge Holcolmb had started his own investigation to seek out the answers to these and many other questions. He centered his investigation on Evelyn Varsario Patterson to find out what was her history and background. So far, he found out that Evelyn had grown up in Flat Run, Wyoming, born May 5, 1955 to Paul and Betty Varsario. Evelyn did not have any brothers or sisters, and Paul died in a car accident in 1962. Betty died of kidney failure in 1970, leaving fifteen year old Evelyn to fend for herself. Evidently, she didn't have any relatives. The records indicated both parents were buried in Flat Run. As far as the investigation found out, after funeral expenses, which were paid by small life insurance policies, there was very little money left. The home they lived in was rented, so there was no estate to speak of.

Evelyn had been a good student, never in any trouble at school or with the law. She did not graduate from the local high school and, as a matter of fact, she had no history for the next seven years of her life, up until the time that Jodie was entered in school with the fake birth certificate. Which came back to the question, why a forged birth certificate?

"I have some people trying to find out where Jodie was born," the judge continued, "They have been checking various hospitals and cities within a four state area using Evelyn's maiden name and her married name. We have concentrated on the three months preceding the birth date on the forged birth certificate as well as the three months after the birthdate."

Cole asked, "What are you doing to investigate Dawson?"

"Nothing really, as of yet. We have been relying on the police for that. What I am trying to do now is to get them to work on tracking his earlier travels back during the missing seven year period in Evelyn's life," a sigh came over the phone. Then the judge added, "They are not too willing to investigate any earlier time period than when the car ran over Evelyn. I am going to continue to call them until they get sick of taking my calls."

"Well, let me know if there is anything I can do. I imagine this will hold up the adoption process, right?"

"Unfortunately, yes. We have to have all of these questions answered, as you can understand."

"Right. Well let me know if I can help in any way."

As the weeks passed, everything continued to go along smoothly for Cole and Jodie. But for Allison, the turmoil within her soul created by trying to restrain her love for Cole, while allowing enough time for him to acknowledge his love for her, had reached a point that made it necessary to make some important decisions in her life.

The airplane crash made Allison look inward at herself and her life. In the past, she had been taken care of by her dad and, to some extent, Cole. Everything had been laid out for her. She would go off to college, get her degree in Veterinary Science, probably meet a nice young college student, get married, have kids, have a career, and live happily ever after.

Reality had not gone along with the plan exactly. And this kept eating at her. She knew whom she loved. But she had been unsuccessful in getting Cole to express his feelings toward her. Cole was not cooperating, either because he didn't love her or because he wouldn't admit it. Allison felt deeply that it was the latter reason.

One of Allison's dreams was to have a family, be a mom, raise kids and have a loving husband. She now came to the realization, because of the crash, that all of that could be snuffed out in a split second. Just as her mom was taken from her and her dad, she too, could have her dreams lost in an instant. It was time for her to get on with her life and live life to the fullest. She wanted Cole as her husband and she now knew her love for him was genuine.

But if Cole did not love her as much as she loved him, then she would have to let that love go, and move on with her life. So, she had made up her mind that she would try one last time to talk things over with Cole, and try to get him to tell her his true feelings. That day was today.

The cold January day started out bright and sunny. But as the day progressed, the weather deteriorated rapidly. Earlier in the day all the kids went down to the lake to skate on the ice and slide down the gentle slopes on their sleds. Sunday was always a pleasant day around the station, since only the necessary work had to be done, such as feeding the horses and other farm animals. Ally had joined Cole and Jodie and the others in an informal hockey game using branches for hockey sticks and a flat, round rock for the puck.

When the weather began to close in, the kids gradually disbanded heading back closer to their houses to play. On the way up the slope from the lake, Jodie got between Cole and Allison as the threesome climbed the gentle incline arm-in-arm. Almost as if on cue, but not planned by Allison, Jodie said, "I love you two." She looked up at Cole and Allison, "Maybe someday we can be a regular family!"

Allison looked down at Jodie, who was still looking up at her, then she looked over at Cole. Cole glanced nervously at A.J. The statement by Jodie had shocked him, and he nervously blurted out, not really thinking, "Jodie, that is nice, but you shouldn't say things like that. It makes A.J. and me uncomfortable because we are just good friends."

Allison stopped walking, bringing the threesome to a sudden halt. Looking at Cole, she said, angrily, "Obviously Jodie has more common sense than you do! If it makes you uncomfortable, then I'll leave!" She turned to her right stomping off through the snow toward the horse barn.

Cole stood motionless as A.J. climbed the small hill to the gravel road that led to the maintenance barn and the horse barn beyond, puffs of white smoke billowing from her mouth as her warm breath met the cold Alaskan air. "What'd I say? Why did she get mad?" he muttered, in disbelief.

"Cole, you are a typical man!" this young-girl-turned-young-lady spouted out. "I'm just a little kid, and even I can see she really cares for you."

"I care for her, too!" he said, defending himself.

"I don't mean like a friend, you jerk! I mean, I think she loves you!' she let go of Cole's hand stomping off toward their cabin, disgusted with him. Looking back over her shoulder as she shuffled through the deep snow, she said, in a loud voice, "Like a grown man loves a grown woman!" As she made her way up the slope he could hear her muttering under her breath, "Stupid men! They gotta be the dumbest animals on earth!"

Cole stood motionless for several minutes trying to figure out what he had said that was so offensive. He knew Allison had crushes on him in the past, but they all passed. He had never given her any reason to think he loved her in any way other than as a friend. What was going on here, anyhow?

He looked around the station grounds. No one was visible. Patting his glove-covered hands together, he caught himself talking out loud, "I don't get it! Why does everyone think I said something wrong? I thought Jodie spoke out of turn, not me!" He dragged his boot back and forth in the snow trying to figure out what to do. He knew he had to go talk to A.J., but he didn't want to. What was he going to tell her?

He realized they were right. He did care for A.J. more than just as a friend. He had been fighting back his emotions ever since A.J. came home from school. But he felt it was wrong to help raise a kid and then fall in love with her. For this reason, he had decided he would never let anyone know he loved A.J. and he would repress that emotion somehow.

"Oh shucks!" he muttered, starting off following A.J.'s tracks toward the horse barn. Halfway there he made an abrupt turn heading to the dining hall. He quickly made two large cups of hot chocolate, then trampled through the snow to the horse barn.

Once inside the darkened horse barn, he called out for A.J.. But there was no answer. The barn was warm inside compared to the nineteen degree temperature outside because the barn had a small coal burning stove located in the center portion that kept the stalls at a cozy fifty degrees. The horses loved it.

He stepped further into the barn on the hay strewn floor between the stalls, "Hey, A.J.. You here?" No answer. The low ceiling in this part of the stables made everything close and dark. Every twenty feet, a sixty-watt bulb hung from an electrical cord producing a dim, eerie yellow cast light. The smell was of hay and manure.

He walked to the end of the stalls, looking in each as he went. Occasionally he petted one of the horses on the nose. Not successful in finding A.J., he walked back to the steep stairs that gave access to the hayloft above. He slowly climbed the stairs to the second level peering into the darkness, "A.J.?"

"Yes, I'm here Cole," a soft, put-out voice answered.

"Oh, good. Can I come up?" he asked.

"I guess," she mumbled, "You'd probably come up anyhow."

Cole climbed the remaining three steps to the loft, slowly walking over to A.J., who was sitting cross-legged on the hay covered floor. He held the cup of hot chocolate out for her to take, "I thought you might want something to warm up your insides."

"Oh, I'm warm all right!" she hissed.

"I'm sorry if I said something to offend you. I certainly didn't mean it to hurt you," he apologized, waiting for a response. Not getting one he said, "What exactly did I say that was so wrong that it made you and Jodie leave me back there?"

Allison looked at Cole for a long time. The pause was very awkward for Cole. But since he didn't know what to do, he waited it out. Finally, Allison said, "We really need to talk, Cole." She sat real still not saying anything thinking what to say, but having a hard time getting started. Then she began to speak slowly and distinctly, "I mean, we really have to resolve some issues that have been building up within me for a long time."

Her heart pounded fast and her breathing became irregular as she got up enough nerve to confront Cole. At the same time, he became increasingly more nervous, too, as he tried to figure out what he would say to A.J.

"Cole, I am really upset right now. I will talk to you only if you promise to answer my questions honestly and tell me your true feelings. Will you do that?"

He tried one last attempt to dodge the questions by answering, "A.J., you know I'm not good at this kind of thing…"

She held up her hand to stop his sentence, "If you cannot agree to these terms, then we have nothing to say to each other," she emphasized the word "nothing".

Shaking his head and exhaling heavily, he sat down on the floor facing Allison, crossing his legs Indian-style. They both continued to look directly at one another, not saying a word. Cole's thoughts reflected on the scene a few minutes earlier when Jodie was naïve enough to speak the truth, expressing her love for him and A.J. He realized she had unwittingly exposed this "can of worms" and, now, he was going to have to confront A.J. about a subject he was trying to hide from everyone, including himself.

He thought about what Jodie had just said to him, and he was becoming more confused as the minutes rolled by. Did Jodie think it was all right to be in love with A.J.? In his thoughts he answered, "She probably does. But, she is just a little kid, and doesn't understand about the past and how A.J. was just ten years old when he came to Alaska." Then, he thought, "What would Bill think if he found out he loved his daughter?"

Perspiration began to bead up on his forehead so he unzipped his coat, removed his gloves, and peeled off his coat. The heat from the stove in the center of the barn collected at the ceiling, raising the temperature to about seventy degrees up in the hayloft.

Still keeping his eyes locked onto Allison's, he sucked in a deep breath of air and answered reluctantly, "Okay….Okay…I'll do it!" He thought to himself that he had to get this over with sooner or later. It might as well be now.

"Good. I was hoping you would say that." She breathed a sigh of relief as she unzipped her coat, removing it to expose a bright red sweater that accented her figure immeasurably. She removed her fur-lined hat, and undid the braid that held up her hair, allowing it to drop loosely to her shoulders.

Cole took in the beautiful woman in front of him, as if it was the first time he had actually seen her. It may have been the darkened lighting, the quiet warmth of the hayloft, or the amount of time he had been by himself out here in the middle of nowhere. But whatever it was, Cole, for the first time, saw A.J. as a woman...a very beautiful woman.

Her shoulder-length, sandy-blonde, straight hair was curled under at the ends. Her brilliant-blue eyes caught the dim light in the loft, giving the effect of almost leaping out at him. Her fair skin, short, straight nose, and her soft, thin eyebrows accented her pinkish cheeks and thin, soft, pink lips. Her long, thin, very feminine neck disappeared into the bright-red sweater, which did a marvelous job of accenting her firm, petite figure and tiny waist.

Allison, too, was looking deep within Cole and, as she did, she was aware that Cole was taking her in. She remained posed, allowing him time to observe her femininity. It felt good to have him look at her in that way, and she let him. This was the first time that she noticed him looking at her the way a man looks at a woman.

Allison ran her fingers through her hair, and slightly shook her head to make her hair fall back in place. Then, after what felt like an eternity, but was only a brief time, Allison slowly lifted her hand out to take the cup of hot chocolate from Cole. As her hand touched the cup, she wrapped her fingers over Cole's, taking her other hand and placing it on top his outstretched hand.

Cole's heart was pounding. He was totally immobilized by the situation. His mind was racing wildly out of control. What was happening here? This was wrong! He helped raise A.J. he cannot think of her in this manner! But, she is so beautiful! He thought to himself, "I have to stop this now!"

Cole pressed the cup of hot chocolate into A.J.'s hands, then pulled his hands back placing them safely in his lap. They were trembling slightly as he rubbed them together to hide his nervousness. "There you go!' he blurted out, referring to the cup of hot chocolate.

Allison set the cup on the hay-covered flooring, slowly reaching both hands out to grasp Cole's. In a low, almost whisper, she said, "Relax....relax, I just want to have some uninterrupted time to talk with you," she giggled softly, "I promise I won't bite you!"

Cole released her left hand from his right. Reaching down to the flooring, he picked up his cup and took an awkward swallow of hot chocolate, gulping loudly. A.J. left hers on the floor, still taking this opportunity to caress his left hand and stare romantically at the handsome man facing her.

Setting the cup down on the floor, Cole's mind was once again sidetracked by his emotions and passion. He reached over to A.J., touching the tiny scar on her jaw created by the plane crash, the only visible sign of the traumatic experience. Her skin was so soft. Her eyes so bright. Her lips so tender. He felt a stirring deep within, and suddenly he realized he was letting the situation get emotionally out of control. So he jerked his hand back. Once again, he thought, "You cannot act like this!"

"I'm..I'm sorry! I..didn't mean to be forward!" he stuttered.

"Why would you say that? You act like you're afraid to touch me. Are you?"

"No, of course not! he said, defensively.

"Then why did you pull your hand back and act so embarrassed?

"Because...because it isn't...right for me to...to..., you know...," he looked at her sheepishly, "you know, I shouldn't be thinking of you other than as my little sister."

"Oh, really? Why?" she asked, raising her voice a little.

"Because I have known you since you were a little girl!" he said, thinking that would answer all future questions on that subject.

Allison grasped his hands again, "You mean, that if you know someone since they were a little kid, you cannot carry that relationship any
further. You can only consider me your little sister. Nothing more?"

"That's right!" He felt proud of himself. He figured that answered all
the questions.

"Why?" she asked.

He hadn't figured on that question, and now he had to answer it. He
swallowed hard, then started to explain, "A.J. you know I love you. But
I love you as a sister. I have enjoyed watching and helping you grow up,
and I enjoy remembering all the good times we have had. I enjoyed
struggling through some of the difficult times, too. But, A.J., I was
twenty-two when we met. For Pete's sake, I had been in a war already,
and now I am thirty-two. You are only twenty-two." He looked down
at their hands and continued, "Even if I did love you in a different manner, our age difference is too great, don't you see that?" he looked up
into her beautiful eyes again, his eyes begging for her understanding.

Allison's fingers gently squeezed his hands. In a consoling manner she
answered, "Cole, I understand what you are saying, but your logic is not
good." She shook her head back and forth several times. "Let me ask
you a question." She took a deep breath, "If you had met me under different circumstances, would you be in love with me?"

Smart enough to know that this was a loaded question, he immediately answered emphatically, "No! Well maybe!" he said, spitting the
words out in machine-gun fashion, "That is not a fair question. You are
asking a question that is make believe."

"So?"

"So I cannot answer that. It is all made up...a childish question," he
retorted.

Allison thought a moment, then tried a new line of thought, "Let me
tell you how I feel. Maybe that will help you tell me how you feel." She
took a sip of her hot chocolate and began, "I will admit that most of my
life I have had a crush on you. And why wouldn't I? You are a very handsome man, Cole Bryant," she blushed a little when she said the words.

This made Cole even more uneasy. He cleared his throat, looked down at the hay strewn floor muttering, "Aw geesh! This is embarrassing."

Allison continued, "I am sorry if I made you feel uncomfortable. But it is the truth, and we are being completely honest with each other, right?"

"I guess," he said, sheepishly. Then thought better of it and added, "Yes, completely honest." He looked back at her, then quickly looked away in embarrassment.

"When I went away to college I did not have a crush on you. As a matter of fact, I just considered you a very good friend, a brother. But the longer I stayed away at school, the more I realized that I love you." She took another sip of hot chocolate, cleared her throat and continued, "I came home that second summer, and had a very difficult time hiding my feelings for you. You didn't know this did you?"

"No." He looked at her with a surprised expression on his face.

"Well, I decided I would stay at school the whole two semesters my last year in school to test my feelings for you. I even dated a lot, trying to see if someone else would be right for me. But the more I dated, the more I fell in love with you, Cole Bryant," she gently rubbed the backs of his hands with her fingers, her eyes filling to the edges of her eyelids with tears, but not spilling over onto her cheeks.

Cole sat motionless, not saying a word. "I have been fighting back my true love for you for the past three years. I cannot help myself. My love for you grows deeper every day," she sniffled as she spoke. "Finally, I have been able to tell you that," she exhaled as if she had released a great burden from her soul.

Cole was stunned by what he heard. He just sat there trying to absorb what A.J. had said. Trying to get up enough nerve to open up to Allison. He began to speak, stumbling along trying to gather his nerve, "A.J...A.J..." he exhaled a nervous chuckle, "A.J....I don't know what to say..." he tried to catch his breath.

"Just say what is on your mind...in your heart...be honest with me, as well as yourself." She pulled his hands up to her lips, kissing them softly.

Cole pulled his hands slowly away from her lips, brushed his tongue over his dry lips, and chuckled shyly. Allison said, once again, "Be honest. It will be all right."

But the fact was, Cole knew he could not be honest. Since he felt this kind of love would be wrong, he knew he would have to lie. It would be the first time he lied to Allison. Finally, he said, "A.J. you are very special to me, but I have always thought of you as my little sister. To be honest, I have noticed a difference with us this summer. That is why I have been afraid to be alone with you because I thought you might have these feelings for me. I just never knew your feelings were that deep. I am sorry if I did something to encourage your love for me." He waited for an answer, but Allison sat motionless, listening to his every word. A small tear raced down her cheek dropping silently onto her sweater.

"Let me ask you a question. What would your dad think if I told him I was in love with you?" But before she could answer, he added, "He would kill me! He would think I was some kind of a pervert!"

"That is where you are wrong," she said, sniffling. "He thinks it is all right for us to be in love with one another. I know because I asked him about it!"

Cole shouted out in disbelief, "You talked to him about us?"

"Yes."

"Oh my God! Oh my God! He began to get up, holding his hand against his forehead.

Allison grabbed his arm, keeping him from rising off of the floor. She repeated, loudly, "Yes! Yes, I did!" Cole sank back to the floor, still holding his head. "I talk to my dad about everything!" she exclaimed.

Cole continued, "Oh my God! He is going to kill me! I just know it! He is going to kill me!'

"No he isn't! Now stop it! Stop acting like a little kid!" she insisted, still holding his arm so he wouldn't get up. "Now listen to me! You feel like it is wrong to fall in love with someone you have known as a little kid. That is just the point I am trying to make. It isn't! Even my dad sees nothing wrong with it."

"What did you say to your dad?" he asked, shaking his head from side to side in disbelief.

Allison took a breath. In a calm, controlled voice, she answered, "I told my dad about the feelings I had for you. I, too, questioned whether or not these were feelings I should have. My dad listened to what I had to say. He told me that if I was sure that my feelings for you were genuine, then I should follow my heart." Pausing a moment, she added, "It isn't as if we are blood-related and it isn't as if we had these feelings when I was just a little kid. Cole, please tell me how do you feel about me?"

He stuttered, "I...I...can't really say." He decided he would continue the lie he started earlier. "A.J., my feelings are as I told you before. I think of you as my little sister...that is all," and then, as if it wasn't a good enough lie, repeated, "That is all."

Allison didn't believe it. She tried to convince him to open up, "I am not asking you to marry me...I am saying...maybe we should..., you know, get to know each other on a different level. Maybe get to know each other as boyfriend and girlfriend. What would you say to that?" she asked. Her heart felt as if it were in her throat.

Cole thought a moment, "A.J. I do love you very much. You know there is not a thing in this world that I wouldn't do for you," he exhaled loudly, "But right now I am at a different place in my life than you are." Looking past Allison blankly into the hay bales behind her, he explained, "You see, I have a lot on my plate right now. I have Jodie to think about."

He digressed a little, saying, "She is quite the kid, you know!" Looking back at Allison, he added, "Right now, Jodie is about all I can handle physically as well as emotionally. I really want to adopt her, you know. And I want to provide the best home I can. So, for right now, I cannot take on another emotion. It's a timing thing. The time is just not right for me. Believe me, it is not you. You are a beautiful, intelligent, exciting, vibrant woman. Any man would be proud to have you as a wife. But if you need me to commit to you today, I will have to decline." He squeezed his lips together in an upturned smile, "I'm sorry A.J...I cannot commit to any other relationships right now." It was very quiet.

"I am...very...very...sorry," he whispered.

It was Allison's turn to sit motionless this time. The barn was silent, except for an occasional noise from the horses downstairs. Cole, once again, looked longingly at the beautiful woman sitting across from him. He was thinking he must be crazy to turn her down on her proposal. But he had to think of Jodie, and his quest to give her his undivided attention. Deep in his heart, he remained convinced it wouldn't be right for him to pursue A.J.

Allison was devastated. It felt as if Cole had just ripped her insides out. She had thought he would tell her he loved her once he realized everyone approved. She thought she knew Cole better than this, but evidently she was wrong. She sucked up her hurt feelings, gathered her composure and collected her thoughts. She decided she would let Cole off of the hook politely. After all, it wasn't his fault he didn't feel the same way she did.

Finally, Allison spoke very softly, "Yes...yes, you are right. Jodie is a great kid. She deserves the best." She sniffled a little, dabbing a handkerchief at her tear-filled eyes. "I really love Jodie, and I think she really likes me. What do you honestly think?" she asked.

"Oh, I know she likes you! She loves you! She talks about how great you are and all of the girl things you two do together," he said, trying to lighten the conversation.

"Yeah, we do have fun. It is nice having another lady around." she said, chuckling softly, sounding congested from the tears. She thought to herself that what Jodie and Cole needed to complete the family was a wife and mother, such as herself. But her "timing" was not right, and she was not part of the plan.

"Thanks for having this conversation with me, Cole. I know it is probably silly. I just had to know how you felt about me. You do understand, don't you?"

"Yes. I hope you understand what I am going through right now and I hope I haven't hurt you," he said.

"No, not at all!" Then holding his hands in hers, "I think I want to be left alone for a little while to collect my thoughts." Looking toward the open area above the stalls, "I want to spend some time with Cinnamon," her favorite horse at the ranger station, "if you don't mind?"

"I understand. Okay. You gonna be okay?" he asked, as he stood up brushing the hay off of his trousers.

Allison stood up, her head coming to just below Cole's shoulders, "Yeah....Yep...I am okay!' she reached up putting both arms around his neck, stepping on her toes she gave Cole a short soft kiss. Moving her head back slightly, she whispered, "I love you, Cole Bryant." She gazed into his eyes.

Cole put his arms around Allison's tiny waist, pulled her hips close to his, feeling the warmth of her body against his, "I love you too, A.J. If things were just a little different..." he stretched out the sentence, then came back to reality, "but they aren't."

Allison parted her soft, tender lips, pulled herself closer to Cole giving him a long, passionate kiss that seemed to last for hours. Cole's brain went wild with passion for her, making him feel as if he were spinning around the room. He returned the kiss moving his hands up and down A.J.'s slender back, finally breaking away when he felt he couldn't take anymore without loosing total control.

"Wow! he gasped, "Wow! I don't think we should do anymore of that!" he chuckled, releasing A.J. from his grasp.

Allison caught her breath, lowering her hands to her sides, "Yeah, let's just say that was my goodbye kiss."

Cole, thinking she meant it was a kiss to send him on his way, turned around, galloped down the stairs and headed back to his cabin and Jodie.

Chapter 14

Cole entered the cabin letting in a gush of cold air. Removing his boots he gleefully said, "Halloo, there!"

Jodie was seated at the table bent over a writing tablet putting the finishing touches on her homework. "Uh huh," she mumbled, disgustingly, still not looking up.

Cole sat down at the table next to Jodie, "What's up?" he said, continuing the gleeful tone. He knew he was in the "dog house".

"Not much."

"What is the matter, little girl?" he put his arm on Jodie's back, rubbing it gently.

"You know by now, don't you?" she asked, looking up from her papers.

"Well, kinda'," he said, frowning. "Why did you get so mad at me? Huh?" placing his left hand on his chest to illustrate who he was talking about.

"'Cause sometimes you act really dumb! I don't mean to hurt your feelings. But, sometimes, you act just like a "typical" guy." She placed the pencil she was writing with on top of the table.

"I am a guy!" he chuckled.

Jodie didn't find that amusing, "Cole, do you love Ally?" she asked, looking into his eyes.

"Sounds like my little girl is growing up way too fast!" Cole exclaimed.

Jodie retorted, "That is not answering my question. You said I could ask you anything, didn't you?"

Cole knew another woman was being developed before his eyes, so he decided to answer. "Yes, I love her. I love her like a sister, Jodie. Why do you ask?"

She thought a moment, answering, "Well, Ally and I are really good friends. She shows me all kinds of neat things, like you do. Only, usually, they are girl things, you know? Since we spend a lot of time at the campground together, it is just natural that we would become good friends." She looked at her fingers, spreading them out on the tabletop, "Like my fingernails. Ally showed me how to cut them real nice and then, sometimes, she will let me use her fingernail polish to make them look real lady-like. Things like that."

She played with her pencil a little trying to say the proper words, "Well, since I like Ally and you like Ally, and Ally likes you and me, I kinda' thought it might be nice if you two became, like, boyfriend and girlfriend." She looked up at Cole sheepishly.

"That is nice." Cole leaned over kissing Jodie on the forehead, "That is what A.J. and I just talked over in the barn. See, I am not too dumb!" Gathering his thoughts, he continued, "When you get older you are going to find out that being boyfriend and girlfriend sometimes is not too easy. But for now, let's just say that Ally and I agreed that it is best to wait a little bit on being boyfriend and girlfriend." Grabbing her tiny, outstretched hands in his big callused hands, he asked, "Can you trust me on this one?"

"Yes, sir. But I want you to know that it would be nice to have you and Ally as my mommy and my daddy."

"You're a great kid." He hugged her across the shoulders.

Three days later, Cole was working in the office when he heard one of the airplane engines on the frozen lake come to life. He instinctively looked at the logbook on the far corner of his desk. Whenever one of the rangers would fly somewhere, they would write in the log the time they were leaving, where they were going, and when they thought they would return.

Cole did not remember any entries in the log for the day, so he double-checked to see if he had missed an entry. Sure enough there wasn't an entry. He walked through the open doorway into Ranger Defreese's office to the far side where the large windows faced the lake.

Looking through the cold windowpanes, he noticed the engine was running on A.J.'s Cessna. The airplane was facing his way so he could make out the face in the cabin as that of A.J. The engine increased in rpm's flinging the loose snow under the wings and out past the tail of the airplane. The airplane moved slowly forward turned around, then headed in the opposite direction out into the wide, open area of the frozen lake. The powdery white layer of snow that covered the frozen surface continued to be blown rearward as the rush of air created by the propeller slowly increased the speed of the airplane. When the airplane reached mid-lake, the engine revved higher, and the airplane sped even faster down the lake, finally lifting off of the frozen surface, climbing higher and higher until it disappeared on the other side of the mountain.

Cole continued to stare out the window as he muttered to himself, "I wonder where she is going?"

"What?" Cole had not noticed Bill Defreese come into the office and stand next to him at the bank of windows. Cole, deep in thought, kind of jerked when Bill had spoken.

"Oh, nothing," more plainly this time, "I was just wondering where A.J. was off to."

"Oh, yes," Bill continued to look at the lake as if waiting for another airplane to taxi down the makeshift runway.

Cole didn't say anything, waiting for Bill to continue. But, he didn't say anything. Just silence.

"Well?" Cole asked, "You gonna tell me where she is going?" looking at Bill, with a disgusted frown.

"Oh, she is going to Juneau," he turned around and headed to his desk. Sitting down, he pretended to be working.

Cole, still at the windows, turned around facing Bill. He didn't say anything for quite awhile. He knew something was happening here. He just had not figured out what was happening. "You gonna tell me why she is going to Juneau or am I going to have to ask you every little question to find out what is going on here?" he demanded, sternly.

Bill slowly looked up from his desk. Cole could sense by the expression on Bill's face that he wasn't too pleased with him. Studying his face, he took a deep breath, and exhaled, then folded his arms across his belly, leaning back in his chair.

"What?" Cole asked, "What?"

"You have no idea?" pausing, "You really have no idea, do you?"

"I guess not! What on earth is going on, Bill?"

"Allison is moving to Juneau," he stated flatly.

"What? Juneau? Why?"

"I think maybe you should come over here and sit down, son," Bill instructed.

Cole did as he was told, settling uneasily into one of the big leather chairs in front of the desk.

"Allison has decided to go work for Dr. Lerner, the veterinarian in Juneau," Bill started. "You see, she wants to get the experience of working with many different kinds of animals."

"Gee, I thought she would be right here forever." Cole said, almost as if he were asking a question. "You know how it is. You just never figure a person you have known for so long is going to move away," he said, slowly, reflecting on the past.

"Well, she is moving to Juneau!' Bill said, matter of factly, "You better get used to it!" a kind of bitter tone to his voice.

Cole sat quietly for a minute thinking something was still not quite right about this sudden move for A.J. "I wonder why she didn't say anything to me about this?" and then, "How long has she been planning this move to Juneau?"

Bill leaned forward in his chair placing both elbows on the desk, "She didn't want you to know."

Cole was shocked, "What?...Why?"

"Well, Cole, it seems you two don't see eye-to-eye on some very important matters," exhaling he asked, "Do you know what I am talking about?'

Cole's mind was racing through his last conversation with A.J. three days ago. He was thinking, "What am I going to tell this man? More importantly what did A.J. tell him?" He stuttered at first, "She thought we should get more serious.....you know what I am saying?" He looked desperately at Bill, shifting uneasily in the big leather chair, picking aimlessly at the crease in his pants with his fingers. Cole was hoping Bill would show some sign of acknowledgement that he knew what he was talking about. But, Bill was upset over Allison leaving the station and he was not going to give Cole any breaks.

"Bill...I have always thought of A.J. as a little sister, nothing more. I want you to believe that, do you?" he begged.

"Yes," he sat motionless, staring directly at Cole.

"Well, evidently A.J. has had different thoughts for quite sometime." He swallowed so hard it could be heard across the desk. Beads of sweat started to form on Cole's forehead, "Sunday afternoon she confronted me with her feelings," he took a deep breath, "and she wanted to know how I felt." The room was very quiet, the grandfather clock on the far wall could be heard ticking.

"So?" Bill asked, raising his eyebrows.

Cole swallowed hard again, this time rubbing his neck with his right hand, "Well, I told her that I wasn't ready to commit to another relationship right now. I have my hands full taking care of Jodie, and trying to get the right to adopt her."

Bill said, bluntly, "Do you love Allison?"

For the first time in his life, Cole was petrified with fear. He stammered when he spoke, "Bill...Bill, this very awkward. I have never...I have never made a...pass at your daughter...

"Is that what this is about?" Bill interrupted, "You're afraid that I won't like the idea of you falling in love with my daughter, right?"

"Yeah, kinda'."

"Let me ask you a question. You answer it completely honestly. Promise?"

"Yes, if you promise not to hate me?"

"Deal." Bill quickly answered.

"Do you love my daughter as a more that just a good friend or brother?"

Cole sat up straight in the big chair, "That is hard to say for sure, Bill," leaning forward, he continued, "You see, every now and then the last couple of years, I would feel a little funny around A.J. You know, strange! I couldn't put my finger on it because I have not thought of her as a girlfriend. He got up from the chair, walked to the windows and stared out into open space, not really seeing anything, still deep in thought. "The other day when A.J. insisted," he put extra emphasis on the word insisted, "we have our little pow-wow, it was like I saw her for the first time."

He turned around facing Bill, "I saw her as a woman. Like I would see any other woman I would meet. I saw A.J. as a woman for the first time ever!" Looking down at the wood floor, he said, "That is when I knew what those funny feelings were. It was me being attracted to your daughter."

Cole returned to the big leather chair, sitting gently down into the soft cushion, but not leaning back, "So, to answer your question, I think I may love A.J.. But I am not ready to commit to any new relationship right now," he paused, "It is just not the right time, if you know what I mean?"

"Yes. Yes I do know what you mean," Bill answered. "Unfortunately A.J. has decided time is passing her by. She wants to get her life on track, so to speak. She is afraid she may end up an old maid if she continues to live out here in the middle of nowhere waiting on you."

Cole looked depressed, "I can understand. It is just not the time for me...not the time."

Bill agreed, then added, "I just want you to understand that if you ever decided to marry my daughter, I would be proud to have you as a son-in-law. But, that is between you and Allison."

The winter months passed dark and slow. After the winter solstice passed, the daylight hours slowly increased. Sometimes, even the weather would pretend that spring was not too far off. Sunday March third, though, opened with a blizzard brewing outside. The winds gusted as high as fifty-three miles an hour, blowing the wind driven snow horizontally across the landscape. Cole had wanted Jodie to spend the day indoors, out of the wind. It was dangerous to go outside with such high winds for fear of being struck by a fallen limb or even a tree blowing over, weighted down by the snow and ice on the limbs.

Jodie had adopted some wild rabbits that had strayed out onto the frozen lake. Evidently the mother rabbit had become disoriented because she kept taking the baby rabbits in circles. So, Jodie had brought the family of rabbits to the pen, since it was unoccupied at the time.

She told Cole she needed to go to the barn to make sure they had food and water. Cole said he would do it, since he had to go out anyway. Jodie said they were her bunnies and she was going to take care of them. Reluctantly, Cole agreed.

This time of year, the campground was occupied by only a few brave and hearty soles that love to trap and hunt, or ice fish in the frozen lake. No one paid much attention to the hairy faced, big man that occupied one of the small travel trailers at the outer edge of the campground. The stranger kept to himself, very rarely being seen by any of the workers around the ranger station for the seven days he had spent there.

However, the big man was watching everyone else at the station. As he sat out on the ice-covered lake fishing, next to the round hole he cut in the ice, he was also observing the movements of everyone at the station. Even at night, if someone had been watching the big man, they would have seen him crouched beside a tree or behind a bush tracking his next victim.

So, early that Sunday morning, the big, hairy man cranked up his old Chevy 4x4 truck, letting it warm up as he finished packing his things into the enclosed bed at the rear. He looked around with his dark eyes thinking the weather had turned out perfect to carry out his plan. When he was finished loading the truck, he drove it through the foot deep snow to the unoccupied maintenance barn.

Getting out of the truck he held his back to the gusty wind, made his way to the big barn door, unlatched it letting it swing wide open. He climbed back into the truck, and carefully backed the Chevy into the maintenance barn. Then, he quickly got out of the truck, hurrying to the big door. Taking a quick look around the area outside the building, he satisfied himself that no one saw him enter. He pushed hard against the big door to overcome the force of the wind until he got it shut. Then he ran a big board through the door to lock it shut so it couldn't be opened from the outside.

The big man walked to the small door that opened out into the fenced in pen, slowly opening it making sure no one was nearby. Seeing no one, he leaned out into the cage, grabbing one of the baby rabbits. He quickly closed the door. Tying a string around the rabbit, he cracked the door open wedging a small stone beneath the door to keep it from closing. Then he placed the rabbit inside the barn just beyond the door opening, but still visible from outside.

Patiently, he waited in the freezing barn, the rabbit frozen in fear and restrained by the string the big man held in his hand. Twenty minutes passed and, as if on cue, Jodie approached the pen trudging through the deep snow leaning her tiny body into the wind to keep from being blown away. She wore her thickest coat and pants, two pairs of long-johns underwear, a thick fur-lined hat with attached earmuffs, and a scarf wrapped around her head covering her entire face except for her big, brown eyes.

Smoke, now a "teenage" wolf, was unaffected by the chilling cold. He bounced around Jodie running in circles glad to be out of the house. Occasionally, he would run off to a bush or a tree to investigate an unusual movement, which to him, could be a bug or small animal he could play with. Every now and then he would jump up towards Jodie to see if she would play with him. But she wasn't in the mood for that. All she wanted to do was to make sure the rabbits were taken care of, then head back to her warm, safe cabin.

Opening the gate to the pen, Jodie told Smoke, "Stay out her Smoke. Stay!" Closing the gate behind her she walked softly to the small wooden house where the rabbits had been staying. Peering in the house, she saw the mother rabbit and five babies. She could not find the sixth bunny.

Suddenly, Smoke started acting funny. He paced up and down the fencing, emitting a low growl, his eyes took on an intense, evil look.

Turning around, Jodie asked, "What's wrong boy?" She stood up, went to the fence poked her glove-covered hand through the wires of the fence to rub Smoke's nose. Smoke became more agitated growling louder and deeper, sometimes putting his two front paws up on the fence. "You want to get into the pen to play with the rabbits, don't you?" Jodie giggled, "Well, not today. You just calm down. I'm missing one of them. Let me find it, okay?" She drew her hand back from the fencing and turning back to the building she noticed the barn door partially opened.

"That's odd," she thought. Then, she noticed the baby rabbit just inside the door. Crouching down she slowly walked to the rabbit, her hand slightly extended as if calling for the rabbit. As she reached down to grab the rabbit, a lassoed rope dropped around her arms and body and was instantly drawn tight making it impossible for Jodie to escape. She let out a scream, "Eeek! Smoke!"

Smoke went crazy outside the pen, growling and howling angrily as he raced back and forth around the fenced in area trying to get to Jodie. He literally climbed the fencing, trying to find a way into the pen. But there was no way to get to his master. Foam and saliva covered his mouth, dripping to the white snow, as he continued to try to get into the pen.

The big man with the lasso whirled the tiny girl around to face him, pulling down the scarf to expose her mouth. Her eyes, big as charcoal briquettes, looked at her attacker, "Daddy!" she shouted in shock.

He stuffed a handkerchief in her opened mouth growling, "Shut up!" Tying another large handkerchief around her head to hold the handkerchief in her mouth, he slung her under one arm, still holding the lasso tightly as she twisted and turned trying to get loose. He quickly made the distance to the open door of the Chevy truck.

He pushed her into the seat of the truck, quickly fastening the seat belt. Her arms were still trapped beneath the lasso and now, the seat belt, making it impossible for her to squirm loose. Quickly running to the driver's side of the truck, he removed the big board locking the barn door shut, then jumped into the truck closing the door quickly.

As soon as Smoke heard the noise at the big barn door, which would have been imperceptible for a human to detect with the howling wind being so loud, he raced around the building to meet the attacker. The barn door was still closed when the wolf bounced against it. The dog's weight was not enough to move the door, it only shook a little. Again the enraged wolf hit the door. Nothing.

The truck engine roared to life. The wolf ran in circles, bounced against the door, and leaned on the door with his front claws digging at the worn wooden surface, leaving big trails of dug up wood. Dawson put the truck in gear, eased out on the clutch to move the truck slowly forward, pushing the big barn doors open.

As soon as the barn doors opened enough for the wolf to squeeze through, Smoke ran to the driver's side of the truck, leaping up at the closed window, leaving big wet trails of saliva streaking down and long, deep scratches in the faded, black paint of the door. Bashing his head against the window in an effort to break through, the wolf snarled and howled viciously like a rabid dog.

"Ha, ha, ha! You stupid mutt!" Dawson growled, as he drove the truck through the partially opened doors. A gust of wind caught the left-hand door swinging it on the hinges and slamming it noisily against the barn wall. The other door dragged along Jodie's side of the truck until the truck cleared the building.

Dawson turned the vehicle to the right, picking up speed as he drove down the snow-covered gravel road that led to the paved main road. The tracks made earlier by the truck coming up to the barn were almost swept away by the continuously falling snow, and the gusty wind coming off of the lake. Smoke continued to run beside the black truck leaping at the driver's door, sometimes running around the truck to the front, standing in the road in an effort to stop the vehicle.

But, of course, Dawson was not stopping. As a matter of fact he wanted the dog to stay at the front of the truck so he could run him over. The wolf even tried to break down the rear gate of the speeding truck.

Dawson wickedly chuckled, "That wolf of yours sure is dumb. Look at it! It thinks it can stop this truck!"

Jodie twisted and turned in her restraints trying to scream, but only muffled sounds came through the handkerchief.

"Shut up you little pest!" he shouted, as the truck came closer to the intersection at the main road.

The gravel road was stable and passable with the loose snow covering it. However, the main road was constructed of asphalt. Since asphalt is black in color, it retains much more heat than the white gravel, also when the temperature rises just a little the snow melts. Then when the temperatures drop below freezing, the water on the surface of the asphalt freezes forming ice.

Such was the case today. The snow covered asphalt road looked the same as the snow covered gravel road, only underneath, was a thin layer of ice that had formed the day before when it was warmer and sunnier. Dawson, not being a great driver, had not considered this when he started to negotiate the left-hand turn onto the main road.

Touching the brakes as he entered the corner to reduce the speed of the truck, everything was fine until the wheels passed onto the ice slickened paved roadway. Instead of continuing to turn left, the vehicle continued straight passing across the width of the roadway into the shallow ditch on the other side, coming to rest in an awkward tilted position.

"Oh crap!" he said, as the truck came to a stop killing the engine. He quickly restarted the truck, shifted into four-wheel drive, put it in first gear, and attempted to power out of the ditch on the other side. The truck, at first, responded slowly, then the wheels dug in as the overhanging front bumper caught on the mud-covered side of the ditch.

He shifted to reverse applying power as he let out the clutch. The wheels caught instantly pulling the truck slowly out of the ditch onto the paved road, "Ah ha!" he laughed, sounding really relieved. Leaving the truck in four-wheel drive, he shifted to first gear. This time, he let the clutch out slowly, so as to keep the vehicle from sliding on the slick roadway.

The truck began to pick up speed as it headed down the main road that led out of the valley. The wolf was still snarling and jumping at the side of the truck, and Jodie still restrained in the seat.

Dawson was real proud of himself. Everything had gone according to plan. The little girl had shown up at the pen right on time, and his plan to avoid the wolf had worked flawlessly. Plans are only good until something unknown happens. The unknown in this case was the next reaction of the wolf.

Smoke was beginning to tire, as Dawson had figured he would. But the wolf was a hunter by nature. And nature took its course in the next two minutes. The wolf, also, realized he could not chase the truck much longer so he reverted back to his hunter instincts, slowing down, and turning away from the speeding truck.

Dawson looked in his mirror as the dog disappeared into the ditch along the road, "Well, Jodie, your dog is not going to help you anymore 'cause it just ran out of steam..ha, ha, ha.." His laugh was evil sounding.

Dawson was not a good driver. He was a person that held onto the steering wheel, turning it back and forth erratically. He was not "one" with the vehicle, so to speak. As he preceded down the road concentrating on keeping the truck between the evenly spaced sticks that pointed out the direction of the road, his lack of driving ability was evident by the jerky motion back and to of the truck.

Several minutes passed. Suddenly out of nowhere, the wolf leaped onto the hood of the truck crashing into the windshield, smashing it into millions of small pieces directly between the two occupants in the seat of the truck.

Smoke had used the inbred hunter instincts to catch up with the truck by disappearing behind the cover of the surrounding hills, taking a more direct overland course to intersect with the unsuspecting prey, Dawson Patterson.

After crashing into the windshield, the wolf continued to slide across the top of the truck falling into a deep snowdrift on the far side of the road. Totally taken by surprise, Dawson jerked the wheel to the right.

The truck spun out of control turning around several times, but luckily for him, not leaving the road.

Bert had the watch that morning, and had spent the first hours patrolling the lake area making sure the airplanes were tethered good against the gusty wind. He had heard the truck engine rev up when it had skidded into the ditch, but he had not seen the truck or the wolf from his position on the frozen lake. Then, out of curiosity, wondering who would be out in this kind of weather, he had remained on the lake looking toward the main road to catch a glimpse of the vehicle.

Just as the truck appeared in his field of vision, the wolf sprang from the hilltop crashing into the windshield, falling limply into the snowbank. Bert witnessed the truck spin out of control, then restart and continue on its way down the road.

Bert immediately spoke into his walkie talkie. "Hey! Hey!' he said, still shocked by what he had seen, "We have a major problem on the main road! Can you hear me?"

An instant later the radio came to life, "Yes, this is Emilio", "This is Cole", "Josh here."

"Everyone, something really odd is going on out by the main road. I just saw a speeding black truck that got hit by a wolf," he said, frantically.

Cole being first in charge asked, "You mean a speeding truck hit a wolf?"

Bert answered, quickly, "No. I mean a wolf purposely jumped off a hill into the windshield of a speeding truck!" he thought a moment adding, "Where is Smoke?"

Cole still trying to grasp the situation blankly responded, "Smoke is with Jodie at the pen." Then it began to sink in, "Wait a minute do you think...?" he left the sentence unfinished, "I'm going to the pen now!"

Bert shouted over the whistling wind, "I'm going to check out the wolf." As he walked toward the sight of the collision Bert could hear several conversations going on over the walkie talkie, "All men report to the maintenance barn with survival packs and weapons in ten minutes," he heard someone say.

Bert approached the wolf slowly, not knowing if it was dead or just wounded badly. The wolf was motionless, but as far as he could see, not bleeding. He now knew it was Smoke by the big red collar around the wolf's neck. He bent down just as the dog regained consciousness, letting out a soft howl. He petted the dog and spoke into the walkie talkie, "Cole, this is Bert. The wolf is Smoke. Have you found Jodie?"

Cole was breathless by the time he reached the pen area. He could see the tracks of the dog and Jodie going up to the pen. Jodie's tracks continued across the pen into the barn. The wolf's tracks were everywhere around the pen, having pushed the snow aside in every direction, then led off around the side of the barn.

Cole went through the pen into the barn where he saw the rabbit attached to the string, "Oh no!" he muttered. About that time Bert's message came over the walkie-talkie, and he realized Jodie had been abducted. He shouted into the walkie–talkie, "Someone has taken Jodie!"

He quickly ran through the barn to the open doors that were now swinging wildly back and forth being pushed by the gusty wind. Once again, the wolf's tracks met up with him. He noted the truck tracks heading down the gravel road, "Someone has taken Jodie!" he shouted again into the microphone.

Bert's voice came over the speaker, "I have Smoke, he appears okay just was knocked out from hitting the truck. He must have been trying to save Jodie."

"Who was in the truck? Anyone know?" Cole asked, over the walkie talkie.

Bert answered, "I don't know who it is, but the truck was an old black Chevy with a topper on it, I think."

A moment or two passed. Emilio answered, "There was a loner in the campground staying in a small trailer that had a black truck with a topper. I will go there now."

Cole ran across the station to the dining hall where he had seen the jeep parked. He quickly started the jeep, checked to make sure it had gasoline and a survival pack in the back. Then he ran to the cabin, grabbing his rifle, pistol and hunting knife. By the time he got back to the jeep, the engine was warmed up, so he put it in four-wheel drive and sped down the path to the main road.

When he arrived at the crash site he brought the jeep to a quick stop. Bert had Smoke by the collar, the dog barking loudly. "He wants to run down the road, Cole! I don't think I can hold him much longer!'

Cole jumped out of the jeep dashing over to the ditch where the wolf was being contained by Bert, "Is he hurt?", he shouted over the wind.

"I don't think so. He is very strong, you know!"

Cole took Smoke by the collar, and led him into the jeep telling the wolf to stay. The dog did as he was told. Cole gave Bert instructions to get a search team together and follow his tracks on the road. Bert was to notify the state police to be on alert for the black Chevy truck. He, also, told Bert, since he would be out of walkie talkie range, if he ever had to leave the road, he would leave some sort of a sign for him. Bert agreed heading back to the maintenance barn where the others were beginning to arrive.

Cole jumped into the jeep with Smoke, and sped down the road in search of Jodie and her abductor. The canvass top on the jeep did not do a good job of keeping the freezing air out, so Cole had the heater blasting hot air out from under the dash as they picked up speed following the tracks cut through the snow by the Chevy truck.

The only way to know the direction of the road was to stay between the markers that had been placed at evenly spaced intervals along the outer edge of the asphalt. The deep snow made it impossible to follow the road without the markers. It was apparent to Cole that the driver of the other vehicle was having a hard time keeping the truck in the center of the roadway. The tracks he was following weaved from one side to the other between the markers.

As the jeep climbed to the higher elevation of the mountain, not only did the road begin to twist and turn more up the side of the mountain, but the wind picked up, sometimes gusting over fifty miles per hour. Cole figured he was gaining slightly on the Chevy because the tracks in the road appeared to be fresher and less covered by the newly fallen and wind blown snow. The visibility had decreased to almost zero, as he drove through Gold Diggers Notch. The wind raged, blowing the snow so fast that it actually stung a little when it hit his face as it blew in from the open sides of the jeep.

He slowed the jeep to a crawl, not only because of the poor visibility but, also, the wind threatened to blow the small vehicle off of the extremely slippery road. At one point, he saw the Chevy's tracks twist in a circle, then continue across the pass weaving back and forth between the markers. To Cole, this was both a good sign and a bad sign.

It was good because it meant the driver of the truck was having a hard time keeping the truck on the road. That meant, perhaps, he would end up in a ditch, and Cole would be able to catch him. It was a bad sign, on the other hand, because the other driver may end up driving off of a cliff or rolling the vehicle over, hurting or killing Jodie.

As he drove along, his total concentration was to catch the truck ahead somehow. But, occasionally he would try to think of the reason someone would want to abduct Jodie. This was a question he just could not answer. However, it was apparent to him that Jodie was not taken by coincidence. Thinking back to the scene at the barn, it was obvious that this abduction had been planned out. The abductor had laid the trap to catch Jodie, but why?

The wind blew hard and steady against the black 4x4 driven by Dawson as he headed down the outer slope of the mountains into the flat plain ahead. Visibility was limited to twenty or thirty yards because of the blizzard conditions as the wind blown snow flew horizontal to the ground. Heading down the curving road from Gold Diggers Notch, Dawson almost mistakenly drove into the deep ditch on either side of the road.

Jodie had remained silent, her mouth stuffed with the handkerchief, her hands bound by the lasso and seat belt. She was silently praying that Dawson would make a mistake sliding them into a ditch. She had cried, silently, a long time thinking that Smoke had given his life to try to stop the truck. She was worried that Cole would not know what happened to her until he missed her coming back to the cabin. Then that would be too late to figure out where she was.

At that moment, a huge gust of wind caught the truck from the side making it swerve to the left. Dawson over corrected for the blast of air, turning the wheel sharply to the right. Just as he did this the wind ceased, causing the truck to make a sharp right-hand turn running straight into the deep ditch on the right side of the road.

The truck stopped instantly, as it hit the bottom of the ditch, throwing Dawson forward, his chest hitting the steering wheel, and his head crashing into the windshield. Jodie was jerked forward, but since she was tightly held in her seat, she did not strike anything.

There was a short period of silence as the occupants regained their senses. The wind still whistled around the truck. Dawson slowly realized what had happened, pushing himself back from the steering wheel. Small droplets of blood formed on the left side of his forehead. The truck was at a steep angle pointed forward. The front of it in the bottom of the deep ditch, the rear still up at the road level.

Dawson attempted to start the truck, but too much damage had been done at the front. The engine would not crank. "Crap!" he shouted, "Crap! You stupid kid caused all of this!" he shouted. He took the back of his hand and hit Jodie across the face in anger.

The force from the blow knocked Jodie's head towards the door turning her cheek red. Jodie began to cry. He had hurt her. She thought to herself this was just like him always blaming his mistakes on someone else. He used to do that with her mother all the time. Suddenly, she had a flashback to when he was beating her mom. She remembered it was late at night in the hallway of their house. Dawson had come home drunk, as usual. He was yelling at her mom and beating her. She began to cry even harder. She missed her mom so much.

Dawson opened the door on his side of the truck. It creaked and popped as it opened having been jammed between the fender and the body during the violent descent into the ditch. He grabbed the rifle from the rack at the back of the cab jumping out the truck sinking up to his chest in snow. Slowly he made his way up the side of the ditch to the roadway hanging onto the side of the truck as he went.

He opened the back gate, extracted two sets of snowshoes and two backpacks. Laying them in the road, he made his way down the right-side of the truck, unbuckled Jodie, and hauled her up to the frozen, windswept roadway. After they put on their backpacks and snowshoes, Dawson removed the handkerchief from Jodie's mouth, and released her arms from the lasso, keeping her body still securely fastened by the rope. Holding the rope in one hand, Dawson grabbed a map of the area from the cab of the truck, telling Jodie to cross the ditch and head cross-country.

Slowly they made their way through the wind driven snow. Dawson checked his compass every couple of minutes, for he knew if he stayed on a northwest course he would, eventually, come to the Great Alaskan Railroad. Once there, they could hop on the train, which would slow down to take on passengers as it made its way down the state to the Canadian border.

This area of the country was fairly flat, treeless, with small gentle slopes that formed shallow valleys, all of which were covered deeply in pure white snow. Visibility was held at no more than thirty yards because of the blinding wind and snow, and because everything, the ground, the sky and the background, was coated in white.

As Cole pushed the little old jeep to the limits trying to catch up to the black Chevy truck he noticed that the tracks were appearing to be fresher. Smoke had regained full consciousness, and appeared to be helping Cole find his way, sitting straight up in the front passenger seat. The winds had been the worst as he passed through Gold Diggers Notch, but the visibility coming down the mountain was still very poor.

Suddenly out of nowhere, the rear end of the black Chevy truck appeared to his right. Shocked by the sudden sight, Cole slammed on the brakes putting the jeep into a four-wheeled slide on the ice slickened road. As the jeep slid by the other truck, Smoke jumped out of the jeep, rushing up to the closed doors growling and howling. He circled the old truck ready to pounce at the enemy that had taken his master.

The jeep continued down the roadway several hundred feet, finally coming to a stop in the center of the road still pointed in the right direction. Cole, his adrenaline flowing viciously, grabbed his rifle, cocked the mechanism, and jumped from the jeep in a crouched position using the vehicle as a shield. Through the blizzard conditions, the black truck remained fuzzy to his sight. But he could make out Smoke ranting and raving beside the truck. No life could be seen moving inside the vehicle.

Gazing around in all directions, Cole did not see anyone, so he slowly approached the vehicle. When he was within twenty feet of the rear of the truck, he made a dash to the left side of the truck. Peering through the windows, he discovered the cab and rear of the truck were empty.

By this time, Smoke had started across the ditch following the tracks made by the snowshoes. Cole made note of the tracks, headed back to the jeep, backing it up to the 4x4. He removed his snowshoes and backpack from the jeep. He placed the shoes on his boots, picked up the backpack, slinging it over his shoulder, and headed off in the direction of the other tracks.

"Smoke!" he said, quietly. The dog appeared almost instantly from the veil of wind and snow. "I want you to guide me. Stay with me, okay?" he said, calmly, holding his glove covered hand down for Smoke to sniff and lick. He didn't know if the dog understood, but it made him feel closer to the animal.

Cole knew the others from the station would be along shortly, see the trucks and follow his tracks through the snow. About that time, Cole noticed a small, red patch in the pure white snow. He bent down to get a closer look.

Dabbing his fingertip in the red liquid, he muttered, "Blood!". He could only hope it was the abductor's blood. Again the thought crossed his mind, "Who would want to take Jodie? For what purpose?"

As he struggled through the freezing cold he kept trying to answer those questions. He tried to keep his emotions in tack mentally and, also, pace himself physically so that he would have enough energy to bring down his "prey" when that time came.

As the day wore on, the wind began to subside, and the visibility increased. He could tell he was slowly catching up to Jodie and the mystery person by the crispness of the tracks he followed.

Late in the day, as he began his way up a small rise, he noticed Smoke standing motionless facing him. He slowed his pace as he approached closer to the wolf, who had now lain down in the snow. Thinking this odd he, too, crouched down beside the wolf.

Smoke stayed down on his belly, crawling up to the apex of the hill. Keeping his head down. Cole imitated the wolf up the hill until he could see beyond the knoll. There, in the shallow valley below, Jodie and her attacker could be seen walking away from them. The wolf crawled away from the hilltop and, once clear of the view from below, ran around in circles a moment or two. Then Smoke headed off around the side of the hillside, out of site of the attacker.

Cole could see what the wolf was up to. Smoke was going to use the cover of the hills to get ahead of Jodie and her abductor, like wolf packs do when they hunt, creating a trap.

Cole peered back over the hilltop, estimating the man and Jodie were about a half mile away. Looking skyward, he figured he had, at best, an hour of daylight left. As soon as the two passed over the next small hill, Cole headed out following the tracks at a much faster pace to shorten the gap between them.

The wind had subsided now and the snow had stopped falling. He covered the distance across the shallow valley in half the time it took Jodie and Dawson. On the other side of the valley, he once again peered over the next knoll. The two of them were no more than three hundred yards away, sitting down taking a break.

Cole looked around. He noted daylight was fading fast. So he decided to take a break, also, and wait for darkness to give him cover so he could possibly get closer. The problem was not catching up with the pair, which he had done, but surprising the man so that he would not harm Jodie or use her as a shield to protect himself. As of yet, Cole had not figured out a way to surprise the unknown abductor.

During the day as they had trekked across the deep snow, Jodie had asked her dad why he was doing this? Why would he take her when he disliked her so much? Dawson had answered, "Look kid, this is nothin'

personal. Just keep your mouth shut and do as you're told and nothin'
will happen to you!"

"But I don't get it!" she exclaimed, "If you hate me so much, why did
you come all the way up here to grab me?"

"I said shut up!" he bellowed, "All I'm gonna say is if you do as
you're told, nothing will happen to you. Once you get me what I want,
you can go back to this God forsaken place!"

She kept on, "What do you want me to get for you?" he didn't
answer so she asked again, "What do you want me to get for you?"

Dawson blurted out in anger, "Money! Money, stupid!"

"Money? Did you say money?" she asked, "I don't have any
money!"

"That's right you little pest! You don't! But the insurance company
has plenty. All I want you to do is sign a paper that gives me the insurance money!"

"I still don't get it. What insurance money?" she asked, with a puzzled look on her face.

"Your momma had insurance, and you are going to sign the money
over to me!" his voice was evil sounding.

Jodie began to cry when she thought of her mother, and the way her
dad treated her. She missed her mom so much.

"Mommy left me some money?" she asked, through the tears.

Dawson jerked on the rope pulling Jodie along, "That's right! Seems
as though your mom thought she could hide the insurance policy from
me!" he chuckled, in a low voice, "But I found it, and now you're gonna
sign it over to me."

"So give me the paper and I will sign it."

"I wished it was that easy. You gotta do that in front of the man from
the insurance company, so I'm taking you to him." he growled.

As daylight quickly faded into darkness, the moonlight cast a pastel
blue glow on the snow-covered landscape. The pair continued toward
the railroad tracks, now just two miles away. Cole remained in close pur-
suit, but out of sight. He could see Jodie and her abductor silhouetted

against the snow. Now that he had figured out where they were headed, he realized he had to find a way to surprise the man soon.

Cole caught a movement out of the corner of his eye, off to his right. He froze in his tracks peering into the darkness in the distance. Suddenly, over the crest of the hill he saw Smoke rush diagonally down the hill toward the backside of the abductor, not making a sound.

Cole immediately cocked the rifle he was carrying, and headed toward Jodie and the man as fast as he could. The wolf sprang from the ground, running at full speed, grabbing the man at his neck. The man's head jerked back, not knowing what hit him. The force of the big dog's speed and weight knocked the man forward into the snow. The wolf continued running forward when he landed on the snow. Turning around abruptly, Smoke headed back for a second strike at the fallen man.

Dawson instinctively tried to get himself up off of the ground, trying to figure out what was going on. He looked back at Jodie, who was frozen in her tracks with terror trying to understand what had just happened. He felt an agonizing pain in his neck, where the wolf's teeth had punctured the skin, and the force of the attack had nearly broken his neck. Reaching up to the back of his neck with his hand, he felt the warm blood gushing from the wounds.

Just as Dawson got to his knees, the wolf attacked him from the front. This time Smoke's mouth opened wide capturing Dawson's whole face. The teeth punctured the skin in a dozen places across his face from below the chin, across his cheek bones, to just below his left eye. This time the force of the attack pushed Dawson over backwards, buckling his legs under his torso. Dawson, now more aware of what was happening, let out a horrible scream, not only of pain but, also, of fear.

Cole arrived at the sight of the attack, "Run over the hill Jodie!" he shouted, "Run over there, quickly!" She did as she was told.

The wolf was now heading back for a third attack, "Smoke! No!" Cole commanded.

The wolf slowed slightly but the animal instinct was to kill his prey. Smoke grabbed Dawson one more time, this time attacking the man's

flailing arms. The teeth ripped away the sleeve of the heavy coat and
the glove.

"Smoke, no!" Cole, again, shouted. This time the wolf obeyed,
snarling loudly, the first sound Smoke had made during the attack.

Dawson was writhing in pain, his blood staining the pure white snow.
"Oow...oow...help me...ow...argh," he was screaming. He picked his
head up slightly to see what had happened to him.

Smoke came closer to Dawson, glaring at the downed man with his
evil looking eyes. The dog's mouth remained half-open, tongue hanging
out, salvia foaming from his mouth, and traces of Dawson's blood spat-
tered on his nose. A deep, angry growl emanated from Smoke's throat.

Dawson put his hands to his face screaming, "Kill him, don't let him
kill me...please get him out of here!"

Cole quickly removed Dawson's rifle from the area and threw it
toward Jodie. "Shut up and don't move or the wolf will make mince
meat out of you!" Cole yelled, still pointing the rifle at Dawson.
"Good job Smoke...very good job!" Cole reached over, patting the
wolf on the shoulder.

"Okay mister, sit up, but don't move!" he commanded, "Come on
sit up!"

Dawson did as he was told, keeping a fearful eye on the menacing
wolf. He didn't say a word.

"Who are you? And why did you abduct Jodie? Cole asked, the rifle
still pointing at Dawson.

Dawson moaned a little, finally answering, "My name is Dawson
Patterson. And the girl is my daughter!" Then getting up more nerve, he
raised his voice, growling, "And you are in deep trouble, mister. I'm
gonna sue the pants off you and the National Park Service!" Gathering
even more strength, he continued, "Who the heck do you think you are
attacking me and my daughter like this?" He started to move a little. But
Smoke growled, scaring Dawson back into submission.

Cole looked at the bleeding man, his jacket sleeve torn away exposing
a badly bleeding, tattooed arm. The disgust swelled up inside him. This
was the low-life that abandoned his child on the docks of Farrow's

Patch. The man that told his little girl that he hated her, and didn't want to see her again. And now, he was professing to be an innocent, loving father…the gall!

"Shut up you low-life! You abandoned her, and now you have the nerve to say I am the one in trouble. I oughta' let this wolf finish you off!"

Partially turning around, Cole shouted over his shoulder to Jodie, "Jodie, are you all right?"

In the distance he heard her answer, "Yes sir!'

"I'm sending Smoke to stay with you while I take care of Dawson." He could not bring himself to call Dawson her father. "Smoke, go to Jodie," he pointed toward the girl as he spoke. The dog obeyed, leaving the two men alone.

When Cole had turned his attention, briefly, toward Jodie, Dawson slipped his hunting knife out of the sheath attached to his belt, holding it in his hand hidden under his body. Cole turned back to Dawson crouching down on his knees beside the wounded man. He laid his rifle in the snow out of reach of Dawson. Cole removed his backpack, set it on the snow, opening the medicine pack.

As Cole bent over Dawson to administer first aid to the badly bleeding man, Dawson pulled out the knife he was hiding under his body, and thrust the six-inch blade into Cole's abdomen.

"Oow…Argh..!" Cole shouted, as he felt the sharp blade penetrate deep into his gut. He let go of Dawson, jerking backward trying to get to the rifle.

Even though Dawson was wounded badly, he had an amazing amount of strength. He withdrew the knife from Cole's body attempting to strike again. But Cole had fallen backward just beyond the immediate reach of Dawson. Dawson may have had his strength, but because of the neck and arm wounds, his limbs did not move too well making his movements haphazard and clumsy. The two men thrashed their way toward the rifle, Dawson still trying to get a second stab into Cole.

Smoke heard Cole yell out, turned and rushed toward the two men. Once again, the wolf grabbed Dawson's neck attempting to kill him, as his natural instincts told him to do.

Dawson had reached a frenzy. His neck was now bleeding profusely because the wolf had made a direct hit on his neck, severing his jugular vein. Blood gushed from the wound in spurts, as Dawson's heart pumped rapidly. He was a dead man, but he didn't know it yet.

In a last desperate attempt to win the battle, Dawson flung himself toward Cole. Cole had reached the rifle by this time, pointed it at Dawson's chest, squeezing the trigger. The rifle went off blasting a hole in the lunging man's chest.

Dawson fell face down in the snow beside Cole. The wolf attacked again and again. Blood spurted from Dawson's body, splashing across Cole and Smoke, melting the snow with the heated deep-red liquid.

"Stop Smoke! No!" Cole moaned, just before he passed out.

Jodie ran as fast as she could down the gentle hill, snowshoes flopping loudly, "No! No! Cole are you all right?" she cried loudly, "Please be all right!"

"Stay!" She shouted at Smoke, as she slid in beside Cole.

He was unconscious, but breathing. The wound in his abdomen had soaked his thick coat in red blood. Jodie, still crying, attempted to wipe the tears from her eyes so she could see better. She peeled Cole's jacket back, opened his shirt and pulled the top of his long-johns back to expose the nasty knife wound.

Grabbing the medical kit Cole had pulled out of the backpack to aid Dawson, she pressed gauze over the wound. She remembered how Cole had done this to Strike when they found her on the mountain with the deep wounds from the fallen tree.

Then she grabbed the army blanket and the one man tent Cole carried on his backpack, and quickly placed the blanket on top of him, then draped the tent over top of the both of them. Jodie remembered to do this from the airplane crash when she covered Ally to keep her warm. She held the gauze tightly against the wound to stop the bleeding as she curled up beside him to help keep Cole warm. Then, she laid her head on Cole's chest almost passing out from the sight of the wound.

She cried heavily, "Please don't die!...Please don't die!...I love you, Cole, please don't die!" she kept repeating.

She could hear Cole's heart beating deep in his chest. Soon Smoke crawled in under the tent, lying next to her and Cole, satisfied that Dawson was dead. All through the rest of the cold, dark night, the three-some clung to life. The combined body heat was just enough to keep them from freezing to death.

Soon after daybreak, Smoke jumped to attention growling and bark-ing in a low tone awakening Jodie. She came to consciousness with a start, trying to figure out where she was. Quickly remembering the situ-ation, she checked Cole to see if he was alive. He was, his heart still beat regularly and strongly.

Smoke, wagging his tail, ran to the crest of the hill they had last passed over the night before. Howling loudly, the blood-covered wolf escorted Bert and three other men to the side of Jodie who, once again, was crying uncontrollably. Cole was still unconscious and very weak from loss of blood. Dawson was dead, his body frozen stiff.

Chapter 15

"Well Ranger Bryant," Dr. Ross said, taking his glasses off, placing them in his white hospital coat pocket, "you are definitely a lucky man! The knife cut through the muscles in the abdomen just missing the colon and the kidney. If the wound would have been as little as one-quarter inch off in any direction, you would have been in serious trouble, maybe even dead."

Cole moaned a sigh of relief, still groggy from the anesthesia the doctors had given him for the surgery to repair the knife wound." Gee, that is good news!" then added, "So why do I hurt so bad?"

"Oh, I didn't say it wouldn't hurt," the doctor chuckled, "You'll be sore for several days, no doubt."

"Yeah, I believe you."

They wheeled Cole into a room to stay three days to make sure no infection got started. "Where is Jodie?" he asked.

"I'm right here!" she answered, stepping closer to his bedside. A nurse brought a step stool to let the little girl climb up to the side of the bed. "I will stay right here with you, I promise." she continued, "I hope it doesn't hurt too bad. Does it?"

"Now that I know you are okay, it hardly hurts at all honey."

When the rescuers had arrived, Cole was close to going into a coma from hypothermia. Lucky for him, the body heat provided by Jodie and Smoke had saved his life. The men had cranked up the big two-way radio one of them carried on his back, calling for a helicopter to pick up the wounded ranger. Thank goodness the weather had broken so the helicopter could come in right away.

Since there was a total of seven people and a wolf, an army Chinook helicopter was dispatched from Eielson Air Force Base. The twin rotors thrashed up a whirlwind of snow from the ground as it landed one hundred yards away on the crest of one of the small hills. The four rescuers very efficiently carried Cole on a stretcher to the waiting craft, then returned with a body bag for the frozen body of Dawson Patterson, who died as viciously as he had lived.

After all of them were on board, the big helicopter slowly lifted off, rotated one-quarter turn, then headed for Fairbanks General Hospital. Jodie had thought to herself that in the past several months she had been on two helicopter rides. Neither one was a pleasant flight because of the circumstances surrounding the rides.

After Cole had been home recuperating for several days, Bill came by to see him one afternoon. "I have some news on all of this Dawson Patterson stuff," he started.

"Like what?" Cole asked.

"Okay, you know that Dawson abducted Jodie to collect on some insurance policy that Evelyn had taken out on her life leaving Jodie as a beneficiary, right?"

"Right."

"Well, I have the insurance policy here." He pointed at a folded, wrinkled, official looking document printed in blue ink, "The face amount of the policy is twenty- five thousand dollars. The owner of the policy is Evelyn Varsario, the date of the policy is July 17, 1971. You wan'na know who the beneficiary is?" he asked.

"Don't toy with me Bill," Cole said, in an aggravated voice, "I'm not in the mood. We know who the beneficiary is," he continued matter of factly, "It is Jodie, of course!"

"Not exactly!" tapping the folded document on his free hand, "The beneficiary of this insurance policy is Mary J. Varsario."

Cole thought a moment, "And who is Mary J. Varsario?" he asked, a surprised tenor in his voice.

It seems we now have discovered Jodie's real name!" He looked down at the printing on the document reading it out loud, "Mary J. Varsario."

Cole responded in a puzzled voice, "So my little Jodie is really Mary?"

"Apparently so." They both reflected on this awhile.

"How do we know that Mary is Jodie and not someone else?" Cole struggled to get out of his chair to secure the document from Bill. Bill quickly stepped closer to Cole handing him the policy.

"Well, I did a little investigating on this myself." He sat down in a chair next to Cole, "If you notice on the document, it was purchased in Junction City, Wyoming. So I called the hospital there to see if they had a record of a baby being born by the name of Mary J. Varsario in 1971. Guess what?" he asked.

"There was?"

"That is right. Mary Josephine, six pounds, four ounces, was born June 8, 1971 at Junction City General Hospital," he spouted the facts rapid-fire style.

Cole ran the facts through his head, "So, that still doesn't prove it is Jodie, does it?"

"No, but this does. The little girl was born to one Evelyn Varsario, born May 5, 1955." he paused, proud of his investigative prowess.

"So…Jodie is…Mary." Cole whispered, deep in thought. Rubbing his chin as he sifted the new information through his brain, he leaned back in the big overstuffed chair. "You know, at some point, we have to let Jodie in on this information."

"I know. But I think it is better if we unravel some more questions first, don't you think?" Bill asked.

"Yeah, like is Dawson Jodie's real father? And, why did they get a fake birth certificate?" he scratched the side of his face, looking puzzled. "Hey, you didn't mention the father's name on the birth certificate!" he exclaimed, raising his voice.

"That is right. It seems the birth father is listed as 'Unknown'," Bill raised both hands forming imaginary quotation marks with his fingers, "on the certificate."

"Oh great!' Cole exclaimed.

"One other item," Bill continued, "The coroner in Fairbanks said there was a key in Dawson's belongings along with some other things not of any interest. He said he was sending the key, which had the name 'Ralph's' printed on it to the Portland police to see if they can figure out what it unlocks. Maybe we can find out more about Jodie...er...Mary then."

"A key...huh?" Cole pondered, "Anything else?"

"The only thing I would like to do is pass this information on to Judge Holcolmb. Do you mind?'

"Absolutely. He needs to know," he paused, "Oh, by the way, find out if he has any updated information on his end."

That day, Bill passed the information on to Judge Holcolmb who said he would try to put more pressure on the Portland police to resolve the case. He said he really had not gotten any new information in weeks. He was glad to hear that Cole was not injured any worse than he was and that, finally, Dawson Patterson wouldn't be hurting anyone anymore.

As Cole began to feel better, Jodie had started to talk more in depth about the abduction. She had told Cole she was scared a little when Dawson had taken her from the barn, but the worst part of the ordeal was during the attack by Smoke and Cole.

"When Smoke first hit my dad..." she broke the sentence off holding off a tear, "Cole, would it be wrong if I didn't call him my dad anymore?" she asked.

Cole took a deep breath, letting it exhale slowly, "No...no Jodie, after all you have been through with him, it would not be wrong," he spoke, softly holding his arms out for her to come to him. Jodie gently climbed into his lap curling up with her back against the side of the overstuffed chair, her legs curled beneath her, she put her right arm around his neck.

"I just cannot bring myself to call him Daddy anymore," she repeated. "He really did hate me, you know." A tear ran down her freckled cheek. "Do you know what it is like to be hated by your daddy?" She wasn't looking for an answer, "I think I will call him by his first name, Dawson."

"Okay, Dawson it is then!" He rubbed the little girl's back to comfort her.

Jodie gained her composure, then spoke again, "So, as I was saying, when Smoke first hit..." she hesitated before she said, "Dawson..., it took me by surprise. But, when Smoke turned around, and I realized it was Smoke, and he headed back for the second strike...," she used her hands to demonstrate the motion of the wolf, "I caught myself hoping he would kill...Dawson." She wiped more tears from her eyes with the back of her left hand, sniffling a little. "Am I a bad person for having that kind of feeling about my....dad?...er...Dawson?"

Cole shook his head from side to side. Jodie continued, "I didn't see Dawson when he stabbed you with the knife because I was greeting Smoke when he came up the hill. When I heard you yell out, that is when I saw him take the knife out of your stomach...I wanted to run down the hill and kill him myself!" she blurted out, "And, then, when I saw you shoot him, I wanted to tear him apart...just the way Smoke did!" entwining her hands and pulling them apart to demonstrate her anger. "Smoke ended up doing what I wanted to do! Does that scare you?" she looked deep into Cole's eyes searching for any kind of answer.

He hugged the little girl tightly. Releasing his hold slightly, he answered, "Honey, you have gone through a very tough year," pausing to select his words, he added, "Let's face it, you have had a very tough childhood. Dawson has lied to you, abandoned you, mistreated you and your mother, and abducted you. So, any bad feelings you may have I don't think are necessarily wrong. I think anyone would want to get rid of that man out of his or her life. I will tell you this, wanting to kill someone and actually carrying out killing that person are two different things."

"I thought he had killed you...and if he had, I know I would have killed him!"

"Well, he didn't. That's what matters." he held her head against his with his hand, softly kissing her on the forehead.

It was very quiet in the cabin, neither one saying anything for a long time. Both reflected on the ordeal as they had over and over again since it had happened.

Jodie put her finger in her mouth, looking embarrassed, "I can ask you anything, right?'

"That is the deal. Anything!"

Slowly, she said, "Can I call you Daddy now?"

Cole considered the question, looking down into that little freckled face and those big brown eyes. "Before I answer that I need to ask you a couple questions, young lady."

"What?"

"If I take the title of Daddy, it means you intend to have me as your daddy for the rest of your life." He winked at her.

"I know that!" she giggled, finger still in her mouth.

"Are you sure that you know me well enough that you know I will take care of you, and watch after you forever?"

"Don't be silly! You already do that!" she exclaimed, still giggling.

"Do you love me more than anyone in the whole wide world?"

"Yes, sir! You're the bestest!" She pressed both tiny hands against his cheeks making his lips form an "O".

Cole chuckled, kind of embarrassed himself, "Then I guess it is official, you can call me Daddy!"

She bounced up and down in his lap loudly proclaiming, "Yea, I have a real, honest-to-goodness Daddy!"

Cole, himself, was having his own emotional problems. Just as the airplane crash had affected A.J. and Jodie, so did this near death experience affect him. Cole realized he had come very close to losing his life when Dawson stuck that knife in him. This thought had made him reflect on his life to date and on his future. He knew he had made the right choice deciding he wanted to raise Jodie. But his other life choices were now being questioned. Did he really want to continue living way out here in the woods? Was he doing all he could for himself and Jodie? Where did he want to be in five years, ten years, twenty years? Was he truly happy? And on and on.

It looked like the adoption of Jodie would be granted, now that Dawson and Evelyn were dead, and there appeared not to be any other relatives. There still was the question of who Jodie's real father was, but based on the fact that the real father had never been in the picture, Cole believed he would be allowed to adopt Jodie.

Cole realized that every major decision in his life had come after he actually first refused to accept it. When he was much younger, he wanted to be a Forest Ranger, but because of his parents' objections, he didn't pursue that course, at first. Instead it took a tour of duty in Vietnam and a near death situation to force him to make the commitment to pursue his dream.

Then, when he first met Jodie, he had rejected his feelings, trying hard not to commit to her. And because of his decision, he almost lost her to some other foster family. Now, he felt he had, once again, rejected his feelings for his love for A.J. And because of that, she had given up on him and moved to Juneau to get on with her own life.

So, as Cole reflected on this, he realized, once again, that he had made the wrong decision. He now had reached the conclusion that he loved A.J., and deep down in his heart, he knew he had loved her for many years. He had just refused to admit it to himself because he continued to think everyone would tell him his feelings were wrong. All of this time wasted worrying about what other people thought. Now he had probably lost A.J. forever.

April seventh broke into a beautiful spring day; clear skies, high thin white clouds streaked the sky above, still reflecting the orange cast of the rising sun. Cole drove Jodie and Smoke down to the bus stop where the other kids were gathered. He kissed her on the cheek, petted Smoke on his thick fur-covered head, and wished them well for the day.

"By the way, I am flying down to Juneau to pick up some supplies. I should be back before you get home," he explained to Jodie.

"Okay, make sure you are safe!" she cautioned.

"I will. You know, you sound more like a little mother every day!" he joked. He put the jeep in gear, slowly turned the vehicle around, then headed off to the administration building waving to her over his shoulder.

Jodie returned the wave, then joined the others as the yellow school bus entered the ranger station.

Cole quietly logged his flight into the book and headed for "Lizzie" down at the lake. The lake was no longer frozen. The skis on "Lizzie" had been switched back to pontoons. After checking the aircraft out, he was soon in the air flying toward Juneau. He had successfully managed to avoid any contact with Bill or any of the other workers for he did not want to explain why he was going to Juneau.

Cole had decided to right a wrong. His plan was to fly down to Juneau, meet A.J., tell her how wrong he had been, and, if she was willing to give it a second shot, have her come back to the station to see if they were really meant for each other.

All the way down to Juneau his thoughts would swing back and forth between committing to his decision and not. He broke out in a cold sweat every now and then as he thought about A.J. possibly turning him down, saying that it was too late, and she had decided to forget him. Other times, he would get nervous thinking of how much he really loved her, and what it would be like if they got married and had kids of their own.

Finally, softly touching down on the smooth blue surface of the cove at Juneau, he taxied "Lizzie" up to Waterman's Wharf, securing "Lizzie" to the floating pier. After stowing everything away, he headed off into the streets of Juneau.

Juneau had turned into a regular big city. Small by comparison to some cities in the lower forty-eight states, but large by Alaskan city standards. Already, several ten-story buildings occupied the downtown area. The paved streets were lined up parallel to the curving bay, broken up as city blocks by streets that ran from the bay to the nearby mountain range. Juneau had numerous traffic lights and, during rush hour, traffic cops. This was a growing city, and the people in the city acted like "city people", not people that lived in the country and sometimes came into town to get supplies.

Cole checked his watch. It was now eleven-thirty. He figured he would go down to the veterinary clinic, find a good view of the front door from across the street, then when he caught a glimpse of A.J. when she left for lunch, he would act like he accidentally ran into her. That way, it would break the ice, and give him a chance to ask her to come back home with him.

Cole walked the three blocks up from the bay to Asher Street, then six blocks to Nanute Avenue, where the Lerner All Animal Clinic was located. Looking around the intersection, Cole noticed a hardware store on one corner, a small, two-pump gas station on another, and a carry-out deli on the third, next to a drug store. The clinic occupied the remaining corner. Looking back at the drug store, he noticed a park bench close to the street at a bus stop. He figured this would be a good place to view the clinic door that opened right onto the corner.

The park bench was occupied for quite awhile by two little old ladies and a man in a business suit. But soon a bus rumbled to a stop, and the three people disappeared into the half-full bus. Slowly, it rumbled away as Cole sat on the now empty bench keeping a close eye on the doorway to the clinic. He noticed a steady stream of people entering and exiting the clinic holding various animals, from dogs and cats to birds, to even one lady holding a small squealing pig under her arm. But, the clock ticked on, and A.J. never exited the doorway.

As he sat there thinking why she had not gone to lunch, he got an idea. Maybe she wasn't working today. So, he went into the drug store, looked up the phone number to the clinic in the telephone directory and called.

"Lerner All Animal Clinic," the female voice on the other end of the line answered.

"Yes, I wanted to bring in my pet today. But I wanted to make sure Miss Defreese is working today," Cole lied.

"What kind of pet do you have, sir?" the lady asked. This was not part of Cole's plan. She was just supposed to answer "yes" or "no". Now he had to lie more.

"Eer...a dog...yes, that's it a dog!" Not a very good start into the world of lying, he thought.

"Miss Defreese doesn't work on dogs, sir. That would be Mr. Peterson. Are you coming in right now?" she asked.

Cole couldn't believe his ears. How could detective work be so hard? His mind raced wildly out of control. Finally, be blurted out, "Oh, really! Well Miss Defreese must have worked on one of my other animals. What kind of animals does she see?" he gulped, loudly.

"Miss Defreese is our livestock specialist. Now are you bringing in your dog right now?" foiled again, he thought.

"Probably tomorrow. But tell me, can I speak with Miss Defreese a moment? I have a question about the calf she looked at last week." The lie just got bigger and bigger.

"Hold one moment, I will see if she is in," the voice responded. A half-minute passed before the female voice came back over the receiver, "Miss Defreese is scheduled to return to the office at two-thirty. Would you like to leave a message?"

"No, I think I will see her when I bring in my dog tomorrow," he hung up quickly.

Cole looked at his watch it was now one twenty-three. He would grab lunch at the drug store, and return to his position outside of the store in time to catch her entering the clinic. Hopefully, this time he would catch her. He had not planned on it being this hard to meet up with her. Of course, he could take the more direct approach, and just wait for her in the clinic. But he dismissed this as being too uncomfortable.

By the time he had finished lunch, it was approaching two o'clock. He resumed his position outside the drug store waiting patiently for A.J. to show. Slowly the time passed until, at two-seventeen, he spotted A.J. walking toward him on the other side of the street.

At first, he almost didn't recognize her for she had changed her appearance dramatically. Her hair was worn down, as she had let it down in the hayloft, almost touching her shoulders. The sandy-blonde hair caught the daylight making it look as though it were luminescent.

She wore a medium-blue, low-cut, short-sleeved dress that had a matching belt accenting her tiny waist, and soft pleats from the waist down to about two inches above her knees, where the dress stopped allowing the observer to take notice of her long, nicely shaped legs. She had a small black purse held by a shoulder strap, which matched her low-healed shoes.

She, evidently, was in a good mood, as she appeared to bounce along the sidewalk with a spring in her step. Every now and then she would greet someone walking in the opposite direction. Occasionally, she would stop at a shop window to gaze at the merchandise, then continue down the block.

When she got halfway down the block, Cole decided it was time for him to make his way toward her. He crossed the sidewalk and waited at the curb for the traffic to clear. His heart pounded with anticipation. He felt like his hands were trembling, and he could feel small beads of perspiration forming on his forehead. He took a deep breath saying to himself, "Okay this is it!"

Just as he started across the street, he once again, took a glance to see how far away A.J. was. He noticed she stopped, greeted a man in a suit who appeared to be around twenty-five, or so. Then, she put her arms around his waist, leaned forward, giving him a rather long kiss.

Cole stopped dead in his tracks not believing his eyes. The lady crossing the street behind him ran into his back. She said, "Oh, pardon me!" as she stepped around him, and continued on her way. Cole, still in shock, didn't even notice the lady or hear her comment.

A.J. slowly turned on her heels as the young man put his arm around her. They casually continued down the sidewalk toward the opposite corner. The couple was engaged in a light-hearted conversation laughing now and then, sometimes putting their heads together and, at least twice, kissing one another on the cheek. When the light changed to stop the traffic on their side of the street, they walked to the front door of the clinic.

There, they exchanged more happy conversation. Then the man in the suit leaned over kissing A.J. passionately on her lips as she willingly and eagerly returned the kiss. They parted, looking at each other, and holding hands until the distance between them became too great. She turned, and entered the building. He walked on down the street whistling.

Cole was devastated. He had come to conquer his true love and, instead, would leave knowing he was totally out of the picture.

"Excuse me sir," he heard a man's voice behind him, "Excuse me, are you going to cross the street?"

He turned, facing the little Oriental man that had spoken to him, "No! No, go ahead!" he said, absent-mindedly. Cole wandered aimlessly through the city streets, his mind racing, confusion and disappointment having set in. He, eventually, ended up at Waterman's Wharf, flying "Lizzie" out of Juneau back to the ranger station.

On the long trip home, he had collected his composure and his thoughts. He was more prepared to face Jodie. Since he was running a little late, he had radioed ahead to the ranger station to let Jodie know he would be home about an hour after she got home from school.

That night he was very quiet. Jodie had sensed something was not right. She, being the inquisitive little kid, tried to get Cole to tell her what was on his mind. But Cole was not about to divulge any secrets. Instead, he wanted information from Jodie.

"So tell me little girl, does A.J. still write you letters?" he inquired.

"You know she does. Why?"

"Oh I dunno. I guess I started thinking about her when I was in Juneau, and was wondering how she is doing," he shaded the truth.

"Did you see her?" Jodie asked, enthusiastically.

"No! Oh, no. As I was leaving Juneau, I happened to think that she was there." He thought it was more than thinking, but that would do for now.

Jodie didn't answer, so Cole asked again, "So?"

Jodie looked at him curiously, "So, what?"

"So does she say how she is doing and all of that?" he acted perturbed having to ask the question a second time.

"Well, she got an apartment real close to her work. She said she likes her work very much. But she says she misses me a whole bunch," she held her hands wide apart as if describing how big a fish she caught.

Cole acted like he was half listening as he pretended to be reading an article out of a magazine, "And...has she found any new friends...or is she lonesome?" he dragged out the sentence like he was reading and talking at the same time.

"Oh, she says she has lots of new friends. She says she has been invited out to lots of parties, and dinners, and things."

Holding back his emotions, he said, "Well, that is real good. I am happy she is enjoying herself." He kept his face hidden behind the magazine to avoid eye contact with Jodie that probably would give away his true feelings.

Jodie came over to Cole, pushing the magazine aside with her small hand. She looked in Cole's eyes with that woman's intuition look on her face, "Daddy, be honest. You miss her, don't you?" she asked.

"Of course I miss her! I helped raise her, you know!" he tried to dodge the question.

"You know that isn't what I mean, buster!" she said, in a pushy voice, "You miss her 'cause you like her a whole bunch...as a girlfriend, don't you?"

This little girl was going to be a handful for her husband one day, because she could read men like a book. He didn't answer.

"That is why you are so quiet. You went to Juneau, and I bet you tried to see her!" She thought a moment, "Did you? Did you see her?" the pitch in her voice getting higher and higher as she figured it out.

"Look, honey, I went to Juneau to pick up supplies. That is all! And, I don't appreciate you grilling me like this!" he tried to intimidate her.

"What happened? Huh? Tell me what happened? she continued to quiz, "Did she tell you to take a hike?" she chuckled.

"No!" he committed a mistake answering that question. Now he had to explain what happened at Juneau. "No, it's...just...it's just...I saw her...walking down the street...and was wondering about her. That's all!"

"So you didn't talk to her?" She was on a roll now.

"No! It is just like I said. I was picking up supplies and happened to see her walking down the other side of the street." He swallowed hard. Telling white lies was not easy for him. "There wasn't really anytime to talk, and I was too far away to get her attention anyway."

"That is too bad." Jodie didn't believe a word of it. So, she decided to bait him a little, "She really likes you, you know? I bet she would have her feelings hurt if she knew you had seen her and not spoken."

"Yeah, well there just wasn't time," he repeated.

Jodie knew Cole loved Ally, but she just didn't know how to get them together. Jodie didn't tell Cole that Ally had started dating down in Juneau, and she wasn't about to tell him. But, she thought to herself, somehow they have to get together before it is too late for both of them. The problem was how to do that.

Another month passed before news came back from the Portland Police Department. One afternoon, Cole was in Farrow's Patch, picking up supplies from the general store when he dropped in on Judge Holcolmb. The judge had told him he now had enough paperwork complete to start the adoption process.

"Good day, judge!" Cole extended his hand to shake the judge's hand.

"Hey, Cole. I'm glad you waited until today to come in because I just got the missing pieces of the "Jodie" puzzle in the mail yesterday. The Portland Police completed their investigation, and the case is closed. They took the mysterious key to Ralph's Storage Center where they found all of the information to solve the case," he said, turning toward his office, and walking to the chair behind the desk. "Come. Come sit down with me, and I will give you pretty much the whole mysterious story."

Opening a large manila envelope, he extracted some official looking documents. "The first missing piece was who was Jodie's...er...Mary's real father?" holding a paper in front of him, he read off, "John Sherwood".

Cole repeated, "John Sherwood?"

Sliding the document across the desk to Cole, the judge said, "Yep, that's right," he leaned back in his chair clasping his hands together across his fat stomach. "It seems that Evelyn Varsario had a boyfriend named John Sherwood about the time her mom passed away, leaving her all alone. She took up with John, and they kind of roamed around. He would do odd jobs to keep them in food, but basically, all they really did was have a lot of sex," he raised both hands palms up in the gesture, "What you gonna do?".

"Well, needless to say, Evelyn gave birth to Mary, a.k.a. Jodie, when she was just sixteen. But before she gave birth to the baby, it seems the second missing part to the puzzle, how did she get hooked up with Dawson Patterson?, came into play."

"So, you're saying the couple met up with Dawson before the birth of the baby?"

"Right," still leaning back in his chair, hands clasped together across his stomach, he continued, "the roving couple ran into Dawson somewhere in Washington State. They started robbing small businesses as they traveled the roads."

"Oh boy! They were robbers?" Cole said, raising his voice.

"Well, Dawson and some other guys actually did the robberies, and John drove the car. It seems that John really knew how to handle cars." Judge Holcolmb pushed another sheet of paper across the desk toward Cole, "This is a picture of the automobile." The picture was a black and white print of a 1966 Pontiac GTO coupe.

"Wow, quite the car," Cole exclaimed, looking at the photo.

"That was the one possession that John had to his name. He used that as the getaway car in approximately seven heists he was involved in."

"What about Evelyn? What was her part in the robberies?" Cole asked, leaning back in the straight chair in front of the desk.

"She only participated in one heist, as far as we know. It was the last heist. It is believed that she didn't want to be involved in the robberies at all. But the last heist was the biggest one the gang pulled off and they felt she needed to be along for some unknown reason." He pulled out a newspaper clipping from May 11, 1971, shoving it across the desk.

Cole leaned forward reading the clipping out loud,

> "Today three men and a young lady attempted to rob the State Bank of Worchester leaving one man dead and two others captured. The woman is still at large, at this time.
>
> After two of the men entered the bank, they made the customers lay on the floor, and demanded a teller hand over three bags of money, valued at approximately $15,000. Soon after that, the two men fled to a waiting car driven by the third man with the lady in the back seat. Just as the car pulled away from the curb, Frazier Simons, a security guard

at the bank, stepped out of the doorway firing his gun at the fleeing vehicle.

It is said the bullet passed through the rear window missing the two occupants in the rear seat, but striking the driver in the back of the neck. The automobile sped down the street, the driver having been killed instantly, eventually striking a utility pole at the corner of Ash and Blakely. The force of the crash threw the passenger in the front seat through the windshield onto the pavement, knocking him unconscious, where he was later arrested.

The two occupants in the rear seat, a young woman and a large, longhaired male exited the vehicle and ran down the alley behind Parson's Hardware Store. The male was captured two hours later in a pasture on Slater's farm. The female is still at large. The woman left a purse that contained a wallet in the rear seat of the car. The identity of the woman is Evelyn Varsario. All of the stolen money was retrieved from the vehicle."

Cole set the paper aside, "So she was there. But not one of the robbers?" he asked.

"We are not sure of that, yet. I have the connection with Evelyn and Dawson here," he pulled out a thin book, holding it up for Cole to see. "This is Evelyn's diary."

"Evelyn had a diary?"

"Yes, she did!" the judge exclaimed. Handing it across the desk to Cole, he said, "At least she had a dairy for the first two years of being with Dawson."

He leaned back in his chair once again, "The gang had a ring leader. His name was Dawson Patterson. He was not in the car and, evidently, according to the newspaper, they never knew about him. According to Evelyn's diary, she joined up with him shortly after the robbery. She was very distraught over John's death because, according to the diary, she had loved John since grammar school. He was the love of her life. Apparently, she met John in fourth grade."

Cole browsed through the yellowed pages reading excerpts from the book, as he slowly turned the pages.

"According to the diary, Evelyn was taken in by Dawson, who was a mean man even then. He felt society owed him something because of how poor he was as a little kid. She was in a bad way at the time. She didn't have any family or money and she didn't have a place to stay. To top all that, she was eight months pregnant. So Dawson took her with him."

"If Dawson was so mean, why didn't he just leave her on the side of the road?"

"That was my question, too. I figured maybe he did have some redeeming quality. But according to the diary, Evelyn later found out two reasons he helped her. The first, was he wanted to sell the baby to someone to get some 'real money' and the second, was simply so he could have an indentured servant to look after him, and do anything he requested. It made him feel good to have power over someone else."

"What?" Cole blurted out. "You mean this guy held her as a slave?" He could not believe what he was hearing.

"That is right. Look here," he pushed a photograph across the desk. Cole picked it up looking at the fair-skinned, young woman standing in front of an old house.

"This is Evelyn?"

"Yes. On the back it has her name and the date the picture was taken," the judge pointed across the desk.

"She is a nice looking girl. Too bad she met up with that loser!" He put the picture in his lap with the other items the judge had given him.

"Yeah! And when she would not sell the baby, things got a little violent. Evidently, he would beat her up quite often," he said, pounding his fist into his other hand to emphasize his point.

"Why didn't she just leave? What kept her with Dawson?"

The judge breathed deeply expelling the air slowly, then answered, "That was my question, too! The diary tells of the last robbery, and Evelyn having the baby, and Dawson taking her in. But later in the diary, it explains that Dawson told Evelyn that if she ever left him, he would go to the authorities and reveal that she was the female in the rear seat of the getaway car. He told her that since a man had been killed during the robbery, she would go to jail for a long, long time," he paused.

Cole interjected, "So if she went to jail, Dawson probably convinced her she would never see the baby again!"

"Bingo!" the judge held his hand in the air forming the okay sign with his fingers.

Cole leaned forward in his chair now understanding the name change for Jodie, "And she got the fake birth certificate because the child could possibly lead the authorities to Evelyn, right?"

"That is the whole story." The judge stood up from his chair walking to the front of the desk next to Cole, who was still pondering the revelation of the diary.

"Congratulations! I am pretty sure you are going to be a father!" he held out his hand for Cole to shake.

Cole placed the documents, pictures and diary on the desk, rose from his chair tears forming in his eyes, shook Judge Holcolmb's hand heartily, and gave him a hug with the other arm. The judge returned the hug.

Chapter 16

Cole spent the afternoon going over Evelyn's diary knowing that now was the time to inform Jodie of her history. Before Cole left Farrow's Patch to return to Chisano Station, he stopped by the post office to have copies made of some of the pages from the diary. He used the flight-time back to the station to reflect on what he had read, and to prepare his thoughts for the inevitable meeting with Jodie.

Later that evening, as the two sat in front of the hearth, Cole encouraged Jodie to relate her experiences of the day to him, as they always did before retiring for the day. Then she asked him how his trip into Farrow's Patch had worked out. He told her about his errands while he was there and mentioned that he had stopped by to see Judge Holcolmb.

"You know, I was surprised to find out that they have completed their investigation in Portland," he began.

"You mean the investigation to see if you can adopt me?" she asked, enthusiastically.

"Yes, that is the one," he answered, "You see, because Dawson abandoned you, and your mother had passed away, they needed to investigate to make sure someone else should not be the one to adopt you. You know, like a relative that no one previously knew about."

She quickly asked, "They didn't, did they?"

"No!" Cole chuckled, "you're kinda' stuck with me, if you'll have me!" He touched his chest with his left hand.

Jodie leaned over, stood on her knees, kissing Cole on the cheek, "Don't be silly, Dad!" she giggled.

"Well, do you want to know all about your mother and Dawson?" he asked, a little nervousness creeping into his voice.

"Yes, sir. That would be real nice."

Cole began by opening the big manila envelope that he had set on the sofa. One by one, he pulled out pictures that had been taken of Evelyn over the years. Jodie would gaze at them with great interest making comments about each one. On many of the pictures, a brief description of the place or date was handwritten on the back of the picture.

"Oh, this is Mommy when she was about my age," she said, holding the picture up for Cole to see. "It says the man next to her is her dad."

Then, they would look at the next picture until most of the photos in the envelope had been laid out in front of them. Cole removed another photo that pictured Evelyn and John together in front of Evelyn's parents house. She was about fourteen when this photo was taken. The two of them were standing next to each other with their arms around each other, and John was kissing Evelyn on the cheek. Evelyn was looking straight at the camera, with an embarrassed expression on her face.

Jodie carefully studied the picture, then flipped it over to read the writing on the back, "July 4, 1970...my true love, John." She flipped the photo back to the front to look at the couple once again, "Mommy looks happy in this picture, doesn't she?" she asked.

"Yes, she does," Cole answered. Pointing with his finger at John, he said, "That young man, there, is your real father."

"What?...my...father?...I don't understand," she said, looking up at Cole, "My father is Dawson."

Cole shook his head from side to side, his eyes meeting Jodie's confused gaze, "There is a long involved story here. But your real father is John Sherwood," he pointed his finger at the young man in the photo, again. Cole began the story of Evelyn's past, taking his time developing all of the important points that led up to Jodie's birth, and Evelyn's difficult decision to stay with Dawson Patterson.

Jodie had a lot of questions as Cole explained why Evelyn had done what she had done. After a considerable amount of time, she came to realize that her mother had given up a lot to keep her safe, and make sure she grew up as a good person. Cole concluded the story by pulling out one of the copies he had made of the pages of the diary.

"Jodie, as I told you, your mother kept a diary. I will let you read the complete diary when you get a little older, and you will know what a terrible life she had with Dawson. For right now, I can only say that I have told you the truth about everything that is important about your mother and Dawson. I made a copy of one of the entries in the diary that I feel will let you know how much your mother loved you." Holding the sheet of paper in front of him he began to read,

"*March 10, 1973*

A Letter For My Daughter

Dear Diary,

Today I had a quiet moment with my most prized posses-sion, my daughter, Jodie. Dawson has finally found another job, so he is at work. Last night he hit me again several times in the face and back. So, once again, I have to stay in the house so I do not have to explain to the neighbors why I am black and blue. Sometimes, I feel like I should just leave him and run away. But I have tried that, and he has found me, and beat me even more. I just wish I could change my life...but I don't know how.

As I sat in the rocker holding Jodie, I looked into her soft, sweet, peaceful face realizing how happy this tiny per-son has made me. Because of her, I can endure all of the pain that is thrust upon me by Dawson. Today I reflected on the day that I found out I was pregnant with Jodie, and realized what a blessing she had been to me.

Naturally, when I found out I was pregnant, I was scared because I was so young, and had not been around babies too much since I was an only child and didn't have any cousins or anything. When I told John the news, he was immediately prepared to quit school, get a job, and support me and Jodie. He never once had a second thought about keeping the child. He was a very good person. I love him so much, and I miss him terribly still. But I have dedicated myself to Jodie because she is the combination of our love.

So today, diary, I am writing this for Jodie, so she will understand my love for her, and the love I have for her father, John.

Jodie, I wish you could have met your dad because he was the kindest, lovingest, most considerate person in this whole, wide world. I have known him since we were in grade school. He always looked out for me, and I could count on him for anything I needed. He loved you very much, even though he never met you face-to-face. He made sure I took good care of you while I was pregnant, and if he would have lived one month more, he would have had the pleasure of seeing your darling face. But that was not to be and that makes me very sad. For, if you had not been born, I am sure my life would have ended when he died.

I am praying that you will grow up to be a good person with good moral values and the strength to not allow anyone, like Dawson, to control your life. I know you probably want to know why I let Dawson keep me here. All I can tell you is sometimes people are drawn into a bad situation through no fault of their own. That is when a person must be responsible, and move on with their life...something I am not able to do myself.

I am sorry.

I love you with all my heart and soul...Mom"

The two of them sat for a long time not speaking, tears had welled up in Jodie's eyes, and she sniffled softly as she looked at the page in front of her.

"I miss my mommy very much!" Leaning over, she put her head against Cole's chest. He wrapped his arms around the tiny girl rocking her gently back and forth.

"I wished I could have helped your mom. She was a really brave person, you know," he spoke softly, "and your dad would have been proud of her for raising such a good kid."

"I miss my mommy very much!" she repeated, still sniffling, head against his chest.

"I promise, I will take care of you forever," he whispered. She hugged him tightly. Finally, she felt totally secure for the first time since her mom passed away.

Six weeks later Judge Holcolmb called to tell Jodie and Cole that the adoption could be completed now. They set up an appointment for the following Tuesday in Farrow's Patch. The judge requested Cole, Jodie, Bill, and Allison to be present to sign the necessary papers. Also, he said after the official signing he would be buying lunch for all of them. That would be his little present for putting up with him all of these years. He had chuckled when he made the invitation.

The weather behaved and all of the parties arrived on time. The adoption papers were signed, notarized and legally filed. There had been much excitement and jubilation as the final papers were signed. The tension was released and all of them gathered in the judge's office to talk and reminisce about the unusual events that led up to the adoption today.

Cole had been exceptionally nervous, not only because of the adoption but, also, because he wanted to talk with A.J. by herself. He could hardly look at her across the chamber table for fear he might give away his true feelings. So, as the group moved down to the Madison Rooming House for the lunch that Judge Holcolmb promised, Cole jockeyed for position to steer A.J. away from the main group so he could be alone with her.

"So, A.J., how are things treating you in the big city?" Cole inquired enthusiastically, trying to remain calm.

"Great!" she replied, her hand on Jodie's shoulder. "Just great! I have really enjoyed being in the city environment." She looked at Cole. Gathering her thoughts, she added, "You know, I wasn't sure I would like having all those people around. It really is kind of nice for a change."

"Really?" Cole returned her gaze, "You don't miss home?" He was hoping for a positive response.

"Well, a little. I really do like it in Juneau," she lowered her head, glancing at her left hand. She couldn't resist telling them any longer, "I am engaged to be married!" she held her hand up to show Jodie and Cole the engagement ring that adorned her hand, her face glowing with excitement.

Jodie and Cole stopped dead in their tracks staring at the ring. Neither one said anything for the longest time. Cole finally blurted out, "Wonder...ful! That is...wonderful!" he lied, as he tried his hardest not to show his shock and disappointment.

Jodie gazed at the ring even longer than Cole, then said, softly, "That is real nice, Ally. It's just...uh...it really is a...shock...eer...surprise. It really is a nice ring!" She looked up at Cole, then glanced back at Ally. An awkward silence came over the threesome.

Cole asked, "Who is the lucky man?" his voice an octave higher than normal from the stress.

A.J. giggled, wiggling her finger for the diamond to catch the sunlight, "Chad Nimmons!" she said, excitedly, "He is a banker in Juneau!"

"Ooh! A banker, huh?" Cole said, smiling back at his lost love.

"Yes, he is a banker. He has put money down on a piece of property just outside..."

Jodie interrupted her in mid-sentence, exclaiming loudly, "For two people that really care about each other...you two sure do try real hard to hurt each other!" she pulled away from A.J. and Cole, turned around with a scowl on her face, adding, "I just don't get it!...Why do you hurt each other all the time?" Cole and Ally stood motionless, still in shock. "Somehow...I...thought you would quit this...and get together once and for all!" Tears welled up in her eyes as she turned around, and ran to catch up with the others as they headed into the Madison.

Cole responded first, "Jodie! Jodie come here!" she kept running away not paying any attention to him.

"Jodie!...I...Jodie, please!...I..." Ally tried to get the little girl's attention. Turning to Cole, she said, "I am sorry. I didn't mean to upset anyone. I thought it would be good news. I mean, I thought everyone would be happy for me!" Tears began to well up in her eyes.

"Now, now. Don't you go getting all upset. She is just a little kid, you know." He patted A.J.'s shoulder. "You know she really loves you a lot, don't you?" he asked, softly.

"Yes...I suppose I do," she opened her purse pulling out a handkerchief, dabbing the tears in her eyes.

"Well, she probably thought you'd come back to her at the station. So, naturally, she is upset."

"I...I guess you are right," she paused a moment, "Are you upset with me, too?" she looked up into his brown eyes with those brilliant blue, teary eyes.

Cole looked down at the most beautiful woman he had ever seen. The woman he had let his heart fall in love with. "Why had it taken so long for him to realize A.J. was the woman for him?" he wondered. Her soft pink lips parted slightly as she waited for his response. In that brief moment, in which time seemed to stand still, he gazed at all her perfection. The high cheek bones, the soft blonde hair...he thought to himself, "Oh how I want this woman!" But, he had to put that out of his mind now. She had met someone else, and he was not going to spoil her decision to marry Chad.

He took a deep breath answering, "No," he lied again, "I am very happy for you, A.J. I am very happy you found someone that you love enough to spend your life with." He grasped her hand in his, gently picked it up to his lips, and kissed her hand softly. "Congratulations, Allison Joanne Defreese. You are going to make a beautiful bride," he smiled down at her.

A.J. curtsied, "Thank you, kind sir," she mocked him.

"When do I get to meet the future groom?"

"Oh, I dun'no. I thought I would bring him to the station to meet everyone soon."

"Have you set a date?" he asked, a nervous bubble coming up his throat feeling as though he might choke.

"Kind of, I want to wait a while. So I tentatively have set it for late October," she answered excitedly. "So much planning to do and all, you know."

"Right!" he answered, as he walked her slowly toward the others who were patiently waiting on the porch. "Do they know you're getting married?" he asked.

"Daddy knows, of course. The others are about to find out, unless Jodie told them when she came up."

When they joined the others on the porch, Allison broke the news, and everyone congratulated her. Cole excused himself making his way over to Jodie, who was seated in one of the porch rockers aggressively rocking back and forth in anger, her arms folded and a big scowl on her face.

Cole leaned down on one knee so he was at eye level with the tiny girl, "How is my favorite daughter?" he asked.

Jodie looked at him, and began to smile, "That is right! I am your daughter now!" she giggled.

"Not just my daughter, but my fav...o...rite daughter!" he stretched out the word.

She reached over, giving him a big hug. Then she got serious again, "I'm mad at you and Ally!" she said, forcefully.

"Honey, some things are just not meant to be." He put her hand in his rubbing the back of her hand with his thumb. "It's a..." he searched for the proper wording, "It's a timing thing. You know, the timing just hasn't been right, for one thing," he looked at her for understanding. Seeing none he continued, "Even though A.J. and myself have known each other for a long, long time we are really just real good friends." Again he looked for a reaction and got none from Jodie.

He exhaled quickly, "One day...when you are older...you will under-stand. But for now, just believe me when I tell you this is good for A.J." He looked across the porch to the noisy group as they entered the Madison, "So, please don't be mad at A.J. or me, for that matter. And believe me things will be all right. Okay?" he begged.

Jodie looked down at her lap, "Okaaay." She couldn't stay mad at Cole or Ally.

Just as they were starting into the Madison, Ally exited the doorway. "Jodie, can I have a word with you, please?" she said, softly.

Jodie looked up at Cole. Cole nodded his head, "I'll just go inside and entertain the judge," he said.

Ally sat in a rocker next to the one Jodie was in, and slowly rocked back and forth for several minutes, not saying a word. Finally, she looked over at Jodie who was looking up into her face. "Jodie, you know I love you, don't you?"

"Yes."

"I always thought we were best girlfriends," she stated.

"Yes, we are," Jodie answered.

Ally rocked some more, then reminisced, "We have really had some good times at the campground, haven't we?"

"Yes, I really like hanging around with you," she looked straight ahead, rocking a little faster.

"I know you think your daddy and I should get together, but sometimes it is not possible. I love Cole very much, Jodie, but to say I love him anymore than as a good friend would not be right." She put her hand on top of Jodie's tiny arm, stroking it softly. "It is kind of like you and Cole. You love him as a daughter, he loves you as a father. Do you see what I am saying?"

Jodie looked up at Ally, "Yes, I do," she hesitated, then added, "It's just that I would like to have Cole as my daddy and you as my mommy."

"I understand that, Jodie. But I have to ask you to settle for me as your best friend, or your big sister," she leaned down, kissing Jodie's forehead. "Just remember this. I will always be around whenever you need me."

Jodie got up from the rocker, and gave Ally a big hug. "Let's go inside and have a fun lunch," Ally said, gleefully.

The next several weeks went smoothly around the ranger station for Cole. Jodie got out of school for summer break having completed a successful school year in which she made new friends and became part of the community. Jodie had really flourished in the year that she had spent with Cole. All of her nightmares had gone away, and she was looking forward to traveling with Cole throughout the park system.

Allison had brought Chad to the ranger station to spend a weekend with his future father-in-law, and to show him the surroundings she grew up in. Chad was about six-foot tall, light build, dark, short hair, tapered at the base of the neck, parted down the left side, with dark brown eyes and thin eyebrows to match. He was fair-skinned with freckles across his nose, which made him appear younger than his twenty-eight years.

Chad had grown up in Los Angeles, California. He had not spent very much time in the wilderness, so the trip was a new experience for him. Although he tried to have a good time, he appeared to be stiff and uncomfortable. Chad had very little in common with the others at the ranger station, so the conversations between Chad and the others were strained and short lived.

Even though Allison hung on his every word, and was obviously very interested in Chad, the gulf between their lifestyles was apparent. She was from the country and nature, he from the city and urban life.

While they stayed at the ranger station, Jodie made it clear, through her actions, that she did not care for Chad. She did everything in her power to make him look badly. She, also, put an extreme amount of effort into getting Ally and Cole off somewhere alone, without Chad around. But the two of them could see through her manipulations, and went along with her every now and then just to make her feel good.

The summer was racing past. Soon it was approaching July. This year the people of Farrow's Patch were planning a July Fourth Festival. The timing must have been perfect because Cole had never seen so many people so full of excitement about the upcoming event.

Johnny and Tyrus, the owners of the Yukon, had started the idea back in March when the cold arctic blast was still freezing the population of Farrow's Patch. They suggested that what everyone needed was one good warm weekend of fun. One thing led to another until it finally matured into the July Fourth Festival, as it was now promoted.

Johnny and Tyrus had booked some bands from Fairbanks and
Juneau, and invited everyone to camp out on the mossy flats surrounding Farrow's Patch. Then, someone got a carnival vendor to agree to
come that weekend, and soon others joined in. Unbelievable as it
seemed, a high school band and a group of Shriners were going to march
down the main highway in a parade. The owners of the Settlers Feed
and Supply Warehouse, located on the main highway next to Greta's
General Store, said they would clear out a space in the warehouse for a
dance floor where the bands could play.

As all of those plans were moving ahead, Jodie was trying to develop
a plan of her own. Jodie had never said anymore to Cole about him and
Ally getting together. Unknown to him, she had been talking to Ranger
Defreese about the subject. After Ally and Chad returned to Juneau,
Jodie had talked to Ranger Defreese in his office one day when Cole was
busy doing maintenance on "Lizzie" at the lake.

She had eased her way into Bill's office while he was working over
some papers on his desk. She quietly made her way to the big row of
windows overlooking the lake.

Bill looked up from his desk, following her progress to the windows,
"Yesss?" he said, softly drawing out the word.

Jodie quickly spun around, "Oh, am I bothering you?" she acted surprised he had noticed her.

"No, not really." He removed his glasses laying them on the desk.
Leaning back in his chair he locked his fingers together behind his head
using them as support. "And exactly what are you doing, young lady?"
he accented his words as he spoke.

She looked down at the floor as if looking at her shoes, "Nothing."

"Nothing? Then why do you suppose you are in my office?" he
inquired. He slowly twisted the swivel chair back and forth.

Jodie turned around, looking out the window down toward the lake
where she could see Cole working on "Lizzie". "He works really hard,"
she said, softly.

Bill rose up out of the chair, made his way across the large room to stand beside Jodie, hands in his pockets. He looked down at the freckled face, and asked, "What are you up to?"

"Well, nothing," she fibbed.

"Look, midget," he called her that when he played with her, "you're gonna have to come clean. I don't have all day, you know!" he jingled some change in his pocket.

"Can we talk?" she asked, looking up at Bill.

"Of course! What's on your mind, honey?"

She looked toward the open office door, "Can we close the door?"

He looked down at her a moment, then said, "This must be really serious. Is it serious?"

She nodded her head, then whispered, holding her finger up to her mouth, "Yes sir, real serious!"

Bill grumbled a little, as if he was a little annoyed, as he walked to the door, closing it slowly behind him. Facing Jodie, he motioned for her to sit down in one to the big leather chairs in front of the desk. She did, and he joined her, sitting in the matching chair to her right. "Now what is the matter? Tell me," he encouraged her, compassion in his tone.

Jodie wiggled her legs, as they dangled from the big chair, thinking what she was going to say. "So, how do you like Chadwick?" she asked, using his given name to display her dislike of him.

Bill stared back at her, not answering.

"You know, now that you have spent a weekend with him, how do you like him?" she repeated.

"Little, little girl. You know I don't tell little girls things like that," he said. "That would be for me to know, and you to find out," he chuckled.

"You know what? I don't like him very much!"

"Why?" he asked.

"Well…he just don't fit in," she paused a moment to collect the proper words, "He doesn't seem to do too well around animals and nature," another pause, "He isn't very outdoorsy. You know what I mean?"

Bill laughed out loud, "Yes, I know what you mean. But why are you so interested in Chad?" he probed.

Jodie pulled both legs into the chair, sitting Indian-style. "I just don't think he is the right person for Ally."

"Oh, I see. This is really about Allison, huh?"

"Yes," a short pause, then, "and Cole."

Bill chuckled again, "You mean you want Allison and Cole to get together, right?"

Jodie jumped down from the chair going to Bill's chair leaning on the armrest. "It is the natural thing, don't you see?" she begged, sounding so grown up.

"Jodie, you cannot be a matchmaker. It never works. It never, never works!" he held Jodie under her arms, slinging her up onto his lap. "I know you mean well, but if Allison and Cole are meant to be together, they will find a way to make it happen."

"Don't you agree they belong together?"

"That is not for me to say."

Jodie gazed at Bill with a serious look on her face. She needed to get his help. But she wasn't having much success. "Just between you and me, wouldn't you like to see your daughter marry Cole instead of Chad...wick?" she stretched out his name in a mocking manner.

"Sorry. Cannot answer that."

"Come on..." she begged.

"You just tell me what you have on your mind."

The little girl thought a moment, then said, "Okay, here is my plan." She rubbed her hand on her chin, plotting her plan. "I don't think Ally really loves Chad...wick as much as she loves Cole. And I think Cole loves Ally a lot more than he lets on. He is holding back on his feelings 'cause he doesn't want to upset Ally." She studied Bill's reaction. There was none that she could see. But in his mind he was thinking the very same thing.

"I think we have time to get them together. I just don't know how to do it? Do you have any ideas?"

"Well, I...," Bill stopped the sentence. This girl was good. She almost got him to say something. "I...am sure you will come up with something," he regained his composure.

"Maybe, but what?" she quizzed.

Bill was interested enough to plant a seed for Jodie. "Well, I know Allison and Chad are coming to the July Fourth Festival," he blurted out, "I don't know what you could do." He looked slyly at the freckled-faced little girl. "You know, all the games and things...," he left the sentence dangle.

"Yeah! That is it! You will help me then?" she asked, enthusiastically.

"I already told you, I am not a matchmaker," he said, winking at her. "I cannot promise anything. I still say it is up to Allison and Cole to work things out. I just want you to promise me that if they do not get together you will leave well enough alone after this one attempt. Promise?"

She thought a moment, then said, "I promise. But will you help me?"

"Only a little. I am not a matchmaker," he repeated.

Jodie talked to Bill for quite sometime about the July Fourth Festival, coming up with some ideas to get Cole and Ally together. The main focus of her plan was to get Chad out of the picture somehow.

The second day of July had come rapidly, and the Alaskan weather had cooperated nicely. It looked like the next three or four days were going to be perfect weather for the July Fourth Festival. The whole community surrounding Farrow's Patch had begun preparing for the big event. Everything was abuzz with activity, from the men hanging flags and streamers down the main street, to the group that had set up a makeshift campground for the out-of-towners.

Johnny and Tyrus were busy coordinating all of the activities, including a small fireworks display that would occur late on the evening of July Fourth. Since the sun would only be down for five hours, the fireworks would occur at about eleven p.m. that evening.

Down at the Settlers Feed and Supply Warehouse, the floor had been cleared of all of the stock and a clean layer of sawdust was being put on the floor for people to dance to the sounds of small bands that had signed up to play throughout the day and night. A disc jockey from Fairbanks had offered to play records during the breaks and the periods the bands were not playing.

Cole, Jodie and Smoke arrived at Farrow's Patch at mid-morning July third. This was one of the arrangements that Bill had agreed to do for Jodie. She wanted to make sure that Ally and Cole would be at the festival. So Bill told Cole his assignment was to help with crowd and traffic control during the three days beginning July third.

As Cole, Jodie and Smoke crested the mountains in "Lizzie" to the east of Farrow's Patch, they could see the increased activity. The main highway seemed to have a considerably greater volume of traffic and the cove was occupied by at least twenty airplanes, about twice the normal number.

Cole eased "Lizzie" into a gentle downward spiral until she finally splashed onto the smooth surface of the water in the cove. All the while, Jodie had been plastered to the side window taking in all of the activity below. He was pleased to see her get so excited with anticipation of being able to enjoy the upcoming activities.

After they had put their belongings in the room at the fully booked-up Madison, Cole headed out to help set the festival up and make sure that everyone abided by the law. He was not an official police officer, but he did have the authority to detain someone if it came to that.

He met with Troopers Davis and Imakamu of the Alaskan patrol, who were the official police officers, and several other volunteer deputies. After a brief meeting going over the various events, the men headed out to help the community have a good, fun time.

Allison and Chad arrived in Farrow's Patch around ten the morning of July fourth. It was an absolutely beautiful day with virtually no wind coming in off of Icelander Bay. The temperature was in the high sixties, but as the day wore on the temperatures would "soar" into the mid to high seventies.

Allison had to circle the cove four times before it was her turn to land. The cove now had more than fifty airplanes floating on the gentle swells. From the air, it could be seen that the makeshift campground had run out of space with campers packed in neat tight rows and people milling all about. And the main highway actually had traffic backed up for a half-mile in either direction, a first for Farrow's Patch.

As Allison and Chad made the last step up the stairs from the cove to Main Street, she took in the bazaar atmosphere. People were milling about everywhere. Various booths had been set up on each side of the street for people to play games or buy food and souvenirs. The street had been closed off at the intersection with the main highway so the crowds could mill about freely. Music blared through speakers, and the crowd noise sounded as if it was trying to win a battle to be heard over top of the music.

"Wow!" she exclaimed to Chad, "I cannot believe my eyes! This is the busiest I have ever seen this street!"

Chad was not extremely impressed. This, to him, represented a minor event. Nothing like the Los Angeles Olympics or a Super Bowl event. Everything looked so corny to him. He lied a little, and went along with her excitement, "Yeah, really popping around here."

"Let's walk down the street and see if we can spot Daddy. He said he would stay close until we got here." She excitedly bounced along towing Chad behind her as she held his hand.

They found Bill leaning against the banister on the porch of the Madison. He had seen Allison's airplane circling so he waited patiently, while watching all of the activities, until she came down the street. Of course, at his side, stood Jodie and Smoke.

"Hey everybody!" Allison shouted, as she approached the porch. She was wearing a gray sweatshirt with "I love Juneau" printed in dark blue letters on it, jeans and brown work boots. "Wow! This is really a big crowd," she held her arm outstretched as she turned a circle to take in the view.

"Hey Allison!" he shouted back over the noise of the crowd, "Come here and give your old man a hug!" he held out his arms to Allison. "How are you, Chad?"

After Bill hugged Allison, Chad, dressed in casual tan slacks with a narrow brown belt, dark green shirt with narrow white stripes, and brown loafers, shook Bill's hand, saying, "I understand this place is not usually this busy?"

"You got that right! Usually there are no more than three cars and, maybe, six people on the street at any one time."

Chad asked, "Do you all have this event every year?"

"No, this is the first time ever," Bill shouted back over the crowd noise, "I bet it won't be the last one with the response we have had."

Jodie reached up hugging Ally as she bent down to greet her tiny little girlfriend. "I have missed you, Jodie," she said, as she gave her a kiss on the cheek.

"I have really, really missed you, Ally!" she closed her eyes as she hugged Ally with all her might. "I want you and Chad to play some of these games with me...Will you? Will you, huh? Please?" she begged.

"Of course we will, won't we Chad?" Allison looked over at Chad, winking.

Chad looked down at Jodie with a slightly disinterested look on his face, his hands in his pants pockets, "Oh, yes. Certainly," he said. From the tone in his voice it was apparent he wasn't too warmed up to Jodie yet.

"But where is Cole?" Allison asked.

"Oh, he has to do crowd control for a little while. He said when we run into him he will join us," she waved her arm toward the crowd illustrating that Cole was out there somewhere.

"You're coming, too, aren't you Daddy?" Allison asked her father.

"Not right now. I will be along after awhile. I'm supposed to keep an eye on this part of the street," he answered. "You all go on and have a good time."

The threesome headed through the crowd, stopping at various booths, looking at souvenirs, and playing games as they slowly made their way toward the main highway. The more games they played, the more obvious to Jodie that Chad was very disinterested in this whole affair. It was, also, more and more obvious to Jodie that Ally was trying her best to keep Chad interested in the events. As a result, she was overcompensating for his lack of enthusiasm.

Eventually, they ran into Cole, and he joined them in playing games and having fun. They ate lunch on the steps to Greta's General Store joking and poking fun at one another. Chad was obviously left out of much of the conversation because most of the topics were related to reminiscing about old times at the ranger station and Farrow's Patch.

Jodie kept pushing all of them to do more activities. One of them was a softball game with fathers and sons or daughters. So they looked up Bill. Cole and Jodie, and Bill and Allison, signed up on the blue team. Chad sat in the stands watching the foursome and others poking fun at each other.

As Chad sat there, it became more and more obvious to him the genuine attraction that Cole and Allison had between them. They seemed to know what each other was thinking and their attitude toward each other seemed so natural. As he watched, he noticed several times, Allison would hang onto Cole after a big play in a manner that seemed to be more than just as if from one friend to another.

He noticed how much time Allison spent with Jodie, coaching her, consoling her, teasing her, and hugging her. When the game finished, he told Allison he would like to go back down the main street, just the two of them, to get an ice cream at the vendor close to the Yukon. So, he and Allison left Jodie and Cole, going their separate way.

Afternoon turned into evening. Cole had agreed to take Jodie to the dance that night. She had told him that a lot of her friends would be there and she promised that she would bring her dad. So, after they ate dinner, they freshened up, and changed clothes.

Cole wore a new pair of blue jeans held up by a wide hand tooled belt and silver buckle, new work boots, and a blue striped short-sleeved shirt. Jodie put on a pastel yellow dress that stopped just above the knees, tied at the waist by a matching yellow cloth belt, white shoes and a small yellow bow in her hair. Ally had helped pick out the dress for her, so it was special to her.

They arrived at the Settlers Feed and Supply Warehouse to find a line of people outside waiting to get in. The music from within the building echoed its way outside getting everyone's emotions in gear to have a good time. Cole looked around and thought it was really nice to see this many people having a good time.

Inside, the warehouse was rustic, to say the least. They had done a good job decorating the place with American flags hanging from each building support throughout the dance area. Someone had hung colored lights around the large space giving the dance floor and surrounding tables a multi-colored tint. And they had roped off the dance floor with several openings to enter and exit.

The band was at floor level on the far side of the dance floor. The DJ had his booth off to the side, slightly elevated so he could be easily seen as he introduced the bands or the records he was going to play. At times, during some of the fast dances, the noise level was so high it made hearing the person next to you impossible. Other times, the music was soft and soothing, so that was the time most conversations occurred.

Jodie acted very nervous until Ally and Chad arrived. Jodie explained her nervousness to Cole as that of being anxious for Ally to see the dress she had helped her pick out. As Jodie nervously watched the door, Cole took the opportunity to walk around talking with old acquaintances. Soon afterward, Allison and Chad arrived.

Allison was wearing tight-fitting blue jeans that enhanced her long, slender legs, held up by a wide, brown, leather belt. The jeans were tucked into brown boots that covered half her calf. A red, low-cut blouse with ruffles around the collar that flowed down the plunging neckline exposed a good portion of cleavage, accenting her firm, well proportioned figure.

Chad wore a solid blue shirt, dark blue dress-slacks, black belt and matching black dress shoes.

After looking around the room slowly, Ally saw Jodie. She waved, and headed toward the table where she was sitting, Chad in tow. "Don't you look adorable!" she exclaimed. Looking at Chad she continued, "Doesn't she look cute?"

Chad's attention had been on the couples on the dance floor. So, he responded, "Huh?...Ooh yes....adorable!" He barely looked at Jodie, turning his attention back to the dance floor.

"I bet you catch yourself a man tonight, Jodie!" she said, smiling at Jodie.

"I was thinking the same thing about you, too!" she answered, then, "You look really nice!"

"Thanks. Where is Cole?" she asked Jodie.

Chad turned around to face the two girls interrupting Jodie's answer, "I was wondering how long it would take you to ask that question," he blurted out.

Jodie and Ally returned his look, both with a look of astonishment on their faces. "What is that supposed to mean?" Ally demanded.

Chad, taken aback by her sudden response, answered, "It means…it means exactly what it sounded like."

"Explain. I don't get it!" Ally insisted.

"All day long, all I have heard is Cole this, and Cole that. Cole can we do this, or Cole is so great at that. I am kinda' tired of it," his voice had raised an octave higher than his normal tone.

Ally didn't say anything right away thinking what she was going to say. "Look Chad," her voice carried a mean tone to it. A tone that Jodie had never heard before, "you have to realize that Cole has a long history with me and my dad. You have to realize that we are in my hometown. Naturally, we are going to talk to one another and about one another. And naturally, I want to spend time with him today. I don't get to see him much anymore. So, I am going to take this opportunity to have fun with him." She stopped to take a breath and collect her thoughts, then continued, "It would be no different than if we went to Los Angeles and saw your family. I am sure I would hear, somebody this and somebody that. I would expect that." She looked at him with an expression of dismay.

Chad stood motionless, returning Allison's stare. He drew her close to him, saying, "I am sorry. I guess I got a little jealous for a moment."

"You shouldn't be jealous, silly. You're the one I am going to marry, you know!" she said softly, standing on her toes so she could kiss him.

Jodie couldn't stand to see this, so she plopped down in one of the chairs next to the table putting her elbows on the table, and resting her chin in her hands, a put-out look on her face.

"Come on, this is a slow dance. Let's go on the floor," Chad said. Holding Allison by the hand he led her to the center of the dance floor.

Shortly after that, Cole arrived at the table. Seeing Jodie's disgusted scowl, he asked, "What's wrong, honey?"

"Oh nothing, really. It is just I don't like Chad-wick too much," once again stretching his name out mockingly.

Cole sat down in a chair next to Jodie, turning around to observe the couple on the dance floor. Cole let out a catcall whistle saying, "Wow! A.J. is pulling out all the stops for this guy. She looks like a real lady tonight!"

"The only problem is, she is Chadwick's lady!" she muttered.

"What did you say?" Cole spun around to face Jodie.

"Nothing," she said, then added, "I said, the only problem is she is Chadwick's lady."

"Well what is wrong with that. She is going to marry him, you know!"

"Yeah, that is the problem. Don't you see? She should be marrying you!"

"Jodie! I thought we covered this already!" he raised his voice, sounding annoyed.

"Yes, sir. I'm sorry."

A little later, the couple came off the floor to join Jodie and Cole. Polite chatter continued until Bill arrived at the table.

"Hey people!" he said, enthusiastically, raising his hand, waving it back and forth. "Wow, honey, you look marvelous in that outfit!" he whistled, as his eyes scanned his daughter, then winked at the group.

"Oh, stop it Daddy!" Allison blushed red, lowering her head in embarrassment.

"Hey Chad, can I borrow you for a moment. It seems Mr. Unaku, the local pharmacist, would like some investment advice. Would you mind adding your insight?" Bill asked.

Chad was thrilled that his future father-in-law would ask him his opinion on a banking matter. "I would be honored," he answered. "Do you mind, Allison?"

She looked up at her dad, who was smiling back at her, "Only if it doesn't take too long because I am in the mood to dance the night away," she joked.

The two men left through the front door. Bill quickly stole a glance over his shoulder at the group at the table as he disappeared through the crowded doorway, winking at Jodie.

A moment of silence came over the table. Finally, Cole asked, "A.J., would it be improper for me to ask you for a dance?"

A.J. winked at Jodie, answering, "I think it would be impolite for you not to ask me for a dance." She rose from her chair taking Cole's outstretched hand as they made their way to the dance floor.

Cole gently placed his right hand on A.J.'s back at her waist, holding her right hand in his left, bodies slightly apart facing each other. The couple picked up the slow beat of the music as it echoed in the big warehouse. They moved in unison, gently, smoothly, as they glided with the music through the slow dance.

"This is nice," Allison said, softly. She looked up into Cole's brown eyes.

"Yes it is," he answered, looking down into her brilliant blue eyes.

Allison moved closer to Cole, allowing their bodies to touch, laying her head against his chest. He could feel her warmth through his clothes. His hand moved slightly at her waist sensing the soft skin beneath her blouse. His heart began to pound, his palms began to sweat slightly. They continued to move as one on the dance floor.

A.J. looked up into Cole's eyes, again. In a voice that was half voice, half whisper, she said, "I have missed you. Have you missed me?" Her brilliant blue eyes had a misty look to them.

He returned her gaze, looking down at this beautiful woman in his arms, "Yes, I must confess, I have missed you a lot," he emphasized the word "lot". They continued the slow dance in silence both enjoying holding each other, both secretly hoping the song would go on forever.

Allison felt secure in Cole's arms, as her mind raced through all the good times the two had together throughout the years. Cole always had made her feel secure. It was then that she realized she still loved this big guy. And it was then that she realized she would not be marrying the man that she really loved. "If only Cole would have admitted his love for me, I would be marrying the man of my dreams," she thought, to herself.

When the first song ended, it was followed immediately by a second slow dance. They remained on the dance floor holding each other close, moving gracefully to the beat of the music, enjoying the moment.

Cole, too, was thinking how much he loved A.J.. He tried to gather up enough nerve to tell her of his true feelings. But he had convinced himself that A.J. had chosen another man for her husband, and he didn't want to do anything that would confuse her, and possibly ruin the relationship between her and Chad.

Chad had returned to the table just as the second song began, observing Cole and Allison as they danced. It was obvious to him that the relationship between Cole and Allison was much deeper than just good friends, or for that matter, big brother and little sister. As he sat there, he began to ponder the situation when a little boy came up to the table to speak to Jodie.

"Hi Timmy!" Jodie said.

"Hi Jodie," Timmy nervously answered. "When the next dance starts would you dance with me?" he blurted out, machine-gun style.

"Sure," she answered, excitement showing in her eyes.

The slow dance ended. Cole and Allison remained embraced in one another's arms for a considerable time before even noticing the music had stopped. When they came to their senses noticing almost everyone had left the dance floor, they quickly walked back to the table, embarrassment on their faces.

Cole seated A.J. next to Chad, saying politely, "I'm going to get all of us some refreshments. I'll be right back."

He walked off to the temporary refreshment stand at the rear of the open area. As he stood in the long line, he turned around to steal a glance back at the table. He observed Allison and Chad holding hands across the table carrying on a quiet conversation. Once again, Cole admitted to himself that he had made a mistake not accepting A.J.'s invitation to carry their relationship to the next level. He realized he really did love her, and now, he had lost her to another man.

Cole was surprised to see A.J. sitting all alone at the table, when he returned with the tray of refreshments. "Where are Chad and Jodie?" he asked.

"Oh Jodie is still on the dance floor with that little boy, Timmy. They are so cute together! And Chad had to step out to get some fresh air or something," she pointed toward the front doorway.

Cole looked down at her as he set the tray of drinks and popcorn on the table. He looked into her eyes searching for some sign of trouble. "Everything okay?"

"Yes, why do you ask?"

"Oh, I dun'no, your voice sounded a little strained."

"Yeah, really everything is fine. Chad just needed to get outside," she tried to disguise her emotions, as she answered.

Cole eased himself into a chair across the table from A.J. taking a sip of his soft drink still trying to size up the situation. Allison patted the empty chair next to her's, saying, "Why don't you sit here, closer to me, so we can talk. The music gets very loud sometimes."

Cole changed chairs sliding his drink around the table to be in front of him. Then, he removed a soft drink for A.J., placing it on the table in front of her.

"Thanks," she said, softly. "You said you missed me. Did you just say that or did you really mean it?" she probed.

The music started again, so Cole leaned closer to A.J.. He spoke just loud enough to be heard above the music, "I really meant it." They stared into each other's eyes, looking deep within one another, their faces just inches apart.

"Remember our conversation in the hayloft, Cole?" she paused, thinking back to that day he had told her he wasn't ready to add another commitment at that time, "If things were different now would you still feel the same?" She put her hand on his leg as it rested next to hers.

Cole's mind raced through his options in answering this question. He could continue to deny his love for A.J., and give up the last chance he may ever have to win her over or he could, once and for all, level with her and accept whatever resulted from his honesty.

"What do you mean, if things were different now?" he asked, with a puzzled look on his face.

"I mean, if I were not engaged to Chad, would you still feel that you could not carry our relationship to another level?..eer..you know, that you could not consider me as a girlfriend?" Her pulse pounded with nervous anticipation to a possible answer that she would not like to hear.

"Once again, you speak in 'if and buts', A.J., and I will not be part of that." Her face showed disappointment with his answer. Then, he continued, "I'm tired of talking 'if this, then that'. So, I am going to tell you what I feel right now."

He looked down at his soft drink, drew it to his mouth taking a drink, then set the cup back on the table. Once again, looking A.J. square in her beautiful blue eyes, be began, "A.J., I realize now that I made a mistake in the hayloft that day. Oh, it appeared to be a good decision at the time. But since then, I have thought about you and me a lot."

"You know, I probably should have said more to you that day in the hayloft. I just wasn't ready...you know, I was afraid to commit. The feelings I had toward you were new to me. I just had not paid attention to what was going on inside myself."

"Now I am ready to tell you what is on my mind because, later, it may be too late. So, even though I may confuse you and your feelings for Chad, I feel it is important for me to speak my mind." Keeping his eyes focused on A.J.'s, he put his hand on top of her's, which was still resting on his leg.

Squeezing her hand gently, he cleared his throat, then continued, "You see, I felt funny every now and then when you would come home on school breaks. Probably the same way you felt, I guess. I just thought it was because I had not seen you for a while that it made me have that kind of feeling for you. It wasn't until you mentioned how you felt about me in the hayloft, that I began to understand those feelings of mine were more serious than I figured they were."

"Several times I was gonna' tell you how I felt. But by then, you had gotten engaged to Chad. So, I decided if Chad made you happy, that was all that mattered. Now you have asked me point blank, do I feel differently about you?" Cole reached over, taking both of A.J.'s hands in his big callused hands. He leaned closer to her, saying, "No I do not feel differently!"

Allison looked shocked, "You mean, things are exactly the same?" her tone was two octaves higher than her normal voice.

"Yes, exactly the same," he paused leaving her hanging for what seemed to be an eternity to Allison. "I loved you then and I love you now!' he exclaimed. "The only difference is, I didn't realize I loved you then. Now, I know I did...and I do!" he smiled at her.

Still trying to make sure she understood what Cole had just said, she asked, "You're saying you have loved me the whole time, right?"

Cole took a deep breath, expelling it slowly while he gathered up his nerve, saying, "Yes...Yes, Allison Joanne Defreese, I have loved you the whole time."

He looked around the room at the people coming and going to see if Chad was nearby. Not seeing him, he said, "I hope that doesn't mess things up with you and Chad. But you asked, so I answered. I don't ever want to get in the way of your love for Chad," he said.

A.J. sat motionless, staring into Cole's big brown eyes. She touched his cheek with her right hand, gently stroking his manly face. "No, no you won't get in the way of me and Chad." Her pulse was pounding uncontrollably in her ears. Her voice cracked a little as she continued, "I really appreciate it that we can talk honestly to each other, again. Like we used to before I messed things up by falling in love with you. But, it is a relief to know that you feel the same about me."

Now it was Cole that had the puzzled look on his face. He said, cautiously, "How do you figure me loving you and you loving me make it easier. Doesn't that present a problem with you and Chad?"

Allison got up slowly from her chair grasping Cole's hands in hers as she faced him. He took in her beauty again as she stood in front of him. She leaned her head down close to his ear, and asked, "Cole, can I have this dance?"

Cole rose from his chair, holding her hand he escorted A.J. to the dance floor just as the DJ put on the next record. They held each other close, A.J.'s head tightly against Cole's chest as the record began to play a romantic slow dance.

Allison looked up at Cole and said, softly, "May I have a kiss?" Cole's lips met her soft pink lips, gently kissing her as they moved back and forth to the music. Allison felt the pounding of her heart, and the throbbing of her pulse. She partially opened her eyes. The colored lights draped around the dance floor appeared to her as multi-colored streaks of light. Things began to swirl around her as her deep love for Cole took control of her mind and body.

The kiss became more passionate as the two forgot their surroundings and all the other people crowded on the dance floor. They were totally emersed in one another.

Allison slowly pulled her head away from Cole, whispering in his ear, "I love you, Cole Bryant." She engaged Cole, again, in another passionate kiss as the couple continued to dance slowly to the music.

Cole responded, "A.J., we shouldn't continue this...," he kissed her again, holding her close to him, "...I think...we are...getting...out of control," he whispered, between kisses.

Allison gently eased her head away from Cole's, saying in a voice that was more whisper than voice, "Cole...Chad broke off our engagement tonight."

Cole smiled back at A.J., saying, "Chad who? Kiss me my love!" They embraced once again, as the song in the background continued.

Jodie walked over to the front doorway, having observed Cole and Ally on the dance floor. Smoke followed her, as he always did. Tugging on Bill's pants leg, she looked up at him and said, "Hey, I thought you told me matchmaking never works?"

Bill looked down at Jodie, patting her on the head. He winked at her, replying, "Good job little girl. I think you pulled it off."

Jodie reached down to pet Smoke, then she looked up at Bill again, exclaiming, "I think I now have a complete family!" she paused, then added with a wink and a smile, "Right, Grandpa?"